Voices Beckon

VOICES SERIES
BOOK 1

LINDA LEE GRAHAM

VOICES BECKON is a work of fiction.
Names, characters, places, and incidents either are the product of the author's imagination or are used fictitiously. Apart from well-known historical figures, any resemblance to actual persons, living or dead, events, or locales is entirely coincidental.

Print Book ISBN 978-0-9832175-9-6
eBook (Kindle) ISBN 978-0-9832175-0-3

Published by Repository Press LLC

Linda@LindaLeeGraham.com

Cover design by Razzle Dazzle Design
Cover image: (ship) © Jeff Wickham
Interior Format by The Killion Group, Inc.

For my mother, who did all the hard work:
how it might have been

Also by Linda Lee Graham

VOICES WHISPER
VOICES ECHO

Set in the late eighteenth century, Voices Beckon spans seven years in the lives of three young Britons who form an unwavering bond of friendship, love, and loyalty while on a life-changing voyage to a new nation. Rich in historical detail, this sweeping romance chronicles their coming of age against the vivid backdrop of the emerging United States of America.

1

River Avon, Bristol
November 1783

ELISABETH LONGED TO RETURN HOME, and it had been only days since they'd left—two days, nine hours, and heaven knows how many minutes, every last one of them biting cold. She stood aside the stacked trunks, her foot tapping a quick rhythm beneath her skirts, and closed her eyes, briefly blocking the chaos of the quay. It would be months now, not days, before she would receive a letter from her best friend, Rhee, telling her if Rhee had managed to snare William's attention at church on Sunday. Together, she and Rhee had devised a foolproof plan; it couldn't have failed. Well, unless he—

"Elisabeth!"

At last, her father's voice. Opening her eyes, she quickly spotted him in the crowd. Given his grim expression, it wasn't the first time he'd called her, but in the midst of this mayhem, he ought not to have expected she'd hear him. Pushing back the hood of her cloak, she waved to acknowledge his approach.

She shook her head, smiling. He was practically in full

dress to board a ship, for mercy's sake. The cut of his coat flattered his tall, slim frame, and the garment hung without a hint of strain about his shoulders. His shoes were spotless, their silver buckles gleaming, and the ornate black clocked stockings displayed beneath his coat stretched taut to his breeches. To top it off, his new hat hid his thinning hairline quite nicely—a must, given she'd finally convinced him to discard his wig.

Thin lips pressed tight, he clutched a fistful of papers in one hand and gestured impatiently with the other. "We're to board, Elisabeth. You must pay close mind to me. You wouldn't want to get lost in this rabble now, would you?"

"No, of course I wouldn't."

He grabbed her elbow, holding her tight. His stride was purposeful and sure, and others, less sure, moved out of his way as he pulled her toward the longboat.

"What of our luggage, Papa?" she asked, looking over her shoulder at the pile they had abandoned.

"It's taken care of. Now, put your hood up. The wind is rising, and I won't have you taking ill."

"Mr. Hale!" one of the seamen called, motioning them forward. Her father raised his handful of papers to acknowledge him.

She pulled the hood of her cloak up and turned toward the trunks again, feeling as if she were watched. Two men, members of the crew, she hoped, were loading the trunks onto a cart. Neither of the men paid her the least mind. Her father tugged, and she followed him onto the wharf. The man who had called out reached for her, and with large, bony hands, guided her onto the boat that would transport them to the *Industry*.

She wished she had thought to grab a bit of Bristol sand. She may never return; it would have been nice to have a small piece of some part of Britain. She looked back at the city, saying a silent goodbye.

There! That man slumped against the side of that warehouse, his thumbs hooked in the waist of his breeches—he was the one staring.

She frowned. No, not quite a man; he probably wasn't much older than she. But he was as big or bigger than most men. Even slouched, she could see that he was tall, his shoulders broad, and his chest wide. He didn't glance away when he saw her turn; he met her gaze directly.

A lock of dark hair escaped his cap and hung low over his brow. If his meager possessions were anything to judge by, he was likely one of those steerage passengers her father had named 'rabble.' Or perhaps he was merely boarding one of the ships sailing to Ireland and didn't need to carry much. She was too far to make out the detail of his features, but his bearing intrigued her. He conveyed confidence; he hadn't lowered his eyes when she'd noticed him watching her. Not arrogance. Not a challenge. Merely curiosity?

She felt an odd pressure beneath her stays, and her hand rose without thought to push back at the sensation. Her father urged her to sit. Dropping to the bench, her gaze stayed locked with the boy's while the crew rowed the longboat toward the waiting brig.

DAVID PACED THE QUAY, watching for his uncle. The innkeeper had handed him Uncle John's note first thing that morning, so David knew that his uncle had had to take care of some last minute details, and that he wanted David to board the *Industry* when he could. The man likely thought he was doing David a favor, letting him sleep, but David could have done without that extra hour. He wasn't keen on boarding the brig alone.

Besides, if Uncle John was planning to abandon him, the night before would've been the time for it, when David had

had the opportunity to while away some time with one of the inn's barmaids. Betsy, her name had been, just here from Bath.

She'd been an agreeable lass. Pretty, blonde, and plump; she had laughed at everything he'd thought to say. While she lingered over pouring their ale, she'd hinted she'd still be about after the kitchen closed later that night.

Which hadn't been as pleasing a prospect to Uncle John as it had been to David. Uncle John hadn't cared much for Betsy the barmaid, and he'd stuck by David's side until long after the kitchen closed.

David and his uncle, the Reverend John Wilson, had been traveling for close to three weeks now: on foot, by water, and by coach. His uncle had had the worst of it, traveling all the way from Ireland, stopping in Scotland to collect him. And though Ma's lectures had always been delivered by Da in the past, she'd apparently taken advantage of that brief time to pass the obligation on to her brother. Uncle John had taken the duty to heart many a time over the last three weeks.

Hands in his pockets, David rolled up off the balls of his feet. This was his last day in Britain—for seven years if not for a lifetime. He added it to his round of 'lasts.' His last Sunday spent with his family in kirk. Ma's last home-cooked meal with all his favorites. One last tussle with Cousin James . . . one last night tucking in his younger brothers. Then there was that last lecture from Da as they fished a lazy morning away. But Da could write as well as talk, so no, that likely wasn't the last. And that final hour spent with Alice Ennis. He grinned as he thought of her beckoning him into her barn. Now that had been a sweet leave-taking, for sure.

Sailors called down from a nearby ship as they repaired its rigging, mocking him, David supposed; he couldn't make out the words, but he knew the tone. He ignored them. The early morning fog had lifted some, and he had a clear view of the *Industry* now. The brig had a tidy look to it; two masts, an uncluttered deck.

Tidy was good; meant someone was minding things.

As the quay filled with more travelers, David moved to stand alongside a warehouse, keeping the ship in view.

Then he saw her.

She was standing alone next to a large heap of baggage, framed by the passel of gulls screaming and diving at the leavings of the fish trade on the sand behind her. Well dressed, her dark cloak was tied with bright blue ribbons, a color he thought might match her eyes. Bonny lass, a slight smile playing around the corners of her lips alternated with a grimace of impatience as she looked about. She seemed out of place, standing there alone, though he thought her family must be near, given the number of trunks she guarded. He wished his family were near, but they'd had a hard enough time scraping to save for his passage alone.

He watched her turn when a man called out, and his mouth curved in a grin of anticipation. Elisabeth, the man had called her, was boarding the transport for the *Industry's* cabin passengers.

She turned as she boarded, as if sensing his scrutiny, and met his gaze. He thought briefly of looking away; he'd been taught better than to stare. But he didn't.

And then he couldn't. He felt her gaze as it shot straight down to his boots, then meandered back up to scurry to and fro across his back and his shoulders, before it darted down to his fingertips. He flexed his fingers, staring at her, watching the longboat as it shoved off.

Had he just imagined that?

He narrowed his eyes, puzzled. He must have.

The clouds began to disperse, the strengthening breeze chasing them about. He grabbed the bags and joined in the push to the loading queue, the worry leaving him as he moved forward, the excitement growing as he listened to the chorus of voices around him.

The man in front of him was struggling to keep three boys within arm's reach. Not brothers, for they were nothing alike and addressed the man as "Mister," not "Da." The man was of middling age, his kindly round face surrounded by a full head of sandy hair beneath his tricorn hat, hair he wore loose and wild about his shoulders. David guessed he was their guardian.

The tallest boy, the one they called Liam, appeared to be David's age. He grinned when he caught David's eye and pointed down the river.

"How long do you suppose before we get to Philly? Sean here says a fortnight," Liam said, tousling the youngest boy's curly red hair. The boy grinned up at Liam, his round, freckled face coming alight at the touch. "Rob says it'll be three to four times that. There's a ha'penny banking on it, for them that's closest."

"Mind your grammar, Liam," the man said, sorting through the untidy heap of papers in his hands.

"Aye, Mr. Oliver," Liam said obediently, winking at David. "Well, what d'ye say, mate?"

"It'll be at least eight weeks, I'm thinking, being as it's winter. Mayhap longer, if we hit more than a bit of weather," David said. "And you, your wager?"

"None. Canna risk what I dinna have, and I dinna have a bawbee to spare. But I don't mind risking what these two have," Liam said, slapping the backs of his companions.

The one named Rob rolled his eyes and turned toward the water. David noticed he had a pronounced limp in his walk, evident each time they took a few steps forward. He appeared to be the oldest of all three, a sturdy and serious lad.

"Where's your family, young man?" Mr. Oliver asked, peering at him over his spectacles, seeming to notice him for the first time. "You best stay close to them in this crowd if you don't want to risk crossing on your own."

"I'm not with my family, sir. Well, that is, just my uncle, Reverend Wilson. He had some last minute things to take care of, and I'm to board so as he doesn't have to waste time finding me. I have all my tickets and letters," David said, patting his jacket with confidence.

"Aye, well, he can follow us, canna he, Mr. O, just in case that hawker up there gives him trouble?" Liam said, canting his head toward the man incessantly shouting, "All aboard, have your tickets ready or step out of the way."

"I suppose," Mr. Oliver said, his gaze sweeping the crowd, apparently looking for anyone resembling a reverend searching for a boy. He clearly didn't relish the prospect of another charge.

David also scanned the crowd. It was easy enough to spot his uncle, his height being the one thing they shared, though of course his collar set him off as well. The resemblance ended there, his uncle being fair of skin and hair, his features rounded and pleasant, always friendly and approachable, reminiscent of his mother.

David's coloring was dark; his own features with more of an edge to them, at times appearing brooding and unapproachable, reminiscent of his father.

What would he do if his uncle didn't arrive by the time he reached the transport? Board as he had instructed?

With an effort David returned his attention to Liam. It was hard not to like the lad straight away; he was alive with an excitement that was contagious. He was almost as tall as David himself, but of slighter build, with jet black hair that brought to mind the tales of the sleek coats of the silkies off Orkney. His dark blue eyes were bright with intelligence.

"Rob and I are going to help Mr. Oliver set up a school

in the states. As soon as he heard the war was done he just upped and decided to leave and start over, didna ye, Mr. O? Ye can do just about anything you want in Philly with an education, says Mr. O. Sean here will be going on toward Pittsburg, to meet up with his brother and help him on his farm, maybe end up with a farm of his own. Land's free for the taking I hear, if ye can work it. Are ye aiming to stay on in Philly?" He paused for a breath and introduced himself.

"Liam Brock," he said.

"David Graham," David responded. "I'm to apprentice to printers Hall and Sellers in Philadelphia. Mr. Hall's da knew my kin from the university in Edinburgh." As they were pushed forward he turned to scan the crowd again and spotted his uncle. He closed his eyes in a quick prayer of thanks, then grinned broadly.

"Uncle John! Uncle John, over here," he called, waving his hand high above his head.

John Wilson hurried forward with a small trunk, his brow furrowed with concern.

"There you are, David. I was worried, what with the sail being so close. If I didn't see you, I was in a quandary whether to board or not. I should have arranged it better to assure myself of your whereabouts." He paused, setting the trunk down as he hunted for his handkerchief. "What was I going to tell your mother if I ended up in Philadelphia and left you here, or if I should stay and you ended up in Philadelphia on your own?" He took off his hat and wiped his hairline, his blond hair dark with perspiration born of worry.

"Dinna fash, Uncle. I did what ye told me and here I am. Did ye find what ye were looking for?"

Noticing David's curious companions, Wilson set his hat back atop his head. "Are ye planning to make the introductions, David?" he asked, ignoring his query.

"Oh, aye, of course," he said. He introduced Mr. Oliver

and the others.

"Well, ain't this cozy. This ain't a tea party; are ye boarding or not?" They had reached the front of the queue and the ticket collector. "Plenty behind you want your space if not, so make it quick. Where's your docs? That's not them. You're not getting far with your lodging receipt. Stop wasting these good people's time; there's a windward tide to catch, man."

Mr. Oliver continued to fumble through his paperwork, dropping several pieces in his search for the tickets. Reaching over, Liam quickly plucked the tickets from amid the scramble of documents and moved his foot atop the fallen papers before the breeze could take them.

"Here they are, ye old sap, and don't forget ye kept us waiting these last three days for the sail."

"Liam, tis better to return discourtesy with courtesy," Mr. Oliver said quietly.

"Right, Mr. O, sorry. Sometimes I get me back up and forget." He bent and retrieved the papers beneath his foot, then took the balance of documents from Oliver, carefully placing them in the case at the man's feet. He nodded toward the waiting barge. "Let's board then, aye?"

David passed the ticket he'd been safeguarding to his uncle, who handed it, along with his own, to the ship's employee. The man motioned them along impatiently, "get on with ya man, keep it moving."

THE DECK OF THE *Industry* was a passel of passengers moving every which way, and seamen shouting orders. David grabbed his uncle's elbow, steering him to an unoccupied spot along the rail. They stood silently for several moments, watching the pandemonium on the quay.

"Well," Wilson said, sighing and turning. "No looking back, aye? Let's go below and claim a berth, shall we?"

Even midmorning it was dim between-decks. Only a weak

bit of sunlight shone through the small open hatch, and it took David's eyes a few seconds to adjust.

The space was filled with people clamoring about in confusion. The berths were stacked two high on either side of the hold, and four long tables ran the length of the center. A man was already making use of the slop bucket behind a board serving as a makeshift water closet.

"Uncle," David asked quietly, "will the women bunk here as well, then?"

"We're all in this together son, although we shouldn't have to share a bunk with any women, since we've none traveling with us."

"Share . . . ye mean there'll be more than the two of us in one of these?"

"Aye, David, we'll probably share a berth with two other men, maybe more."

Studying the size of the berths, David shook his head and led his uncle toward the other end of the hold, where not as many people had gathered yet.

Wilson laughed. "It'll fill up over here as well, but aye, this will do." He set his bag on the top berth.

"Won't ye be more comfortable on the lower berth?"

"At first perhaps, but not when the seepage from the sick above makes it way down to those below."

David quickly lifted his own bag, storing it next to his uncle's, hitting his head as he did. He looked up at the low-lying timbers.

"Ye'll only be able to stand up straight in the middle of the hold, David."

"'Pears so." He asked about the small locked trunk his uncle had added to their gear.

"It carries our dishware, as well as some provisions."

David lifted it to the foot of the berth. "It's heavy. What kind of provisions?"

"Mostly oatmeal, but there's cheese, biscuit, flour, a bit of butter, some vinegar . . . in case rations are tight."

"I thought all was provided?"

"I heard talk. Tis prudent to have something to supplement your rations, due to the uncertainty of the winds. Now, if ye don't mind, I'll rest a spell. It was a long night spent worrying. Why don't you go on up and watch our departure, while I close my eyes a bit?"

David raced up on deck before his uncle reconsidered, and nearly collided with a young sailor who was carrying a log-line and sand glass.

"Best be making yourself invisible abaft bucko, or Mr. Ritcher will have ye below faster than ye can say 'but suh'," the boy said, placing the items near the wheel. David nodded and moved farther aft. He supposed that was abaft; there were fewer seamen in that direction.

"Loose sail!"

Canvas cracked overhead and sails unfurled. The sound sent his blood racing, made it all real. After months of endless talk and ceaseless planning, he was truly sailing to America.

Several sailors dropped from the rigging and raced to the front of the ship, hoisting two of the ship's boats up from the booms and over the larboard side, down to the river to join the three boats secured to the ship with tow-lines. Men scrambled over the side, dropping into the waiting boats to man the oars. Forgetting the admonition to stay out of the way, David went forward to watch. The anchor now up, the tide and the brig's boats began the laborious task of towing them out to sea.

Great limestone walls rose from the thick forests crowding the banks on either side of them, and as they rounded a bend he spotted two deer taking water at the shoreline, heads rising warily as their eyes followed the ship sailing by.

Smaller fishing boats passed by under sail, and farther ahead he caught a glimpse of another ship being towed out to sea. He briefly considered waking his uncle to witness it all, but that would require going back down into that hold. And the man had said he wanted to rest.

By the time the sun was high in the sky, the young sailor who had spoken to him earlier joined him at the rail. Clad in ill-fitting brown trousers, his coarse linen red-checked shirt tucked haphazardly about his narrow waist, the slight young lad was hatless, his long dark hair tied untidily back. The bright red scarf he wore around his neck was his only concession against the cold. He was not at all in keeping with David's impressions of what a sailor should be: burly, weathered, and mean-tempered.

"Watch all that did ya? Now you can say you know first-hand why the English be the best seamen in the world. Ain't an easy thing to work a ship down a windward tide, backing and filling the length of it, especially not in a channel as narrow as the Avon Gorge, no matter how skilled the pilot. I heard it done, ain't never seen it afore now."

"I'll have to take ye at your word there," David said, "Seeing as I havena a clue what ye're talking about. Ye're American? Have ye been at sea long?"

The boy laughed. "Yes, I am, and no, I ain't. Could be why I ain't never seen it done! Alex Mannus," he said, holding out a rough, wind-chapped hand.

David shook his hand and introduced himself.

"We're at the Bristol Roads now. Soon as the pilot's paid off, we'll be heading out," Alex said. "See? They're bringing in the boats." He pointed to the sailors hoisting in the ship's boats and securing them, each one nestled inside another.

David nodded and then noticed one of the crew bearing down on them, a husky, rough looking man with an air of authority. "I think that man behind ye is looking for ye, Alex.

He's headed this way, and he doesna know me. First mate, is he?"

Alex turned. "Aye, that's Mr. Ritcher. Don't get on his bad side. I'm off then." He ran the short distance to meet the mate.

"Make sail," the captain bellowed at last.

There was shouting from atop the rigging as more sails unfurled, snapping alive. A brisk, salty breeze replaced the last of the river's pungent stench, chasing away the final grey of the sky until all that remained above was a cloudless, brilliant blue. Gulls circled and dived, their screams a chorus of farewells.

Three porpoises kept pace with the ship, sailing into the air from time to time as if to welcome them to their world. The sea was bright with small, white-capped swells, the sky alive with gulls diving now and again to snatch a meal. David savored the breeze, filling his lungs as he took slow, deep breaths.

His hands tightened on the rail as the shoreline slowly receded. What was it Uncle John had said? No looking back?

He crossed the deck and instead faced a horizon full of possibilities, one bounded only by the sky.

Aye, no looking back.

2

Celtic Sea
November 1783

BY DAVID'S RECKONING THERE WERE close to thirty children onboard. He'd wager each of them had cried out at one time or another throughout the night—and not at the same time, mind you; the bairns had it synchronized so that there was never more than five minutes of silence between outbursts.

And that was after the others had knocked about for an hour or two preparing for bed in the dark. Why that was, he hadn't a clue; all one had to do was take a piss and set aside one's boots. No livestock to see to, no barn to secure.

But things were what they were, and thus he'd spent most of the night tossing and turning, little of it sleeping. Especially when the image of a lass called Elisabeth had come unbidden, filling his mind, crowding his dreams, displacing all lingering remnants of Betsy, the barmaid from Bath.

Opening his eyes slowly, he glanced over. Alone. They'd

been fortunate; they had only one other, a man from Galloway, sharing their berth. He stretched out across the full width and length of the berth, pointing his toes and raising his arms above his head in an effort to ease the tightness in his body. His hands slammed into the rafters. Grunting, he readjusted his stretch, lengthening it until he could feel his muscles calling out their thanks. Rolling off the side of the berth, he pulled on his boots and made his way to the bucket that served as the privy.

Someone had thought to hang a blanket for privacy, nice touch. Nicer still if someone had thought to empty the bucket before it was so full it splashed over each time the ship rolled. He grabbed the pail and hauled it up the ladder, emptying it over the side of the ship. Replacing it, he looked for something resembling a wash basin. He'd like to splash some water on his face and hands; he wasn't waking easy today.

A boy was studying him, one he recognized from the inn in Bristol, one of the Germans the place had been full of. "Good morning, lad. Have ye seen any water?" He pantomimed splashing his face and washing his hands.

The boy grimaced.

"Don't care for washing, then?" David said, laughing. The boy rattled off something and pointed to a woman packing away the remains of breakfast. She looked up and smiled, signaling David to wait. Bringing over her small tub, she offered it with a towel.

"Thank ye, Frau—" He looked at her, and she supplied her last name, or so he thought. "Thank ye, Frau Kiefer. Much obliged."

He gulped down the oatcake his uncle had left him on the berth, shaking his head in disbelief at the small amount of water in the cup. Really? He tossed it down in one swallow, then scowled. Foul tasting stuff anyway.

At least he could hold out some hope for supper. He grinned, recalling the stroke of luck they'd had last night when a woman had approached them on deck, timidly offering an exchange of services.

"Reverend," she had said. "Begging your pardon, sir, but—well—it's just I seen you and your boy—I was wondering. Well, d'ye suppose I might take on the cooking for ye, in exchange for your boy taking on the burden of the heavier work the captain be asking of us?" Her hand had gone up nervously as she made her request, shielding a side of her face. She'd been beautiful once, still was on the side unscarred by burns.

Wilson had smiled gratefully. "Aye, I'd welcome such an exchange. Neither my nephew nor I have much experience with the stove. Thank you, madam. I'm Reverend Wilson; this is my nephew, David. And you are?"

"Mary, sir. Mary Andrews. These be my two boys, Adam and Samuel. My husband, he's in America, a year it be now. He thought it too risky to take us, without his having work first, that is. But he's sent for us now, I'm glad to say. It's been hard without him."

"We'll be glad to help ye, Mrs. Andrews. I've two brothers at home. You look to be the age of one of them, Adam," David had said. "And I don't mind taking the meals to and fro the fire once ye have them set. Gives me reason to be on deck, makes it more of a fair exchange."

"Och no. I'll have your meals hot and ready." Thanking them, she had led her boys away, Adam peering back shyly at David from the shelter of her skirts.

"Thanks be . . . huh, Uncle?"

Wilson had smiled. "Aye, David, the Lord provides. And do cart the pots. She doesn't need to be hauling and watching two small lads shipside on her own. Poor lass; looks like she's already experienced her share of mishaps 'round the fire."

But it was a long while until supper. He headed up on deck to search out Liam and his friends, spotting them gathered below the mainmast, a lass among them as well.

Liam called out to him. "David, are ye up for a game of hazard? Come meet Elisabeth. Her pa's not taking the sea well; she's up for a bit of fresh air from tending him."

David stilled as the girl turned to greet him. She was the one he'd seen quayside yesterday.

He could now see her eyes were indeed blue, a startling sapphire blue, flecked with dark specks of indigo. Her flawless skin was creamy white, unmarred by smallpox, touched with just a bit of color along the fine line of the bones above her cheeks. Hair was escaping her cap in the breeze and curling in wisps about her face, some of it caught in the corner of her mouth. Her mouth . . . full pink lips tilting up in a perfect bow. His hand rose to touch her face, to pull back the hair, to test the softness of her skin.

Don't.

He couldn't recall ever seeing hair the color of hers, not the color of wheat as he'd first thought, but that of a pale amber. He didn't recall ever seeing a face such as hers, period. She was the colors of sunrise.

Liam elbowed him in the ribs. How long had he been staring?

He roused himself, taking his cap in hand. "Hello, I'm David Graham. I'm pleased to make your acquaintance," he said, horrified to hear his voice betray him with a slight stutter. He noticed Liam's raised brow and resolved it best to say no more. Elisabeth smiled politely and returned his greeting. There was silence then, an uncomfortable silence, but he didn't trust his voice to speak, didn't know what to say. She was the first to break it, taking her leave to see to her father.

No sooner was she down the ladder and out of sight than the others began their merciless banter at his awkwardness.

Liam played a part of the proper English gentleman, Sean the lass, and Rob provided an amicable commentary, letting him off easy. He shrugged it off good naturedly—what could he say anyway? He had played the fool; he deserved the taunting. Besides, if he resisted, it'd only go on longer.

"Eijits," he said, a wry smile turning up a corner of his mouth. Admiring the effortlessness with which they interacted, he gave them a couple moments before deciding enough was enough. Running his hand back through his hair, he set his cap on, pulling it down tight. "Are we to play, or are ye all too busy acting the goat?"

"Oh, to be sure, we can carry the weight of both, David. Don't ye be mistaking that," Liam said. "But ye seem a bit discombobulated so we'll make it simple for ye and keep it to the bones. Rob, toss 'em, will ye?"

Hazard was a game of chance, though Liam turned out to be a skillful player in his gaming strategy and the play required all David's attention for the next few hours for him to hold his own. The stakes were tiny, but he didn't like to lose. Especially after he'd just embarrassed himself over the chit.

Liam stood when they broke for the midday meal. "D'ye play Whist David? No? Well, we'll teach ye tonight then. Mr. O's always looking for a fourth." Mr. Oliver was also set on teaching lessons in the afternoons, and Liam invited David to participate in those as well.

"He willna mind a bit. He loves to impart bits of his wisdom. He's even arranged with Elisabeth's father to include her," Liam added with a wink and an elbow to Sean. The lad took his cue and pantomimed a swoon.

David grinned, shaking his head at the teasing. He gave a noncommittal answer before leaving to find his uncle, sure Mr. Oliver would be expecting payment, something he didn't have to spare.

3

November 8, 1783—Our first full day at sea passed without event. Weather fair, wind light. A German boy, Paul, from the inn, is on board with his family. We passed a pleasing hour with the language. He'll likely be speaking English like a Scot at journey's end! And I hope to be speaking German like a German. Morning spent gaming with Liam, Sean, and Rob, lads from the country north of Glasgow. Most of the afternoon reading with Uncle. Tomorrow plan to ask the Captain for some chores, so as the time passes less slowly.

BREAKING BRIEFLY FROM HIS MONOTONOUS pacing, David sat on deck and made a short notation in his journal. The ship's bell rang twice, signaling mid-dog watch.

He was beginning to doubt his ability to keep his wits about him for the length of time it would take to reach Philadelphia. Only the first full day, and he was so wound up with the urge to run his skin fair crawled with the wanting of it.

Breathe . . . breathe and look about.

The brig moved swiftly through the water, the sea occasionally blasting him with a light spray of cold, salty water. He focused his thoughts on the motion of the breeze, the movement of the ship.

Breathe.

Aye, so the ship was small. But the ocean, now there was another matter entirely. Imposing . . . without end . . . full of life beneath. Another world just out of sight . . . just had to imagine it. He stood and walked to the rail.

Breathe . . . breathe and look about.

The sun, a huge glowing ball of orange, fell slowly toward the horizon, bathing the timbers of the ship in a soft glow of red, its sails in a fiery orange. All the colors of the rainbow surrounded him as it sank from view, vivid colors intermingling with the flat slate blue of the sky. He turned a slow circle to take it all in, doing his best to be nonchalant about it. It wouldn't help matters any to have the crew start in on him for gawking at a sunset.

Things weren't so bad, only different, just have to look about. A full moon was rising early in the east, a spectacular yellow globe rivaling the sun. He watched the trail of light it left across the water and relaxed his hands atop the rail, welcoming the calm as it washed over him and settled.

He felt her approach, felt her pause before she spoke, felt the tranquility he'd worked so hard to achieve, vanish. She hadn't made a sound, he thought idly, not one that could be heard above the myriad of other sounds aboard the ship anyway.

He kept his eyes on the ocean. The lass likely thought him a simpleton; there was nothing to be gained in passing on how aware he was of her, everything to be risked if her face befuddled him again.

"Are you frightened, thinking of the changes to come?"

Hell. She *did* think him a simpleton then. He managed a snort of contempt before he answered her.

"Frightened? Nay." Turning toward her, grateful the night and her hood cloaked her face in shadows, his eyes scanned the deck behind. "Should ye be out alone after dark?"

She laughed, lowering the hood of her cloak. "I didn't mean to offend you. I apologize. It's just that you appear to be making the trip alone. I'd be frightened if I were."

Her laugh, there was no artifice to it. It tugged at him. My God, she was even more beautiful in the moonlight, her face luminescent. He turned away.

"No' alone. My uncle is traveling with me. And I was serious, lass, what with the seamen, it might no' be safe for ye up here at night."

"My father has made great friends with Captain Honeywell. I'm sure his sailors have all been asked to keep an eye out for me." Her voice carried an odd blend of tones: soft, sweet, yet confident. Mayhap that assurance came with the traveling in cabin class.

"David?"

She was looking at him, waiting. What had she asked? A corner of her mouth tilted prettily as she studied him.

"Do you have family other than your uncle?"

"Aye."

"Well? Why aren't they with you?"

"It's no' the right time."

"Why is that, if you don't mind my prying?"

He smiled, shaking his head slightly. Would it matter if he did? "We just set up in Glasgow last year, when we had to give up the farm in Newry. Ma's kin is all there, and Da thought to try his hand at tailoring again. He says now that he's older and more settled he might be more suited to such. I canna see it, but mayhap . . . ye do what ye must. That I do know."

"He didn't want to start over in the colonies?"

"No' the 'colonies' any longer, lass. Nay, I don't see my Ma ever wanting to leave, especially when Da's trade is uncertain. Since I'm the oldest of my brothers and a bit at loose ends without the farm to work, Da thought it time I learned a trade of my own. When Uncle James wrote that a print shop was looking for young men in America, he decided I should go."

"You're fortunate to have a large family, even if they can't be with you. My mother died, giving birth to my sister, and my sister soon after. I still miss her, but I miss my Papa, as well. He hasn't smiled much since then. He promises things will be different in Philadelphia. I do hope he's right."

He thought about that. Pa's brother, Richard, had left the farm in seventy-five when his wife and baby son had died in childbirth. Took off to France, hadn't come back home since. His mother had retreated deep into the recesses of her own soul when his sister Margaret died of the smallpox. She'd left them for months.

Maybe it was necessary, the licking of wounds on one's own so as they heal. Ma had come back to them, and Uncle Richard was doing fine now, with his new wife, new sons, and new country.

"To be sure, he's right. Everything will be different," he answered.

"The sky is wonderful out here, isn't it? Have you ever seen so many stars?" She set her back against the rail, tilting her head his way.

"Do you remember my name, David?" she asked with a smile.

"Aye."

"Hmm."

Sassy wench, was she flirting with him? Sassenach gentry, not likely . . . mocking him, then? He turned his eyes back to the ocean. The few clouds had disappeared, and she was right; the sky was brim full of stars. "This many stars? It's a rare sight at home, to be sure."

Captain Honeywell walked by, spotting her. Honeywell was a stout, thick man, his booming voice leaving little doubt as to whose word was law on the *Industry*. David hadn't glimpsed his compassionate side yet, though Uncle John had assured him it lay just beneath the man's rough exterior.

"Miss Hale, I'm sure your father will be expecting you. It's late," he said, aiming a stern glance at David.

"Yes, sir. I'll go to him now."

The captain planted his feet and stood his ground, waiting without a word until she started to walk away.

"Elisabeth?" David said, earning another glare from the man.

She stopped and turned, her face alight at the sound of her name.

The lass had been flirting then. Imagine that. "I'm verra sorry about your mother. I canna fathom the loss."

"Why, thank you, David. Good night, Captain Honeywell." And then she was gone.

Breathe. Breathe and look about.

4

Atlantic Ocean
November 1783

"I UNDERSTAND MR. OLIVER IS KIND enough to include you in his daily lessons," Wilson said, rising from the bench, reaching over to grab David's cup and pack it, along with his own, back into their trunk. "He asked if I'd mind sharing a bit of the gospel with you boys in the mornings. I told him I'd be more than happy to."

David grinned, recognizing at once the exchange his uncle had made on his behalf. "Well, I think they got the better end of that, Uncle John, ye've a talent for making the Book exciting."

"High praise indeed," Wilson said cheerfully, reaching out an arm to steady himself as the ship rolled heavily to one side. "But best not to raise expectations too much I've found, especially with young men who've much more on their minds than the word of the Lord. Are ye still hungry, lad?"

He was, but he knew his uncle was worried about the amount it took to fill him. They had already dipped into the supplementary provisions and they were only out a day.

"Nay, I'm good." He grabbed the trunk and hoisted it up onto their berth.

"I'll join you on deck at four bells then. Be careful up there, will you? The sea is rough today."

"Aye, Uncle John." Leaving his uncle to his Bible, he climbed the companionway ladder and walked to the mainmast. Many passengers had stayed in their berths this morning, owing to the weather. He wondered if Elisabeth suffered from seasickness.

Someone needed to kick some sense into him.

"David! You're right on time, man! Can we be getting started then?"

"Morning, Liam, Rob. Where's Sean?"

"He's still in his bunk, no' taking well to the roll of the sea," Rob said, his hand massaging the ankle of his lame leg.

"Ache?" Liam asked. "I can get—"

Rob scowled and shook his head, moving his hand, tucking the leg under his other. "It'll just be the three of us till he wanders up," he said, cutting Liam off. He brought the die out of his pocket, tossing them three times until they read a number from five to nine.

"Six. Shoot this time, will ye, David?"

David took the die, casting a six on his first try. "Nicks. That ship we saw last night? She was a slaver. Alex said so."

"Thought so. She had an evil look about her," Liam said, wrinkling his nose. "Smell as well." He groaned when David won the next toss as well. "Ye take credit?"

"Don't think I know ye well enough to loan ye my stash," David said, grinning as he reached for the balance of the stake. They had found a small dowel down in the hold yesterday and had sliced it into wooden coins, distributing them evenly amongst themselves to use when wagering.

"Hmmph," Liam said. He looked up as Wilson joined them, Sean in tow. "Rev'rend Wilson, good morning."

"Good morning, lads. Gambling with the ship's timber I see."

"Just waiting for ye, sir. Mr. O warned us ye'd be by."

Wilson chuckled. "Oh? Ye needed fair warning, did ye?"

"No' me, Rev'rend. Canna account for what Mr. O thinks I might need. I'm willing enough to listen to any wisdom you're willing to toss my way, so's Rob here."

"Rev'rend Otter often thought Liam's questions rude, sir," Rob offered.

"I welcome your questions, Liam, as well as the segue into the story of King Solomon and his gift of wisdom," Wilson said. "But I can't promise I can give ye an answer to all of them."

"Fair enough, sir. And tomorrow, mind, I think a chat on charity wouldn't come amiss. Remind your nephew here on the meaning of the word." Liam motioned to the empty spot that had held the stash now in front of David. David rolled his eyes.

"Best carry on, Rev'rend. He'll talk til ye forget what ye were about," Rob advised.

Wilson skillfully steered the banter to the story of King Solomon, two mothers, and one baby. The conversation was lively as they discussed the wisdom of Solomon and the merits of his actions, Wilson contributing only when he thought it necessary to keep the exchange on track. David kept silent, listening to the responses of the others.

"The odds were against the man. No woman alive would willingly see a child cut in two, her own or no'," Liam said.

"Mayhap the King just gave the bairn to the Ma that spoke out the quickest?" Sean said. He spoke haltingly, pressing his lips tightly together after the words were out.

"Ye're spilling too much sentiment into it, Liam. There's plenty enough women do 'bout anything to achieve what they be after," Rob said.

"Half a bloody baby's an achievement?" Liam said, scoffing. "Off with ye, Rob."

"Liam does have a point," Wilson said. "But I think we're best served not to belabor the details and take away, instead, the message intended."

Liam nodded, considering, then stood, grabbing Sean by the hand. The boy's eyes had gone round, the muscles in his throat visible as he gulped convulsively. Leading him to the rail, he took off Sean's hat and placed a hand under his chin, aiming his face to catch the cold spray of the sea.

"Aye, I'll give ye that then, Rev'rend. In this case the message is clear," he said, turning back to look at them. "Tomorrow, then, come with one a bit more untidy in the interpretation, then we'll talk."

Wilson laughed. "All right Liam, I'll give it some thought." He stood and announced with a wink at David that he was needed elsewhere. "Sean, ye look a wee bit green round the gills. Would ye want to join me then? Lie down in your berth for awhile?" Sean managed a nod and Liam handed him over.

Liam looked at the sun, gauging the time. "D'ye want to keep playing?"

"Nay." Rob eyed the mast before them. "Ye think we'd see land from the perch atop the first yard?"

David grinned, thinking it a grand idea, wondering why it hadn't occurred to him first.

"Mayhap. I'll go first." He started up the ropes, welcoming the pull in his muscles as he climbed.

"I'll have ye all locked below," one of sailors bellowed from above, "iffin you don't keep your bloody feet on the bloody deck."

David dropped.

"Can he do that?" Rob asked, squinting up at the man high in the yards.

"Dinna ken. Though Ritcher likely can, well enough," David answered, watching the First Mate march toward them.

"JUST IN CASE we were feeling homesick, aye, Davey?" Liam said as he shoveled, mucking out the livestock hold. Ritcher had descended fast upon them, grumbling he had no use for idle hands on his deck. Rob had made his getaway timely, claiming Mr. O needed his help.

"Ye don't want to be getting soft as a lass on the passage, do ye?"

"Och, I wasna complaining, mind ye, just making conversation. And don't be mixing soft lassies in with the manure. It's no' right."

David laughed. "We're done here. Suppose we ought to go below so ye can rest up a bit afore your class."

"Hmmph," Liam said. He sprinted past David and leapt into the hold, missing the ladder by a mere fraction of an inch.

"Eijit, I'm no' nursing ye if ye break a leg," David said, climbing down after him.

"I expect not, Davey, but there's where I give ye leave to mix in the soft lassies."

ELISABETH STOOD TO CLEAR the evening meal from the tiny table, catching her plate just before it crashed to the floor. Bracing her feet against the roll of the ship, she quickly grabbed the bowl that had held the stew, pouring the small amount left into her father's bowl.

He'd been on her mind for days now. David.

She had recognized him immediately. He was the boy on the quay, the one she'd caught staring; the one she had stared back at. And couldn't seem to stop staring back at.

And it wasn't his appearance she was drawn to, though David was every bit as handsome as Liam was, if one took the time to look. And she was taking the time. Too much time, she was afraid. She'd do well to take a page out of Rhee's book before she made a fool of herself. Rhee could be head over heels with a boy and he'd have no inkling of it.

But his face was such a study in contradictions, who could blame her for noticing?

It was a stern face; full of harsh lines. Full lips formed a mouth that often rested in a scowl, a scowl that could change in a heartbeat when it lifted and the lines rearranged themselves into the deepest dimples she'd ever seen. Heavy dark brows framed his eyes, large doe-brown eyes lushly fringed with thick lashes. And the curls he kept hidden beneath his cap . . .

"Elisabeth, be careful. You're spilling it."

"Oh, I'm sorry, Papa." She took her cloth and wiped up the stew that had spilled. Maybe they should just eat bread. Surely it was less of a mess.

He'd smiled at something Liam had said today, and she'd been relieved that smile and brief display of dimples hadn't been turned on her, for she suspected her knees would have turned to pudding if it had.

But no, it wasn't his appearance that was responsible for her fascination. It was his strength. It was a quiet, inner strength, and it drew her in.

"Elisabeth, the captain said you were talking to one of the boys on deck last evening." Her father pushed his empty bowl away, folding his well-manicured hands atop the table, calling an end to her distraction.

"Yes, Papa, I was. He's one of the boys I met in Mr. Oliver's group." She went to him and straightened his cravat. He was usually so impeccably groomed; he must still be feeling poorly. "He's on the ship without his family. He's headed to Philadelphia to become an apprentice to a printer; I thought he might be feeling alone." Timing the movement so she didn't drop it, she quickly picked up his bowl and wiped it clean, storing it back with the others in their small box of kitchen ware.

Hale stood and reached for his book and bottle of whisky from the shelf. "Well, be that as it may, you need to remember your place. You're aware, are you not, of the social status of an apprentice? Be sure he's someone you have no cause to spend time with." He carefully poured out a measure of whisky into his cup. "For that matter, most of these people you have no cause to spend time with."

"Papa! You know Mama always said you could learn something from people in all walks of life. Why, learning a trade to support one's self is nothing to be ashamed of. It's quite the thing in America." She put the last utensil away and paced back and forth in front of her father, her fingers pulling at the cloth in her hands. At the sound of it ripping, she set it aside. Calmly, she must approach him calmly, or she would be spending the next six weeks in this room. She stood in front of him, placing her hands gently over his.

"The trip is to be so long, Papa, and there are only a few people my age. I miss my friends, I miss home. No one here would cause me harm."

Her father sighed, softening immediately. "There are many ways to invoke harm, Elisabeth. Ideas may harm. Whether employment in the trades is 'quite the thing in America' or not, it shall not be for you, nor for the people you choose to surround yourself with once we arrive." He reached over to set the bottle back on the shelf. "But I've no wish to lock you up in these wretched circumstances. I only mean for you to remember your place. You mustn't form any attachments on this ship, is that clear? Absolutely clear?"

It was clear. She nodded, hugging him tightly. "Thank you, Papa. You know I'd never want to disappoint you. Would you like to walk on deck?"

"Oh. Well, all right, I suppose. The book will keep." He set it and his cup in a secure spot and donned the overcoat and hat that hung from the rack at the foot of the companion ladder, taking care to straighten the white ruffles at the edge of each of his cuffs. Elisabeth threw on her cloak and followed him up the stairs.

Placing her hand in the crook of his elbow, she guided him in a slow circle of the deck. Mr. Oliver stopped them as they passed, delivering news of the day's class. She suspected Mr. Oliver was hoping she would be one of the students at his new school in Philadelphia, but even if her father allowed her to attend a school, it would depend less on the teaching skills of the schoolmaster and more on the attributes of the other students enrolled. Which was a shame, because one had only to talk a brief time with Mr. Oliver to be impressed with his depth of knowledge.

Liam, David, and Rob were just behind Mr. Oliver, and Elisabeth took care to introduce her father formally to the boys. She wasn't quite sure she could count on him to be polite, and she held her breath as he shook each of their hands. But he made courteous inquiries about their trip so far, and Liam, not as reserved as David and Rob, actually made him laugh at one of his anecdotes. She tried not to look at David any more than she did the others. Papa wasn't stupid.

The wind picked up as they continued their walk and the roll of the ship made each step a little more difficult. When they reached the companionway again, Elisabeth suggested they go below.

She was anxious to be alone with her thoughts, to mull over everything David had said to her. She and Rhee used to talk for hours at a time about a boy one or the other of them might have a fancy for on any given day; analyzing and deciphering the meanings that might be read into each phrase the one in question had uttered. Eventually they'd laugh and give up, deciding that the boys were much too simple to have their words taken at anything other than face value.

Somehow, she didn't think that was the case with David. Actually, she was quite sure there was nothing simple nor superficial about him.

Heaven help her. She didn't want to make a fool of herself, but, mercy, he did intrigue her past reason.

November 9, 1783—Cold today. Started classes with Mr. Oliver, passes the time.

November 10, 1783—The day promises to be a fair one, although again cold. Wind strong and steady, and according to Mr. Ritcher, we are on course. Alex says the log reads nine knots with regularity, which I gather is a respectable speed. Some of the passengers have an ongoing wager on the distance traveled each day. Many still confined to their berths, unable to recover from the constant roll of the ship. Deck has been empty of passengers for the most part.

November 11, 1783—The sea has stilled some, will be a relief to many. Wind steady.

5

"ARE YOU KEEPING A JOURNAL, David?" Her voice flowed over him, fluid and feminine. He closed the journal and looked up. "Morning, Elisabeth. Aye. Ma gave me this to keep a record, something I can hand her next we meet. She says someone working in the printing business best be comfortable recording events."

She sat beside him. "Would you mind telling me about her?"

He smiled, thinking of her. "Ma's the one ye ask permission or forgiveness of, the one adamant we attend school and kirk. She'll see through any excuse 'fore ye even have time to think it up. She holds the family together; not the one of us has a chance to forget it. I had a heck of a time convincing her to allow me to go to America. Without the persuasion of Da and Uncle John, it ne'er would have happened. I've only seen her weaken one time, and that was when Margaret, my sister, died of the fever two winters past. Margaret was less than a year old when we lost her."

"The only girl . . . I feel for your mother. The loss would

be that much harder. I'm sorry for that, David, the loss of
your sister."

"Good day, Mr. Hale. Up to catch a wee bit of the fresh air,
are ye? It's a fine morning, to be sure." Elisabeth jumped up
as the sound of Liam's voice carried across the deck.

"May we talk later, David? I ought to go."

"Of course. Are ye feeling poorly then, lass?"

She smiled. "Oh, no. But I must see to my father."

He saw Liam wink as she passed, then heard her greet her
father. "Wait for me, Papa. I'll walk with you. You remembered Liam, didn't you? He's the boy traveling to Philadelphia
with Mr. Oliver to open the new school?" Her father's reply
was lost as they walked away.

David looked thoughtfully at the ocean, his journal forgotten for the moment, forearms resting on his knees as he
twirled his pencil round and round in his fingers. Dropping
down next to him, Liam took out his knife and began working a piece of bone.

"So . . . ye'd be thinking her Pa wouldna want her to be
passing the time with me?" David finally asked.

"Aye. Ye'd have noticed yourself, if you weren't so caught
up with the wee lass." He was silent for a moment, as if
mulling it over. "Well, to be fair, I have had the pleasure of
a bit more dealings with the cull than ye, on account of his
talks with Mr. O."

David pulled a piece of straw from the bale behind him
and stuck it between his teeth.

"It's not ye, David; it's the lot of us. He willna be pleased
to be sharing her company with the likes of us, no' any of
the Scotch. Nor the Irish, I'd be guessing."

He pulled the straw from his mouth and glanced at Liam,
searching his face. This was the first he'd seen Liam serious. Bitter, even. He exhaled a long, slow breath, conceding
Liam's assessment, resigned in his acknowledgment that it

was no surprise, nothing he hadn't encountered before, the only wonder being that she had even approached him in the first place.

And she had. First.

"Aye, well, be that as it may, I don't think I can see my way clear to stop talking to the lass, long as she be willing." He took his cap off and ran his fingers through his hair before setting it back in place, then put his pencil and journal into his pocket. "Mayhap I should, Liam, but I don't think I will. It's just a conversation. I'm free enough to have a conversation with the likes of anyone willing to do the same, Sassenach wench or no'."

Liam grinned. "Aye, that ye are."

"What're ye working on there?" David asked, pointing a finger at the bone and knife in Liam's hands.

"A die. Mr. Oliver should have a new seal for his new Academy, aye?"

David leaned over and took a closer look. It was intricate work, and Liam's long slender fingers were sure and quick as he went about it. He had the letters naming the Academy all formed precisely, up through the letter 'v' in 'Oliver's', the space of each calculated to leave ample room for the remainder. He frowned, looking up at Liam.

"That's incredible. Where'd ye learn that?"

Liam shrugged. "A fellow I knew once." He pocketed the die, stood, and stretched, bouncing from one foot to the next, full of restless energy. "There's the Reverend, searching for ye. Dinna be forgetting, the lads from Kilkenny are playing tonight. Lively boys; they're sure to take the edge off. And the lass with them . . . Annie . . . well." He sighed dramatically.

David laughed. "And ye'd best no' be forgetting those lads are her kin, and not likely to take their eyes off her. I'd hate to see that pretty face of yours colored purple."

"Don't underestimate my charm, Davey," Liam said, grinning. "And bye the bye, ye're going to need to work on yours, ye be thinking ye can keep your hands full of that Wallace chit whilst your thoughts are full of the beautiful, proper Miss Hale. She gets a whiff of that, the rest of your passage will be miserable. Trust me on this."

He frowned. Which "she" would be the one making him miserable? There was nothing between him and Sarah Wallace. Nothing. Admittedly, she'd caught him watching her dress the other day. Mayhap he'd kept his eyes on her a bit too long. Blonde, rosy, and plump, with a bosom one could lose himself in—well, there was a lot to look at. And she'd certainly made no effort to be modest about it. He could almost suspect she'd planned it.

Which could absolve him . . . mayhap . . . of the brief groping that took place last night when she cornered him up here by the livestock. Though truly it was more of a thought than an action, owing to the sound of Uncle John's voice drifting from across the deck.

How had Liam known?

Liam laughed at his expression. "Finish your business with the Reverend, Davey, then come. It's time for me to recover my stash from ye."

"Aye, soon after our meal." Zounds, this ship was small.

November 12, 1783—The ship is full of those from all walks of life and all manner of looking at it. The man who shares our berth has indentured himself for a year in exchange for passage. He seems honest and steadfast, and likely to benefit in the end. Others, maybe not so much. The Germans, particularly the women, are a hardworking bunch. Few gentry on board, Elisabeth among them. The friendship of a lad called Liam Brock shows promise to last well beyond the length of the passage. Ma would name him sauce-box, and she'd be right. But there's more there, much more.

6

"YE'RE OUT EARLY." LIAM YAWNED, crossing his hands over his forearms and hunching his shoulders in an exaggerated shiver.

"Aye, 'early to bed, early to rise' and all that—Da's favorite adage for saving tallow," David said, his head bent as he worked on the rope he held.

"I think Franklin was considering more the health of a man's mind than his pocket."

"Mayhap he was, but ye don't know my da."

"What's that ye're so intent on there, Davey?"

"A different meal, I'm tiring of the fare. The sea, she's calm early on, the ship still. I think I can catch a fish or two 'fore the wind picks up."

He'd pulled out a few strands of his hair and was carefully inserting them into a loose knot in a bit of weighted twine, finishing by tying the knot to the hook he'd fashioned. Breaking the loose end with his teeth, he grabbed a small piece of the galley refuse he'd set aside and stood, walking over to the rail.

Liam followed, reaching over to finger the strength of his line, eying the drop from where they stood to the surface of the water below.

"Hmmph, a wee bit different from the loch. Ye'll no' be wading in after it, I expect." He grinned, looking back at David. "You don't have a net, do ye? I can hang ye by your toes should ye need help bringing one in."

David looked down to the water and took a small step back. Calm or not, its vastness was still daunting.

"I'll be letting it go first. See that bucket over there? I'm thinking I can bring it up with that. It may take a bit of trying."

"Aye, a bit," Liam said. He turned his gaze to the sea, suddenly alert. "Now! Drop your line, Davey. See the porpoise over there?" He pointed to a spot several yards out. "Maybe there's more! They're sure to be tailing something to eat."

David tossed out his line, and they watched it disappear under water. A minute passed, and he started to pull it in to check the bait, then stopped, transfixed, as a porpoise sailed out of the water directly in front of them.

"Whoa!" Liam said, jumping back.

David didn't move. The porpoise hung suspended for a moment, the playful glint in its eye belying the grey corpse-like mantle it wore. It tossed its snout up into the air, and David heard a rush of air as if it were snorting, then it glided gracefully back into the sea, leaving nary a ripple as evidence.

"Did ye see that, Liam? Did you see? He looked right at us!"

"Aye, and I think he made an offering as well. Pull up your line."

David had felt the tug and was already doing just that while Liam ran to retrieve the bucket and another bit of muck to bait the hook. He brought in two more in quick succession, keeping his eye on the porpoise as it circled back round again, chasing the smaller fish toward the line.

"Holy hell. Bring all the bait over, Liam."

He could hear the crew in the rigging cheering them on as

the catch piled up. Twice more the porpoise herded round the fish. Then, on the last loop, it came in close and sailed high out of the water. Chattering, it tossed its snout again, telling them what, he hadn't a clue. Then it landed with a great splash, completely soaking them with icy seawater. Laughing, they called out thanks to the creature as it sped away.

"Well, I'll be damned, what d'ye make of that, Davey? What do ye think it said?"

"When I know, I'll let ye know. Though it appears it thought we needed a decent meal and a bath." He stood at the rail, watching the open sea thoughtfully. After a moment, he turned and looked at Liam, grinning.

"Don't know about you, but I need to get into something dry. Then let's find the cook. He made a promise to fry up the catch for a fair share. And mayhap that was the beast's message; he offered up more than enough to share, aye?"

November 15, 1783—Luck was with us today. Liam and I caught many fish with the help of a friendly porpoise. It was an unusual situation to be sure. Even the sailors were agog. A welcome respite to the provisions we have been provided.

DAVID POCKETED THE JOURNAL, taking his now habitual stance against the rail as he watched the moon rise. The water was calm, the reflection of the moon unbroken as it laid a glittering white carpet across the black sea.

"They say with each new moon, souls return to the earth for another try."

Liquid softness, that's what it was. There was no mistaking her voice. He hadn't seen her alone since that morning she'd scurried away at the approach of her Da.

"Aye, well, don't be letting Uncle John hear ye say that; ye'll be setting yourself up for a sermon."

"I wait for it each month, for a sign of my mother."

He looked at her, drawn by the sadness underlying the words. "Will ye know; if she comes back, I mean?"

'I don't know. I like to think I will. But I hope it's not for some time. I prefer to feel her presence as it is now, watching over me. Look!" she said, pointing out the bright trail of a falling star. She turned to him. "At supper this evening the mates were full of the story of you and Liam fishing. They say it's a sign, a good sign, that the fairie-folk are watching out for you, and therefore this ship."

"Hmmph." He looked away, his eyes back on the moon. Best not to comment on souls returning and the blessing of the fairie-folk in the same conversation. Uncle was not keen on that vein of talk either, to say the least.

"I should leave you to your thoughts. I told Annie I'd meet her later. Good night, David."

Should let her go. Plenty of agreeable lassies aboard this ship.

"No! I mean . . . don't go just yet, Elisabeth. Let's step out of the wind, sit for a spell."

He reached out to grab her elbow, drawing his hand back instantly before touching her, remembering his resolve to keep her at arm's length. He pointed to a spot sheltered from the wind. "Here, ye can still have a view of the moon, and it's a wee bit warmer."

She sat, and he dropped down beside her, drawing up his knees and crossing his arms atop them. They didn't have to talk of fairie-folk; there was plenty other to talk of.

"What d'ye think it'll be like, Philadelphia? I spend a lot of time wondering. I expect the town is full of important men. I may even have the opportunity to meet Dr. Franklin, if he returns. He's ties to the *Gazette*, where I'm to be indentured."

Elisabeth looked at him, eyes narrowing. Quicker than he'd given her credit for then, seems she realized his use of the word 'indentured' had been deliberate.

"Well, if you do, know that I expect to be introduced as well."

"The people. How different they must be, to have accomplished what they did."

The treaty between Britain and the colonies, or rather the United States of America, had been signed in France a couple of months ago, and King George had relinquished all claims to the thirteen colonies. Had actually acknowledged them to be free and independent states. It was nothing short of remarkable. What of the people who had brought that about? Why had they succeeded where so many others had failed? How long had Scotland been at it? What made the Americans different?

"Why, just on this ship alone, Elisabeth, we're but a small group among many. The Germans, the Dutch . . . I know some French, a few words of German. It's so different from home, where ye know the intent of those around you."

"Well, just knowing the language doesn't mean you know your neighbor's intent, David."

"To be sure . . . but it helps, if ye can match the eyes with the words." A tinder box slid past him as the ship rolled. Recognizing it as Alex's, he reached for it, pocketing it before it landed in the sea. Lad had enough trouble starting the evening's fire.

"And it's no' just the language. What of the customs, whose shall prevail? Or do ye think we'll mingle and take a bit of the best from each?" he asked, turning to look at her.

"I think it's likely that people will congregate into groups where they share something in common, don't you?"

"Now that the common cause has been won, they'll go their separate ways? Live with those with whom they belong, ye mean?"

"No, I didn't mean to imply that."

She shifted, as if he were making her uncomfortable. Well,

he wanted to hear her say it. Again, plenty of agreeable lassies aboard this ship.

"David! There you are. Good evening, Elisabeth. I'm sorry to interrupt." Mr. Oliver, looking harried, paused to tip his hat to Elisabeth. "David, have you seen Sean? He disappeared shortly after supper. He's been full of talk about your fishing experience; I'm afraid he might try to replicate it. I've sent Rob to search. I haven't been able to find Liam; however, I expect I know his whereabouts."

"And which whereabouts d'ye have in mind, Mr. O?" Liam said, striding up with Sean in tow.

"Sean, I've been looking everywhere for you! Ye had me worried. Thank heavens you're in one piece."

"Course I am, Mr. Ol'ver. I was only talking to one of the sailors 'bout his work. I didna know ye were missing me, but then Alex, he's the sailor, ken, he saw Liam and Annie trying to keep each other warm, that's what he said anyway. I don't think that's what they were doing, but he talked to Liam and then Liam wanted me to take a walk with him. Did ye know they climb up that mast to the very top to fix the sails when they be needing to? And last week he did that twice, but I didna get to see cause I was in lessons. Don't you think that would be the best lesson, Mr. Ol'ver, learning how the ship sails? He said he would take me up there if I wanted to and if ye said I could. I do want to, Mr. Ol'ver!"

"No, Sean, I think not. My charge is to get you to Pennsylvania in one piece. You may climb all the masts you like once you're in your brother's care." Mr. Oliver put his arm around Sean's shoulders and guided him toward the companionway.

"But there won't *be* any masts with my brother, Mr. Ol'ver!"

Mr. Oliver's reply was lost as the two of them descended.

"Elisabeth, did Davey here tell ye all about the porpoise and the fish? I tell you, David had those fish landing filleted into the skillet for the cook to fry faster than we could eat 'em! It was a sight to see. One I'll ne'er forget, I'll tell ye that now."

"Good evening, Liam. Well, actually, he didn't have much to add to what little I'd already heard from the crew."

"Aye, well, that's David, the strong, silent type. Keep in mind ye'll need to see me whenever ye require a full accounting of events. Now, come, the both of ye. Rob's waiting. A cèilidh of sorts is underway on the aft deck. Annie says ye were planning on singing with her tonight, Elisabeth. Is that so?"

"Nay? Truly? Annie did?" David stood, offering his hand to Elisabeth.

"Yes, I suppose there might be a bit more to me than you're aware of." She stood without taking his hand and turned on her heel, walking toward the aft deck.

Liam laughed. "I think ye offended her."

"Aye, well mayhap," David said, "Let's go, I don't want to miss any if she sings."

The musicians were running through the motions of tuning their instruments, matching their notes one against the other. "The lad with the flute, he's called Ewan. Thomas is playing the accordion, and ye of course know Sarah and Annie. The one with Elisabeth in his arms is Seamus. He plays the fiddle," Liam said, with a discreet eye to David's reaction at the last.

David whipped his head around to follow Liam's gaze. Eyes narrowed and jaw tensed, he watched as Seamus swung her round and round.

"David, you're here. Good, I took the liberty of bringing this up from your case," his uncle said, coming up behind him, producing a harmonica from his pocket.

Seamus released Elisabeth at Annie's side, and David turned slowly, taking the harmonica. "Thanks, Uncle John," he said, glancing back to see that Seamus still had his hands off her.

"Ye play, David? Well, well, cull of many talents. Let's give these Irish lads a helping hand then, aye?"

Liam quickly tested the heft of a few of the smaller barrels in the vicinity, choosing one that was half empty to serve as a drum. They waited a few beats into the first song, then joined in, the drum setting a rhythm the harmonica answered, delighting the others. Annie and Elisabeth joined in at the chorus.

She set his blood dancing, just looking at her. He hadn't meant to set about her earlier; he had no quarrel with the lass.

He couldn't keep his eyes off her as she sang song after song, not even when Sarah Wallace came and sidled down between him and Rob. As soon as he saw her step aside to take a break, he pocketed his harmonica and went to her, grabbing her hand and startling her into a laugh as he swung her round and round in step with the music.

He kept her dancing for near an hour, until she finally begged, breathless and laughing, to sit for a spell.

"I'm finally warm, David, for the first time since the ship has sailed."

"Aye, well, it does feel good to be moving, doesn't it?" He struggled to keep his arm on his knee instead of drawing her closer. She was a bonny lass at any time, but more so now with her cheeks flushed, her eyes bright. "Your voice is a wonder Elisabeth. What other talents are ye storing?"

She laughed. "Not too many actually. I do love to write poetry, though. My friend Rhee and I would while away hours reciting our poems to each other."

"Aye? Recite one now. If ye don't mind, that is."

"Oh, I think I'll save that for another day. It won't serve me well to reveal all my secrets in one evening. Besides, I should be seeing to my father before he seeks to find what's become of me."

"Another evening then." He stood and offered her a hand. She took it this time, jumping to her feet at the same time the ship rolled, tossing her toward him. Gently, he steadied her, reveling in the sensation of the warm, soft weight of her.

She backed away slightly and looked up at him. Keeping one hand around her waist, he moved the other to her face, pulling a bit of hair back from her eyes.

"Aye, but ye are a bonny lass, Elisabeth," he said quietly, losing himself in her eyes, his hand cradling her chin while his thumb caressed her cheek. He could kiss her. She wouldn't mind, he could tell. And Uncle John had retired an hour ago.

But there were more than a few eyes on them, that he could also tell.

Might be worth it.

Then he thought of her father and dropped his hand from her face, pulling her closer for a brief instant before releasing her and guiding her toward the companionway leading to her cabin.

At the open hatch Elisabeth turned and gave him a dazzling smile. The force of it startled him, and once again he found he had lost his tongue. How did she do that?

Why did he let her?

"Good night, David. Sleep well!" she said. She didn't wait for a reply.

He let her because he didn't seem to have a say in the matter.

He rejoined the others, dropping between Liam and Rob on the deck. Liam looked at him, opening his mouth, then closing it as he seemed to think the better of whatever he'd intended to say. He passed over a cup of water, and David drank from it gratefully.

"She's an acid tongue, that wench," Rob said.

David turned on him, not certain he heard right. "Say

again?" he said, his hands curling into fists at his side.

"Sarah . . . ye left me at her mercy. And she has none."

David relaxed, remembering Sarah had come to sit between them. He grinned. "Just sparing ye time with an agreeable lassie, Rob."

"Dinna need no favors, lad."

David pulled out his harmonica and played softly. He watched as Annie beckoned and Liam went to her, holding her close as she whispered in his ear. Laughing, Liam turned to Sarah and hauled her up and into a dance.

Sweet, the lass had been aiming daggers his way for hours, since he'd first taken hold of Lisbeth. Hadn't been much more than a few glances between them, and she thought to make something of it. And there'd be no more of that now, besides.

Elisabeth hadn't pulled away.

"He's always been one to attract the lassies, or anyone for that matter. Fate's way of evening up the score, I suppose," Rob said.

David continued playing, though he glanced at Rob, signaling his interest. He was curious about Liam. For all his loquaciousness, the lad sure didn't speak much of himself.

"I met him a few years past, when Mr. Oliver bought out my indenture. Liam's had a rough time of it. His ma took to the gin when he was but a wee bairn. He ne'er knew his pa. Some say his pa was an English gent, one who tarried in the village a bit too long whilst on the way to his estate. Mayhap so. Liam doesn't have the look of most. By the time I met him, he was taking more care of his Ma than she of him, with necessity causing him to become very resourceful. Even so, Mr. Oliver has always had an eye out for him—for all those who be needing a little looking after." Rob paused, running his hand down his leg before he caught himself and removed it. It seemed Rob had needed a 'little looking after' himself at one time, and he didn't want to be reminded of it.

"He made sure Liam had enough to eat and attended his school. His ma passed last year. Tongues wagged she overdosed herself with the laudanum. I don't know if it was true, but the time was right when Mr. O decided to make his way to America and asked him along."

The ship's bell struck three bells, and Rob nodded.

"Tomorrow then, David." He got up slowly, steadying himself with his hand against a crate before he walked to the companionway.

Rob was a good, steady sort. He'd likely do well in America.

Annie's high, clear voice rang out with the verse to a melancholy song, signaling the end to the evening. Ewan and David accompanied her, David's thoughts racing as he played. His family; they didn't have much, but they always had food and shelter. If they were ever short of anything, it was Da who did the worrying and providing. If Da hadn't been there, would he've been able to? To provide? He'd like to think so, but truly, would he?

Elisabeth . . . she'd been in his arms. She hadn't pulled away. He was apt to lose sleep over just the thought of it tonight. You'd think she was the first lass he had had in his arms.

Somehow she was.

November 16, 1783—The passengers put together a cèilidh on deck. It is not unusual to have music; it passes the time. However, this one taking place on the fifteenth instant was of a more organized nature. It served to spread goodwill amongst all, I think, and lightened the tedium some are feeling. I've been fortunate to date as I've been able to keep busy with new friends, lessons, and some chores assigned by the first mate. I'm appreciative of the chores—this ship

is very small for one used to having five hectares to work
daily. Uncle John has arranged for me to participate in afternoon lessons given by Mr. Oliver (Liam's guardian). The
mathematics comes easy, but the Latin is requiring a bit of
thought. Liam, in spite of his flippancy, is proficient in all.
The younger ones are most affected by monotony as they
are not allowed on deck without supervision. This morning
Liam, Rob, and I fashioned a stash of logs from a bit of
flotsam and have been encouraging Sean and his friends to
build miniature cabins and such. Mr. Kiefer showed us how
the log cabin was configured. It seems an economical way to
build a lodging fast if ye but had the timber.

*November 17, 1783—We are all feeling the cold overmuch as the
wind is constant and fires are allowed for a short cooking period only,
due to the danger they present. Needless to say, we'd all perish should
the wind carry the fire across the ship. We sighted another ship heading
to London. The captains compared calculations, and Captain Honeywell was satisfied his were accurate. They communicated by means of a
board. Alex, the youngest member of the crew, is helpful when we ask
for clarification of the 'goings on' aboard. I often feel that the language
the crew speaks to one another is something entirely other than English.
It's helpful to have someone interpret. I mean to ask if he lives in Philadelphia when not at sea.*

*November 18, 1783—Elisabeth shared one of her poems with me
last evening while we took exercise on deck. I wasn't sure of the meaning, but I did appreciate her company. I've come to look forward to
spending time with her.*

*November 19, 1783—This morning the sea was much calmer. I
tried fishing early on, but without luck. I told Liam if he had but risen
from the berth at first light, he could have applied his charm again, and
we would be eating other than oatcakes. Uncle John's wee 'sermon' was*

particularly agreeable this morning, especially as he joined us in a game of hazard first. Prior to this trip, I hadn't known he played, much less that he enjoyed playing. It's something I would have thought the kirk to frown upon.

November 20, 1783—The sailors are forecasting a storm tomorrow based upon the look of the moon tonight. Fishing may be good if it holds off until the afternoon. They say it may cause us to be confined below for our own safety if it is a powerful storm. I pray not.

7

"STORM COMING," DAVID SAID.

The *Industry* struggled as she flew across the ocean in a valiant effort to outrun the white-capped swells battering her on all sides. The crew was lively about the ship, busy preparing for the imminent onslaught, and frigid seawater was flying over the deck in all directions.

"Ye lured me up here at the crack of dawn with false hopes of catching breakfast," Liam said, watching the activity with interest.

"Aye, well, not today, I'm thinking. How's Sean managing?"

"Flashed his hash twice already. Had to leave before I did as well."

"Ye've a stomach like a rock. More than likely ye didna want to help Mr. O clean the lad."

"No' for the third time anyway."

The first mate eyed Liam and David.

"You lads aim to be on deck; I aim to get some use out of you. Mannus!" Richter shouted, calling Alex to his side.

David and Liam ran to and fro across the deck as Alex

assigned them tasks. They hauled the hammocks down to the shelter of the crew's quarters, then they found him pieces of tarpaulin that he placed up in the weather rigging so that the watch would have some shelter from the wind and driving rain. He took them forward to check that the boats were secure, shouting orders as he showed them how to clear the drain holes and cover them with canvas. David lost hold of a sheet of canvas as the wind whipped it from his hands, sailing it straight into Liam, knocking him down. Alex ran around the boats to retrieve it as Liam struggled to free himself from its bulk.

"Thanks, Liam," Alex said, laughing. "Lucky break there, David. Ritcher wouldn't take lightly to us losing a bit of canvas to the storm." The ship rolled heavily, and David and Liam both lost their footing and slid toward the rail. Ritcher gave a signal to Alex.

"You're gonna need to get below now," Alex said as they rejoined him. "It's coming fast." He ran to check that the lifebuoys were secured to lines, then went aft to fasten the hatch cover.

The boys started toward the companionway, stopping as they spotted a passenger climbing out.

"Sean? What's he doing? Sean!" Liam shouted, the wind drowning out the sound of his voice. "Sean, over here!" Sean set his hands on the rail, peering into the water below. "Ah, hell." Liam ran to fetch him.

"Hang tight! All hands, hang tight!" one of the sailors bellowed.

The ship canted heavily, and David turned, facing the mountain of water that towered over them, dwarfing the ship.

Holy Christ, they were going down.

He took ahold of the mast he stood by, bracing his legs, ducking his head and praying. The wave burst across the ship with a roar, covering him, soaking him through, crashing over the deck and sweeping away everything loose in its path. David lost his hold on the mast and was tossed in the grip of the water as it battered him to and fro across the deck. His legs straddled the rail as the ship rolled high and he clung to it as she trembled heavily and settled. Stunned and shivering, he struggled to unwrap himself.

"On your feet, lads! Ain't paying ye to take a morning swim," someone called out, likely Ritcher. The crew had been knocked about as well. David looked for Liam and Sean.

My God . . . Liam and Sean.

"Man overboard!" Ritcher shouted as the bell rang. "Heave to!"

"Let go the lifebuoy!"

"Man overboard! Heave to!" shouted a sailor from the mizzen rigging.

Liam was swimming. Swimming. David blinked, struggling to focus. Sean was in the water, not far. A seaman had thrown a lifebuoy out, though Liam hadn't seen it, focused as he was on reaching the boy. Liam couldn't swim well; well, neither could he for that matter, and he looked to be tiring. Alex ran up beside him. David stood, pointing toward the boats.

"Why havena ye launched one?" he shouted.

Alex shook his head. "They won't."

"What d'ye mean, they won't? They'll drown!"

Alex just looked at him, helpless.

"Hell. Keep them spotted. Don't let them out of your sight!" David ran toward a seaman who was barking orders up at the men in the rigging. He grabbed him. "Launch a boat!" he shouted.

"No," the sailor said. "Cap't will crucify the lot of us for risking the boat and the crew. It can't be launched in this weather. He needs to grab the buoy. We'll bring him in, he does it quick enough."

"He doesn't see it! Surely ye can see that. There's no time; he's foundering now! Someone's got to help them! He needs it brought to him!" It seemed as if hours had passed, though it had been less than a minute. But even seconds in that roiling black sea . . .

Someone? He ran toward another buoy, struggling with the ropes, releasing it from the rail.

"Get below! They be lost; ye'll only be joining them to their fate." A sailor had run up behind him and wrapped an arm around his neck.

He recognized the sailor, a small man, one who used his acid tongue to make up for what he lacked in size. David had always taken pains in the past to avoid the man. Not now. He broke his grip easily and turned, drawing back his fist. He hit him hard, sending him sailing back onto the deck. Two more sailors approached, one to grab his fallen mate before he slid off the deck, the other with his hand up in a conciliatory gesture as he motioned to the buoy.

"Ease off, lad. The reach of the rope may be long enough. We'll add to it if we can and tow you back."

David grabbed the buoy and ran aft, past where Liam and Sean had drifted. The sailor followed, handling the rope. "Stay afloat, let the lads drift to you. Don't tire yourself."

He stood at the rail, buoy in hand, frozen in place as huge swells of inky black water rolled up to meet him, the frigid spray soaking him through afresh. A minute now; they had been in a minute and counting.

He couldn't go in there; he just couldn't. The man's right, they're lost in that. There's no point in his going in. None at all. He swallowed hard and looked toward Alex, to see if he had them in sight. If he didn't . . . nay, he was pointing.

White-livered, yellow-bellied eijit, jump in there, *now*, damn it. Already wasted a minute just making a damn decision should have been second nature, didn't need deciding in the first place. He wrapped the buoy's rope around his wrist and vaulted over the rail, jumping as far from the ship's side as he could manage.

Good God Almighty Holy Mother of God. Water—hurt. He gasped frantically for air. Nothing but water—and it hurt. Hurt. Thousands of tiny knives piercing his skin. He couldn't see, the towering wall of water in front of him dwarfed him. Tremendous waves swelled around him, caging him. Caging him. He couldn't breathe—the knives—suicide's a sin. What in God's name had he just done?

The only thing.

Liam and Sean, is it even possible they're still conscious? He looked back at the ship as a swell carried him high. Aye, Alex was still there, pointing. They were still above water. He forced himself to kick, trying to maintain his position like the man said. His teeth chattered convulsively, the pain shooting about his head. Seconds passed and the sea tossed him back, plunging him once again into a deep abyss.

Don't panic. Kick again, don't panic. Same waves be tossing Liam and Sean this direction as well. Stay put, conserve energy. He rose to the top again. There, Liam had Sean in one arm and was using the other to pull himself forward. Sean didn't look—nay, don't think. They're above water, not far, not far, not far at all.

He didn't dare call out. He would only end up with a mouth full of water and couldn't be heard over the wind anyway. He waved his free arm high above his head, holding tight to the buoy.

Liam had seen him! He held the buoy in front and began to kick with every ounce of strength he had left. Closer, closer . . . A tug pulled him back and he panicked, suddenly recalling the shark he'd seen trailing the ship the day before. Would he even feel the teeth of the beast, atop the knives? He circled to the front of the buoy and looked behind. The rope was stretched tight all the way to the ship. No shark.

"Eijit," he spat out through his chattering teeth. He looked back to Liam. Still too far. Why hadn't they added to the line? Because this was pointless; they were right—why waste the rope?

Maybe, maybe not. He reached for his knife and began sawing at the rope. Don't drop the knife, don't drop the knife, don't drop the knife.

Suddenly it was no longer taut. Had they just cut him loose, save him the trouble? He followed the line of it to the ship. No, one of the sailors was motioning him forward. Thanks be, they added another length after all.

Putting his knife away, he began moving again, kicking until he reached them. He grabbed Sean under his armpit, pulling half his weight up onto the buoy. The lad was unconscious, and Liam refused to surrender his hold.

"Let go, Liam, I've got him," he tried to shout. "Hang tight to the buoy. It will hold us all. We've got to get back to the ship. Liam! Pay heed man, I have got hold of Sean. Just grab his free hand if ye will. We have to hurry." His voice was hoarse from the salt water he had taken in. Liam wasn't listening.

"Liam." He reached out, touched his face, and turned it toward him.

Recognition dawned slowly in Liam's eyes. The lad barely had the strength to keep himself above water. He nodded slowly, placing a hand on the buoy. David signaled, and the crew began towing them in.

Cold . . . ache . . . sleep now. There'd be no shame in it, not now, none.

Liam's holding on. Liam'd been in the water twice as long. Liam could hang on, well then, so could he.

How much longer, though?

Ma, her pain when his little sister died of the fever, think what the loss of another child would do to her. His brothers, why, they'd not be allowed out of the house forever. They'd never forgive him. America, what of the plans he'd made, all for naught if he slept.

Sleep, no shame in it now . . .

The rope, had it weakened at all when he'd tried to cut it? Might still end for the lot of them in a watery grave, a new beginning indeed. Mayhap Elisabeth could look for their souls to return with the next new moon.

Was she right? Would they return with the next new moon? He could find out if he surrendered.

No. How it had felt to hold her. There. Aye, that was sweet. Why hadn't he kissed her when he'd had the chance? That was surely one of the more stupid decisions he'd made.

The ship. Good God, we made it.

Two sailors had climbed down the ropes and were waiting for them. They reached for Sean first, and Liam helped David push him up and over to the men. One of them slipped a harness over his chest and under his arms and gave a signal to haul him up. David looked at Liam in relief as they pulled Sean over the rail, then watched in slow horror as Liam's eyes lost focus, and he let go of the buoy, slipping underwater.

"Nay!"

Adrenalin raced through him, and he dove without thought, thrashing his arms about to feel for him. He grabbed Liam's hair and reached for his collar. Which way now—up was which way? He couldn't remember; both ways were dark. Forcing the terror down, he chose a direction and kicked toward it, gulping greedily at the air as soon as he broke the surface. He didn't see the wave coming, wasn't hanging tight to the buoy. It picked him up high, slammed him full force against the side of the ship. He dimly realized he'd lost his grip on Liam.

Raining now. Sea is warmer, warmer than the rain. Can sleep now.

8

FRIGID SEAWATER MISTED HEAVILY THROUGHOUT the hold as the storm continued to batter the *Industry* the next two days, adding to the despair of those trapped within. The ship pitched violently, throwing possessions and those passengers still standing against the tables, bunks, and floor. Those in bunks were tossed against the side of the ship and each other, rolling in their own or their mates' vomit. The two sloop buckets had long since overturned, the stench of their contents overpowering all others in the cold, airless shelter.

Children cried, women screamed, some prayed earnestly; most just moaned in misery, pleas for water repeated over and over in vain. The water barrel was empty, with no hope of getting another while the storm raged. When it finally began to abate that second night they were all too exhausted, sick, and frightened to do more than lie helplessly in their berths until morning came.

ELISABETH PRESSED A COOL CLOTH against her

father's forehead, then down along his face and throat.

"Can you drink, Papa? Just a few sips?" He opened his mouth slightly, and she held up the back of his head, pressing the cup to his lips. He closed his eyes and mouth after a swallow, and she lay his head back on the pillow, waiting. Good, it stayed down. He'd been vomiting for hours. Maybe it had been days, she'd lost track of time.

Captain Honeywell and his first mate were coming down the ladder. She stood and went to the door, listening. The captain was speaking, his words slurring from exhaustion. "Confounded fool lads, damn near brought my ship down. If they make it through this, they'll wish they hadn't. See to it, Mr. Ritcher."

"Yes, sir."

"Well, speak up, man, will they?"

"Sir?"

"Make it. Have you checked on them or not, damn it?" the captain asked, turning back to face Ritcher.

Ritcher had noticed her and nodded in her direction. The captain turned to look, set his mouth in that way he had, then turned on his heel and disappeared into his quarters.

"Mr. Ritcher, who? Who is he talking about? Mr. Ritcher, please!"

Ritcher had mumbled something unintelligible and hurried back up the companion ladder, dropping the hatch down after him.

David. Or Liam. Why else would Mr. Ritcher behave in such a manner? My God, what had happened? Not David; please not David. Then, ashamed, she bowed her head and said a short prayer for the safety of them all.

But please, not David.

Her father moaned, and she walked back into their room. Alex; Alex will know. Alex would be down soon to see to the captain. She just must stay awake until he did. She mustn't miss him.

Oh, God, please not David.

9

DAVID LAY STILL, HIS EYES shut as he tried to put a name to his surroundings. His head pounded, every muscle in his body, clenched rigid against the cold, ached. His teeth chattered, poking away at the ache in his head. The cold . . . the sea! His eyes flew open as he raised his head. There was something he needed to recall.

No, the pain . . . he quickly fell back, turning his head to his side, retching. Someone, his uncle maybe, murmured words of comfort as he cleaned him. He tried to concentrate, tried; there was something important he should know. The effort was too much. He slipped back under.

Later, minutes, maybe hours, he woke to the smell of soup. Someone put a spoon full of it to his mouth. He felt his stomach heave again; nothing left to vomit, vomited anyway, felt the cloth around his face. He turned his head away from the smell. No more, didn't want more. Soft hands.

Someone was talking quietly; he couldn't make out the words. Soft hands, soft words, then nothing but blackness.

No, no water. Didn't want anything. Stop. Hurt.

Again, he surrendered, welcoming the blackness.

"DAVID, DAVID? Come on, mate. It's been more than two days now, ye need to wake up. Ye're worrying me, man."

Liam. He tried to answer, but the words wouldn't come. Two days? Why? Not possible.

"David, if ye can hear me, press my hand," Liam said as he grabbed David's hand between his own two.

He made an effort, but his fingers wouldn't move. Tried to open his eyes. Maybe just looking through his lashes wouldn't bring that awful pain. Nay, not worth the effort. He tried his fingers again.

"Elisabeth, he moved!"

Loud. He winced, then he felt a soft hand across his brow, smoothing back his hair, and a cloth moving gently round his face.

"I'll go find the Reverend. He's only just left. I'll be right back," she said. "You'll stay with him?"

Silence. David moved his fingers again, stronger this time, questioning.

"Aye, well, ye remember the storm coming, I expect. Sean had come up on deck to find us. He wanted to try his hand at fishing, ken. Sick as he was."

David tried his fingers again, an urgent press.

"He's fine now, Davey, no small thanks to ye. Don't be worrying over him. Mr. O has him chained to his side. Otherwise ye'd find yourself sharing that bunk, so troubled is he that ye may not wake. When ye got us back to the ship, some of the crew were waiting to hoist us up. Story is, I went under again, you dove to fetch me. When ye brought me up, a huge swell claimed the both of us. Ye ended with your head slammed against the side, the both of us headed under again 'fore the sailors took hold and hauled us in. Sean and I, we recovered by the next day, but the storm still kept us down. Ye, on the other hand . . . ." Liam stopped, his voice breaking.

David tensed, the terror of those few moments washing over him afresh.

"I don't mind telling ye, Davey, we've all been worried. That's a harsh way to get the lass's attention. Once they let her down here, she's only left your side to tend to her Da. The storm made him awfully sick," Liam said, curling his fingers tightly around David's hand.

"That was a damn fool thing to do Davey, and I . . . I thank ye for it."

David returned the pressure, then surrendered again to the blackness.

ELISABETH TIPTOED BACK into her cabin just before her father woke. She'd spent the night in steerage, helping the Reverend and Liam with David. Liam had tried to convince her to sleep in the berth, "only to keep the lad warm Lisbeth, no one can find fault with that. Ye've more padding than the rest of us when the ship tosses him." But she didn't, as much as she wanted to. She contented herself with rubbing his hands to warm them and sponging his face to cool his forehead and keep him clean as he continued to vomit up whatever remained in his stomach. He didn't wake all night long, but she thought his fever broke.

She'd been so frightened when she found out what had happened. Reverend Wilson had told her that at the onset of the storm Paul had stuck his head out the hatch door to look for Sean and had had just enough time to see David go over the side before his mother grabbed him by the waist and pulled him back in. He'd told his mother what he'd seen, and she had gone to Wilson.

She knew the German mothers on board had a soft spot for David and Liam, both of whom had spent hours below entertaining the children with games and card tricks. They were doing what they could to help David recover.

She prayed they knew more of how to go about that than she did.

ANOTHER DAY, another night; still, he was down.

"Elisabeth, are you leaving?" Papa asked from his bunk.

"I'm going to get you some broth, Papa. You should try to keep something down now that you're feeling better."

"Later, not now, Beth. Now I just want to sleep. Thank you for keeping me company. You're a good daughter," he said, his voice trailing off, his eyes closing.

She hoped he still felt that way in a few days when he was up, hearing the talk that was making its way through this ship.

Should she sleep as well? No, how could she, as worried as she was. Grabbing a book from the shelf, she headed to the kitchen to talk the cook out of some broth. The Reverend had told her David had kept some water down last evening. So far he had yet to speak, but he was waking briefly. That had to be a good sign. Please, Lord.

The cook gave her a broad smile as she entered the kitchen. "Aye, Miss Elisabeth! Cap' says to give ye my best for your Da. Here it is a'waiting. More than enough for ye, too. And how is Mr. Hale?"

"He's much better. He's sleeping now. Thank you, Mr. Grimes," she said, reaching for the soup.

"Sleeping, eh? Well, he can't eat if he's sleeping, can he then? Here, I think the lad may be wanting something to settle his stomach 'bout now. This will surely tempt him. Have him eat the broth while it still be warm," he said with a wink, handing her a loaf of fresh bread. It smelled wonderful. "I hear he's keeping water down now. That's a good sign."

Elisabeth looked at him, opened her mouth to reply, then closed it, not sure of what to say.

The cook laughed. "Come back later. There'll be more waiting for your da."

"Thank you, and I'll thank the Captain for this," she said, smiling as she backed her way out of the kitchen.

"Oh, I'm thinking we'll keep the Captain out of this, if it all be the same to you."

She hoped God didn't judge her too harshly for all the deceit she'd carried out these last few days. And now she was taking food from the Captain's table. But David would never get better if he didn't start eating something. The aroma of the food roused even her stomach to attention, making her wonder when she had last eaten.

"DAVEY, LOOK what an angel has brought us!"

Elisabeth looked up, her heart jumping to her throat. "David, you're awake!"

"No' sure; thought I smelled fresh bread, likely dreaming."

"This looks to be straight from the Captain's table, Davey. I think it really *is* bread, fresh bread. Can ye believe it? It pays to have friends in high places, aye?"

"To be sure. Hello, Elisabeth."

Warm brown eyes met hers as Liam helped him sit up. She looked away, hastily busying herself with the food. "Good morning." Good heavens, why was she flustered? Surely he couldn't remember if her hands lingered as she had soothed him and cleaned him. Nor the prayers she had whispered. Could he?

She handed the food to Liam and climbed on the berth. "Where's your cup, Liam?" He pointed, and she poured some broth into it and handed it to him. "Eat."

She turned to David with her bowl. He grimaced each time she held the broth to his mouth, his eyes not meeting hers. But he swallowed. Was he embarrassed? Or would he rather someone else held the bowl? She looked toward Sarah's berth, finding her fast asleep. The poor girl had been suffering alone for days, vomiting whenever she woke, though she scorned Elisabeth's offer of water last night, so maybe she wasn't completely alone. Annie was up and around a little, she likely cared for her. It was certainly not her father. He'd been insensible with drink since the storm. Well, it wasn't her concern. Sarah had certainly made that clear since the cèilidh.

She broke off a few chunks of bread and put them in David's hand.

"Make shares, Lisbeth. I havena seen ye eat in days," Liam said, reaching for the piece she handed him.

She did, taking as small a portion as she could.

After the last bite, David lay back down, looking at Liam. "Liam, go on deck for a spell for me, will ye? Your stories are getting stale. Ye need some new tales."

"Aye, well, I could be using a wee bit of fresh air, if ye're sure you're not needing me for anything."

"Go!" David said.

Liam grinned, jumping off the berth. "I'll send the Rev'rend, Lisbeth."

"You've a friend for life, you know," Elisabeth said quietly, climbing down from the bunk after Liam had left.

"Aye, I know, one I be proud to claim." He moved gingerly, readjusting his position, closing his eyes. "Don't go, Lisbeth." He reached out a hand, and she took it in hers. "Can ye stay? Will ye read?"

"Yes, of course I will. I've brought a book."

"I enjoy hearing your voice. Start where they bring Gull'ver to the city gates."

She had thought him asleep, but he had known the book, had known where she had left off. He did want her here.

"Of course." She let go of his hand and sat, opening the book to read aloud.

"The emperor, and all his court, came out to meet us; but his great officers would by no means suffer his majesty to endanger his person by mounting on my body . . ."

10

LIAM HAD HEARD THE RUMORS. He and Sean owed their lives to these men, after David. No one would openly acknowledge it, but Rob had told him it had been whispered about that the Captain was within seconds of giving the order to make sail. Would have, too, if David hadn't reached them just when he had.

He understood. It was the man's duty to weigh one, or as the case may be, three, lives against a hundred and fifty. A ship can't hove to in weather like that without great risk. And if the crew hadn't been quick about towing them back and hoisting them up, they would have been left.

And if that didn't leave a rock of terror low in one's gut, nothing would.

So he'd clean when the captain gave the order to clean.

A crew of women organized the effort, sending men up on deck with buckets of grime and orders to replace it with sea water. Over and over. Those staying below were put to task scrubbing and repairing, taking care not to use so much water that it leaked into the cargo hold below and incited the

Captain's temper. Not a one of them balked. The hold was days past the point of becoming unbearable.

And he'd help with the crew's quarters as well, something the Captain hadn't ordered.

Some had realized early on that helping the sailors with domestic chores got them small favors in return. Extra fires for cooking . . . sweeter water for a sick child . . .

Sometimes even a hand up from a roiling black sea.

UNCLE JOHN HAD MOVED him to the forecastle so he could sleep during the cleanup. But he'd had his fill of sleeping, he needed some air. And it looked as if the sun might be shining. He rolled out of the hammock, stretching his hands high above his head, then down to the floor. He looked up as Liam walked in with a passel of women, toting an armful of supplies.

"Liam, good, you're here. Have ye had breakfast? I'm near famished."

"Hmmph. 'Bout time ye got out of that bed. Breakfast was hours ago. I notice ye waited till just after the cleaning was done, nothing wrong with your senses."

The women patted him about the head and shoulders, speaking quickly amongst themselves in German. He'd picked up enough of the language to understand the gist of what they were saying and smiled, thanking them for their concern before turning back to Liam.

"Can ye grab something and meet me on deck, Liam? I canna face another minute 'tweendecks, even to find grub."

"Ye need to face another twenty minutes. Sit back down till we're done. This willna take long."

Hell, he was hungry. He glared at Liam.

"I can make ye, easily enough," Liam said, shrugging.

That might be true. At the moment, anyway. He hesitated.

"I'm helping these women David, so dinna make me worry after ye."

David lay back in the hammock, hands behind his head. "By all means, Ma. This I have to see anyway."

HE BLINKED SEVERAL times against the brightness, steadying himself at the top of the ladder.

"David!"

Sean broke from Mr. Oliver's hold and ran, vaulting up into David's arms, careening him backwards into Liam, throwing his arms tightly around David's neck. Laughing, Liam came around and grabbed Sean.

"Here now, squirrel, ye dinna wanna be choking the life out of him, d'ye? He just got it back inta him."

"David," Mr. Oliver said solemnly, taking his hand. "I am more grateful than you can ever know." He threw his arms around David in a strong, brief embrace.

Somewhat uncomfortable, he returned the man's embrace, mumbling a reply before sliding down against a crate.

"How have ye been keeping busy, Sean? Think ye can best me in chips yet?" he asked. He glanced at Liam, who gave a mock salute before heading back below toward the provisions.

"It's been awful without ye, David. Liam won't play, so I canna practice as good. Rob doesna spin the yarns Liam does, and we had to stay below for days while the ship was tossing. I got to sleep with you, only ye didna know so it didna really count . . ."

On and on Sean went. David leaned back, grateful to feel the sun on his face and the boy in his lap.

"The water was awful cold, wasn't it David? I was really scared," Sean said, his voice dropping to a near whisper, the change rousing David.

"It was the coldest I have ever been, Sean, and I was really scared, too."

"You were?" The lad's eyes searched his face, his blue eyes squinting in disbelief. "I'm not going to do that again, go near the rail without Rob or Liam or Mr. Ol'ver or you. Mr. O don't believe me, I think, but I'm not, I promise. I'm sorry I made ye and Liam come in with me and that ye got so awful sick."

David looked at the boy, his tears threatening to spill over freckles as he gave the speech he'd obviously been thinking over for days. He grabbed him close and murmured, "We're all fine now, Sean, dinna fash over it. It was only an accident, it wasna your fault." Sean held on tight, shoulders shaking as he nodded.

David pulled back and tapped Sean's nose with his forefinger. "Look, there's Liam, and he's brought some oatcakes. Grab some for me, will ye, 'fore he claims them all?"

"Take a break, Mr. O, will ye? Find Rob for us and send him over," Liam said.

"I'll bring Sean when I head below," Wilson said.

Mr. Oliver glanced at Sean, who was hanging tightly to David's leg, and nodded. "Aye, then I will."

Minutes later Rob limped up on deck. "Finally, man, ye gave us all a scare."

"Did ye bring the chips?" David asked before Rob could think to coddle him as well. "Well then, toss 'em, man; let's play 'fore Sean forgets all I taught him. Will ye join in, Uncle?"

He did, surprising them again with his luck as he beat them handily.

"Just another example of experience gentlemen, winning out over the enthusiasm of youth," he said, standing to take his leave, reaching for Sean's hand.

"I don't wanna go, Rev'rend Wilson," Sean said, his arm still wrapped around David's leg.

Wilson bent to whisper something in his ear, and Sean glanced at David. David winked at him, and Sean tightened his lips rebelliously but didn't protest further as he rose and followed.

One game was enough. David leaned his head back, closing his eyes as he raised his face to the sun.

"I'm well enough Liam, just enjoying the gift of the sun and fresh air. Leave me be," he said, before Liam could ask.

He listened idly as Liam and Rob rambled on about the virtues of one of the lassies Rob had fancied back home, and he himself daydreamed about the virtues of a lass on board this ship. He must have drifted to sleep, as he started a bit at the sound of Liam's voice.

"Good afternoon, Elisabeth. It's a fine day to be up on deck. How's your father faring?"

He opened his eyes as Elisabeth sat next to him, a spot Rob must have vacated.

"Papa is fine, thank you for asking, Liam. He rose this morning feeling much like himself again and made his way to the Captain's cabin for the afternoon."

"So, ye'll be having the afternoon free to spend with the likes of us, then?"

"Yes, I do. Have you anything entertaining planned?"

"Nay, and the truth of it is, David's tiring of my entertainment these past days."

David snorted. "Liam, sounds like Elisabeth will act as nursemaid now. You can take some time off."

"I don't need time off, David. Ye're no' a chore."

"Go find Annie, or Eliza, or what about the lass yesterday, the one who offered—"

Liam quickly stood. "Stop, Davey, no' in front of Lisbeth. Ye'll have her telling tales out of school. I'll be back in a bit. Behave yourselves, now."

He left, and David turned to Elisabeth. "Ye don't have to

stay if ye've things need doing. I know you've been nursing both your da and me the past few days. Ye're likely weary. I didn't mean to volunteer your time without asking. Just that Liam wouldn't have left otherwise, and he needs to. And I don't need a nursemaid." He paused. Maybe that sounded ungrateful. "Not anymore, that is. I didn't mean to imply I don't appreciate all that ye did. I do. Appreciate it, that is."

Hell, maybe it was better when he lost his tongue.

"Do you want me to go?"

"Not unless ye need to."

"All right," she said, looking at him uncertainly.

Ah hell. His fingers found hers, and he grasped her hand tightly. "Stay. Please."

She looked at him and smiled. "I'd like to."

He spent the rest of afternoon listening to her talk of home, contributing to the conversation now and then, dozing off now and again. He was glad of her company. Glad she didn't seem to expect much else. He kept ahold of her hand, all the while stroking the base of her thumb with his own in a slow rhythm until the sun was low in the sky.

"Papa will begin to wonder where I am soon. David?"

"Hmmm?" He stood, helping her to her feet. He looked at her face, waiting.

"David, I want you to know I'll always treasure this afternoon. I'll always remember it." She looked around quickly, then rose on her toes, her mouth aimed for his cheek.

He wasn't one to make the same mistake twice. With lightning quickness, his hand cupped her chin, moving her face so that her mouth met his lips instead of his cheek. He'd meant it to be a quick kiss, and he was prepared for 'nice.' Maybe something a bit more; after all, just touching the lass was beyond nice.

What he wasn't prepared for was the slow spinning sensation that enveloped him as everything about them receded, leaving nothing but her: the sweet taste of her mouth, the warmth of her body as she pressed against him, the softness of her skin under his fingers as he caressed her face. Her scent marked him, filled him, drowning out all others.

"Ahem. Hello? David?" Liam tapped his shoulder. "David!"

He drew back slowly, his eyes searching her face.

"Elisabeth, thanks for watching over the lad. Mr. Ritcher says your da is looking for ye. I told him if I saw you, I'd send ye directly."

He couldn't believe it; he'd forgotten where they were. Completely, utterly forgotten. The bump on his head, it must have lingering effects. Except she had felt it as well, he could see the confusion in her eyes as her fingers went to her lips. She nodded without speaking and pulled away, walking quickly in the direction of her cabin.

No sooner than she was out of earshot did Liam begin his tirade.

"Jesus, Mary, and Joseph, David, what if I had been her da? Or one of the captain's men who reports to her da? Are ye mad, man? Isna one near-death experience in a week enough for ye? Where's your sense? I know I haven't known ye long, but I had ye figured for the cautious, careful type. Ne'er the type to grab a lass whose da disapproves of the likes of ye and kiss her like she was your next meal, in broad daylight no less, for all to see. What were ye thinking, man?"

It was clearly far from 'broad' daylight. David grinned as he faced the sea and made a point of watching the sun disappear.

"Well, it's light enough that all but a blind man can see, and her da is no blind man, ye can be sure of that."

David laughed. "What am I thinking? Aside from the fact that ye're making a lot of fuss over a wee peck? Aye, well . . . I'm thinking here's a bonny lass, one I happen to fancy no less, standing in front of me, one who clearly willna mind being kissed. And I'm thinking who knows what the next minute will bring." He looked past Liam. Something had caught his eye in the gathering dusk. Squinting, he raised a hand and pointed.

"Mayhap that monster over there will swallow this ship, and I'll have missed my chance to kiss the bonny lass I happen to fancy, for sake of prudence. And what little comfort that will be as I wallow in the belly of that monster fish."

Liam lowered his head, shaking it from side to side in mock disgust and resignation. David grabbed him by the shoulders and turned him to face the sea, just as the whale rose alongside the ship with an audible snort. Liam jumped back, knocking the both of them off their feet.

"Oggh." David grumbled and pushed. "Ye weigh more than a boll of wet oats. Don't forget I'm but barely an invalid."

"Invalid, my arse." Liam said. But he moved off and over, never taking his eyes off the monster fish.

"It's a whale. At least I think it is," David said. "I don't believe it'll harm us. I just said those things to make my point."

The whale kept pace with the ship, its bulk dwarfing the *Industry*.

"Point taken," Liam said slowly, his eyes still locked on the whale. "Ye know Davey; there's never been a dull moment with ye."

"Me? I thought it be you. My life was steady 'fore I met you on that quay."

Then, with no more noise or warning than it had given upon its arrival, the whale submerged.

"Ye don't think it'll come up under and capsize us, do ye?" David asked.

"Nay, it's no' our time to die quite yet."

David looked hard at him. "Really now, is that so? Well

then, I ask ye give me fair warning when you determine the time has arrived."

Liam laughed. "I don't think so, no' and have the responsibility of the virtue of the lass that may be within arm's reach of ye."

"Hmmph." David braced himself against the crate and stood. "Let's find some supper. It's been a fair while since I've eaten. Looks like Mrs. Andrews is taking a turn at the fire already. Maybe I'll share with ye."

"Mr. O's a bachelor as well, dinna ken why she couldn't have offered an exchange with him. He's as harmless as the Reverend."

"Mr. O comes packaged with a wild black rascal like you, as opposed to a sweet, angelic youth like me."

"Mr. O's saddled with three lads as opposed to one. She can figure that out quick enough," Liam countered. "Though she probably didna count on ye eating as much as three."

November 30, 1783—Rob says we are on track to arrive in about six weeks, having lost some time due to weather. He spends a good amount of time with the seamen talking about navigation, ship routes, and such. We suffered through a terrible gale, and I lacked the opportunity to write, but all is well now.

11

December 1783

HE HADN'T SEEN HER IN days. In quarters this snug, that was likely by design. Hers?

Had the kiss embarrassed her? Angered her? Disappointed her? Left her indifferent? He could think of nothing other than her and that kiss—didn't mean she couldn't.

She may have simply been playing at nursemaid, a way of passing the time when naught much other was available. Now that he was on his feet, she had no use for him?

Maybe she'd been curious. Consort with the lower sort and all that. Now she'd satisfied her curiosity and had negated the need for more. Well then, maybe his curiosity was satisfied as well, and he'd negated his need for more.

"Have ye heard a word I've said, Davey?"

"Sure, ye said ye willna be missing home." Best pay attention on who was in front of him; stop worrying over who wasn't. "I can't think on it too much, though, Liam. I've no sense what life will be like once we've landed. There's no anchor to it, aye?"

"Hmmph, well, Mr. O feels like home to me, and ye'll be around, so I've no worries on that score. Ye'll be my anchor if I be needing one. I can count on that; I can count on you. Look, here comes your uncle."

"Morning, Uncle John, what brings ye up so early?

"It's Sunday, and it looks to be a fair day. Mayhap we should have service up on deck."

"That's a grand idea," Liam said. "Reverend, have ye by chance met Elisabeth's da?"

"I have. Why is it you ask?"

"I've seen neither him nor the lass on deck in some days now. I was thinking it would be the Christian thing to ask him to service also. He's the type would appreciate a personal invitation."

Ahh, hell, Liam. All the pains he'd taken to keep his uncle from guessing he was partial to the lass.

"I miss the lass. We grew . . . ahh . . . close. Whilst nursing Davey here, ken?

Taking care to keep his own face impassive, David watched his uncle's as the man's eyes darted from Liam to David, then back to Liam. Uncle John was no fool.

"Aye, well, surely ye know the Hales are Catholic, Liam. I'm not so certain he would accept the invitation, personal or not," Wilson said.

What? David's head whipped around to Liam. He hadn't known that. Liam had?

"Oh, to be sure, he wouldna," Liam said. "But he couldna deny his daughter outright the chance to worship, should she choose to, do ye think? It's the same God, right?"

Wilson laughed outright. "There's a bright future for you, Liam, I've no doubt of it. Very well, I'll extend the offer personally to Mr. Hale. I'm heading back below. You lads join me shortly to begin preparations?"

"Aye," David said. He turned to Liam.

"Can't have ye losing focus, man. Like I said, ye're my anchor." Liam shrugged. "'Sides, I *do* miss the lass."

Forget the missing her. Everyone knew this but him? "She's papist, Liam? How long have ye known that?"

"Dinna ken, no' exactly. Does it matter?"

"Does it matter? Are ye daft?"

How could Liam even think that? Hell, he'd have thought someone could have mentioned this before . . . before what?

"Pete's sake, Davey." Liam looked at him, bright blue eyes assessing. "Same God, right?"

No. Well . . . yes. Mayhap. Hell, he didn't know.

ELISABETH HAD COME to the service, alone as Liam had predicted, and was sitting with Annie a short distance away. And was paying heed to Uncle John, just like everyone else.

Or mayhap the others were just outwardly showing respect, and their thoughts were occupied elsewhere while their blood danced about with frustration. Liam frowned pointedly at him, cuffing his knee to point out he'd noticed the fidgeting.

Sean ran to greet Elisabeth as soon as it was over.

"Elisabeth, where have ye been? Ye missed my reci . . . my recit. . . I memorized my six times multi'cation and told the class yesterday. Only ye weren't there to hear it, and ye helped me learn them!"

Elisabeth grabbed Sean, laughing. "I'm sorry, Sean, my Papa had some work he needed my help with these last few days. Would you like to recite them for me now?"

"Now? Nay, it's Sunday. Dinna have to know them on Sunday; ye're supposed to rest on Sundays. Ye don't rest on Sundays?"

"Yes, yes I do. I suppose I was thinking it was more like

talking than work at this point, since you've already memorized them."

"Nay, ye have to wait till the morrow. Are ye coming to
class then? Is your Da done with ye?"

Elisabeth ran her hand through his mop of red hair, then
patted the curls, smoothing them down. She reached for his
hand, taking the cap he held, placing it back atop his head.
"Yes, I believe he's finished with his letters, for a few days
anyway. Hello, Rob, Liam, David."

"We've missed ye, Elisabeth. Glad to hear ye'll be back
tomorrow," Rob said.

"Aye, the young ones are a bit harder to handle without ye,
that's the truth," Liam said. "Were ye feeling poorly?"

"Oh, no. My Papa wanted my help with some of his correspondence. I believe we've finished most of it, though, and
he won't have need of me quite as much."

"Sean! Wait, ye know ye must wait for Liam or me," Rob
said, hurrying after Sean. "It was good to see ye out again,
truly, Elisabeth."

"Thank you, Rob. Goodbye, Sean!"

"Bye Lisabeth. Don't forget tomorrow."

"All right, Sean, maybe we'll have time to start on the sev-
ens," she said, waving a hand.

"I heard tell Mrs. Reid has taken an interest in ye," Liam
said.

Elisabeth looked back at Liam, surprised. "Is there anything you *don't* know, Liam?"

Liam shrugged. "I've always found it helpful to keep my
eyes and ears open."

"Who's Mrs. Reid?" David asked, speaking for the first
time since she'd joined them. It was irksome the way her
presence had sent his blood racing. He was grateful Sean had
gotten to her first. The lad saved him the embarrassment of
running to greet her like a lovesick fool. He had the sink-

ing feeling that without Liam there to make conversation he might remain tongue-tied for the duration. He hoped she hadn't noticed. Of course, Liam had.

"Annie mentioned that the widow Reid was spending a lot of time trying to catch the notice of Mr. Hale and his poor motherless daughter. I gather she tried to ingratiate herself with the father by carrying tales of the daughter?"

"Tales? Of what?" David's dark brows came together in a scowl. "Are ye meaning this widow made something of Elisabeth spending time with me while I was down? Is that true, Elisabeth? Is that why ye've been confined to your cabin?"

"Not confined, precisely, but Papa did suddenly need a lot of help with his correspondence."

"And?" David said.

She raised her brows, questioning.

"*Why* was it that he needed ye close, of a sudden?"

Liam excused himself to see if the Reverend needed help.

"Nay, stay. If ye don't mind, that is. I'll no' be the cause of her being shut in again."

"David, it's not important, really. Mrs. Reid ended up with much less than she bargained for. Having a daughter around full-time doesn't make for ease in romancing. She's the one who convinced Papa I should go to Sunday service, in spite of—never mind. She won't be bending my Papa's ears again with tales of my 'transgressions.' Quite the opposite, I should imagine."

"Lisbeth, I'm sorry for the trouble I've caused ye. Ye need to be doing as your father expects." He put his hands in his pockets to keep from reaching for her and looked at her, rocking back on his heels.

Her eyes snapped, darkening to a deeper blue. "Oh no you don't, David Graham. I'm not a small child. I do and have done many things without my father's express permission. And as of this point in time he hasn't forbidden me to spend time with anyone, *anyone* on this ship. If you choose to no longer spend time with me, then come out and say so, don't hide behind my father. Do I make myself clear? As a matter of fact, there's Sarah standing with Annie. Mrs. Reid was full of talk about—never mind, if I'm not mistaken, Sarah appears to be waiting for you. She'll be much less troublesome. From my understanding, *her* father is much too taken with the bottle to know or care *who* she spends time with."

She stopped, her hand flying to her mouth and her eyes widening in horror. Flushing, she turned and hurried away.

David blinked, taking a step back. She had made it so easy, he hadn't even used the words he'd crafted, explaining their differences.

Liam looked at him, grinning. "She told ye, didna she?"

"David? I need you. Can you come over here?"

David scowled at Liam. "Aye, Uncle John."

Why didn't he feel relief?

December 7, 1783—Uncle John held a service on deck this morning, which was well attended as the day was fair. Some started music on deck for the afternoon, probably not in keeping with the Sabbath, so I didn't attend, but enjoyable for others nonetheless.

December 8, 1783—Full moon last night, bright enough to play cards, and a group of us did. I wish Elisabeth had been able to make it. She may have considered it if I hadn't been there as well.

December 15, 1783—We have had the blessing of a strong wind the last week, and the crew thinks it may be enough to make up for time lost during the gale in November and the stillness after. Many have been ill from seasickness, and the first mate sends us below when the ship rolls overmuch.

12

"LIAM?" DAVID WHISPERED. "YE AWAKE?"
Liam was out of his berth instantly, finger to his lips, shoving David to the companionway and up the ladder.

"Ye wake up Sean, Mr. O will be forgetting he favors ye."

David snorted. "He ne'er loses his temper." He took a deep breath. "Aye, much better. The smell below was stifling this night. At least the wind had kept it down some."

"Country boy."

"Hmmph, and you're no'?"

"Och. Nay. Me, I'm from a thriving city of one hundred or so. Well, mayhap fifty. Varies upon the number of gents passing through for sport. I never much thought on it."

David grinned. "Aye, well, city boy, it's glad I am then, that I brought you up here to observe a clean night sky." The night was brilliant with stars, and the small whitecaps atop the water glowed with a phosphorescent fire. They spent a good while in silence, pointing out falling stars.

David yawned and stretched out his arms. "One night I'm hoping to be lucky enough to see *na fir-chlis*." Alex had explained the phenomenon to him as a strange fire atop the mast, visible only at night.

"Ye willna, ever—it needs to be storming. This crew willna let the likes of us on deck again in a storm, you can be sure of that," Liam said. "Are ye still writing daily in your journal?"

"Aye, I try. But I think I need to slow it down a bit so my pencil makes the entire journey. Why d'ye ask?"

"Elisabeth. She was in a lather about the paper ye had given her. Ye do know her da has much more paper at his disposal than ye?"

David chuckled. "Aye, well, it made her happy." And had taken the look of studied indifference from her eyes for a brief while. It was difficult for her to avoid him on a ship this size, but she was fairly good at ignoring him. "I asked her to write out a wee bit of her poetry."

Liam grunted, but didn't make more of it than that. "She's a good sort. Did ye see her today, watching Alex eat the maggot from his biscuit? She barely flinched." He laughed.

"Aye, well. He didn't have to savor it like it was a delicacy. I'll admit I was feeling a bit queasy myself by the time he was done."

"He did allow as how it was the better variety of the beast," Liam said. "I think mayhap man can eat 'bout anything, he gets hungry enough. And this crew has been hungry enough at times."

"Have ye?"

"A time or two. Well, just be knowing I was hoping to have a copy of it, your journal; forget the poetry. To read when I'm old and grey, ken?"

"It's no' much, I'll be warning ye in advance, but course I can be writing ye out a copy." He elbowed Liam, pointing at one of the figures pacing the deck. "That's Hale coming this way, aye?"

Liam looked, then nodded. "With Wallace. Now that's an unlikely pairing. What do ye make of that?" They inched back further into the shadows, keeping quiet while the two passed, wondering what business Sarah's father could possibly have with Mr. Hale.

"Begging your honor's pardon, don't mean any offense by it, for certain I don't . . ." Mr. Wallace could be heard saying as the two passed by.

"Bumming a bottle, ye think?" David asked softly.

"Could have picked a more generous mark, if so."

13

Christmas Eve, 1783

December 24, 1783—I have missed recording many days, as not much of note has happened. I will try to make up for the loss in this entry. Our progress is finally steady. The days have settled into a predictable, albeit pleasant routine. I always join Uncle John for the noonday meal. The late afternoon is spent in class with Mr. Oliver. His curriculum is limited due to the restrictions and distractions of the ship; however, it does pass the time, and I come away with a bit more knowledge than not each day. Liam and I try to entertain the children on the ship. We found it helps reduce the amount of crying at day's end and makes the evenings easier for all of us. Often we spend time with the Germans and try to extend our knowledge of the language—as do they.

Yesterday there was a cry of "Sail Ahoy," and a great commotion among the crew. The ship was the Ceres, on her way to London, carrying troops. The crew speculates she was carrying the last of the British troops from New York. This being an American vessel, that was cause for an extra ration of rum for the seamen.

This evening the children are putting on a play to commemorate the birth of Jesus. Hymns for both adults and children are planned; it will be held betweendecks as the weather is too frigid for most once the sun goes down. Elisabeth will be able to participate as she is to manage the play. I'm glad of that, as I don't often see her past supper. She avoids me when she's able.

ELISABETH HURRIED DOWN THE LADDER into steerage, smiling to find it chaotic as always, loud with laughter and good natured jests. Someone was playing melodies on a harmonica, and one of the MacTavishes was tuning up his fiddle.

"*Frohe Weihnachten!*" Mrs. Kiefer said as she passed.

"Did you do this, Mrs. Kiefer?" she asked, fingering the decorations strung along the berth. She started to struggle with the German, then settled on English to try to tell her how impressed she was. David came up behind her, rattling off something, and Mrs. Kiefer laughed, embracing her. Hopefully he'd only repeated what she'd been trying to say. It sounded rather long, more than a mere 'they're beautiful.'

Politely, she took her leave and continued on toward the children. She made it as far as the next berth before he stepped in front of her, walking backwards so that he could face her as they moved.

"Lisbeth, the wee ones, they all be wanting to know the plan, lass. Liam and I havena a clue."

"David, good evening, you seem rushed," she said, struggling to keep her eyes off his face. Her resolve to stay away would falter if she looked directly at him. She'd already made enough of a fool of herself. She blushed as she was reminded once again of her uncharitable remarks regarding Sarah and her father.

And his complete lack of denial. She mustn't forget that.

"Just anxious to see ye, lass."

"Lisbeth, at last! Davey and I are ready to go swab the deck or scrub the galley, something a wee bit more relaxing. If we tarry much longer with this bunch we'll no' have energy left for caterwauling." Liam pulled two small boys from around his neck and set them on the floor.

"Lucy, you know all the parts well; didn't you want to help David and Liam?"

Lucy giggled and hid her face in Elisabeth's skirts. Surprised at the girl's uncharacteristic shyness, Elisabeth looked up at David, forgetting her resolution. Faith, but he did make her heart skip a beat, his shoulders so wide and strong, straining against his white linen shirt. Mischief sparked from his warm brown eyes as he grinned at her, and she felt the spark all the way to her toes. That grin transformed his face, the hard lines that usually settled into a solemn mask, erased, as his dimples appeared and took over. Her hand itched to reach up and push back the lock of hair that had fallen across his eyes, separating from the tangle of soft chestnut curls that never seemed to stay put within his cap.

She'd known better than to look.

And Liam, with his impish charm, well, there weren't many females who could resist taking a second glance there, those piercing blue eyes all the more remarkable against his raven black hair and brows, framed above the fine line of his nose, the high set of his cheekbones.

Mercy, she supposed she knew how little Lucy felt. They made quite a pair, the both of them.

"Well, all right, no matter, Lucy. Let's let them go off and do boy things. I see Annie now; she's headed this way. We best get started." She arranged them in rows according to order of appearance. She felt David behind her, whispering in her ear, asking her to please not disappear after the play. He hadn't waited for her to say no. She turned to watch them saunter away, rubbing her arms to subdue the goose bumps he'd raised.

They owned their world, those two, no doubt of that—and it wasn't the same world as hers. She'd do well to remember that.

Annie joined her, looking festive with a garish green cap atop her red curls.

"Where did you find that, Annie?" Elisabeth asked, laughing.

"Oh, and don't ye like it, love?" She pirouetted on her toes, hand to her head.

"Oh, yes."

Annie clapped her hands. "Lovely, Lisbeth. Now, where's my Mary and Joseph?"

"Sean, are you ready?" Elisabeth asked. Sean, the oldest of the bunch, was the master of ceremonies. He nodded, bouncing with excitement.

Elisabeth and Annie stepped to the side and let the children carry on. And so they did, almost flawlessly, with little prompting from Elisabeth. Annie sang to aid in the telling of the story, her beautiful voice resounding around the confines of the hold, and at the end of the play the children received a thundering round of applause.

"Oh, Annie, thank you so much. You made it so much easier for them," Elisabeth said.

"I enjoyed it just as much as they did, Lisbeth. Your lad's headed this way. Merry Christmas, love. Say hello to your father for me now."

Her lad? Was she referring to David? How was it possible the gossipmongers weren't up to date? Certainly, if anyone's, he was 'Sarah's lad'.

"That was wonderful, Elisabeth," Mr. Oliver said. "I know first-hand what a difficult task you set up for yourself, and you made it look easy. That's a talent you can be proud of."

"Oh, but I love it, Mr. Oliver. If you had told me six months ago that I could have arranged this, well, I'm not sure I'd have believed you."

"Now, you're not leaving, are you? There's a long evening ahead, I'm hoping you can share in a wee part of it."

"No, she's not leaving as yet, are ye, lass?" David said, appearing at her side. "Your play was wonderful, Elisabeth."

"Thank you, David. I wasn't sure you saw it."

"Every minute of it. Now come eat. Liam's got a plate ready for ye, Mr. O."

She supposed it couldn't hurt. The women had put together such a festive spread. She didn't know much about preparing meals, but surely it'd be impossible to prepare the items they were serving with the rations provided. They must have been prepared to have Christmas onboard. She wasn't; she'd been certain she and Papa would be spending Christmas with her grandparents.

The smaller children called to her, asking her to sit with them. She acquiesced, not turning to see if David followed.

"Sean! You were wonderful. Would you mind if I sat with you?" she asked, squeezing between him and his friend, the German boy, Paul. "Hello, Paul, I wanted to let you know your voice is beautiful. Such notes you could reach! Had you studied that at home?"

No matter the poor boy couldn't understand much of what she was saying, especially as fast as she was prattling. She risked a glance at David from beneath her lashes. He had followed and settled in the spot next to his uncle across from her. Drat, he had caught her peeking and was turning that grin on her.

"Your mother has such lovely decorations, Paul. She's quite talented, isn't she? Wouldn't you agree, Sean? Now, Lucy, tell me what you'd be doing right this minute, if you were home for Christmas Eve."

The children were delighted to have her full attention on them, showering her with questions as she told them stories of celebrations she had had at their age. Some knew so little of her Christmas traditions, it was surprising. She would ask David about that later.

No, on second thought, she wouldn't. It would have something to do with the differences between the Catholics and the Protestants. He was only a casual acquaintance after all, and religious differences weren't an appropriate subject of conversation between casual acquaintances.

The children turned their questions on Reverend Wilson: did Jesus speak all the languages there were to speak, what if He didn't, how would one know which language to pray in so He could understand, how old would He be now if He were still alive, did He have to obey his mother and father all the time even though He was in fact God's son, and on and on.

He patiently addressed each question, but she'd aver he displayed a bit of relief when someone announced it was time for all to gather around and sing hymns.

"Elisabeth, are you ready to return?" Mr. Oliver asked, joining them. "I promised your father I'd see you back safely before three bells."

"I am, thank you, Mr. Oliver." She had noticed Sarah was free now, free from attending to her father's meal, and she wanted to leave immediately—before the girl made her way to David. And well before any unkind thoughts made their way from her tongue to his ears.

She understood completely the attraction Sarah carried for David. She'd recognized it from the first. There were plenty of other young men on board who would eagerly accept her attention, should she choose to bestow it. But she didn't, not for any appreciable amount of time anyway. No, Sarah had sensed something in David, just as she herself had. And Sarah needed the haven that something promised. She shouldn't begrudge her that.

"I'll escort her, Mr. Oliver. I'd like to get a bit of fresh air. If ye don't mind, that is, Elisabeth. I promise I'll get ye there without delay," David said. Mr. Oliver nodded before she could think of a valid reason why she'd mind.

She had valid reasons aplenty, just not ones she was comfortable sharing with Mr. Oliver.

THE CAPTAIN AND Ritcher were standing outside the companionway, enjoying a smoke. Rotten luck; he should have let Mr. O take her back. Now her Da would hear first thing she was with him.

David tipped his cap to the men. "Capt'n Honeywell, Mr. Ritcher."

"Good evening, Mr. Graham, Miss Hale. Was your performance a success, Miss Hale?"

"I believe so, Captain, thank you for your inquiry. Is my father awaiting me?"

"He's deep into the cards, Miss. He'll not be missing you as yet," Ritcher said.

"Come along, Sam. It's likely to be your hand by now. Good night, Mr. Graham." They extinguished their cigars and disappeared down the ladder.

Well now, that was odd, wasn't it? Left her alone with the rabble.

Elisabeth turned to him. "I should go below now. I don't want my delay to be the subject of speculation. Merry Christmas, David."

He looked at her, opened his mouth once, then shut it. He took in a deep breath, releasing it slowly as his hands fisted at his side.

"Aye, Lisbeth. Merry Christmas to you as well. Sleep tight."

He hadn't pressed. Given that he'd wanted to drop to his knees begging her to give him the time of day once again, that'd been a struggle.

He'd like to have kissed her good night, to test his memory of that first kiss. He'd had a good knock on the head; the kiss likely wasn't anything like he remembered it. He'd planned to kiss her again, see that it wasn't, get the wanting of it out of his system, stop the dreaming. But the deck was teeming with people tonight. It'd have to wait.

He grinned, walking back to the other companionway. There was also the minor hindrance she'd likely slap him, should he even venture close.

He found his uncle alone. "Uncle John, why is it that we don't celebrate Christmas like this at home? It seems happier, the way the Germans mark the occasion. Elisabeth's stories as well, don't ye think?"

"The Church feels that a lot of the traditions observed prior to the Reformation had no relevance to the birth of Christ and more relation to pagan celebrations."

"Aye, well, I'm thinking there's no harm in a wee bit of decorating and plenty of good food. The carols the Irish are singing, I hear references to the birth of Christ, as well as to general goodwill."

"I'll no' argue the fact, David, I don't believe there's harm in this type of celebration. But history has shown a more riotous type of revelry at Christmas, one that had little to do with the birth of our Savior. The Church thought it best to put a stop to it all, in order that we could remain focused on our service to God."

David nodded, unwilling to dispute the point. He had to believe, however, in the possibility the Lord had nothing against celebrations centered around family and the singing of hymns.

14

"LOOK AT THE BRIGHT SIDE, David," Liam said, as they played yet another game of cards. "The wind's at least moving us in the proper direction."

"Aye, and it's moving the air below as well. Could be worse."

"Aye, we could be swimming," Liam said, grinning.

David laughed. Or drowning. Life was good. It was the day after Christmas, and the Captain had ordered all passengers confined below, owing to the strong wind coming out of the east. Most didn't notice, too seasick to move from their berths.

The game of choice below deck was Whist, and they never lacked for partners in the long evenings aboard. Mr. Oliver had indeed seen to it that David was taught the game, and he had learned it quickly and well, albeit not as well as Mr. Oliver and his boys.

As closely as he'd observed Liam's swift calculations and strategy, he didn't think he'd ever match him. And some days there wasn't any point in playing against someone he hadn't a hope in hell of besting. He'd suggested they play Loo this morning.

"Where are we, Rob? Did ye find out?" Liam asked, looking up from his hand as Rob joined them.

"Dinna ken, no' for sure."

"Ye? Or the crew doesna?" David asked. Rob was normally full of the particulars, given he spent a fair amount of time with the seamen.

Rob shrugged. "They're no' sharing."

There was talk amongst the others that they were only a few days out from Cape Henlopen. David thought that might be true; they had begun to see smaller craft in the sea and birds as well. The crew was reluctant to discuss their position, though, even Alex, and the talk amongst the passengers was just that, talk.

Sarah sat next to David.

"I'm so cold, David," she said, hunching her shoulders in a shiver, surprising him as she moved in close. She hadn't spent time with them in the last few weeks; he figured she'd lost interest. It wasn't a secret he fancied Elisabeth, not anymore. He gave her a brief smile, turning his eyes back quickly to his cards. No wonder she was cold, the cut of her gown as low as it was. Lass needed a mother.

"Ye're feeling well enough then, are ye, lass?" Liam said. "Angus over there's been trying to keep you warm for days now, darlin'."

She ignored him, entwining her arm with David's. "Are you sure you want to be playing cards again, David? It's all you've done for hours." She pressed up against his arm, scooting closer. "There's ways more entertaining to pass the time. Cozier ways."

He grunted, not answering.

Liam laid down several of his cards.

David groaned at the set and reached for another card. If he ignored her long enough, she'd go. Wouldn't she? Wasn't that the way of it?

He didn't know; how would he?

"Angus?" Rob asked. "Ye're meaning the lad that won the deed to that German fellow's farm last night?"

She put her other hand on his thigh beneath the table, and the cards in his hand curled as his grip tightened.

"One and the same," Liam said. "He's riding high. Word is that farm 'bout runs itself. He'll just have to sit back and count the profits."

David concentrated hard on his cards, choosing one and discarding it. Hell, he could have laid down the key to his game, for all the sense he could make of the figures. He risked a glance down at his arm. Sure enough, those lovely breasts pressed up against him were threatening to spill over. She was actually a sweet lass. They could pass the time together. She could erase the spell Elisabeth had cast.

Now . . . there's a thought.

"That and watch his back. The German's wife was fit to be tied," Rob said.

Her hand moved higher, her grip on his arm tightening. His eyes crossed. Mayhap . . . it wouldn't hurt to just . . . it couldn't hurt just this once.

"Willna do her much good. The man won it fair and square. *Right, Davey?*"

No. He clenched his teeth, reaching below the table to move her hand. Even if he could be sure Lisbeth wouldn't hear of it, Uncle John sure would, and he'd have his hide.

"Davey?"

"What? Oh, aye, right."

He lay down a set and deliberated on the remaining cards in his hand.

"I think ye already lost, David," Rob said, his voice laced

with amusement.

"Do you only plan to play at cards, David? Maybe I should go."

He turned to her, managing a weak grin. "Sure, Sarah, wish me luck for the next round."

She stood, her pretty pink lips puckering in a pout as she turned and headed in Angus' direction.

"Do you two rehearse in advance?" David asked quietly.

"Deal me in, will ye?" Rob said. "Think the lad'd be more appreciative, wouldna ye, Liam?"

"Indeed I would, Rob."

"I'm verra appreciative. Just was wondering, that's all."

"'Specially seeing's how it'll only be 'bout twenty minutes afore she realizes ol' Angus hasna more than the shirt on his back," Liam said, "and likely ne'er will."

David looked around, spotting his uncle. "Uncle John," he called. "Up for a game?" He patted the empty spot next to him.

"Sure, David. What's the choice, gentlemen?"

"Whatever Liam prefers," David said, tossing in the balance of his useless hand. Sarah hadn't gone to Angus, her father had waylaid her, and he looked a bit angry. Good, he was paying heed.

15

"SAIL AHOY!"

Captain Honeywell took out his glass and trained it on the ship in the distance. "Well, Mr. Ritcher, can you make her out?"

"Aye, sir, it's the *Liverpool*."

"That will be Darcy then, I'll want to talk to him."

"Heave to!" Ritcher bellowed. "Looks as if they're preparing to launch a boat, sir."

"Good, better him than me."

A short time later Captain Darcy was welcomed aboard the *Industry*. Honeywell ushered him into his cabin, offering him a cup of wine. "Well now, Albert, what am I up against?"

"Ice. Ice everywhere. Never seen anything like it, Jack. Spoke to Jacob Smith a few days back. He left London fifteen weeks ago—"

"Where, Albert? Where did you see him? He's bound for Philadelphia as well."

"Latitude 30, 40, longitude 74, 30. The *Brothers* was drove off the Capes, lost her top-sail yard and sails. Now she's headed to Charlestown. Smith said he'd spoken to twelve or thirteen vessels what had been drove off the coast."

"God Almighty, all going to Charlestown, I expect. And you're still headed north? Why?"

"Have cargo waiting in New York. Haven't encountered anyone yet said there's a problem there."

"Charlestown? You heard anything about that?"

"You shouldn't have a problem with that, Jack, not with ice anyway." He drained his cup and stood. "I need to get back. Much obliged for the drink."

"Thank you, Albert, I'm indebted for the information." They left the cabin and climbed up on deck. "How did you find Jamaica?"

Darcey laughed. "Warm." He paused as he prepared to scale down the ropes and into the waiting boat. "For your ears only, Jack. Seems the governor has orders from the King not to trade with the Americans. Had to sell off my cargo at half the price on the black market. This whole damn trip, nothing but a waste of time and money."

"But you still have your ship; appears to be more than some can say. I hope to be able to say the same in several weeks."

"God willing."

"Aye. God speed."

16

New Year's Eve, 1783

RUMOR WAS THEY NO LONGER headed to Philadelphia.

"I was hoping to be celebrating the New Year with my feet on the ground, American soil, as it were," one of the passengers grumbled as he paced.

"It wouldn't be so bad, not if we knew what the trouble was," another answered.

David lay in his bunk, his arm over his eyes, trying to lose himself in sleep. The not knowing, aye, that was always the hard part. But he'd heard it over and over again these last two days. Each time it only served to set his nerves further on edge.

He didn't trust himself to be civil during yet another conversation of useless speculation or another game of cards or dice. So he'd retreated to the solitude of sleep early last night and did his best to keep up the illusion well into the day. Better that than risk making things worse by alienating a friend.

He missed seeing something other than this blasted hold. He missed his freedom to move about.

But most of all he missed seeing Elisabeth. He'd counted on the chance to talk to her again before they parted. She was in his thoughts constantly; he needed to resolve it. Somehow.

"DAVID, UP WITH YE, the Cap'n's here." Liam shoved at David's shoulder.

"I trust you would like further information of our voyage. Gather round so I don't have to be repeating myself." Honeywell's loud, booming voice filled the hold.

Instantly all were quiet and moved to the forefront. David jumped off his bunk, following Liam.

"We've been advised the Delaware is full of ice, and we won't make it past the Capes. Several ships have been anchored outside the Capes for weeks, without movement and with little shelter. Not only will it put us at undue risk to follow suit, it will sorely test our store of provisions. Therefore, we're heading to Charlestown to reprovision. We'll make sail for Philadelphia again when the weather clears."

The Captain ignored the groans and questions, continuing with his announcement. "This being New Year's Eve . . . Hogmanay," he said with a nod to the Scots. "I've allowed for the distribution of a quantity of rum from my private store. Should this be deemed insufficient later in the evening, the purser has been instructed that a certain quantity shall also be available for purchase."

He paused briefly as the noise in the crowd altered to grunts of appreciation, and his eyes searched out David and Liam.

"I've also lifted the restriction against the more hardy of you wishing to venture on deck. I believe the danger of encountering ice has passed for the time being. Be advised we should reach Charlestown within the week."

Cheers rose as the Captain ascended. David and Liam tore up the aft ladder and immediately encountered Mr. Ritcher.

"Mr. Brock, Mr. Graham, 'bout time ye lads came up from yer napping. See Mannus over there and make yourselves useful. I ain't got no use for idle hands on my deck."

"Aye, aye, sir!"

Alex talked nonstop, and the afternoon passed in a blur, punctuated only by the freezing downpour they worked through the last half hour.

"We've had the luxury of a bath for the New Year, eh, Davey?" Liam said when they finally sat, choosing a spot somewhat sheltered from the wind. Even so, it didn't take long for the chill to set in once they were idle.

"Hmmph," David said, shivering. "Did ye check the barrel, Liam?"

"I did. Maybe enough for a cup, no more."

They had taken the top off a used barrel and set it out during storms, hoping to collect rainwater to supplement their tiny water ration. The first couple of times they had set it under the mizzenmast, but found the water collected there tasted of tar. And that was only if the barrel didn't get kicked away by one of the crew climbing the mast. Now they had fixed it in a more open spot, forgoing the benefit of runoff, settling for a meager amount that at least tasted somewhat pure.

"Mayhap it'll keep raining awhile. We'll likely want it tomorrow, after rum. Let's get dry," David said. "What d'ye think my chances are of retrieving Lisbeth from her cabin?"

"Oh? The lass is back on your mind?"

David ignored the taunt. He knew darn well the lass was on his mind. He never lost an opportunity to point out any number of God-fearing actions taken by the Irish-Catholics they bunked with. Same God, right? Right.

Liam turned to him once they had climbed back down into

the hold. "No' good, Davey. Maybe I can, I'll think of something to do with the wee ones that involves her help. Get me after ye change. And hurry, looks like we're behind. Rum's been flowing for awhile now."

He hurried. He was colder than cold. Felt good though, once he changed into something dry. The exercise, the fresh air—he felt better than he had in days. He scanned the crowd, searching for Liam. His uncle caught his eye and beckoned him forward.

ELISABETH MADE HER ESCAPE as soon as her father joined the Captain for a drink, asking the widow Reid if she'd mind telling her father she was spending the evening with friends. She'd suspected Mrs. Reid would be only too happy to do so, and she was right. The forced confinement had strained all their nerves.

She wanted a chance to thank Mr. Oliver, in the event she didn't see him again; a chance as well to say goodbye to Annie. And Liam and Sean and Rob. She had even steeled herself against the possibility of seeing David with Sarah. It was New Year's Eve, after all, a time to be with those special to you. She thought she might manage a credible goodbye to the both of them, if she left it until last, right before she made her escape back to her cabin.

The hold was noisy and chaotic, though nothing like the Christmas celebration of last week. These were loud, hard drinking men, the women blending unnoticed into the background. For the first time, she didn't feel comfortable being there. She hesitated.

"Miss Hale! Don't be leaving yet! Your friends will be so disappointed to have missed you. Come with me." It was Mrs. Andrews, the woman with the burns, the one who cooked for David and the Reverend. She let her take her hand and lead her to the midsection where she and her son bunked.

"Don't worry, love. They're just letting off some steam. Your lad's no' been joining in. Here, have some. Welcome in the New Year." She handed her a small cup of warm spiced wine.

Elisabeth sipped it. "It's good, Mrs. Andrews. It's not what they're drinking, though, is it?" Taking another small sip, she nodded toward the bowls lined up and down the centers of the tables.

"No, lass," Mrs. Andrews answered, laughing. "That would be the captain's rum. This is just a wee bit of wine. Mrs. Drecker fixed it up. One of her family secrets she claims it is. I aim to have your David write it out for me. I watched her make the second batch, so as I'd know what's in it. I've taken quite a liking to it."

'Her David.' She liked the sound of that, but he hadn't been her David since his recovery from the near drowning, if even then.

And there he was. Seeing her, he grinned, pushing his way toward her. That grin; my word, those dimples would be the undoing of her yet, if she didn't soon develop some backbone. She raised the cup for another sip, finding it empty. Laughing, she handed it back to Mrs. Andrews. That certainly wasn't the route to more backbone.

"It's too good, I'm afraid, I didn't mean to gulp it down. Thank you, ma'am. I'll have to ask David to write out the receipt for me as well."

She moved through the crowd to meet him, declining a cup of the grog when offered. "I'd better not, sir," she said, laughing. "Faith, I'll have a difficult time enough holding to my senses after the wine." One of the men shouted something to the effect that the "lad shouldna be minding that a bit" and was hushed quickly by the others. She decided not to take offense, waving him off with a small smile.

David came up beside her and took her elbow. Surprised, she searched his face. Maybe he *had* been joining in with the men and their toasts. Because he hadn't touched her since that first and last kiss a month ago.

She'd thought often of that kiss. He had done a much better job of kissing than—well, she couldn't seem to recall his name now, and never mind, he wasn't important. But David's kiss had been special, she knew it had. Why hadn't he sensed it as well? Why hadn't he wanted to kiss her again? Why had he preferred Sarah?

Well, now's now, that was then. She smiled at him, then remembered her promise to herself. She struggled to keep her expression neutral.

Had Mrs. Andrews actually said the wine was not as strong as the rum?

He grinned. "It's good to see ye, lass. I've missed you."

"Elisabeth! Top of the evening to you!" called Seamus. "We need ye to fill in for Annie a song or two. She says she's busy. Can you do it, lass?" Some of the passengers were clearing away a small area for dancing. Seamus and Ewan were standing by with their fiddle and flute.

"Go ahead if ye'd like, Lisbeth. I need to see what Uncle John requires of me. I'll be back to fetch ye shortly, if ye don't mind. I'd like to visit with ye," David said, nodding to Seamus and Ewan. "Please?"

Her spirit soared before she stamped on it firmly.

"Very well, David, just for a few minutes."

Thankfully the crowd was lively and easy to please, because her heart wasn't in it as she sang. She needed to say her good-byes, tell Mr. Oliver about Charlestown. When Annie relieved her, she moved back through the hold, searching for him.

Maybe he'd gone up for a bit of air. She'd try the deck. Reverend Wilson called out to her just as she reached the ladder.

"I thought I'd get a breath of fresh air," she told him. "And I needed to speak to Mr. Oliver."

"I think it best if you don't go on deck alone tonight, Elisabeth," the Reverend said. "The Captain allowed the crew some rum as it's Hogmanay. The judgment of some will be lacking."

"Well, all right," she said, glancing toward the ladder doubtfully. She'd never felt unsafe with the crew before. As she looked, she saw Sarah descend, followed by Liam, then by David.

Gracious, what that girl was wearing; she'd catch her death of cold unwrapped like that up on deck. She had the urge to take off her own cloak and throw it over her.

Sarah, seeing her watching, came to her, thrusting her chest out, giving her a small, smug smile. "You be slumming tonight, Miss Hale and Mighty?" She glanced back over her shoulder at David, then leaned in, placing her hand on Elisabeth's arm. Elisabeth struggled not to back away from her touch, tried not to cringe at the overwhelming smell of alcohol as she leaned in close to whisper, "Well now, don't you be tossing yer high and mighty little head, taking yer temper out on our David. He's got more than enough to share, see. And I'm not one minds sharing." She laughed, stopping short at a hiccup, then wandered away without waiting for an answer.

Elisabeth staggered back half a step, her hand going to her mouth, then to her chest as she fought to catch her breath. Why, that . . .

David could bury himself in that tart's bosom, if he was so enamored of it. She glanced down quickly to assure herself her own lace scarf was arranged modestly about her neckline. Why, it was a wonder Sarah's stay could even contain her bosoms, though granted it only contained them by a mere fraction. Mama would turn over in her grave should she even consider wearing something so revealing for everyday wear.

She'd write Mr. Oliver to say goodbye, once they were in Philadelphia. Or maybe she wouldn't.

And David could just wonder about her whereabouts, as she no longer cared to tell him. To tell any of them.

Rabble, indeed.

She tightened her mouth and turned back to Wilson. "Reverend, would you accompany me then? I feel a headache—"

Lord Almighty, him too. Reverend Wilson was walking away, Sarah under his arm.

HE'D SEEN HER AS soon as he stepped beneath the hatch, had seen the stricken look on her face. Torn between slapping Sarah and soothing Elisabeth, he chose the latter. Not that he'd slap Sarah anyway, no matter how sorely he'd been tempted.

"Lisbeth, please don't go," David said quietly, coming up behind her. "Come, sit with me a bit. I'll show ye a trick my ma uses for headaches. If it doesn't work quickly, I'll take you back to your cabin. Or Uncle John will, if ye'd prefer." He didn't allow her the opportunity to refuse; she'd take it in a heartbeat.

"Get your hands off me," she said, pulling away.

"A minute, Bess." He half-carried her to an empty berth away from the others.

"So help me, I'll scream," she said, hissing through clenched teeth, struggling as he held her tight.

He was out of time. Releasing her, he stepped in front of her, blocking her passage, dropping to a knee. He brought his hands to hers, taking care to keep his touch light. "Please, lass. Please."

She darted a glance around. "Get up, you fool."

"There's nothing between us, Sarah and me. Ne'er has been. Nothing but friendship."

"Get up! Are you so intent on making a spectacle of yourself?"

No, he wasn't. But he'd checked before he gone to his knee, no one was looking, not yet. The hold was wild tonight, more than enough to look at elsewhere.

"Get up!" She kicked him, her small foot slamming into him. It caught him off guard; he fell on his backside.

"Oh!" Her hand flew to her mouth. "Oh, my word. I'm so sorry, David, are you all right? I didn't mean to—I'm so sorry." She stooped down to offer him a hand.

"I'm fine, 'specially knowing ye care!" He grinned, taking her hand, debating whether to pull her down into his lap and kiss her—get done with all this talk. "Will ye give me a chance to speak, 'fore ye leave? Will ye listen?"

She stepped back, withdrawing her hand, folding her arms across her chest as she looked away, making a show of tapping her foot. "Do hurry, please."

He laughed and stood, scooping her up before she could think, settling her between his knees on the berth, back against his chest.

"A minute, Bess, only a minute, please. Close your eyes." He brought his fingers to her temples, applying pressure. "Uncle John sent me up there to fetch her. He'd seen her drinking more than a few servings of the grog, ken?" He tightened his legs about her, holding her still as she struggled to rise.

"Uncle John worries over her. He thinks her da doesn't. I asked Liam to accompany me, seeing as she can be difficult." He felt her relax just a fraction.

"She was playing free and loose with several of the crew. Liam talked her way free and we brought her back. Ungrateful lass; she'll probably head back up there within the hour if her da doesn't start paying some mind to her whereabouts. I'm no' sure who told ye what about Sarah and me, but they were wrong, lass. They were wrong." He paused as he felt her settle against him, his fingers now gently massaging circles on the sides of her forehead. "Are ye still mad?"

She sighed. "No, not even at her, I suppose. But don't stop doing that."

He chuckled. "For just a bit longer, I don't want ye falling asleep. I'm hoping ye'll stay for a long while yet."

"Why are you touching me all of a sudden?"

His fingers stilled for a moment, then resumed. He didn't pretend not to understand her.

"Noticed that, did ye? Truth be, I . . . I don't know, Elisabeth. I guess I'm just tiring of the effort it took no' to."

"What?" She pulled away and looked back at him, her mouth open.

He shrugged, having no better explanation. He liked having her near; it was as simple, or as complicated, as that.

"Is it all right with ye then? If I touch ye?"

He watched as the muscles jumped about in her face, finally settling into a smile that reached her eyes.

"Yes, I expect it's all right."

She settled back and he held her, sheltering her with his body as his thumb stroked the back of her hand, soothing her.

She felt right, and for now he was done questioning it.

Just as she was starting to doze off, he prodded her awake.

"Victuals are out, Lisbeth. I'm famished, come. Rob and Liam have saved us a spot."

They spent a companionable hour eating, talking and laughing, and at the end of the meal she rose from the table to help the women clear.

"Mrs. Andrews told ye to stay seated. Ye're a guest." He straddled the bench and pulled her down, back against his chest, wrapping his arms around her. "I know ye've got to get back to your father soon, but I'm not ready to be handing ye over just yet. Can ye stay a wee bit longer?"

"Actually Mrs. Reid seemed anxious to have me out for the evening. I don't think I'll be missed for some time."

"Do ye mind? Her taking him over like that?"

"To some extent, yes, of course. But I admit it makes me feel better about spending time away from him, and I do want him to be happy. It's just that I don't think she'll be the one who makes him happy. She's far too different from my mother."

"But mayhap she can help him move past your mother, and that will be a step forward, aye?"

She grasped his hand and nodded. "Is it hard for you, being away from your family on a celebration like this?"

"No' with you here. Besides, I think the worst of missing them has passed. Time and distance softens that. I know it doesn't ache to be thinking of them now."

"That sentiment will give me something to ponder when the ship arrives in Philadelphia," she said quietly.

She stiffened in his arms and he saw her blush; she hadn't meant to say it then.

"Look at Liam. I believe he's sparking Hilde. Why, I don't think he knows much more German than I do."

"He'll manage, don't be doubting that."

"I suppose you're right," she said as the girl leaned into Liam, whispering something.

"Let me up to help the women, David, I don't feel right just sitting here."

"David! There you are. Paul and me wanna try that trick again. I got the cards; can you show us one more time?" Sean asked. "Hey, Lisbeth."

"Hello, Sean, Paul. What trick does David know?"

"He'll teach you, too, won't ye, David?"

David reluctantly released Elisabeth and turned back toward the table, taking the cards from Sean. "Elisabeth is leaving for just a bit. Right then, all eyes watching closely now, aye?"

He spent the next hour putting the boys, and Elisabeth, once she returned, into fits of giggles as they tried to replicate his tricks and failed each time. "All right, lads, that's enough for tonight. I need to escort Elisabeth to a dance 'fore she has to leave. It's getting late. I should tuck ye in 'fore I go, aye?"

"Nooo!" the boys cried as they ran off into the crowd.

David stood and took Elisabeth's hand, leading her to the music. "Come, Lisbeth, dance with me. We've a bit of the evening left."

MUCH LATER, winded and warm, they stepped away from the other dancers. David filled a cup full of the grog and led her to an empty spot on the bench in front of his berth.

"Will this go on all night, David? No one shows any signs of slowing. It must be getting close to midnight." She took a large swallow of the drink. "This is good. It tastes of lime. I've never had it before."

"It'll continue through Ne'erday if the whisky flows long enough. Or rum, as the case may be. Provisions being light, mayhap only until first light. We don't commemorate Christmas with the same gaiety the English do. This is our annual celebration. If I were at home, I'd have a gift for ye." He pulled her back to rest against his chest and bent to kiss the top of her head. "I'm grateful to have you with me this night. It bodes well for the new year."

How fast things change. Not more than twelve hours ago he lay in this room feeling bad-tempered and sorry for himself, through no one's fault but his own. He reached for the cup, finding it empty. He laughed. "Thirsty were ye then, lass?" The man seated across reached out his hand to take it, refilling it from the large bowl on the table. David nodded his thanks.

Elisabeth squirmed until she was resting closer yet. He tensed, then relaxed as she stilled. She grabbed one of his hands, idly stroking it as she talked about the last few days she'd spent in the cabin, eventually coming around to the subject that had brought her between-decks.

"And my father thinks we'd be better off in Charlestown and arranging alternate transportation. So I may be leaving the ship within the next few days if that's the case. I wanted to let you know, and Mr. Oliver of course. That's why I ventured here tonight." She turned her head to see if he was listening to her, as he hadn't responded. "Did you hear me, David?"

"Aye," he said, tightening his hold.

He struggled with the thoughts running through his head. He couldn't come out and say he thought her father inadequate to keep her safe on the journey from Charlestown to Philadelphia. For one thing, he knew nothing of her father's adequacies or inadequacies. He had to assume the man had been taking care of her all her life. But he wanted to be there as well, just in case. Hale was still feeling the loss of his wife. It was bound to dull his judgment, maybe even his survival instinct, and travel was dangerous. Always had been. He chose his words carefully.

"I didn't think to be losing you so quick. Ye just set me back a bit, lass. Come, let's watch the coming of the New Year from above." He stood, pulling her up. The cup was empty again. He looked at her face closely, hell to pay if he got her lushey. Grabbing the blanket from his berth, he led her up the ladder.

"David, top of the evening to you, bucko! Ye brought someone to keep ye warm this night, eh?" one of the sailors called out.

Elisabeth giggled softly. Giggled? Elisabeth? David swore

under his breath. "Nay, Mr. Parker, just up for a bit of fresh air 'fore the night ends."

"To be sure. I was young once, too. Don't be forgetting it, laddie."

The crew hooted and another chimed in, "I can lend ye a hand if ye need help finding yer way in the dark with the lassie, Davey!"

"Thank ye for the kind thoughts, Mr. Todd, but I believe I'll manage!"

"Aye, well, the boats be occupied, mind ye!" The sailors all laughed as he guided Elisabeth away.

"Sorry, Lisbeth."

"I don't mind. They didn't mean any harm. What did he mean about the boats?"

"The ship's boats. They afford a bit of privacy, being up and stowed."

"Ahh . . ."

"I've never used them, Elisabeth."

"I know."

"Aye, well . . . right then." How did she know that?

"Liam once explained your inclination to avoid confined, close places when I had asked him why I could usually find you on deck. I believe he phrased it, 'Davey doesna care for snug spots, lass'."

He snorted at her mimicry. The night was dark, there being just a bit of a moon. The weather had cleared, not a cloud in the sky and the stars sprinkled light across the sea. It was bitter cold. He'd been planning to keep her warm huddled together under a blanket as they sat on deck, but that was harder now with the audience they had. He led her to the opposite side of the ship.

"It's deserted over here, isn't it?" Elisabeth said softly,

"Aye, it is, being as it's in full view of the captain, should he be coming out for air himself," David said. "Let's sit over here. It offers some shelter." He guided her down and sat behind her, pulling her back between his knees with the blanket covering the both of them, his arms holding her tight.

"Will ye be warm enough?"

"Oh yes, I'll probably be the warmest person on this ship. Tell me what's wrong, David."

"The talk I heard from the crew today. Ships have been lost, waiting to travel up the Delaware these past weeks. Many have died. I believe the Captain's right to travel south to wait it out. It worries me, not knowing your whereabouts, if you'll be safe." He decided it best not to voice any concerns he might have over her father's capabilities.

"Really?" she asked, turning briefly to see his face. "That surprises me, I must admit. I'm sure everything will be all right. Papa's not concerned."

He tightened his arms around her. "I'm sure ye're right. Talk to me of anything, lass, I've been missing hearing the sound of your voice."

His thoughts wandered as he looked out over the sea, soothed by the soft sound of her voice and the feel of her close. He knew he would always remember the start to this new year, this ship, this lass in his arms. A couple was leaving the boats, making a bit of a ruckus climbing out, and he turned his head toward the sound. Well, now, what do you know about that. The Fergusons. Ol' Mr. Ferguson had to be pushing forty. And still catting about—with his wife, no less. Huh. Wait til he told Liam.

The crew began to make more noise, and he suspected someone had determined it was midnight, or close enough to it. He turned Elisabeth so that her side was against him, so he could see her face.

"You're done listening I take it?" she asked.

"Aye," he whispered.

"I think you should kiss me, then. No, I take that back, I'm finished with thinking, I think too much, I think. I should just not think at all sometimes. Lots of people don't, you know, think before—"

He chuckled, lowering his mouth to hers, kissing her. Softly, tentatively, at first, then deepening the kiss as her response assured him more was welcome. Good God, she was magic. The time he had wasted . . . it hadn't been the knock to his head at all; it was her, only her. His arms pulled her closer.

She ran her hands down his jacket, bringing them up under his shirt to run up and down his back.

He'd thought he'd been roused when Sarah had placed her hand on his leg, inching it ever so slightly up his thigh. He hadn't known the meaning of the word. Nothing compared to the feel of Lisbeth's small soft hands on his skin. Every nerve in his body from head to toes was standing at attention. His tongue plunged into her mouth, and he felt her nails as she clung to him.

He'd never claimed to be a saint. Da knew that well enough, which was why he was on this ship sailing to America instead of sitting in a classroom preparing for the clergy like Ma wanted. What's more, he'd never once said he didn't like snug places, didn't know why Liam'd say a thing such as that. He reached under her and picked her up, standing with her in his arms, never once letting loose of her mouth. She made a small mewing sound and pulled him closer.

Sweet, she was so sweet. He could taste the rum on her tongue. The rum . . .

She was lushey. Damn it all to hell and back. Not taking her to the boats, not. He wasn't a saint, but he wasn't a cad either. He set her down.

"Ah, Bess," he said, pulling his mouth away, still cradling her close, "ye are a wonder to me. I don't understand the power you have over me. It unnerves me more than a little, I'll admit, lass."

She pulled back and looked at him, taking her hands up to the nape of his neck. "Rest assured I won't abuse it, David. But I may need help believing it now and then. You're aware you hide it well?"

Well, he surely hoped so. He grunted and pulled away, leading her to the ladder.

"Come, let's celebrate the rest of Hogmanay with the others while there's still time. A wee bit of tea will warm ye right up. The crew still has a fire lit. Knowing Mrs. Andrews, she'll have some tea ready."

"I'm not cold. And I don't want tea." She pulled back. "Are you afraid to be alone with me?"

He grinned. "You're a canny lass, I'll give ye that. I've other reasons as well. Want to hear?"

"I might as well." She crossed her arms and stood her ground. "Maybe there's a small chance my dreams of a big, strong, braw lad won't be soured with the knowledge he's frightened of a girl little more than half his size."

"Ye'll be dreaming of me then, aye?" He chuckled when she shook off his grasp and turned to walk back toward the companionway that led to her cabin.

"C'mere, Bess," he said, grabbing her arm. "The Captain will be coming up for a smoke anytime now and sure to send ye back to your father when he sees you." And send him to the bottom of the sea soon as he notices she's lushey.

"I don't want ye to go yet. Smell the rain in the air? There's a fair chance we could be in for another spell of weather and confined to quarters. I may not see ye again, I'll no' willingly have the little time I can be sure of cut short if there's chance of avoiding it."

"What do you mean, you won't see me again?" she said, her voice breaking and her eyes filling.

"I'll see ye again, I just meant to say no' as often as I'd like," he said hastily. He bent to kiss her.

"Don't. I think I should be angry with you."

Undaunted, he brushed her hair aside and kissed the skin below her ear. She shivered and he raised his head.

"Well, I'd like some tea. Perhaps ye'd consider joining me, lass?" He offered her his elbow.

She ignored it and climbed down the ladder, turning to tell him, "Mrs. Andrews has a receipt we'd like you to copy out. She and I can make it and test it. You will sit and write it."

17

January 1784

January 4th, 1784—Tomorrow we should reach Charlestown, where we will wait out the weather. Lisbeth will be leaving.

"I'LL MISS THIS. THE END of day isn't such a spectacle on land," Liam said.

"Mayhap it is in America. Ye'll note we've seen a lot more of the sun since leaving home, no' near as much of the rain. Things are different. I wonder if it causes much grief to the farmers."

"Jesus, Davey."

"Just wondering."

They sat quietly, each lost in thought, as dusk turned to night and the colors of the sunset faded. One by one the stars appeared, and the ocean soon glittered with diamonds. They had spent many evenings like this in the last two months. Now it was coming to an end, and fast. No longer was there an illusion that they were alone in the world. It was not uncommon to spot another vessel, and land was clearly in sight. He sighed. He, too, would miss this.

He spotted Elisabeth, alone, walking in their direction.

"Lisbeth, are ye looking for someone?" Liam called out.

She jumped. "You startled me. I didn't see you in the dark. I believe I was looking for David." She sat in front of David, resting her back against his raised knees.

Liam cast a puzzled look at David. Likely speculating over her familiarity. David shrugged, and Liam jumped up. "Last night and all. I'll be seeing the both of ye in a wee bit, I hear Seamus starting up his fiddle on the foredeck."

"Aye, Liam," David said. "We'll join ye shortly." He turned back to Elisabeth. "Are ye feeling well enough, Elisabeth?"

"No."

He recognized well the emotions behind the simple answer. Parting his knees, he brought his arms up around her and pulled her back to rest against his chest holding her tight while they watched the night sky.

Just when he thought she may have fallen asleep, she turned in his arms, her face mere inches from his. He loosened his hold. "Would ye like to go listen to the music, dance a bit?"

"No." She reached up and smoothed his hair from his forehead.

He squirmed backwards a bit, and she smiled. "I'm making you uncomfortable."

He chuckled. "And that makes ye happy?"

"Yes, it does. You're always so sure of yourself. I admire it; it's one of the reasons I feel drawn to you. But I do like to think I have some effect on you."

"Oh aye, I think ye can be sure of that."

She brought her hand down to trace his cheek. "Do you?" She put her finger over his lips against any response and lay her head on his shoulder, her palm on his chest. He rested his chin on the top of her head and drew her in close again.

He enjoyed holding her, and if she wasn't worried about her father just now, he'd follow her lead. The weight of her felt good. She was warm, soft, and . . . wet?

"Elisabeth? Ye're no' crying, are ye, lass?" He tried to lift her face from his chest. She burrowed deeper, her shoulders shaking.

"I don't—can't bear—what if you never—" She was sobbing in earnest now. It was difficult to decipher her words.

He gave up trying to lift her face and instead held her, rocking her, whispering all the while. "It's all right, Bess, ye don't need to cry. I'll be doing anything ye ask of me. Just ask, you know that. Stop crying, lass, please." He kissed her forehead and down the side of her face, moving his mouth to the crook of her neck. Eventually her crying slowed and he cradled her face in his hand, kissing each eyelid and the tears on her cheeks.

"No, wait," she said, pulling a cloth from her sleeve. She dropped her head, wiping her eyes and blowing her nose. She hiccupped and looked up at him, mortified, placing her hand over her mouth. He laughed and reached for her hand to kiss her palm, her fingers, the inside of her wrist. She sighed, and he returned his lips to the side of her neck, working his way up and over to her mouth. He felt the tremors run through her as she started to cry again, and he brought his mouth to hers, gently probing her lips open with his tongue. She put her arms around his neck and eagerly pulled him toward her, her crying forgotten.

Later, much later, she pulled away to look at him. He groaned and tried to pull her back. Laughing, she turned her back to him, pulling his arms tight around her. "You *do* like me," she said.

"What nonsense is that? Ye know what I feel for you," he said, returning his attentions to the side of her neck.

"Really? And now how should I know that? To see you, I

have to seek you out. Then most of the time I'm with you, you take undue pains not to touch me. So forgive me for not knowing you like me as well as you like, well, say . . . Mrs. Andrews."

He snorted. "Mrs. Andrews cooks my meals, lass." He held her tight as she struggled against him.

"*And*, I can count on one hand the times you've bothered to kiss me. It's my last night to be with you. Just look at all the time you've wasted."

He chuckled. "Aye, and I'm thinking that's a good thing; otherwise I'd likely be well past satisfied with a kiss." His hand moved up and down her arm, his teeth nibbled the soft spot where her shoulder met her neck.

She shivered. "David? I'm just going to come out and say it, since you won't. Promise me you'll make time to see me, that you won't forget me. You'll have more freedom than I will."

"I promise. I willna forget you, it's no' possible. You're never far from my thoughts. I thought ye knew. I'll no' let ye go easy. There's no' a chance in hell the ache of missing ye will soften." He turned her back to face him. "Now, we have till morning, so who is it that's wasting time now?"

HE WOKE WITH A start at the hand on his shoulder.

"It's almost dawn, David. The lass needs to get back before dawn."

Elisabeth looked up, sleepily, then closed her eyes again, snuggling deeper into his arms.

"Aye, thanks, Liam." He didn't want to take her back. But Liam was right, the ship's bell rang out two bells, and it would be dawn in an hour or two. He stood and carried her, keeping her in his arms until he reached the passageway of her cabin. He set her on her feet.

"Lisbeth, can ye walk? I shouldna be carrying ye to your

doorstep." She turned and leaned against him, looping her arms around his waist, murmuring something incoherent. He pressed her back against the wall and leaned in to kiss her. She woke quickly then, pulling him closer, returning his kiss eagerly.

"Goodbye, Bess," he whispered, pulling away. She didn't speak, just looked at him as her eyes filled.

"Oh no, ye don't," he said. "I'll see ye soon, I promise." He gently grabbed her shoulders, turning her toward the companionway. He waited as she descended, turning only when she was out of sight. He needed an hour or two of sleep himself.

HE STAYED BELOW when the boat came to take the Hales to shore. He couldn't face watching her go, couldn't take the chance he'd cry like a lass.

Liam came down, tried to rout him from his berth. "Up with ye mate, ye need to see her off."

He covered his face with his forearm and turned away. "Too many eyes, Liam. Leave me alone. I said my goodbyes last night."

Liam pulled him back round to face him. "I'm no' suggesting a reenactment of last night, only a wee acknowledgement her going means something to ye. A lass likes a bit of a public declaration, I shouldna have to tell ye that. She's my friend too, and I don't care to see her searching the faces for ye. Ye know well she'll get to thinking ye couldn't be bothered to see her off. Or her da willna miss the opportunity to convince her of it. Is that what you're aiming for?"

David moved his arm from his face and looked at Liam, considering. "The boat; it's still here then?"

"Maybe, was loading just a bit ago. Could be gone by now, though, long as it took to talk some sense into ye."

David leapt from the berth and ran up the ladder. Pushing

his way through the others, he reached the forefront of the crowd just as the crew of the longboat cast off.

"Elisabeth," he called. "Elisabeth!" She looked up and spotted him, her face brightening at once. "I'll see ye soon, lass, aye?" He kissed the palm of his hand and turned it toward her.

Astonished, she gave him a brilliant smile. "Aye, David, soon," she called back. Kissing her palm, she returned the gesture, ignoring her father's admonition not to make a spectacle of herself. The boat cast off, and he watched it go, long past the time he was able to make out her face.

January 5, 1784—Bess and her father have left the ship at Charlestown.

18

America
January 1784

A STRONG NORTHEAST WIND BLEW ACROSS
the harbor the afternoon the Hales left, relentless in
its assault, growing in strength each passing day, until all the
ships in the harbor were in danger of parting from their
cables. The *Industry* stayed anchored as she waited out the
weather, but for those caught between-decks it was small
comfort.

On the fourth day, when the wind was at its most vicious
and cold, the ocean spray filling the air began to freeze, coat-
ing the masts and the rigging with ice. An enormous crash
could be heard over the howling of the wind as the mizzen
mast collapsed from the weight of the ice.

David and Liam were lodged with others under one of the
tables, past caring they were sitting in filth and more than
a foot of icy seawater. Many passengers, David included,
rushed the companionway at the crash, determined to break

open the hatch, determined the hold would not become their coffin. Just as they reached it, a seaman opened it and dropped down.

"Mr. Ritcher says to tell ye all it's only the mizzen mast fractured. The ship is safe, and he believes the worst to be soon over," Alex shouted above the din.

"The water, Alex. We're filling up with water down here. Granted ye canna see it, but ye feel it, surely ye can!" David said.

Alex laughed as the next roll threw David into the side of the ship. "Lubber, still ain't got yer sea legs, eh? The water don't signify, David. It's bound to come through the seams during a storm such as this. Yer safer down here, that's the truth of it, and I'm to stay here for the duration. Now where'd ye stash Liam?"

A WEEK LATER the damage was still being tallied. Two brigs and several sloops and schooners had sunk at the wharves; many smaller vessels were entirely lost. Bodies were being found daily along the shoreline. David was frantic. He asked Mr. Ritcher repeatedly if he'd received news of the Hales and got the same answer each time. Ritcher knew they had made it to town since the lighter had arrived back with their provisions, but other than that, he'd had no news of them.

He shouldn't have let her go, he should have gone with her.

In desperation, he negotiated passage into town with one of the ship's suppliers. Ritcher got wind of it within minutes and threatened to chain him by the ankles in the cargo hold, as well as to tell his uncle. He didn't know if Ritcher had the authority to follow through, but the threat to tell his uncle was enough. It would be bound to set him against the lass.

David had distanced himself from his uncle, Liam, and the others. But no one thought to comment, if they'd even noticed. The violence of this last storm had changed the passengers, stunned them into passivity. They no longer questioned; they simply waited. He struggled with the loss he felt. He'd known her such a short time. He'd likely see her again; the emptiness just didn't make sense. He couldn't talk to his uncle about it; mention of her faith had begun to creep into their conversations, and he sensed the man was relieved the Hales had left the ship. Liam, mayhap, but Liam was antsy with the waiting and out of sorts himself.

BY MID-JANUARY a warm wind blew in from the south, bringing with it a warm rain. Captain Honeywell announced the ships' carpenters had completed the necessary repairs. They would make for Philadelphia once more.

Alone, he stood at the rail, watching the shoreline as the ship made its way north. From time to time they traveled close enough that he could make out the dense forests lining the coast. Not a farm, not a village, not a fishers' cot in sight; what a vast, empty country this must be.

They were close now, he could tell by the watching the crew. Close. A day more? Two?

He drew in a deep breath, relishing the clean smell of the slight breeze. It could be considered warm, he supposed, but only if one compared it to the frigid wind of weeks past. All the sailors were busy: scraping and painting the masts that hadn't already been attended to during the repairs, blackening the yards, tarring the rigging, plus a host of other tasks he still couldn't put a name to. Alex was taking a holystone to the deck; David dropped to his knees to help him.

"Maybe tomorrow, David, we're close now. 'Pends if we can hire on a pilot quick enough."

An hour later they reached the Capes sheltering the entrance to the Delaware. The captain told the passengers to get their belongings in order. They'd likely reach Philadelphia by tomorrow. A month ago that would have brought cheers. Now the only response was noncommittal grunts.

Well, enough was enough. He'd carried this cag too long. He sought out Liam.

"We're almost there, Liam. What's the first thing ye plan to do when ye touch land?"

"Eat."

David laughed. "Aye. And drink. A full pint of anything wet that isn't laced with vinegar or tar."

Liam looked at him, his keen eyes missing nothing. "Ye'll be joining the living again, then?"

"Aye."

Liam nodded, satisfied, and turned to listen to Captain Honeywell. He'd asked the passengers to gather on deck so that he could advise them of the procedures that would be taking place.

"It's been a long journey for all of us," Honeywell said. "I for one am thankful we've suffered no loss of life. Now, we're apt to be put through inspection. You're to have your quarters clean, as well as yourselves. We're subject to quarantine at the whim of an inspector; do I make myself clear? Leave no doubt as to the state of your health. Shouldn't be a problem. We've been lucky enough to have no fever on board as of yet."

The pilot's ship arrived, and the pilot, an unusual looking man considering the primitive circumstances, boarded.

"Will ye look at him, Davey. Did ye ever see such as he? America must be a fine place indeed," Liam said. "Good it is ye swabbed the deck, otherwise he might get the soles of his boots dirty."

"Don't be too quick to judge, Liam, Philly is no small port. I'll wager he knows his trade," Rob said.

In spite of his dandified appearance, the pilot proved more than capable. At long last, twelve weeks after leaving London, the *Industry* began the slow journey through the Capes and up the Delaware.

February 6, 1784—As I write this, the Industry *is finally being escorted up the Delaware to Philadelphia. We took on a pilot last evening on account of the great many rocks at the capes. We should let go the anchor by day's end and all aboard feel thankful and blessed to have made the passage without loss of life. Upon entering the Delaware we encountered eight vessels run ashore on the inside of Cape Henlopen. We learned one was from Bristol, four others from London. I did not learn of the port of origin of the other three. Captain Honeywell took on as many of the survivors as the Industry could hold, I estimate about fifty, and left the remainder of our provisions with the others. Uncle John reminds me of our good fortune to sail with such a compassionate man.*

Whilst we were making these arrangements, a host of ships sailed out of the Delaware. We learned from the pilot that on Thursday and Friday last, Philadelphia experienced southerly winds, accompanied by rain. This opened navigation, and as a result on Sunday between twenty and thirty of outward-bound vessels were finally able to leave Philadelphia to proceed on their intended voyages. These same events have allowed the vessels that had been detained at the Cape by the ice to come up to town.

I'll wager this journey has been the most eventful thing I've experienced to date, and while I don't regret the experience, I am relieved it is finished. Now I wait to hear news of Elisabeth.

19

Philadelphia, Pennsylvania
February 1784

IT WAS CLEAR THE DAY the *Industry* limped into the Philadelphia harbor, clear, still, and cold. Bitterly cold, cold with a crisp white edge to it, no shadows, no softness.

"David, did ye get the trunk? I couldn't find it. Ah, of course ye did. Open it, will ye? I want to add my bowl. Didn't ye eat?"

"Earlier. D'ye see Mr. Oliver and the lads, Uncle? I'd like to cross with them, if that's all right."

"Of course. They're still below; Sean was searching for the logs ye fashioned. Look at that, will you? As busy and rambunctious as Bristol."

He had been looking. The city was to be his home for the next seven years after all. "Aye. D'ye know where we're going, or do we go with one of the greeters?" The baggage of those first off was being grabbed by men swarming the dock, hawkers shouting with offers of bargains on room and board.

"No, not with them. Ye stay close to me. There's Oliver now. Come, we'll join them in the queue.

IT WAS A QUIET CROSSING, each lost in his own thoughts as the crew rowed the boat carrying the lot of them across the harbor. David shook hands with Mr. Oliver once they reached the wharf, then with Rob. Reaching Sean, he picked him up and tossed him into the air.

"Don't be forgetting your promise to write, I want to hear tales of the west." Sean, tears threatening, could only nod as he wrapped his arms tightly around David's neck. "Don't cry, lad. We'll write, aye? And mayhap your brother will bring ye to Philly for a visit. It's no' so far." He pulled the boy's head to his shoulder in a hard embrace, then set him down, tapping his nose. Taking a pack of cards from his pocket, he handed them to Sean.

"Let me know how ye do at remembering the tricks, aye? Ye'll have your brother befuddled, no doubt. Ye learned them well." Sean nodded numbly and turned away, tears streaming down his face as he shuffled through the cards.

David turned to Liam. Not trusting his voice, he offered his hand.

Liam took his hand and pulled him close, gripping his shoulder. "No' goodbye. Ye havena seen the last of me. I know well where to find ye."

"Do, and soon, aye? I'm counting on it." Grabbing his bag and their small trunk, he joined his uncle.

"Look sharp, David, and walk with a purpose. Keep your bag close by your side." Only after they had walked close to a block did his uncle slow, stepping into an empty alleyway to look through his papers.

"I recognize the name of that road there, Uncle. Should we be to the north a couple of blocks?"

"Good memory. Yes, and I believe it's not far from here. Would you like to stop and eat before we seek lodging?"

"Nay, I'd as soon find lodging first and stash our bags," David answered.

Wilson stepped out of the close and continued walking west. "What do you make of the place then? It seems not so different than any city quayside, aye? A bit worse for wear, so soon after the war, perhaps." When David didn't respond, he turned. "Are you feeling well enough, son?"

"I'm just a bit wrought up at the moment, I expect. Nay, it's not so different."

"Wrought up for the last month is more the truth of it. Turn here. Mrs. Andrews recommended a house that's up off that corner I believe. There may be room for us." Wilson pointed. "Her sister-in-law runs it. She and her sons will be staying there until Mr. Andrews comes to collect them."

David brightened. Having Adam and Samuel close would ease some of the emptiness.

"Here, this looks to be the proper street. Right across from that book store it should be. Ah, there's Mrs. Andrews now."

"Reverend, David, come, we've only just arrived—and Eliza does indeed have room to let."

"Come in, come in, shouldn't stand out on the street with your bags. Next thing ye know is a ne'er-do-well will have them. I'm Eliza Andrews, and ye must be Reverend John and young David. I'll show ye to your room. I don't have any victuals prepared, as I wasn't expecting lodgers today, but the Market's close. I can remedy that fast enough."

"Nay, Mrs. Andrews, don't bother. We plan to walk around a bit. We'll eat while we're out."

"That will be Miss Andrews, sir," she said, smiling broadly at Wilson. She was a big woman, and her wild, curly hair fell from her cap as she bustled about.

David ducked his head and smiled. Uncle John's mild way

did elicit interest from women, that was a fact. And they were always wasting their time. He took the bag from his uncle's hand and set it next to his in the room Miss Andrews had led them to, then went to wait outside while they dealt with the financial arrangements.

"CAN WE MOVE IN the direction of the shop, Uncle? So as tae see the surroundings?"

"Aye." His uncle took his elbow, and they moved quickly through the streets, passing several taverns as they headed north, stopping at the sign of *The Brig and The Snow*. "Here David, this place looks to be as good as the next. Let's go inside." A rush of tobacco smoke and warm air greeted them as they opened the door. They chose a table in the corner, and Wilson ordered ale and meat pies from the woman who welcomed them.

"Well, we made it, Uncle John. I have to admit I had some doubts whilst waiting in Bristol," David said. He drummed his fingers absently on the table, anxious for the meal to arrive.

"Truly?" His uncle looked at him, surprised. "I'm sorry I had to leave you alone before the sail."

"I didn't mind so much, dinna fash. 'Sides, we had plenty of company soon enough, aye?"

Wilson's normally pleasant face clouded over. He leaned forward and studied him. "David, it pains me to say this, but I must. Elisabeth is an exceedingly nice young woman, and I don't know what I would have done without her while you were ill. However, we've arrived, and I think it best if you don't endeavor to extend the acquaintance."

"Uncle, but—"

"There's no future there, David. And unfortunately I believe you both think there might be. It will only prolong the inevitable to continue the relationship, and I regret that it went as far as it appears to have while you were under my supervision."

The food arrived, and David was spared a response while the barmaid hovered over them, for which he was grateful. Because he couldn't have promised what his uncle was asking.

"It's just off the ship, are ye? I took the liberty of eaves-dropping some while cleaning the next table." The woman smiled easily as she set the food in front of them, refilling their cups. "She sailed from Bristol, did she? My sister and her family are to be making the trip come spring."

"Aye, she did, and spring is a fine choice," Wilson answered. "The weather we encountered did us no favors on our passage. But our Captain sailed a safe and true journey, I'd highly recommend him." He took a small bite of his food. "We're to find Robert Store, journeyman to Hall, the printer. Would ye by chance know of him?"

"Robby, aye, to be sure. Ye just missed him. He usually comes in for a pint to catch the news of the day. He's been saying as he was expecting some folks from back home soon.

"Molly! It's thirsty we are," a man yelled good-naturedly from across the room. "Cease your dawdling!"

She grinned, waving her hand dismissively at the group. "Ye'll find Robby one street over, on Market," she said, pointing. "It's nae far." She picked up her tray.

Wilson consulted his notes. "Where's High Street?"

"Ye'll be calling it Market. Well, I need to be working. Good luck to ye, and come back."

"This is verra good, Uncle. Aren't you going to eat yours?"

Wilson laughed. He took a few more bites, then pushed his plate in front of David. "Finish it for me, will you? My digestion is a bit unsettled as of now. Not ready to trust the stability of land I imagine."

"Will I be staying with Mr. Store tomorrow?" David asked

between mouthfuls, steering the conversation away from Elisabeth.

"Nay, not yet. I can keep ye with me, as I'll be in Philadelphia a while until my own plans are certain. Then in several weeks ye'll stay with the Halls. Will that suit?"

He nodded. They shared another pitcher, and Molly talked Wilson into trying the cheesecake before they left.

"Ye'll no' have had better, mind." She was a motherly sort, with kind grey eyes and an easy smile. His uncle didn't mind bantering with her and letting the time pass. And she was right about the cheesecake—he was limited to one piece while his uncle finished his own.

"Ready now? Had enough?"

He grinned. "Aye, Uncle John, I believe I can make it til morning."

The streets were full, as the last of the ships had emptied and the markets made an end of day press to unload their goods. Weaving their way through the milling people, Wilson guided them to a small house adjacent to a building advertising itself as the *Printing Office of the Pennsylvania Gazette.*

"I believe we've arrived, David."

20

Philadelphia
March 1784

"DAVID! YOU DIDN'T TELL ME you could catch fish right into your cooking pan!" Robbie shouted, racing out of the house adjacent to the print shop.

David set down his packages and caught the lad up in his arms, Robert Stores' youngest child. The Stores had ties to David's family, and they had taken him into their home for many a meal over the past few weeks. Uncle John had been called to New York a scant two weeks after their arrival.

"Don't be believing everything ye hear," he said, laughing, his eyes searching behind Robbie.

"Your friend, he had to leave. He waited as long as he could, he said." Robbie scrambled down. "But he left you a note." He pulled a small piece of paper from his pocket.

Davey, Mr. O has secured a townhouse on Carter's Alley, east of

Third, two blocks up from the new inn on Front, next to the sign of the Shoe. His name is on the door. Come soon. L.

David whistled softly. They were close, and anything close to Market Street was dear. And Mr. O had traveled in steerage! He grinned, feeling better than he had in days, even if he needed to wait until tomorrow to see them. "I thank ye lad, for being such a good messenger. Now, how 'bout ye help me bring in some of these supplies for your Da, aye?"

"YE RUSHED THROUGH that fast, lad. Looks like you did a fine enough job, though," Robert said, his keen eyes inspecting the shop floor and the ample supply of firewood. Robert was a good sort to work for, and he and his wife had assured Uncle John they'd look out for him if he needed it. He was just about thirty years of age, didn't reach as high as six feet, and was very thin. He reminded David of a hawk with his attention to detail and sharp black eyes, though he wasn't unpleasant about it. He just did a good job and expected no less of anyone else. He had been working for Hall and Sellers since he was an apprentice.

"Robert, do ye think I might take some time then, to see a friend? It's no' far. It willna take long."

"Aye, but no longer than an hour. Thomas will need ye tending the water by one," Robert said, shouting the last of it as David sprinted out the door.

He ran the short distance to the waterfront, wanting to follow Liam's directions exactly. He didn't have time to get mixed up. Plus, this time of day Mrs. Peese's sticky buns would be fresh, if not hot, and he had a couple spare pennies in his pocket.

He loved this city for the Market if nothing else.

"Morning, lad. I'll wager I know what you want." Mrs. Peese handed him a bun and took his change. "Wait just a minute." She cut off a small slice of dark bread and wrapped it up. "Put that in your pocket and try it later. Nürnberg gingerbread, all the way from Germany. You'll like it."

"Thank ye, Mrs. Peese!" he said, grinning as he pocketed it. He ran down Front, turning when he saw the new inn Liam had referred to, and headed up the Alley.

He was in a working class neighborhood now, and one in disrepair at that.

The paper had just printed a satirical piece, a dialogue between one of the dead cats and the dead dogs littering the streets. The cat's spirit was patiently explaining to the dog's spirit that the city tax was levied not to keep the streets free of litter, but instead to enable the street commissioners to keep the streets regularly supplied with dead animals, filth from chamber pots, rotting hides from tanneries, and guts, bones, and garbage from family kitchens, all on the belief that the putrescent substances emitted a powerful antiseptic.

Maybe they were talking about this alley. It wasn't so funny if one had to walk through it.

Dodging the pig rooting through the pile of garbage in his path, he hurried up the hill past Second and began to look for the house, slowing when he spotted the cobbler's sign, stopping when he spotted the two story building with Mr. Oliver's name on the door.

Mr. O was going to need to attract the better sort for his students, and most of the wealth in this city lived within walking distance of the markets. But hopefully he hadn't paid too dear a price for the privilege, given the state of the neighborhood and the townhouse.

He stood in the street and looked at it critically. It was a two story Georgian, no different than the others. The woodwork was badly in need of paint, and shutters were missing, else rotted. The downstairs sported a broken window, and the entrance to the cellar aside the front steps was missing its cover. And that's just what he could see from the outside.

"Mind the way, lad!"

But it was brick, so it wouldn't burn so quick should a fire run up the alley. And he had two brawny lads to help him mend things. Moving out of the way of the fellow carting a load to the shop just past, he climbed the two steps to the door and knocked.

No answer. Disappointed, he took out the note he'd written earlier and left it under a stone by the step.

Liam, will come back Wednesday next—have the afternoon free at three. D

It would have been good to see him. Taking the gingerbread out of his pocket, he took a bite, grinning at the flavor. The trip wasn't a waste then. He started back to the print shop, glad to find it so near when he skipped the waterfront.

"DAVID, COME IN here. I want to talk to you about something," Mr. Hall called.

He liked Mr. Hall. Neat and trim, he had a mild manner like his uncle, though more forgiving, like his Da. And he always went out of his way to make him feel welcome. Now, Mr. Sellers, that man intimidated him, with his piercing black eyes, sweeping white mustache and booming voice. Didn't bother him any that Sellers worked the Book and Stationery over on Arch, leaving the print shop to Hall.

David set down the load of wood he was carrying and walked into the small office. "Yes, sir?"

"It's about your schooling. I arranged for you to start attending the night school come September. A lot of the trade sends their help there. The rates are reasonable, and the hours are set so as not to interfere with work."

"Aye, ye've explained. And if ye ever feel I'm not shouldering my share in the shop, I've only to discontinue the schooling."

Mr. Hall laughed. "No, that's not an option. The terms of our contract require you have the opportunity to keep up with your education."

David held his tongue and waited until Mr. Hall said whatever it was he had to say. After hearing other apprentices disparage the trade school, he dreaded the prospect.

"I had a visitor several days ago, a Mr. Oliver. It seems Mr. Oliver feels he owes you a debt he can never repay, and he'd like to have you attend his Academy without the obligation of tuition. He discussed his plans for the curriculum and convinced me the opportunity is not to be passed up. My only hesitation, of course, was the timing of the classes." He got up from behind his desk and sat on it, looking at David. "However, I've put some thought into this. By the time school's in session you'll have reached the point where you can perform a good bit of your duties without much supervision. And I've seen enough of your character that I should have no qualms leaving you the evenings to do just that. The cost in tallow will be more than offset by the savings on your tuition. Do you have any thoughts on the matter, David?"

"I believe Mr. Oliver to be a capable teacher, and I'd work hard for the opportunity to study with him," David said, struggling to keep his composure.

"Very well then, it's settled. I'll compose a letter later today to accept his generous offer."

"May I deliver it for ye, Mr. Hall?" David asked.

"That won't be necessary. I'll do it while I'm out this afternoon. Now, go on back and finish up with Thomas. By the way, you'll be running the Waterfront subscriber route with him next week. I want you to relieve him of that duty come August."

"Yes, sir. Thank you, sir!" David said.

First the prospect of attending school with Liam, now a subscriber route. And not just any route, but the one he'd been hoping for, the one that had listed a family named Hale. Maybe by Wednesday next he would see her.

21

"WHOA!" LIAM HOLLERED, "MR. O, guess who's here!"

Grabbing David by his shirtfront, he pulled him inside, adding in an undertone, "Man, it's glad I am you're here. I need to escape this for a bit! Be quick in your admiration and duly awed by our progress, aye?"

David laughed, running up the stairs after him. He greeted Mr. Oliver and Rob warmly, telling Mr. Oliver how much he appreciated the opportunity to attend his school.

"You'll no' regret it, Mr. O. I'll work hard for ye."

"I'll never regret it, David, even should you decide to nap through all your classes."

"I wouldn't do that, Mr. O. I'd never mock ye that way."

Oliver laughed. "That was a poor attempt at levity, David, I know you'll make me proud. Come back downstairs. I'm anxious to show you what we've accomplished."

Each floor had two rooms, one in back of the other. They would use the first floor to house the Academy. They had replaced the broken window downstairs and were now working on partitioning the back room into two rooms, one smaller than the other.

"The plan is for the two larger rooms to serve as classrooms, the smallest as an office. We don't need the full yard in back, but I don't think I'll expand out just yet. I don't want to get ahead of myself," Mr. Oliver explained. He walked David around the rooms slowly, explaining what they'd changed and what they still needed to do.

"It's well thought out, Mr. Oliver. I think ye'll be successful. I haven't noted many schools in town. Ye'll fill a need, for sure." He put his hand behind his back, motioning Liam down. The lad was near hopping from foot to foot in impatience. He was anxious himself, but no need to fret Mr. O over it.

"Maybe you could aid me in convincing Elisabeth to help teach the younger children. She had quite a knack with them."

Well. Now Mr. O had his full attention. "Is she thinking of doing so, then?"

"I haven't asked her yet. Liam prompted me into expanding the school to include the younger ones. I hadn't considered it before. But I think he's right; we'll have the chance to keep a student enrolled for a greater length of time. At this point it's only something to consider, as I don't have the enrollment to support the idea. Well, I'll keep you no longer. I can see Liam is barely containing his desire to escape for the afternoon. Off with the two of ye."

Liam shot to attention. "Thanks, Mr. O. I'll be back by supper. I'll bring back some soup, aye? Come, David, let's go to the quay." They exploded out the door and ran down the street toward the river. At the end of the street David started to head south, toward where the *Industry* had anchored weeks earlier.

"Nay, this way, David. Tannery is nasty, plus there're men

working on covering that creek. We'll only be chased away this time of day," Liam said.

David grinned, turning back to the north. "Sounds like first-hand knowledge."

Liam shrugged and pointed. "Up there, see? A spot we can sit a bit and ye can fill me in on how ye've managed without me these past weeks."

They settled under a stand of trees, seeking shelter from the wind gusting up the river. The ferries were busy this afternoon; it hadn't snowed for a week and the ice in the harbor had melted some over the last several days. Robert had said it was the worst winter he could recall, complaining that the city was struggling enough with the return to trade now that the war was over. They didn't need to be worrying over the weather. The harbor was filled with dozens of ships, most sitting idle while the masters weighed the risks against the profits. The risks were winning out.

It hadn't helped matters any that the Confederation Congress had left Philadelphia in a huff, taking with it the business the congressmen had brought to the taverns and innkeepers. Business was lost to the printing trade as well, maybe even more so than the taverns. He was thankful his apprenticeship had been negotiated last year. Any later and there may not have been an offer.

"Geez, it's good to see ye, Liam; like seeing home," David said.

Liam cuffed his shoulder in acknowledgement, his eyes on the river. "Do ye feel it, Davey, the excitement, the possibilities here? At times I feel as if I may burst out of my skin."

He laughed. "Aye, but I've an apprenticeship to serve, so I must postpone my 'bursting'."

"I know; I've years to repay Mr. O, myself. And I don't begrudge them, not a bit. But the possibilities after that, they make my head spin and the soles of my feet itch. If I had stayed, it wouldna be long before I could tell ye what I'd be doing each and every day til the day I died. That's a sobering thought, I tell ye. It's forever I'll be grateful to Mr. O for the opportunity of other." He scooted up a little, seeking a spot in the sun. "Have ye seen the lass?"

"Nay, I havena the time. This is my first afternoon free."

Liam grinned ear to ear.

"What?"

"Your first afternoon off, ye seek me out, no' her. No' that I'll vex her with it, mind."

David chuckled. He watched one of the lighters dock, loaded with iron goods. One of the merchants he recognized from the Market was watching closely as four young men unloaded the goods into his waiting wagon. A laborer was directing the loading of another boat secured at the same dock, a horseboat. Hogshead barrels heavy with something, mayhap sugar.

"I did look up her kin, on the subscriber list. I think I know where I might find her. But I'm at a loss then. I've never courted a lass before, Liam. They've just been there, ken?"

Liam grinned. "Aye, for sure."

David elbowed him. "She's different, and I suspect I can't just go up to the grand entrance, knock, and ask if Elisabeth can—what?"

"Come out and play?" offered Liam.

They roared with laughter. When he could catch his breath David said, "Och, but I've missed ye, Liam. Ye lighten my thoughts."

"And ye elevate mine. It's a fair enough exchange. I'll think on this; I'll come up with a plan. Remember, I have the luxury of direct contact with her da on behalf of the school. He doesn't distrust me for having unseemly designs on his daughter."

David rolled his eyes, not rising to the bait. "No' too elaborate, if ye will."

"No' to worry, Davey, I've a talent for this. My only problem is ridding myself of a lass, no' spending time with one. Look at that, will ye?" He pointed to the horseboat. Fully loaded, several of the dock workers pushed it away with long rods. The three horses tethered to the capstan began to walk in their designated circle. The fellow manning the boat had only to steer and encourage the beasts as they started the short journey across the river to New Jersey.

"I've something for ye, Davey," Liam said, reaching into his pocket.

David extended a hand, his eyes still on the horses. When the fellow was halfway across the Delaware he looked down. His gaze rose to meet Liam's, dumbfounded, then dropped back to the small piece of bone he was holding. He fingered it reverently.

"My God, Liam, ye—"

"Don't. It's nothing."

"Nothing?" he whispered. "How can ye even jest?" He turned the die over and over in the sunlight, marveling at the precision with which it was carved. His initials were elaborately engraved outside a circle. The circle itself contained the Graham family crest, the eagle atop the heron, the motto *Ne Oublie*, all faithfully reproduced. *Never forget*. He blinked, keeping his head down. "How did ye know?"

"The crest, ye mean? Dryman's littered with Grahams, mind. Canna piss for fear of wetting one."

The spell broken, David laughed. "Thank you," he said simply. "I'll treasure it." He brought out his handkerchief and wrapped the die carefully before putting it in the pocket inside his shirt. When he was sure his voice would betray no emotion, he told Liam about his new home.

"I stayed with Uncle John for the first few weeks, with

Mrs. Andrews nearby, no less. It made the transition easier, ye know how I was worrying it. Uncle John was called to New York, though, so I'm lodging at the Halls for now, 'til I start the apprenticeship proper. The lad you left the note with, that was Robbie, Robert's son. Robert's the journeyman running the print shop. His older brother attended University with kin back home."

"What's the work like? Are ye verra busy?"

"It's no' difficult, but the days are long, even in winter. I'm learning the lay of the city and the ways of the Americans, I canna complain. No' much to do with printing yet. My official tenure willna begin until August. Is Sean still in town?"

"Nay, his brother had had a man and his wife waiting to escort the lad as far as Pittsburg. They left within a few days of our arriving. Don't know if he's with his brother yet, no' sure how long it takes."

"I'm surprised they journeyed in winter."

"Aye, well, the man said he'd been waiting over a month, didna have time to dawdle. Sean was pestering the man non-stop for tales of Indians. I expect we'll get a letter come June or so."

David looked at the sun and stood reluctantly. "I have to get back, Liam. Are ye free Sunday, after kirk?"

"For you, aye. Mr. O will be more than accommodating. He thinks ye a good influence on me," Liam said with a wink.

22

March 1784

"WHICH ONE'S THE HALES, THOMAS?"

"Two doors up, why?"

"I think a friend from the crossing may live there," David answered.

Thomas raised his brows, but didn't slow his pace. "This one on the corner—ain't your Hale, no doubt," Thomas said as they came alongside the house and deposited the paper.

David didn't answer, just looked back at the front as they hurried on. It was an imposing façade, to be sure, in the Georgian style, two stories of stately red brick, all tidy and well kept, a large garden with a low wooden fence off around the back. A black man was stepping out a side door to retrieve the paper.

Aye, well, now he felt a bit the fool, knowing where he might find her, knowing he couldn't just call and do so. His Ma would raise Cain if she had any inkling he fancied a lass whose father thought he wasn't good enough for her. No matter, he did want to see her. She'd gotten under his skin; he thought of her all the time. If his pride took a bit of a blow to arrange it, so be it, he supposed. Besides, he'd promised the lass. Hopefully she'd remember that when the time came.

DAVID SAW THE same black man again later that week, playing at a game of dice with others on the footpath outside McTaren's Grocers. He paused, watching the game from a distance. The man wasn't young; his hair was graying, and he moved slowly from time to time, as if an action pained him. He wondered if he was a slave. Some in town still kept them.

After a bit the man stood and walked in his direction. "Ain't playing for cash. Didn't win if I was; you're wasting your time."

"Sir?" David asked, startled. The man gave a grunt and walked on by. He'd mistaken him for a snib? David hurried to catch up. "Sir, no, I wasn't watching ye in hopes of picking your pocket. Truth be, I just was hoping to make your acquaintance as I saw ye outside the Hale home several days ago. I work for the *Gazette*. I was delivering the paper, ken?" He decided he better get to the point quickly as the man kept walking. "I made the passage with the Hales; Mr. Hale and his daughter Elisabeth that is, on the *Industry* this winter, and I would very much like to speak with Elisabeth again."

At this the man stopped. He looked David up and down. "I don't know the man, but I knew his father well. Her pa ain't going to cotton to the likes of you calling on her, boy."

"David, my name's David. David Graham, sir," he said, holding out his hand. It was the black man's turn to be startled. He looked at David's hand a moment before taking it.

"John Black. Pleased to make your acquaintance," he said, shaking David's hand firmly.

"Would ye tell her I asked about her and hope she's doing

well?"

"Can't. She's not here yet. Has Mrs. Hale worried something fierce."

"She's not here yet?" David repeated, turning pale. "But we've been here over a month! They left the ship in Charlestown, see, and were to follow shortly thereafter, by land I'm thinking. Mr. Hale doesna take the sea well."

"Yes, the Capt'n was good enough to send word. I got to be getting along now. By the by, you can't reach Charlestown by land, not by carriage anyhows. Doubt a Hale'd be walking that way, not in the dead of winter anyhows." He walked away, heading to one of the produce stands.

David watched him go, too caught up in his worry to say anything in parting. How could she not be here? They should've arrived before the *Industry*. What did he mean, you can't travel by land? He hurried back to the printing office.

"Robert!" he called out.

"There you are, David, I was starting to wonder. Picked up the dispatches, did ye?" He stopped at the blank look on David's face. "I hope ye didn't forget, David. It's imperative I have those as soon as they arrive."

"What? No, of course I didna forget." Although he might have, had he not done that task before the stationer's shop and John Black. "Ye've one from London, one from Dublin; the rest are local." David brought them out from the packet he'd stuffed inside his shirt and handed them over. "Robert, how does one travel to Charlestown? Is it a long journey by land?"

"I expect it would be a long journey, given there are no roads the length of the distance," Robert said, his head down as he quickly sorted the dispatches in order of importance.

"So one must travel by sea then."

He looked up. "Aye, normally. There's a regular packet that travels back and forth. Why d'ye ask?"

"A group left the *Industry* when we anchored in Charlestown, waiting out the storms. I just learned they've no' yet arrived in Philadelphia. It's been a month since we've come, and a month we were anchored outside Charlestown. I don't understand why they didn't arrive first."

"Well, they would have been subjected to the same weather constraints you were, David, and probably decided to wait out the winter comfortably lodged in Charlestown. It's a fairly pleasant town, so I'm told. It's a bit premature to worry yet." He turned back to the papers.

"Will ye be sure to tell me when next the packet arrives?" Robert didn't answer, so he headed back into the shop. He'd ask again later in the day, when the man wasn't so preoccupied.

"David? Come back a moment. This may be what you were looking for." He handed David the paper he'd been reading.

David read through the dispatch quickly. Ice in Charlestown harbor, disagreeable passage of more than twenty days, uncommon hardships, excessively severe winter in this quarter. He knew she shouldn't have left the ship. He shouldn't have let her. His heart rate quickened as the worry set in. "Where are these places, Robert—Egg Harbor, Seven Mile . . .?"

"Seven Mile is at the cape, Egg Harbour is down the river a ways. You'll just have to be patient. Now head to the back and see what Thomas needs to have done, will ye?"

"Aye," David said, reluctantly handing the paper back to Robert.

THE WIND HOWLING UP THE Delaware was biting cold tonight. David's eyes smarted against the force of it as he made his way to the townhouse. He'd copied most of the dispatch during his dinner and was planning on asking Liam to find out what he could. He knew the lad spent some days quayside, hoping to hire out—and if anyone could dig up more information on Captain Allibone's Charlestown Packet, it'd be Liam.

"David, come in," Mr. Oliver said, swinging open the door.

"I'm sorry to disturb ye at this hour, Mr. O. I was counting on Liam attending the door, so as not to wake ye."

"Liam and Rob aren't in. They went to a late supper. I'm sorry to say I don't know where to direct you."

"In that case, would ye mind handing this to Liam when he returns? And tell him I'll seek him out tomorrow evening when I finish. It shouldn't be too late. I finish up early on Saturdays. I'm sorry I woke ye, sir."

"Not to worry, David. I wasn't sleeping. I'll make sure he receives it."

"EV'NING, ROB. Life of leisure, is it?" David said, motioning to the book Rob held.

Rob answered the door Saturday night, book in hand. "Hah, nay. Mr. O has me studying play writers this week. Not my favorite, but best to be conversant, especially as they're part of the curriculum. Have ye read any?"

"Nay, although I did see a play performed while in Edinburgh a few years ago with my Da. It was entertaining enough. The theatre, that is; no' much of that at home."

"Anything entertaining is too frivolous by half, according to the Kirk," Liam said, running down the stairs. "Have ye eaten supper, David? Rob and Mr. O are finished. I was hoping ye'd join me?"

"Nay, I havena. I came as soon as I finished up."

"Come upstairs. It's nothing hot, but it'll fill ye. I'll relay what I found."

He greeted Mr. Oliver, who was reading by the fire, and sat at the table. Liam set out a small loaf of rye bread, a slab of cheese and a jug of ale.

"It's lucky we were that the *Industry* made it up the river when she did, David. Once she made repairs up in the Whore-Kill Roads, she took off again, but only til the wind ran her aground and the bay iced over. It was just over a week ago that she finally was off that bar. The point being, the same foul weather would have stranded that packet out at the Cape.

"What of the passengers, Liam? Did ye hear any news of them?"

"No' much." He paused to take a bite, and reached for the jug. "I talked to one of the hands from the *Maria*. Her captain, Captain Kelly, he's the one who provided the information for the dispatch ye gave me, he spoke to Allibone, the packet's captain. The sailor told me Seven Mile is one of the barrier islands off the Cape. You'll likely remember it. Several ships were stranded there when we passed, just to the north?" He took another swallow of the ale before pushing the jug across the table toward David.

"Aye, well," he said, "the passengers let off there were most likely those needing relief from the ship. Some were ill. It wasna an easy journey, and that Packet is no' meant for long voyages. Capt'n Kelly left Capt'n Allibone some provisions, which they were in sore need of. The *Maria*, she just made it up the river, dinna forget. None actually saw those stranded, the man said. The provisions were relayed at some distance by the ship's cutter, and visibility was bad. He couldn't tell me how many, or much less who they might have been. There was no loss of life so far as he knew, David. He thought that would have been relayed if so."

"I would imagine the Hales put in on the island, given Mr. Hale's propensity for seasickness," Mr. Oliver said, folding his book closed.

"Aye, I agree," David said. "I didna notice any shelter there."

"Nay, but I'll reckon it's safer than a ship that's not completely seaworthy," Rob said. "It be March now. The ice is likely to melt this coming week, this last storm being winter's last hurrah." David could see Rob's foot was paining him. He had it setting up close to the fire. Winter's hell.

"There are several stands of trees there. I remember seeing them. It'd be possible to make shelter from a few bits of torn sail," Liam said.

David nodded slowly, standing. "Are ye still free tomorrow, Liam?"

"Aye, I'll walk back with ye. Up for a short jaunt, Rob?"

Rob shook his head and held up his book, grimacing. Rob had received the academic side of the bargain in Mr. Oliver's venture.

Outside, Liam shivered, hunching his shoulders against the wind. "It's colder than a witch's teat tonight." Cupping his hands, he exhaled into them for warmth.

"Och, that was thoughtless. My apologies, David. She'll be all right, ken, even if she was on that packet. Lisbeth's a spunky lass, give her that, will ye? She's likely to have supervised the rigging of various fishing apparatus, just as ye taught her, and is now dining on a full spread of fresh cod surrounded by several roaring campfires. She always got the fires going when wee Alex struggled with them, remember? When ye were down she had your care managed with military precision. The rest of us just followed orders. She's a survivor, for all that she resembles a delicate flower. And dinna be forgetting, for all we know she may be sitting fireside, cosied up in a Charlestown parlor, being courted by swags."

"Ye could have stopped midway through that and left it somewhat comforting."

Liam laughed, and they continued the rest of the walk in silence, stopping outside the printing office. The streets were full of people coming and going, cold as it was. "I'm going to come by mid morning tomorrow. Go to kirk early, will ye? And if ye ever need to find me again, try the Man Full, at the sign of the man carting a lass on his back, over on Second and Spruce. I've taken a liking to the place. Food's fair, and it's easy to roust up a game."

"Right, Liam, tomorrow then. Thank ye for your help today, I'm much obliged."

"Ballocks, dinna be forgetting she's my friend, too."

"Your friend first, ye've reminded me a time or two."

"Doesna stop ye from forgetting," he grumbled.

23

Seven Mile Beach
March 1784

THE WIND HOWLED, SLAPPING ABOUT the tat-
tered sheets of sail that made up the makeshift shelter.
Elisabeth huddled into a smaller ball, sure she'd never been
so cold and so miserable.

In truth, though, as often as she'd said that this last two
months, perhaps not. Who's to say one remembers degrees
of misery with any accuracy. She worked to slow the chattering of her teeth. If she were still, if she could control the
shivering that wracked her body, then perhaps sleep would
come. If she were still . . .

First that terrible storm in Charlestown, but they'd been in
an inn. They weren't damp, just cold and terrified. Which in
truth wasn't so bad, not in retrospect. But surely the arrangement of this shelter left a lot to be desired and could have
been better handled.

This morning the captain had left ten of them on the

island, three of them being women, her and two elderly sisters. The men in charge had decided to build two shelters using the scraps of sail and other refuse from the recent shipwrecks. *Two*, for the sake of propriety! She didn't give a hoot about propriety at this point, and shouldn't half that canvas be on the ground to separate them from the damp as much as possible? Not to mention body warmth if they were all sheltered together, which she certainly would *not* mention lest that horrible Horace think she was implying he get close to her.

She should be watching over Papa. He was apt to become ill exposed like this. It was a wonder he wasn't already, given what they'd been through. Maybe he was. He needed her.

Tomorrow she'd try fishing again. It would keep her busy, and maybe the two sisters she traveled with could show her how to clean and cook a fish. Now that she could think clearly, she was sure it wasn't a shark that stole her catch off the line. She didn't know why she was such a ninny as to let Horrible Horace convince her of that. He was just jealous he was unable to even conceive of how to catch a fish without his daddy's tackle at hand.

She missed David so; none of this would be so awful if he were here. She just knew it wouldn't. He'd figure something out. But she couldn't let herself think of missing him. She averred her tears would freeze if she cried.

One of the sisters lifted her head. "Elisabeth? Come between sister and me, darling. We've got enough padding between the two of us to keep a lil' thing like you warm."

Grateful, she moved between the two of them, the thought of protesting for politeness sake not even crossing her mind. "I'm sorry I woke you, Miss Waters," she stuttered. "I swear it's impossible to keep my teeth still."

"Shhh; there now. I declare you're thinking so hard, I can almost hear you."

"Yes, ma'am, thank you, ma'am. I'll try. Miss Waters, would you show me how to cook a fish tomorrow?"

"Surely, darling, now try to sleep."

"I don't know how to clean one either."

"Well then, we'll have a busy day ahead of us, won't we? Now think of something pleasant, and relax that mind of yours."

Pleasant . . . that she could do. She closed her eyes as her body relaxed, burrowing deep in the warmth between the two women. And she allowed herself to think of him.

"DAVID, I'VE JUST received word the Charlestown Packet has anchored, and all the passengers have disembarked. Some a little worse for wear, but all safe. If your friends were on it, you should find they've arrived."

He said a quick, silent prayer in thanks. "Thank ye, Robert."

The Hales had indeed been on that packet, according to John Black anyway. He'd headed to the docks at the end of each day for news, and each day the news was the same: nothing. But now they were here.

Tomorrow he'd seek out John and assure himself of her wellbeing.

24

Philadelphia
March 1784

"BETH, COME, GET IN NOW. We're almost at the end of this God-awful journey," her father said.

Shaken and weary, she walked unsteadily to the carriage and climbed in, grateful for the cushion to rest her head. She searched the quay for a familiar face, even knowing it foolish. He was near now, and she found the thought soothing. Settling back, she closed her eyes.

"Beth? Wake up."

Was the ride that short or had she fallen deep asleep? "I'm awake, Papa." Stepping out of the carriage, she drowsily focused on the house in front of her. The red brick home stood two stories tall. A set of double windows, flanked by shutters, stood just to the left of a large carved door. The door was painted a soft sage green, punctuated with shiny dark green hardware. Grand, though not overly large. She liked it immediately. The front door opened, and her grandmother stepped out.

"Mother!" her father said.

"Edward, my gracious, come in. Elisabeth, how you've grown, child. I scarcely recognize you; you're a young woman now. Lands, I've been so worried, on pins and needles for months now. Tom, take care of their baggage, please. Come in, sit by the fire, the both of you." Tom, a tall, slender black man, inclined his head and stepped around them to walk outside to the carriage.

"How are you, Mother? How's Father?"

Elisabeth followed them through the hall to the front parlor, watching as her grandmother's face clouded, noting for the first time she was dressed entirely in dark colors.

"Edward, you don't know. I confess I forgot the message may not have reached you. Your father passed some six months ago."

Her father's shoulders sagged, and he dropped into a chair by the fire, head in his hands.

"Oh no! Oh, I'm so sorry," Elisabeth said, embracing her grandmother.

"Elisabeth, I'm so glad to see the both of you. You can't possibly know how worried I've been," her grandmother said, her voice breaking as she wrapped her arms tightly around her.

"It'll be all right, Grandmother, we're here now. Papa will take care of everything, and I'll help as well." She patted her Grandmother's back, trying to soothe her. Then she pulled away. "Oh! I must look and smell a fright."

Her grandmother dabbed her eyes and caressed Elisabeth's cheek. "You look and smell wonderful, child." She rang the bell beside the fireplace. "Polly," she said to the young black woman who entered the room, "please send in some tea immediately, then prepare a bath for my granddaughter. Ask

John to prepare something hot and quick. We'll eat supper early so they can retire to a warm bed."

Polly hurried from the room, and Mrs. Hale went to sit in front of her son to offer what comfort she could. Elisabeth sat at the window and wondered if it would be too rude to forgo tea and supper, and opt for bath and bed only.

"HEE HEE, YOU GOTS to be the same boy what my Polly's going on about," John Black said, greeting David outside the grocery. He turned to his companion. "The young miss, she's been carrying on something fierce bout some fellow she met on the ship, ever since she done arrived. I would have expected him to be about ten feet tall, the way she goes on! Her pa don't like it none either, I can tell you that. Hee, she livens up that house, that's for sure."

David grinned. "The lass remembers me then? Is she well?"

"Lessing she cottoned to another fellow named David on that ship, I'll say she remembers you. And she'll be fine soon enough. Ain't nothing but skin on her bones, but I aim to fix that right quick. Her pa ain't going let you call on her, though, that's for certain, boy."

"I'm well aware of that," David said, drawing himself up to full height. "But I'd still like her to know I am thinking of her, Mr. Black, if it'll cause ye no hardship to deliver the message."

"No, no hardship," John said, looking thoughtfully at David. "None at all, son. And it's John, like I done told you already."

25

Philadelphia
May 1784

"TAMMANY WAS AN INDIAN CHIEF or mayhap a King, dinna ken the pecking order of the tribes. I do know he was a friend of Penn, and between the two of them they made peace between the Indians and the settlers here. Somehow the Sons of Liberty are involved as well, I think, but I confess I wasna paying close heed to what Robert was saying. There's an annual celebration in honor of Tammany each May. He was talking of getting an accounting of it for next week's edition."

"I think ye mean the Sons of St. Tammany, not Liberty, Davey. Well now, it's our first American holiday, then."

It was Saturday evening, and they were walking up one street and down the next, covering the city blocks that surrounded the market area, talking of the week behind them. Reaching the riverfront again, they walked past a row of warehouses and turned up Market Street. They could see a crowd of people several blocks away, past printer's square. Cheers echoed down the street. "General Washington has arrived, Huzza!"

"From the looks of them, they've been at it awhile. Culls are lushed," Liam said.

"Oh, aye, the celebration was to have started earlier with a feast by the Schuylkill. A gent stopped by the paper this afternoon and told Mr. Hall that General Washington was expected today. He must be housed near here. Want something to eat?" David asked, stopping next to the young black woman who hawked his favorite version of pepper pot.

"Aye, he is, with Morris I heard. No, and didna ye just eat?"

"Couple hours ago."

The crowd was moving toward them now, and David and Liam moved up against the building, out of the way. A man dressed as an Indian danced down the center of the street, slowly moving toward the riverfront, drums marking his steps.

"Stap me, will ye look at that," Liam said.

"Aye. Wait for me, then." He handed the woman a coin, and she spooned the pepper pot over a bowl half full of cornmeal moussa. He ate it while standing. "Now, more importantly," he said, between bites, "and what I did pay heed to, Robert was willing to share a few fishing spots he favors. Tomorrow's Sunday. Ye'll come?"

"Of course, first light. Net or line?"

He finished the last of the meal and handed the woman the empty bowl. "*Mèsi.*" He turned to Liam and steered him forward. "No' first light; it's Sunday—first thing after kirk. We don't need many for supper. Let's try a line first."

Liam nodded. "Come get me when ye're ready then."

He had waited as long as he could to bring it up, hoping Liam would, but he hadn't.

"Liam, have ye see her yet, or her da?"

"Who?"

David glared and Liam laughed. "No, no' yet, Davey, but I havena forgotten. I know my craft. Ye have to trust me. Timing's everything."

26

"KEEPING YOU BUSY OVER THERE, are they, David? I haven't seen you in a while," the clerk said.

"Yes, sir, I was helping the missus pack up for the summer. She's off to stay with her cousin for a wee bit."

The air hung hot and heavy this morning, thick with flies. He shifted his shoulders and reached back a hand to peel his shirt from his back, wrinkling his nose as his own scent rose above the myriad of others. "It's wicked hot today, isna it?"

"Ahh, this is your first summer. I'd forgotten. It'll get worse. Here you go, only three today. Give my regards to Robert."

"Aye, Mr. Todd, later then." The man was daft; it couldn't get worse.

Elisabeth. He stopped and moved off the footpath. She was just a block down, walking with a young black woman. At least he thought it was her. The way the lass moved, the tilt of her head as she talked to her companion—aye, it was her. Had to be; no other reason his heart would be slamming up against his ribs. He ducked into the close to give himself a moment to think. Should he just let her pass? Would she be embarrassed to be approached by someone of his sort on the street?

"God in Heaven, what's the matter with me?" he mumbled as she approached and passed. He stepped to the entrance of the close.

"Lisbeth."

She stopped, but didn't turn, canting her head as if listening.

"Bess." He stepped out of the shadows of the alley, removing his hat as she turned, watching her eyes carefully as she looked at him. Confusion, surprise, then a vivid flash of joy before shyness won out. She remembers. He stepped toward her, reaching out a hand to cup her chin, running his thumb across her jaw. She closed her eyes, sighing softly.

"You look well, lass." Better than well. God, how he'd missed her.

"You better get your hands off her, mistuh, 'fore I call for the watch." The young black woman grabbed Elisabeth's arm, pulling her back.

"No! Polly, no. This is David. It's all right; this is David."

"Is not all right, missy, it's a whipping I'll be earning, your Papa see you dawdling on this here street with the likes of him while I be standing by."

"Polly!" Elisabeth said, her horror showing at Polly's lack of manners.

"It's all right, Lisbeth," he said, turning to the girl. "Polly, is it? David Graham. It's glad I am to meet ye." He held out his hand and, though she made a point of ignoring it, he thought he could detect a slight twitching at the corner of her mouth. She was a beautiful young woman. He wondered at her place; no slave he'd seen to date carried herself like she did.

"Dontcha be turning your charm on me, mistuh, won't get you anywhere but on your backside. I know my duty."

"I'm sure that you do, Miss Polly, and I'm grateful she has ye at her side. It's only a minute of her time I'm asking for." He looked back at Elisabeth, hoping for help. The intensity of her gaze caught him by surprise as she looked up at him, her lips parting as she met his eyes.

Heat shot through him, pooling in his loins. He turned to Polly, his manner no longer mild. "Ye wait right on that bench there, Polly. I'll have her back to ye in three minutes. Track the time for me, aye?" He pulled Elisabeth into the shadows of the close without waiting for an answer, leaving Polly on the street staring at him, hands on her hips, her mouth open.

His hands cradled her face, and he kissed her, his tongue seeking, meeting, remembering. He moved a hand down her face, fingers following the graceful curve of her neck, gratified as he felt her pulse race at his touch, as he heard her moan of protest when he pulled away. He held her close and spoke, pressing her head to his chest.

"I've missed ye, lass. I was so worried. We've only a minute 'fore your maid calls. Can ye meet me? Later?"

She pulled away, looking up at him, her eyes filling as she shook her head. "I can't. I don't know how I can." She ran her hand across his hair. "You're tying it back now."

"Aye, is it all right, ye think?"

She nodded. "It's only that it no longer curls. I loved the feel of the curls." She ran her fingers across his face, and he felt her touch all the way to his toes. "You've shaved."

He grinned. "Aye."

"I'm sorry, I'm babbling. I've missed you so. I've a mountain of letters to give you. John told me you'd asked after me, but I didn't know what to do with them. It seemed too forward to have them delivered."

"I bring your paper. Leave them with John, and I'll pick them up Wednesday. I'll write ye as well, but think on it, Elisabeth. It's your company I miss as well as your touch. I need to see you. I need to. Your girl is looking worried, I'll no' try her patience longer." He kissed her quickly and turned her, his hands on her shoulders, gently pushing her toward the sidewalk.

SHE LOOKED BACK to say something, but he had already disappeared into the shadows of the alley. Faith, he was even more handsome than she'd remembered. Perhaps it was the clean shave and his hair pulled back in the cue, or maybe the passage of time. But his cheekbones were more pronounced, his jaw more square, his warm eyes brighter, his dimples deeper, his mouth . . . My word, just the sight of him had made her senses swim. She raised her fingers to touch her lips.

Polly grabbed her, turning her. "Look sharp Miss Elisabeth, your Papa's coming up the street to fetch us. Please missy, get that look off your face."

He mesmerized her; there was no accounting for it. It took her a moment to register what Polly was saying, though her Papa's voice brought her to, quickly.

"There you are, Elisabeth. I've finished with the tailor. Is there anything you'd like to do before we return?"

"No, Papa," she said automatically. "I'm ready." Turning to follow her father as he walked toward home, she held back slightly to keep pace with Polly.

"Do you see now, Polly?" she whispered.

Polly giggled softly. "Yes, missy. He's fine."

"SHE'S HERE, LIAM. I saw her, I talked to her," David said.

"Aye, I thought as much." It was Saturday, and Liam was

waiting for David to finish up at the printing office. "Mr. Hale came to the school to talk to Mr. Oliver. Mr. O is beside himself, as it seems she's convinced her Da to let her teach the wee ones in exchange for lessons. The lass appears no' to have forgotten ye."

David stopped abruptly, and the water in the pail he carried sloshed over his shoes. "And ye waited til *now* to tell me?"

"It was only yesterday, David." He grinned as David glared at him. "Well, truth be, Mr. O didna tell me of the visit til this morning. I ran across Mr. Hale in the market a few weeks ago, mind, and cornered the cove with stories of the Academy and our progress. I wasna sure anything would come of it, so I didna mention it. It was only my first go at it, see. I came as soon as I knew ye to be free."

David laughed. "Come, I'll buy ye supper. I'm finished here, and I've something to celebrate." They walked out of the shop and headed down Second. "Don't think I don't appreciate the hand ye had in making this come about."

Liam grinned, pulling David into the first tavern they passed. "Now then, tell me all of it," he said.

"Ye havena seen her yet, have ye? I barely recognized her at first, what with the fancy hat and dress. Have ye tried to kiss a lass wearing such?" David stood briefly and pantomimed the distance the petticoat had kept him from Elisabeth. "Remind me to tell ye news of the *Industry*." He drained his cup, then refilled it from the pitcher.

"You're in rare form tonight, mate. I'd forgotten what it was to see ye in prime twig. And no, unlike yourself, I've no' the opportunity as yet to consort with the 'better sort'." Liam motioned to the waiter to bring another pitcher of ale. "Have ye seen the bloke with the frogs at market? He uses them to scare the ladies to the other side of the street, says they take up too much room 'round his stall, what with their gowns taking the space of three, keeping away the paying customers."

David laughed. "I can see that. Keeps ye at a distance, for sure. She's taller now, or mayhap it was her boots. Carrying a parasol! A parasol—Lisbeth." He shook his head slowly in amazement. "It's a wonder her maid didn't summon the watch when I pulled her into the close." The waiter brought their food and ale, and David piled his plate high. "Och, we're no longer just the 'lower sort', Liam. Robert explained. We're on our way to being the 'middling sort.' On account of our occupations. 'Cept you're still the lower sort when ye work the wharves. So I don't know what that makes you."

"I love America," Liam said drily. "Different, but the same nonetheless. What'd she tell ye of the trip from Charlestown?"

"We didna have time to talk much. Her maid didna appreciate my presence. But I picked up a packet of letters she wrote when I delivered the paper Wednesday. She only mentions it as a 'delay'. She also wrote that her grandfather died last September. They didn't know until they arrived."

"That's hard."

"Aye. And I confess I was worried when I read that, worried she might no' be staying in Philly after all. Her da was to work with her grandfather or some such. But ye've just told me I've nothing to worry about on that score." David drained his cup and pointed at Liam's plate. At Liam's nod, he took some of the food to refill his own.

"How will ye see her again?"

"I was wrestling with that, until ye gave me your news. I don't think I can until the Academy starts up. Mayhap it's enough to know she's safe and close by."

"You're past gone, Davey."

Was that true? He didn't respond for a moment, while he thought. It wasn't.

"Ye're daft. I just said it was no concern to be seeing her, didna I?"

Liam snorted. "Well. The *Industry* then?"

His mood instantly sobered. "The paper received word earlier this week. She was lost off the coast of Drogheda, in the night, on her way to Dublin. Most all the crew perished, dinna ken if she had passengers as well. It was late in March. She must have sailed again as soon as repairs were made."

"Christ. I think if I were Papist, I'd be crossing myself," Liam said quietly. "Honeywell, Ritcher, Alex—all gone?"

"Nay, another captain, probably another crew. I expect the crew we sailed with wasna ready to leave Philly so soon."

"There's that. Well, may God rest their souls, aye? And the ship, I've a soft spot for her. May she provide shelter for thousands of fish for the next five hundred years."

David raised a brow at the toast, but drank to it anyway, having a soft spot for her himself.

27

July 1784

"DAVEY, COME. OH, HELLO, MR. Hall. I came by to see if David could leave a bit early today, to attend an event of some significance to your subscribers, to all the citizens of Philadelphia, no doubt. Even Dr. Franklin's made note of it."

"Come on back, Liam," Mr. Hall said. "I assume the event you're referring to is Mr. Carnes attempt to launch a balloon?" The ascension of the first manned balloon flight in Philadelphia was scheduled for later that afternoon.

"I thought that attempt was aborted on Independence Day," David said.

"Aye, well, he's making another go at it this afternoon. It took longer than he'd planned to make repairs after the Baltimore flight. He's starting off from the prison yard, and I've a spot picked out for the best view without the price of admission. He's threatening to shoot those that watch without paying, ken. What d'ye say, Mr. Hall, can Davey come out and play?"

He laughed. "Go. Do be careful not to get yourself shot, David."

"Thanks, Mr. Hall!"

"Aye, Mr. Hall, not to worry. It's a safe spot I've picked," Liam said, grabbing David and pulling him out the door before Hall could change his mind.

They raced through the streets, slowing when they reached Dock Street. "Where're we going, Liam? The Work House is the other way."

"Hang on, David, we've a wee stop to make," Liam said. A door opened just as he turned up the street.

"I've been watching for you," Annie said, stepping out. "My brothers have already left with the rest of them."

"Annie! Sorry to have made him late. It's good to see ye, lass!"

"David! Look at you! A sight for sore eyes, that's the truth," she said, putting her hand to his face. "Well, let's be going, shall we, before we miss it all. We'll talk along the way."

"IT WILL NEVER rise."

"Of course it will, Papa. That's why we're here. He's done it in Baltimore already."

"No, he hasn't. He sent a boy up less than a third his size."

"It's history, Papa, history in the making. Aren't you excited?" Elisabeth tightened her grip on her father's arm, rising on her toes and pointing. "Look, it's filling. My word, it's beautiful, isn't it? Just look at the colors, and at how big it is. Do you think Mr. Carnes is at all frightened? Can you hear any of what that man over there is saying?" The blast of the furnace drowned out the words of the dignitary speaking.

For days, she had begged her father to bring her. He'd finally acquiesced when the ceremony was switched from

Potter's Field to a more select gathering of paying spectators in the yard of the new work house. She pulled her father closer to the stage as she strained to hear what the gentleman was saying.

The attendants made a show of releasing the ropes from their binding, tossing them in to Carnes. The blast of the furnace again pierced the air, and Elisabeth watched wide-eyed as the balloon filled and slowly rose, rocking back and forth gently.

"See, Papa? Do you see?"

"Like a bird. I'll be damned."

Just then a sudden gust of wind threw the balloon against the prison wall, dislodging Carnes from the basket.

"My word, now what?"

Without Carnes' weight the balloon careened rapidly up and out of the Yard. Shouts of excitement rose from those gathered in Potter's Field as the balloon became visible to all, paying spectators or not.

"I wonder how far it'll go. Does it need a man to blast the furnace?" she asked.

"Of course, Beth."

The balloon continued to rise, growing smaller and smaller in the sky. They watched as its flight stabilized, and it drifted slowly southward, no longer the mad dash upward as when it had first lost its passenger.

"It's on fire! Papa, look!" Elisabeth said, pointing. "That man is lucky he was tossed aside. He would have been burned alive!"

In just a few seconds the whole apparatus was consumed in flames. A horrified gasp rose from those in the field as bits and pieces of what was left fell to the ground.

"Are you ready to go, Elisabeth? There's nothing more to be seen here."

"But don't you want to find out what happened? The

crowd outside probably doesn't even know Mr. Carnes was thrown."

"No."

She turned away reluctantly as he guided her out of the yard. There was nothing to be gained by pressing him. She knew from experience he'd be more than happy to read about the event from the comfort of his study the following week.

"Wait, Papa! Look! Isn't that Annie? Ahead, do you recognize her? We should say hello."

"Absolutely not. Need I continually remind you of your promise to form no attachment with that rabble? We're going home, where you may freshen up a bit before supper. The Hastings are coming over. Their son is your age, and looking forward to your company, I might add."

She looked at him, surprised by the vehemence of his response. The father she'd grown up with was disappearing a little more each day, the loss of her mother still tearing away at the softness that had once defined him.

"I haven't forgotten, and of course I plan to make the Hastings welcome. I thought only to spare Annie's feelings if she'd seen us and thought we were deliberately ignoring her. She was fond of you, you know."

He hesitated. "Of course, I was fond of her as well, Elisabeth. I just . . . well, this evening must be a success, it must. Mr. Hastings is considering inviting me to join in their investment partnership. With your grandfather gone, well, things just aren't the way I had planned them to be when we left home. We need this."

She reminded herself again that he'd lost as much as she had this last year, and he carried the burden of making a life for them here as well.

"It will all fall into place, Papa, I promise you. Think of the conversation you can add after today, especially if they watched the balloon rise from the field. Now let's go home. I can help Grandmother prepare for our guests so everything is just so, all right?"

28

August 1784

DAVID IGNORED THE CLAMOR OF the bell signaling the front door had opened. His only aim was to finish the task at hand as quickly as possible, then eat some supper, read a little, and sleep a lot.

An unexpected bonus was the number of books he'd found at his disposal. Mr. Hall had granted him permission to read them, provided he didn't take them out of the shop and returned them to the shelf looking good as new. He'd started on the new edition of Smith's *Wealth of Nations* a few weeks back; Liam was hounding him to finish quickly so he could read it as well, before the last copy sold. Books were a luxury neither could afford. Though as tired as he was, he probably wouldn't get further than a few sentences.

"Hello? Anyone still here?"

Liam. Saturday; he'd forgotten it was Saturday. Grabbing a towel to wipe his hands, he hurried up front.

"David, you're here. I came round to fetch ye, no excuses.

All work and no play . . . well, there's something bad about it, I'm sure of it, just canna bring it to mind at the moment. Look at ye, you look peaked. Are ye ill?"

"Nay, but it's been a hard week. I just need to get some sleep."

"Wednesday last, your afternoon off, what did ye do? I kept expecting ye."

David sighed and ran his forearm across his brow, mopping up the sweat. "Nothing I can recall. If I had the time off, I probably slept."

"Come, it's four. Hear the church bell? I'm taking ye to eat. Finish up."

"Liam, it's no' that I don't appreciate the offer, I do, but I willna be good company. Honestly."

"Finish up, I no' leaving without ye. Ye can fall asleep on the table, and I'll be content talking to myself. It willna be the first time. But I want ye to come."

"Liam, I just—" David stopped, recognizing the stubborn stance. It'd be easier to just go and get it done with. "Ne'er mind, give me a minute."

"I'm patient. I'll give ye five."

He smiled in spite of himself and went to clean the last bit of type.

Liam held open the door when he walked back up front. "Who locks up, Davey? Are ye the last?"

"Robert just came in. He'll lock up."

They walked toward the waterfront. The breeze coming up off the river was a welcome relief from the heat and stuffiness in the shop.

"There's a place off Water Street with tables outside. We can watch the comings and goings of the harbor while ye regale me with tales of the tyrant ye labor for. They're not stingy with the ale for the price either. I promise I'll have ye back by your bedtime."

Saturday afternoon was always busy on Market Street. Normally he'd enjoy the walk, exchanging small talk with Liam about the shops, the public, the weather, whatever took their fancy. Today he was silent, ignoring the glances Liam sent his way, grunting when his chatter called for a response.

"Grab that table under the tree, Davey. I'll round up the barmaid."

"That was fast," David said, when Liam brought a tray with a pitcher of ale and a plate full of oysters to the table.

"Aye, I could see ye needed something quick to restore ye. I just grabbed the tray she was carrying elsewhere. Drink up."

David laughed. "I'm glad ye had me come, Liam. I feel better already," he said, emptying his cup in a quick few swallows.

Liam refilled their cups, lifting his to David's and toasting. "To your first official week on the job." He took a long swallow, motioning to the waitress. "It was different from your duties to date, I take it. Tell me. Thank ye, darlin'," he said, looking up at the young barmaid who grabbed the pitcher from him, flashing a smile to show his appreciation of her quick service.

David grinned as he watched the effect of Liam's smile on the girl, her color rising, her grip faltering as she took the pitcher. He shook his head, stretching his long legs in front of him.

"It was at that," he said, his gaze following the course of one of the screeching gulls as it veered and dove head-first into the water. "I think I prepared enough ink balls to last the full period of my indenture, even with Monday being such that I could barely lift my head." He reached for an oyster.

"Back up a bit. When I saw ye Sunday last, ye weren't ill. And bear in mind I know nothing of balls of ink or how long one may last."

"Sunday, when I returned, the others had a small celebration planned to commemorate the start of my apprenticeship, at my treat no less. The brandy," David grimaced, then continued, "I felt compelled to drink of it, and I can say without reservation I've had enough of that brew to last a lifetime and more. When Robert woke me Monday, I remember thinking I only wanted to die, or mayhap I had died and was in hell. Then he explained the making of the balls, and I knew I was in hell. The smell of the lye, Liam, ye canna imagine the reek of the pressroom, day after day." He tossed an oyster shell to the ground and reached for another.

"I did notice an odor when I walked in. I thought mayhap someone had been a bit clumsy emptying the chamber pot."

David paused in his effort to free the meat from the shell and lifted his arm, sniffing the sleeve.

"Not ye, David; the shop." Liam hastened to add. "I'm sure ye smell just fine, should I choose to get close enough."

"I hope ye're right. I can smell it in my dreams. I'm not sure what's real. Anyway, I was to take a piece of sheepskin devoid of the wool, soak it in chamber lye, and wring it within an inch of its life. But no, it's still not dry, no' according to Robert anyway. It must be rolled over old papers, and tread—over and over, with my feet, until the last drop of moisture has given up the ghost. The moisture being piss, recall. Only then is it soft and pliable enough to wrap around a bit of wool and hang on a stick."

"Why'd ye do that?"

"Because Robert told me to."

"Pete's sake, Davey. Have ye gone daft? What was the point in treating a wrung out piece of skin as such?"

"Oh. Well, it serves as an ink ball. We use them to ink the type. The piss makes it supple, the imprint cleaner, sharper. But ye know, I think I made more than my fair share. Robert looked unusually canny and kept throwing more pelt my way."

"No doubt. He's recognized ye as an overachiever and knows when to press an advantage."

"My only consolation for the week to come is the remaining skin in stock is still with wool. Divesting it of the wool canna nearly be as unpleasant a task. Other than that, I was just put to skink. Running errands, cleaning type, carrying endless pails of water, emptying the slop buckets, a never-ending round of mindless work that begins again as soon as it's finished. I used to help Ian, the lad just senior to me. There's no one doing it now but me, now that he's moved up the ladder."

The waitress set down the pitcher and asked if they were ready to eat.

"Just in time, lass," Liam said. "My mate was just explaining how a woman's work is never done. I was getting thirstier just hearing of it. Does chicken agree with you, David?" At his nod he turned back to the waitress. "Can ye bring us some supper, then, darlin'?" Liam asked, refilling David's mug.

"You know, alehouses and taverns are forbidden by the terms of my indenture," David said, picking up the mug.

"Signed that, did ye?"

"Da did. Fornication, fraternization, cards, dice—forbidden as well. Mr. Hall went over the terms on Monday to refresh my memory."

Liam laughed. "I trust it's no' a cause for concern. I've come across your Thomas a time or two on the quay, looking a bit worse for wear, bargaining with a lass. Tell me, does Lisbeth fall into the category of fraternization?"

"Aye, probably; should we ever see each other, that is. Robert's counsel was as long as it doesna develop into something Mr. Hall has to deal with, you're free to do as you like on your own time." And Thomas did plenty, he knew. Thomas was the senior apprentice, just about ready to transition to journeyman. He'd likely leave at that point; the shop hadn't the business to warrant two journeymen. "Ahh, here's our food already. I'm hungrier than I thought. 'Cept there's flowers on the salad, Liam. Why'd they do that?" He gathered up the pansies, plopping them onto Liam's plate. "Ye eat those."

An hour later the sun was low in the sky, bathing the river in a soft yellow glow. Sated and relaxed, David stretched, feeling better than he had all week. A group of men, laborers all, had just walked into the tavern, loud in their requests for ale and food as they settled in for an evening of play at quoits. He glanced at Liam to see if he had an interest in joining.

"Nay, Rob's waiting."

"Right then, let's walk."

The wharves were quieting as the dock workers finished up for the day. Small waves lapped against the pilings, lulling in their incessant rhythm. They stopped to watch as a ship was towed into the harbor, staying until it was anchored out amidst the others, sails secured.

"It seems a long time ago, aye?"

"Sometimes, though sometimes it seems we just arrived. 'Cept for you; I feel I've known ye always, David." They turned away. "One of the reasons I came to roust ye out was to remind you the Academy is due to start next week."

"It is, isn't it?" David said. "I can't believe that slipped my mind." He grinned. "Ma wouldna ever have believed that Latin and Algebra could lighten my mood. How did the enrollment tally up in the end?"

"We're full."

David laughed and slapped Liam's back. "Well done. That's quite an accomplishment. Now what will ye do? Spend more time at the docks?"

"There'll be a bit more time to hire out at the quay. I'm glad of that. I've grown accustomed to having a bit of blunt in my pockets. But, otherwise, I'll have to keep the seats full, collect tuition from those not bringing it in, find new bodies for next term . . . I don't think it's ever finished. Right now, though, I have to determine how to keep the trees aside it and still get fire insurance. The fellow Mr. O bought the house from didna have it insured, but Mr. O insists."

"Just cut down the trees."

"I need the trees! Makes us look established."

"What they make is a mess of dead flowers in the spring, scant light to read by in the summer, and dead leaves in the fall."

"It's always a struggle with ye, Davey, getting ye to see the beauty in things."

David took a pencil and scrap of paper from his pocket, writing down a name as they walked. "Go see this man. He's on the corner of Front and Pine. He's collecting subscriptions for a new fire society that allows trees. I read about it last week, though at the time I was sure there were none daft enough to pay a premium price to have a tree. I felt for the man, reason I can recall his name." He handed the paper to Liam. "Have ye seen Lisbeth?"

Liam grinned, tucking the paper inside his shirt, bringing out another. "Aye, she and her maid stopped by this week. She left ye this." David grabbed it greedily, pocketing it. "D'ye want me to tell her anything? She's coming again to get the new spelling primer."

"No, just that I'm looking forward to seeing her soon. I don't have a letter written for her. There just wasna time," David said, adding hopefully, "It would be helpful if ye could plead my case."

"Turn here. I told Rob we'd be by to fetch him." Liam reached down to pet the dog that met them at the corner, one of the strays that frequented the alley. "Next ye know, ye'll be too weary to do your own wooing, and ye'll be asking me for that as well."

"No' likely. Granted, I havena seen her in ages, but I'm still fairly certain I willna need your help should the opportunity arise."

29

"ELISABETH, COME IN. GOOD DAY to you,"
Mr. Oliver said. He struggled to right the pile of
books he was carrying as he closed the door behind her. "To
you as well, Polly. Now, let me see. Did I forget I was expecting you? There's been so much to attend to, I'm afraid I did."

The poor man. He looked frazzled, his sandy hair was wild
about his head. Liam really should talk him into tying it back.
"That's quite all right Mr. Oliver, I didn't specify a time. It
was over a week ago I told you I'd try to come by just before
school started. I wanted to look over the spelling primer you
purchased."

"Ah, yes, I do remember. Liam, show Elisabeth the primer,
will you?"

"Lisbeth, it's good to see ye, lass." He bent to kiss her
cheek. "Hello, Polly."

"Hello, Liam." Liam looked to be lacking his normal
self-possession as well, his shrewd eyes betraying a bit of
tension as he welcomed her, though one could probably
never accuse Liam of looking frazzled. She looked around

the room, taking in the disarray. Running a finger discreetly across a table, she made her way toward the classroom in back, carefully stepping over piles of books and supplies, finding the smaller room in much the same condition. She glanced down at the grime on her finger and retraced her steps.

"Mr. Oliver?"

"Hmm, yes, lass?" he said. "Rob, did ye remember to get that extra slate? I can't locate it anywhere."

Rob was making his way carefully down the stairs, his arms full of yet more books.

"I told ye I'd get those, Rob," Liam said.

Rob ignored him. "No, Mr. O. I don't recall ye asking me to get slate. I've got time, though. It's only just past noon. Hello, Elisabeth."

"I'm sure I did. Well, no matter, write it down and don't go as of yet. We might discover more that's missing."

"There's quite a lot left to do, isn't there?" Elisabeth said quietly to Liam.

"Just a few boxes to unload. We'll be ready in no time, you'll see. Looks worse than it is," Liam said.

"I don't see my globe either, the one I purchased last month. Did either of you boys set it somewhere?"

"I saw it in the back office, Mr. O. I'll bring it out for you in a wee bit," Liam said.

She tried again. "Mr. Oliver?"

"Hmm? Oh, I'm sorry, Elisabeth, you were saying?"

"Well, this is a bit awkward, but it must be said. I know you've a lot on your mind, but the cleaning; have you given thought to the cleaning? With tomorrow being the Sabbath and classes starting first thing Monday morning, well . . . it seems a lot has been left until the last moment, wouldn't you agree?"

She looked at the male faces surrounding her, all of them

blank. She ran another finger across a desk and held it up, hoping she wouldn't have to explain further.

"Are ye saying that you're worried about a wee bit of dirt?" She brightened. "Yes, that's exactly what I'm saying, Liam. It must be cleaned, and it must be cleaned before Monday."

"Well, Elisabeth, I think we have other, more important matters to attend to at this point. The students willna notice it, that I'm sure of," Rob said, dismissing her. He began moving items around the room again, and Mr. Oliver went back to sorting his stacks of books.

She looked at Polly, who only offered a shrug. Perhaps a more direct approach was called for. She went to stand in front of Oliver, placing her hand on his sleeve in an effort to gain his attention.

"Well, perhaps they won't notice, Mr. Oliver. But I believe their mothers will certainly notice. And before you tell me their mothers won't be here, I'll have you remember the clientele you've enrolled. The mothers of the youngest will indeed be here, and they will certainly have somewhat different ideas about housekeeping than a household of bachelors might."

"I believe we've just been insulted, Mr. O," Liam said.

Mr. Oliver peered at her over the top of his spectacles, frowning. Seeing she finally had his attention, she pressed her advantage. "It won't take too much to make a difference, Mr. Oliver. The desks should be wiped, at a minimum, and it would be much cheerier if the windows panes were clean, don't you agree? To let in more light? And perhaps if the fireplace were cleaned, the ashes wouldn't be so quick to coat the desk and the windows again. And the floor most certainly must be swept."

"My word, she's right, lads," Mr. Oliver said. Liam and Rob groaned, mumbling protests. "No, she is. This is to be a bit different than the farm school we had, and I thank you for bringing it to my attention, Elisabeth. You'll have our coop-eration. I only ask that ye assign us tasks, as the necessary ones may not be obvious to us."

Ignoring the grumbling from Liam and Rob, Elisabeth smiled. "Very well then, Polly and I will help." She turned to Polly. "Polly, would you please go home and let Grand-mother know we'll be delayed for a while? And if you can, bring some rags back with you?"

Polly raised her brows, but didn't comment, leaving to do as Elisabeth asked.

"DAVID, STILL AT IT, I see?"

"Just finishing up, Mr. Hall. Robert will lock up in a few minutes. He's just setting the last of the type for a piece."

"He tells me you've done well, claims you learn almost as fast as he did. High praise indeed."

David chuckled. "Aye, well, he feels no hesitation about adding more and more, that's for certain. But none as yet requires much in the way of learning." He held up the broom in illustration.

Smiling, Mr. Hall shook his head. He brought out some paperwork from under the counter and began sorting through it. "Now, don't forget that, beginning Monday, you're on the afternoon shift—Mr. Oliver's Academy opens. Robert will lighten up some then, I grant you. He knows the value of an education."

"Aye, I havena forgotten. I'm headed over there in a bit with a few things for Mr. Oliver and the others. They were planning on working all day today, what with last minute preparations. I may stay the night if that's acceptable. I'll be back in time to attend Kirk."

"Of course. Is that what these items are? Looks like some bread, ale, and a bag of something or other?"

David walked behind the counter and looked. "Aye, I

asked Ian to pick up a few things for me whilst he was out."

Mr. Hall put the papers back under the counter and started toward the stairs. "Enjoy yourself, David. I'll see you tomorrow."

"Thank you, sir." He quickly finished the sweeping and headed to the back office to avail himself of the basin of water to clean his hands and face.

"Are ye going now, then?" Robert asked, looking up from his composing stick, his fingers pausing on their way to the case.

"Aye, Robert, I thought I might, unless ye have something else ye need?"

Robert grinned. "Better hurry, before I think on it too long."

David hung his apron and rushed from the room, stopping just long enough to grab the items Ian had brought.

"David, wait just a moment, will you?"

"Yes, sir." Hell, not fast enough.

Mr. Hall descended the stairs with a basket in his hand. "Eliza baked this earlier today. It's currant bread, currants fresh off the *Brothers*, as a matter of fact. There're a couple bottles of wine as well. I planned to deliver it to Mr. Oliver Monday, but the bread is ready now and will complement the items you purchased quite nicely."

Surprised, David reached out slowly. "Thank ye, Mr. Hall. There was no need for ye to do that. Much obliged, sir."

"Take it with the *Gazette's* compliments, will you? And it's not so much. You'll find the paper makes a point of welcoming new enterprises in town. It makes for good business."

"Thank you, sir. Tomorrow then." He hurried out the door.

The front door was open when he got to the townhouse. Dodging the pieces of refuse cluttering the steps, he sprinted up, pausing at the sound of Liam's voice, his exasperation apparent.

"When we have a fire, the ashes will be right back again. We'll no' have accomplished a thing. This is quite adequate for our purposes."

"No, Liam, it's not. I would speculate it's been left that way since your last fire in the spring, given you gentlemen are not likely to prepare meals. Don't you see? There wouldn't be such a coat of dirt everywhere if it had been taken care of. You comb your hair each morning, don't you? In spite of the fact that it looks as it does now by day's end, and you know you must complete the task again? Consider this the same principle."

David grinned as he watched Liam's hand rise to his hair and his scowl when he caught himself and lowered it immediately.

"She's grown quite bossy, hasn't she?"

ELISABETH FROZE, her back to the door. Her hand went to her face in search of loose dirt as she glared at Liam. He hadn't told her he expected David. My word, she hadn't seen him in months, and he catches her looking her worst, in the midst of haranguing his best friend.

"David, am I glad to see you! She's likely to be sweet as pie now. Ye brought offerings? Let me help you with those." On his way past her, he whispered, "Ye look lovely, lass, no worries."

"For your supper. I thought ye might be overwhelmed with readying for Monday," David said, handing the bundles to Liam.

"Thank ye, I'll take them to Mr. Oliver. He's just in back."

"Elisabeth?"

"David." She turned to face him. "Liam didn't tell me you were coming."

"He didna know. I'm never certain. Should I go?" he asked,

gesturing toward the open door.

"No! It's just, well, I haven't seen you in such a long time, I guess I'd hoped to be more presentable when I finally did. I'm glad to see you."

He went to her, taking her hands in his. "Ye look beautiful, lass, as always. I've enjoyed all your letters."

"Really? I wasn't sure if you'd read them, I had received so little response."

He grinned, dropping her hands, pulling her into his arms, glancing toward the back room. "Now that's an exaggeration, lass. I havena done so badly." He lowered his head, kissing her quickly.

"I suppose you're right, but I find I always want more," she said as she put her hands behind his head, bringing his mouth back to hers.

"Would that I had had *that* method at my disposal for keeping her quiet!" Liam said from the doorway. "Davey, is this food to enjoy now? If so, Rob would sure like to get started. Lisbeth, ye and Polly must stay to eat."

David ended the kiss, pulling back slowly. "Aye, it is," he said, grabbing her hand and turning to follow Liam to the other room. "Hello, everyone."

"David, it was thoughtful of you to provide this meal. It's a timely gift," Mr. Oliver said.

"You're welcome, Mr. O. Mr. Hall and the paper contributed as well, and he sends his good wishes. He said to tell ye he'd drop by Monday."

Liam pulled the items from the basket, setting them around a table. Elisabeth sat and David took the spot by her side.

She found it difficult to keep her attention on the conversation, as David was constantly leaning across her to reach for food or brushing her arm as he raised his hand. He was sitting so close she could feel the heat from his body. What a ninny she was—her presence didn't affect him. He had no trouble keeping up his end of the conversation. Edging away, she forced herself to comment on the bread.

"Aye, it's freshly baked today. Mr. Hall says it was made with currants freshly arrived on the *Brothers*."

"The *Brothers;* she was the ship we watched towed in Saturday last, remember, Davey? She hails from Tenerife. I was able to hire on one afternoon last week to help with the cargo. I recognize the bottle ye brought from Mr. Hall. It was part of the cargo. Pricey, as I recall."

"Which is where, Liam?"

"Pardon, Mr. O?"

"Tenerife; where is it located?"

"Ye quizzing Mr. O?" Liam said as he took another bite. "There's no' a person here doesna know that."

Mr. Oliver just smiled. Liam sighed and obediently replied that it was the largest of the Canary Islands, situated off the coast of Africa.

"Indeed, Liam! It's for things such as this that I must locate my globe. It's essential. What a learning opportunity this harbor represents, wouldn't you agree, David?"

"Aye, why I just learned the Canary Islands export a fine wine."

They all laughed, and Rob went to retrieve the globe. "Here it is, Mr. Oliver. We were just keeping it safe for ye during the preparations."

"Thank you, lads!" He grabbed it from Rob's hands and set it down in front of him, caressing the smooth round surface, absorbed in the images.

Liam stood, reaching for the wine. "I'd say this should be saved until the end of our first day, but David will be unable to join us then. Let's let it sit open a few moments while we finish the chores Lisbeth's assigned us. It can serve as our reward at the end of a long day."

Elisabeth glanced at Polly, who shook her head, her eyes

wide. "Well, I'm not sure. It is getting late, perhaps I should check."

"Elisabeth, if there's only one thing ye learn from me, let it be that tis always better to ask forgiveness than to beg permission."

"Do what you think best, Elisabeth," Mr. Oliver said, looking up from his globe. "I believe Liam's counsel may not always be appropriate for a young woman."

"Actually, I'd like to help finish up, if we can do so within the hour. Liam, you and David work up front. Only the fireplace remains. Polly and I will clean the desks in this room, while Rob and Mr. Oliver can get the last of the books arranged."

"Come, David, we've received our marching orders. You've much experience with fireplaces now. Ye can show me how it's done."

David laughed and stood. Passing behind Elisabeth, he bent to whisper that he'd see her home when they'd finished, his breath on her neck causing a shiver down her spine. He walked out before she could answer. Really now, what made him think she'd allow it? He hadn't even waited for an answer, he was so sure of himself. And after he'd virtually ignored her during the whole meal.

She attacked the cleaning of the desks with a vengeance, working herself into more of a temper, ignoring the small voice that whispered she should show more reason.

"Miss Lisbeth? You'll ruin your hands scrubbing so hard. It ain't that dirty," Polly whispered.

"Who does he think he is, anyway? Does he think he just has to crook a finger?"

"Miss?" Polly looked around the room, puzzled. "Who you done talking 'bout?"

"Elisabeth?" Rob said, coming in from the front room. "There's a man at the door. Says he's been sent to collect ye."

"Very well, Rob, we're finished anyway." Her father's patience must have finally given out. Good. It took the matter of David walking her home right out of her hands.

30

"WILL YOU LOOK AT THAT?" the boy said, adding a soft low whistle of appreciation.

David turned toward the door and his heart fell. Did she have to make such an effort to look 'presentable'? The lass was stunning. Her hair silky and shining, styled to highlight the delicate bones of her face, her gown . . . well he hadn't noticed on Saturday her figure had developed as such. The lads surrounding him would try and make short order of turning her head, no doubt of that.

He'd arrived early at the Academy Monday morning and was making his way round the room talking to others when she showed. He excused himself and walked toward her.

"Bess," he said, quietly greeting her. "How anyone in the room will be able to concentrate on Mr. Oliver's lectures this morning is beyond my comprehension. Ye look extraordinary, lass."

She held both her hands out to him, in the manner of a queen to a subject. "David, look at you, a familiar face! Will you sit next to me? A room full of strangers always unnerves me."

He took her hands without thinking. Surprised at her distant tone, he searched her eyes before she quickly averted them. A familiar face? What the hell type of greeting was that? He thought back to Saturday, retracing the few hours they'd spent together, wondering if he'd somehow offended her. Looking at her again, he was tempted to put a hand under her chin and force her gaze to his. Instead, he dropped her hands, turned, and made a sweeping motion to the empty tables.

"Of course I'll oblige ye, Elisabeth. Choose a spot to your liking."

She chose a table near the back of the room and sat, cheerfully greeting the boy next to her. Judging from the lad's color rising and his inability to form a coherent reply, David had a feeling she'd flashed the full force of her smile at him.

So now she thought to flirt, right in front of him? His hands tightened into fists as he stood, undecided on whether to sit. But Mr. Oliver walked in, so he sat.

Perhaps he'd read too much into a wee sentence. Perhaps the lad was one to stumble over his tongue to any new acquaintance, and she hadn't smiled at him.

Or perhaps she thought she was permitted to smile at whomever she pleased. What the hell was wrong with him? He'd talk to her at the end, get back his footing.

But Mr. Oliver tended to be long-winded when he got to teaching, and even when the church bells started in on the noon hour, there were no signs the lecture was winding down. David's feet started to bounce. He had to get back to the shop. Everyone else here looked to be gentry, which was to be expected, if he had thought about it, most tradesmen being employed at this hour. So maybe no one else had anywhere they needed to be and Mr. O would go on til supper.

No, he needn't worry. Rob stood before the bells stopped,

walking to the door. Must be a signal to rein the man in, as Mr. O called it a day, quickly announcing the assignments due the following morning.

David turned to Elisabeth. "I must get back, Elisabeth. I wish ye all the luck this afternoon, even knowing ye willna need a whit of it."

Not wishing to risk a vapid response to ponder over for the next twenty hours, he hurried out.

31

"OGH, NOT SO TIGHT, POLLY, please!" Elisabeth said.

"That's not what you been saying 'fore, Miss Lisbeth. You sure you wants me to stop?"

She fingered her new stay, her first with whalebones. Grandmother had consigned her old cloth one to the trash as soon as she'd seen it. This one was lovely, and when Polly tightened it, it did lovely things to her figure.

"Yes, I'm sure." She stepped away. "I thought I might faint from the heat more than once the last few days, I could scarcely breathe. It doesn't matter anyway, I'm done with the scheme. It was only making me miserable."

"Did it work?"

"How would I know? Given I haven't been able to speak to him."

Polly patted her shoulder and helped her into her dress, buttoning it up the back. "You don't need to flaunt like that anyhow, Miss. You too smart and pretty, and you not going to school to catch a man. Them games be for the rest of us."

Elisabeth snorted and went to her looking glass, holding it up to Polly's face. "Obviously you haven't had a good deal of time to look at yourself then, have you, Polly? Look at the slant of your eyes, the fine lines of your bones. Your complexion is flawless. You're quite beautiful, you know."

Polly's eyes clouded, and she shoved away the mirror. She pushed Elisabeth into the chair at the dressing table and picked up the brush.

"Polly?"

"You still want it up on the side, Miss, like this?"

Elisabeth batted a slim hand at the brush. "I want to know what I said that offended you."

"Pretty face ain't no gift to a nigger gal. Attracts nothing worth wanting, plenty not wanted. We got to hurry now, Miss Liss. You don't want to be late, do you?"

"Hmm." She sighed and picked up her mother's tiny cut crystal bottle, idly turning it over and over in the path of the morning sunlight streaming through her bedroom window, watching as the wall beside her came alive in a pattern of sparkling multifaceted images. She'd ask again on another day.

"Yes, on the side is fine."

Why had she been angry with David? He'd been nothing but courteous to her that Saturday. True, nothing but. But maybe he just didn't care to wear his heart on his sleeve. She'd always suspected she cared more than he did, had accepted it in the past. It shouldn't make her angry now. Or was she angry he'd caught her at a bad moment, because that certainly wasn't his fault, and besides, she wasn't that vain, was she? Goodness, she hoped not.

Polly was right. She'd been behaving like a silly schoolgirl, attending class only to choose a beau from the best of the lot. Well, she was finished with that as of this morning, and she could only hope she hadn't let Mr. Oliver down in the process.

And besides, she already had the best of the lot. Or she had had.

SHE ARRIVED AT THE Academy early, determined to talk to David before class, resolved she would wait outside until he arrived and walk in late herself if she had to. He'd taken to arriving just after class started.

As luck would have it, he was there, standing outside the school talking to some boys. He broke away from the group when he saw her, as if he'd been watching for her, waiting for her. She said goodbye to Polly as he approached.

It broke her heart when he searched her eyes, uncertainly, as if to determine his reception. What on earth had she been thinking, playing games with someone like him? She spoke first, quietly. "I'm sorry, David. I don't know why I've been behaving so. I honestly don't. I had no call to." When he didn't respond immediately, she quickly added, "Can you spare the time to sit with me tomorrow after class, until the children come for the afternoon?"

"Lass, I canna, I must get back to the paper."

"Oh, I thought . . . Well, didn't you tell me you had Wednesday afternoons free?"

"Aye, but schooling has changed my schedule. I must make up for the time I'm here."

Her eyes filled before she could stop them. "But, so, we'll never talk?"

"Don't cry!" He glanced back at the others. "No' here, Bess, don't cry! Ye . . . please, don't!" He shifted his weight from foot to foot, watching her lower lip tremble.

"Ye'll have me on my knees in a moment. Ye willna do that to me in front of these coves, will ye?" he asked, handing her his handkerchief as her eyes overflowed. "Bess? Please?"

She wouldn't cry. She wasn't keen on making a spectacle of herself. She smiled at him and dabbed her eyes with the handkerchief he'd handed her. "Can I keep this?" She slipped it into her sleeve.

Relief flooded his features, and he chuckled, leading her inside to the nearest table. "And would it make a difference if I said no?"

"No, it smells of you. I want it."

He mumbled something about the timing of the wash, a faint flush rising up his neck. "It's unused, though," he assured her.

Mr. Oliver walked in so she didn't respond. But she smiled at him before she turned to face the front, and the look in his eyes gave her cause to believe everything would be fine. Relaxed for the first time in days, she focused her attention on what Mr. Oliver was saying.

32

"SO DID YE FIND OUT what was ailing the lass?" Liam asked. It was Sunday afternoon, and they were sitting on a riverbank outside of town, their makeshift poles propped up below them, lines drawn out into the Delaware.

David pocketed his harmonica. "No time to talk much. She's fine enough now, though."

"Aye, she came quickly enough to heel."

"Liam."

"My apologies."

"She's not a puppy."

"Again, my apologies. I'm glad, however, ye didna pant like a puppy after her. I've observed that only makes them more contrary. Ye have to admit, David, women can be a struggle to figure out. Sometimes there's no reason to their behavior."

David grinned. "I don't have as much experience as ye, and I don't care to either. I'll just acknowledge your wisdom in the matter. I can tell ye, however, that you will lose that fish if you don't set the hook."

Liam jumped up and jerked his pole. He brought the fish in slowly, releasing his line some to give it play before bringing it in again, over and over, tiring it out before he finally brought it up on shore. Satisfied, he held it up for David's inspection, its iridescent gills shimmering in the sunlight as it danced in protest against the hook.

David grinned. "And she's no' a fish either."

Liam laughed. "I think we have enough for supper, now." He plopped the fish into the basket. "Maybe Annie will feel sorry for us and come cook. I'll even invite her new sweetheart along." He lay down with his hands behind his head and watched the clouds, dappled sunlight playing across his face.

"D'ye find the city wears on you, David?"

"Aye, at times."

"I keep waiting to hear from Sean. Mr. O frets about him from time to time, especially when there's news of Indian trouble. But I feel he's fine and bursting with stories to tell. I'm envious, truth be."

David looked at him, startled. "Liam, ye wouldn't leave yet, would ye?"

"No, no, I wouldna. I'm years from a stash and a plan. Something's starting to pull at me, though. I just enjoy speculating what it might be. Ye'll come with me, marry Lisbeth, start your own paper. I'll be uncle to a bunch of little Grahams, and Lisbeth can warn them daily against following in my footsteps."

David chuckled. "Got it all worked out, do ye?" He wasn't going to spoil the day by pointing out the unlikelihood of that scenario. Liam's response had been scathing when he'd tried to make clear the ramifications of Elisabeth's Catholicism. He knew he hadn't explained it well. He *couldn't* explain what he'd known to be true since before he could think to question it; it simply just *was*. It was the closest they had come to blows, and David had no desire to repeat the con-frontation. Besides, it was pleasant to imagine the picture Liam had painted.

"Well, your part I do. It's easier," Liam said. He sat up and watched as a boat full of Sunday pleasure seekers rowed by. "What was that cull so worked up about yesterday, the one hollering at Robert?"

"The paper didn't print his letter yet, and he was peeved we printed his opponent's letter."

"You're not obliged to give equal time, are ye?"

"No, but it's good business. His letter's scheduled to appear this coming week. Mr. Hall and Mr. Sellers prefer to keep a low profile. They're more than willing to leave the con-troversies to the *Freeman's Journal* and the *Gazetteer*. Hall says there're no thanks to the printer for taking one side against the other and antagonizing half your advertisers."

"What was his letter promoting?"

"He's vocal against the Test Acts, and there's many on his side of the fence."

"Och, myself included."

The Test Acts prevented anyone who hadn't taken an oath of allegiance against the English during the War from voting or holding local office, including those too young to have taken an oath at the time, as well as those not even in the country during the time. It was a hotly contested issue in Philadelphia politics. However, each time their revocation was put to a vote, the issue was soundly defeated.

"Aye, it does smack of unfairness. Mayhap we should feel differently, however, if we lost limbs and property in the war whilst others stood by, now expecting the benefits and rights that come with victory."

"Granted, there's that. But we must unite at some point. The sooner, the better, to my way of thinking."

"Write a letter to the editor. I'll slip it inta Robert's queue."

"When do ye set type? I might have a better chance of having it printed if I wait til then."

David laughed. "The issue will probably be settled by that date, unless they bring on some new apprentices. I'm low man now, and will be until they find a new devil. Ian danced a jig when I arrived. I'm getting hungry; let's start back."

They stood and gathered their gear. "D'ye hunt Davey?"

"Och, and where would I be doing that now? Lessing ye're counting rabbit snares."

"I did a wee bit, escorting some of the gents for sport back home. They taught me some. It seems, though, maybe it's a skill needs some practice. We should spend some time at it. I'll teach ye. We're no' going to live in the city forever, aye?"

"I've never gone after big game. But I'll try, should ye find me a rifle or bow, and land that's free to hunt. Who's going to cook the meat for us? Your sway with Annie willna hold forever."

"I'm a fair cook. Ye'd be surprised."

Recalling Rob's revelation about Liam's mother, he supposed Liam had had to learn to cook, as well as to provide. "Really? Well, teach me, then, starting with this catch, aye? If Annie doesna agree to your plan, that is."

"My plans always work out, Davey. But I'll teach ye, seeing as how Lisbeth likely doesna know the first thing about it."

33

July 1785

"DONE," DAVID SAID.
  "We'll see," Ian responded.
  He'd spent hours covertly studying Robert. The man never wasted a motion, the composing stick in his left hand following his right, his fingers nimbly selecting a letter, placing it quickly into the stick without striking the others, even while his mind moved to the next, directing his fingers on without a fumble, without a glance. He wanted to do that; to be that fast, that sure of himself. But it was taking some time.
  "Let her go, Ian," Thomas said, standing back. Ian pulled the crank to lower the platen and make the impression.
  Thomas pulled the copy off and sat down to proof it, mumbling aloud as he read it. Eventually he nodded at David. "Good job, lad."
  David grinned. It was accurate! Ian gestured his approval while he got ready to pull the crank again.
  "All right, Ian, let's move," Thomas said. Once they got

their rhythm in sync, they could print up to 240 sheets an hour. Then trade positions to begin again, with Thomas pulling and Ian inking. Even Ian, strong as he was, couldn't keep at the crank for much more than an hour without tiring. But switching positions didn't help the unbalanced look some of the older pressmen carried. David watched them for a minute until Thomas looked up. "Start on the next form, David. Keep at it now."

The process would be repeated for the opposite side of the sheets, and David would be left to fold the sheets into individual newspapers with the new lad. Thomas had given him a go at the press yesterday, but they fell behind because of it, so it would be a while before he could try again. He found it monotonous, but he'd get it. There was no reason he couldn't be as fast at it as Ian, given time. Which reminded him, he needed to speak to Mr. Hall.

"MR HALL, MIGHT I have a word with ye, sir?"

"Of course, what's on your mind?"

"Mr. Oliver's Academy will begin a new term in a little more than a month. I realize I won't be able to continue with the press and the type if I'm to be absent half the usual workday. And at sixteen, well, I don't know that it's necessary for me to continue in school. Besides, I can see from Ian's school work that Mr. Oliver's lessons are some terms ahead, no offense intended to Ian or his school master, sir. But perhaps my time will be better served here during the day."

"Not anxious to start back carrying water pails, are you, David?"

"No, sir. I mean, I will if ye need it, of course, but . . ."

"Be that as it may, my agreement is with your father, and you're entitled to two full years of instruction. If you want to work the day shift, I'm obliged to send you to the school for the tradesmen in the evening."

The conversation wasn't going the way he'd intended. He couldn't see wasting three hours an evening at night school, not when he'd be repeating lessons he'd learned years ago. He thought quickly. Mr. Oliver was tutoring Rob and Liam; maybe that would suffice.

"Perhaps a bit of self study, in the evening, assigned by Mr. O would be adequate to fulfill your obligation, sir. It would save you the tuition."

Mr. Hall looked at him, laughing. "I tell you what, David. You explain the situation to your father, and I'll comply with his decision."

"But that'll take months!"

"I'll sign you up for the evening school in the meantime. If your father concurs with your assessment, you can discontinue attendance once we receive word of such concurrence. I think Mr. Oliver will be disappointed in your decision."

David grimaced. "He's likely to, at first, I agree. But I can convince him to see the benefit of it and gain his support."

"No doubt."

"YE'LL NO' BE TAKING class either, Liam, Mr. Oliver told me that himself. He said he was going to include ye in Rob's tutoring sessions."

He'd gone to the townhouse to roust up Liam. He hadn't seen him in weeks. As soon as the summer break had rolled around, Mr. Oliver had insisted Rob and Liam take advantage of the free smallpox inoculations the Philadelphia Dispensary was offering. Then he insisted the both of them be kept isolated to prevent the spread of infection.

Liam sat at the table, eating his supper. "True, but I've had the benefit of Mr. O's scholarship for years, remember. You just took me aback a bit, David. It was pleasant seeing you most days during the term. And I've no' heard much of note about the tradesman school. But no worries, ye're learned

enough. Much more so than most in the class, anyway. I can
agree with your reasoning."

"I'm glad you're feeling better." David retrieved a letter
from inside his shirt. "Here, give this to Elisabeth next ye
see her, will ye?"

"Aye, I expect she'll be by in a few weeks to inspect our
housekeeping, 'fore classes resume. She'll likely be put out
with you."

"Probably. I've tried to explain it in that letter. I hear Mr. O
downstairs. Will ye talk to him with me? I've a second option
if he agrees to tutor me, long as my Da agrees. I'll probably
regret it, being as he's a hard taskmaster, but I'm thinking, as
long as I have to be schooled, I may as well learn something."

"Aye, then, let's go to the Hound."

"Why there? Why not the Man?"

"There's a lass I met last night who works there. She's off
shift after supper, and I've offered to accompany her and her
friend on a walk along the river. There's a full moon tonight.
It promises to be fair."

"Ye just got up off the floor. Why canna ye meet me at the
Man when ye've finished your walk?"

"Let me back up and rephrase. I've offered myself and a
friend to accompany her and her friend."

David groaned. "I don't suppose ye've met her friend,
have ye?"

"Nay, no matter. Ye're the one accompanying her and ye
won't care if she's bonny or looks like a cow." Liam stood
and put his dish away. "Ye ready? If Mr. O agrees to the
tutoring, ye'll be free a night or two for my dancing lessons.
I need more lads, tae draw in the lassies."

"God Almighty, do ye lay awake thinking of new ways to
torture me?"

"Aye, and just think, I've had weeks with nothing else to
do. Why, if they came out with an inoculation for the French

pox, there's no telling what I could accomplish over the summer."

David couldn't help but laugh.

Liam had hired a dance instructor for two nights a week during the last term. David had thought it risky. Who had money to spare for dance lessons? Turned out quite a few did, and the school now generated revenue during the evenings as well. Mr. Oliver's scholarship had begun to attract some notice in the community, largely through Liam's efforts. He'd been able to convince Hall to publish several small pieces throughout the spring on the more noteworthy accomplishments of various students, which, of course, pleased the parents of the students who'd been mentioned, while inspiring competition among those who hadn't.

Mr. Oliver had made a wise decision when he'd decided to sponsor Liam.

"GOOD MORNING, DAVID, I think I have what you've been waiting for!" the postmaster said, holding up a packet of letters for the *Gazette*. "They were delivered but an hour ago from the *Hope*. She's just arrived from Glasgow, only forty days out. Can you believe that?"

"Och, a walk through the park, forty days," David said, adopting the tone of an old man reminiscing. "Why, in my day, one would have to wait up to six months for the return post."

"Off with ye, ye impertinent lad, 'fore I have the watch pick ye up for vagrancy."

David laughed. "Aye, Mr. Todd, thank you!"

"Give my regards to Mr. Hall and Robert."

"I will, sir." Hurrying out, he thumbed through the letters. Finding the one he was looking for, he stepped into a nearby close and opened it.

September 20, 1785
Glasgow, Scotland

Dear David,

We just received your letter Monday, and I wanted to respond as quickly as possible. You will see a letter from your mother in this packet also, a letter begun last month to which she adds more nightly. Don't delay in responding to her. She misses you so.

We didn't tell you we were expecting another child last spring. I regret to tell you now we have lost another daughter, and it wears heavily on your mother. I am heartily grateful we made the decision to leave Ireland when we did. It is a comfort to her to be close to her mother, and your brothers to their cousins.

Yes, I've adjusted well to my transition back to taylor. Of course, I miss being out of doors, but it's easier as I get older to rely on a steady trade versus the vagaries of the weather.

Well, I know you will be quickly scanning this letter for an answer to your request. Your mother and I were of the mind Monday evening to deny it, much as we regretted sending you disappointing news. Were it not for two letters we received on Tuesday (three letters in a week from America! How the world changes.)

David paused in his reading—two additional letters?

You well know how we feel about your education, David. But Mr. Oliver has taken pains to assure us that he will not let you slacken in your responsibilities toward it. If anything, he looks forward to the opportunity to tutor you individually, as it gives him the chance to challenge you further, though he does suggest an additional two years over one, given the time constraints on his side and yours.

He groaned.

Apparently the gentleman thinks highly of you and your chances for success in the States. We also heard from Mr. Hall, who explained that you had presented a fair and well thought out case to proceed with this endeavor, and he wanted to assure us that he thought you capable of it and the enormous discipline it would take to approach your studies in this manner. He also was complimentary of Mr. Oliver and his standing as a scholar.

Well, to close, both letters were such to cause us to reconsider our first position. We grant your request, on the condition that you work with Mr. Oliver for two years, instead of one, as he suggests. I have enclosed a less personal letter with this letter, addressed to Mr. Hall.

I don't mind telling you also, David, that it made your mother and I proud that these gentlemen think so highly of you as to take up your cause. It eases your mother greatly to know you have people who care and watch over you so far away. I send you the love of all your family.

Yrs, Father.

P.S. Did a Mr. Erskine contact you? Your mother made you a new shirt. He offered to take it on his passage. He was to give you a small amount of money from us as well. Let me know in your next letter.

He closed his eyes briefly, thanks be. And Ma, I send my love to my newest sister in Heaven.

He supposed he'd better let her know the stitches on the new shirt had ripped the first time he'd moved his shoulders. Otherwise she'd be sending more to fit a lad the size he'd been when he left home.

34

March 1786

DAVID PICKED UP HIS PACE as soon as he heard the church bell. He didn't want to miss Elisabeth. He needed to ask her something; the answer would likely be no, but he'd ask anyway.

He'd been delayed at the shop, listening to an argument. Both the men were successful merchants, always cordial should one run into either of them on the street. But they were on opposite sides of the political fence, and neither could be swayed from his viewpoint, no matter how loud or abusive the other was in having his say. Not that they could hear each other, so intent were they on being heard themselves. An argument such as this always provided fodder for one of Mr. O's endlessly assigned essays. And Liam was always good for additional insight, just enough to make the arguments sound more reasonable than the two coves had. So he had stayed.

The politics of Philadelphia intrigued him. He'd spent a

good deal of time on the passage wondering how people from different countries would meld, but it seemed it was politics that separated the people, much more so than their backgrounds. Being at the paper day after day put him right in the middle of it. Two of the publishers in town had gone so far as to fight a duel over their bitter war of words, leading Liam to remark drily that perhaps David didn't have the passionate temperament of others in his chosen profession and that he might want to reconsider his path in life.

Her class was emptying out onto the steps. Good, he wasn't too late to catch her. Some of the children knew him by name and called out to him as they ran by. They teased Elisabeth about having a 'sweetheart,' and that was fine by him, so long as they were clear on who it was. He stepped back to avoid being trampled.

"Angus, I'm here to fetch ye for help in checking the spelling of the paper's submissions this week. Miss Hale said ye did very good on your exam Friday last," David called after one of the more rowdy boys. Angus reminded him of Sean, with his freckles and lively curiosity.

"Noooo, David, it's done I am with school work for today! Fetch Miss Hale to help you!" Angus called back, running down the street.

"And ye William; are ye available? Hmmm, I guess not," David said, as the boy ran squealing after Angus.

"You'd better be careful, David. One of these days they'll take you up on it. What will you do with them then?" Elisabeth stood at the top to the steps, arms crossed across her chest.

David grinned, bounding up the steps. He took a quick look up and down the street, then pulled her into his arms and kissed her. "I'll have to count on ye to rescue me with reminders that their Ma expects them home promptly," he said, releasing her. "Ye look particularly beautiful today,

Bess."

"You always say that. I'm glad to see you, David. Can you spare time to share a meal with me?" She reached up and smoothed a lock of hair out of his eyes.

"Of course I will," David said, surprised by the invitation. "What of Polly? Will she be allowing it?"

"Goodness, I wish you'd stop that. She's not my master and you well know it." She opened the door, and they walked quietly through the front classroom, where Rob's class was still in session. He taught an afternoon class filled with those too old for Lisbeth's class and too young for Mr. O's. David acknowledged Rob with a nod before Elisabeth swung close the door to her classroom, leaving it a bit ajar for the sake of propriety.

"I was hoping you'd come early today. I haven't seen you in a fortnight, and I've missed you! Polly won't be here to pick me up for awhile yet. Will Liam be allowing it, d'ye think?" she asked.

"Verra funny." He laughed and grabbed her, swinging her around as he kissed her. "Ahh, Bess, I've missed you, too. Before I forget, here's a letter I've been writing you these two weeks past. I hurried to see ye. I've something to ask."

She snatched the paper from his hand and started to read it. "Later, save it," he said, covering her hand with his. "What'd ye bring? I'm famished."

Laughing, she reached under the table for her basket and set the contents out on her desk. "Take your fill. I asked John, our cook, for some extra food. He asked if it was for 'young David,' I suppose Polly gossips some. Anyway, he filled it with his best when he found out it was to be shared with you. You seem to have made a lasting favorable impression; it's been well over a year since you delivered our paper."

He didn't tell her he knew John well, that he made a point to stay in contact with the servants of her household whenever he saw them in the market. He figured if she knew the extent to which he kept tabs on her, she might misinterpret it. How, he wasn't sure, as he himself wasn't sure what to make of it. But best not to chatter about some things, so he grabbed a bit of the food, mumbling something noncommittal about her cook being a good man.

They talked while they ate. She told him about her day, how the children were progressing, and how Mr. Oliver rarely watched over the class anymore. She was starting to feel as if she could be a teacher. He told her stories about the paper and his increasing responsibilities on the floor, as well as how demanding a taskmaster Mr. Oliver could be on a one to one basis.

"Oh, you exaggerate, I'm sure. He has nothing but the highest praise for the way your mind works. I hear it often."

"Hmmph." He took a last swallow of the ale and repacked her hamper. "Thank you, Lisbeth. That was thoughtful of ye to bring food enough for the both of us."

"No, selfish; it afforded me an hour of your time."

"Have ye heard that Annie is marrying this Saturday?"

"I did. She came by to tell Liam last week. He said she's happy."

He picked up the abacus on her desk. "Aye, well, I was hoping ye may be able to find a way to attend. I would verra much like to have ye there." He busied himself with spinning the beads, not looking at her, waiting for her answer.

"Why, thank you, David. But I didn't see Annie. I'm not sure she even remembers me. More to the point, I don't have an invitation from her."

"Aye, well, I'm inviting ye. She told me to bring a guest." He set the abacus down and stood, walking to the door and back, his hands in his pockets. "I want to escort ye from your home, but I can leave that decision up to you. At the verra least I'd escort ye into the celebration after the wed-

ding. Will ye come with me?" He might have laughed at the
look of shock on her face if he wasn't so nervous about
being refused.

"Why . . . my . . . I can think of nothing I would enjoy
more, David. I'm not sure how I'll arrange it, but I will.
I'll need to meet you at the church, however, I know my
father will forbid me to go with you, and I apologize and am
embarrassed for that. I pray you see it only as a reflection on
his small mindedness and not on you."

"Dinna fash, Lisbeth. I'm just glad ye said yes," he said,
refusing to dwell on the fact that she wouldn't, or couldn't,
spend time with him openly. He pulled her up from her chair,
relieved he'd got that over with. "Come now and show me
how the wee rats are improving in their handwriting."

"I can't, David. We haven't had paper all this week! Well,
Charles and Stuart, of course, did, but none of the others,
and I couldn't ask them to share again. So we've spent all
the last three days in recitations and reading aloud. Have you
heard which stationer might have paper in stock?"

"Nay, but I'll ask. Did ye try Styner? He's lots of school
stock, most times. We're expecting some blank books on
the next ship from London, but that could be in one day or
twenty days. We do have slate and slate pencils, if ye need
them."

"No, they all have that." She heard Rob's class emptying
and went to the rack to retrieve her hat and cloak. "As long as
some is available well before their term book reports are due,
I'll be happy, I suppose. I just wanted them to have plenty
of time to practice with pen and ink. Did you remember the
ink?"

He smiled and tied on her bonnet, kissing her briefly. "I
did. Ye said by next week, remember? I'll make ye some Sunday."

Liam walked in, leading Polly by the elbow. "Here she is

Polly, just look. She's in the capable hands of my good friend David. Nowhere in Philly safer than that. I told ye there was no worry."

Polly refused to be drawn in. "We should be going, Miss Elisabeth, if you're ready. I supposed to help Jane finish up the laundry. I gonna be outside." Polly's eyes didn't leave the floor, and she walked back to the door as soon as Liam released her.

"I'm ready, Polly. I'll meet you out front in just a minute," Elisabeth called out after her. She turned to Liam. "Don't you have enough women falling at your feet without tormenting her? Leave her be."

"He's only teasing her, Bess, he didna mean harm."

"Aye," Liam said. "I like the lass. It's no' in me to ignore a beautiful woman. Does she mind so much?"

"She doesn't care to be singled out. Please, don't tease her."

"Very well, Elisabeth, I'll try to oblige ye. I'll drop this off at my desk, David, and be right with ye," Liam said, disappearing through the door to his office.

Elisabeth turned to David. "I'm looking forward to this Saturday. It'll be the first real time we've spent together outside of this classroom since we were on the *Industry*. I'm so glad it's me you asked to accompany you."

"Aye, well, and who else is it I'd be asking?" he said, cupping her chin. "The wedding is to be held midday, the celebration, right after, at the MacTavishes. I imagine it'll last well into the night, but I'll escort ye home when ye need be." He kissed her goodbye as Liam came back into the room.

"Good day, then. I'll see you tomorrow, Liam," she said.

"Aye, Elisabeth." After she left, he turned to David. "Did ye ask her?"

"Aye, she says she'll find a way to meet me there."

"As I told you, no? It'll be interesting to see how she manages it. Her da still bristles at the idea of her sharing her days in the company of Scots. Mr. O says if it weren't for the Sangham and the Trestle children attending, he wouldn't be able to convince her da to let her stay. Quite a task I set up for myself, filling the school with gentry, just so my mate can court his lass."

David chuckled. "Oh, the things ye do for me, Liam, I'll be in your debt till the day I die, there's no doubt. But mayhap the swells wouldna send their bairns without her as their teacher?"

"Fly cove, are ye? Aye, well, she's a feather in Mr. Oliver's cap, that's true enough. Let's go, time's a wasting."

"PAPA, DO YOU REMEMBER Annie from the *Industry*? She was the young lady with the beautiful voice. She helped me some when you were so ill. She sang to distract you from your misery." Considering the matter for days and finally deciding on a plausible version of the truth, she approached him Friday evening, shortly after he went to his study to relax with his whisky and his book.

"Ah yes, the Irish one, with the rabble for family," her father said, barely glancing up from his book.

"Well . . . yes, yes, I suppose so. She's marrying tomorrow." Elisabeth paused, gathering her wits for the tricky part. She actually had no idea who Annie was marrying, so it wasn't too farfetched to select a completely Anglo-Saxon name.

"She's marrying Henry Williams. You know of the Williams?" In for a penny, in for a pound. "His father works for the Bank. Anyway, my friend Amy knows his family, so she's also invited to the wedding. She invited me to attend with her, and to stay the night. Someone from Amy's family will be there to escort us home."

Oh, my, how easy this comes to me. Amy did agree to cover her in her lie should Elisabeth's father ask her directly, but she didn't expect that Amy would ask her parents to be

complaisant. She selected Amy as their fathers didn't social-
ize on a regular basis.

"That sounds like an agreeable outing, Beth. Annie's done
well for herself then, hasn't she? Be sure to check with your
Grandmother, will you?" her father said, turning the page of
his book. "Amy comes from good stock. You should spend
more time with her and less at that school you're so fond of."

"Yes, Papa, and thank you. Can I get you anything before
I go to bed? No?" She kissed his cheek and walked quickly
from the room. Out of sight in the hallway she leaned back
against the wall, placing her hand to her heart.

"Forgive me, Lord," she whispered. But she'd do it again.
She'd go to most any length to attend this wedding. Rob
and Liam weren't always discreet in the conversations she
managed to overhear. She knew others had begun pursuing
David. Heavens, he got more handsome each day; how could
they not? She didn't know the extent, if any, of his reciproca-
tion, but she saw no need to deliver him into waiting hands.

She ran up the stairs and into her room, collapsing on the
bed and laughing softly, raising her arms to embrace her
good luck. She would tell her Grandmother at the last minute, and *only* if she happened to see her as she left tomorrow.
Something along the lines of 'Papa said he told you about it.
I'm sorry, Grandmother, but you know I shouldn't walk in
after the bride, I must go.' Go to hell maybe, such falsehoods
she had told.

She stood and walked over to her trunk, digging until she
found the box of David's letters. She picked the one with the
most wear, the one where he veered from the simple relaying
of events and told her how often he thought of her. Collapsing on the floor, she read it again and again. He'd asked her
to go with him! She grew giddy every time she remembered
it. My, how nervous he'd looked. She smiled, replacing the
letter in the box and burying it again in the trunk.

Polly knocked and opened the door. "You needs me to help you get ready for bed, Miss Lisabeth?"

"Polly, I'm glad you're here. Come in and close the door. I need you to help me pick out something special to wear to a wedding tomorrow. Something that makes me look spectacular, but not too fancy. Something simple, but beautiful. Let me explain, and I'll warn you in advance you're not going to like it."

She told her about the wedding, that David would be there, and that she was going with Amy and would be staying with her family for the night. She usually told Polly everything. She was a discreet and reliable friend. But she needed to make sure her father couldn't hold Polly in any way responsible for Elisabeth's transgression should her lie be uncovered. He wouldn't be above punishing her, if he thought she were in any way involved.

Polly had pulled back the bedcovering at the foot of the bed while she listened and was tugging at the ropes under the mattress, turning them tight. She smoothed the quilt back down and faced Elisabeth, her hands on her hips. "You're right, I don't like it cause I know there's something more, something you're not telling me. But I don't wanna know it, so don't be telling me."

"But I need your advice with the gown, Polly. Will you help me there?" She walked over to the wardrobe and opened its doors, quickly glancing over its contents. She turned back to Polly. "All Liam's and David's friends will be there, and the girls will be looking their best. I want something that will keep David's eyes on me, but not too fancy as I don't want to be accused of showing off. Do you know what I mean?"

"Miss Elisabeth, that boy is more stuck on you than ticks on a hound. There ain't no way he's gonna take his eyes off you, don't matter if nine gals standing round him buck naked and you're dressed in a sack."

"Why, Polly . . . I . . . that's the nicest thing you've ever said about him. I think. Are you finally warming up to him?"

Polly walked to the head of the bed, picking up the pillow, plumping it high. "Well, don't be telling him, but he's growing on me. He's been helping John get the produce back since he done hurt his back falling on that ice over by the Market."

"He has?" Well, that explained John's extra special rations for David this last week. "You never told me that."

"I was just waiting and watching, you know. Maybe he was doing it just to impress you. But it's been two months now. John is just starting to feel better, so maybe he won't do it no more. But he did it without any asking and without telling, and he's got more than enough of his own work to do. That says something 'bout a man."

"It does, doesn't it?" Elisabeth said, dropping to the bed and reaching for the pillow, hugging it close.

"All right, you be snapping out of it now. Let's get to work so that boy don't stand a chance."

She stood and followed Polly to the wardrobe. "Liam's a good man as well, Polly. He doesn't mean to make you uncomfortable, you know."

"I figured that, Miss Liss. He don't, really. The way he goes through the gals, though, down one street and up the next, well, I reckon I ought not to make it so easy for him."

Elisabeth laughed. "My, you think things through. I should learn to do that as well." She fingered the gown Polly was holding up against her, Polly's sharp eyes measuring the color against Elisabeth's own. "Are you sure this one? David's already seen it a hundred times, it's so ordinary."

"No, it ain't. This color be good on you, and when I finish fixing this here bodice, there won't be no 'ordinary' about it."

35

DAVID POCKETED A BIT OF the savings from the jar hidden in his trunk, then stood in front of the looking glass, inspecting his shirt and neckcloth for stains. Good enough. He ran a hand over his face—he'd have liked to have visited the barber, but there hadn't been time—then hurried out the door.

He'd been ready to lay Ian out across the shop floor earlier when he'd told him he was feeling peaked, wanted to keep his Saturday afternoon off, didn't want to trade with him after all. Lad thought he was being funny; didn't know how close he'd come to truly feeling peaked. *Nothing* was going to keep him from spending this afternoon with her. It'd been all he could think of since she'd said yes.

He reached the church the same time as Liam and Rob.

"Are we to be segregated then? Where's the fun in that ? Where are all the lassies?" Liam asked.

"They be in helping the bride. She's been in there for close to an hour now, by my calculations," one of the boys said, one David didn't recognize. He looked to be dressed in a borrowed suit. Grand enough; just didn't fit the lad. Seamus introduced him as Angus, the groom.

"Not quite," Seamus said. "You're just getting nervous. It's been less than that." He rolled back his shoulders, then shook them, as if he found his clothes constricting. "The lass Elisabeth is in there with them. I'd forgotten how lovely she was. I don't think I've seen her since the crossing, not that I can recall anyway. And she's a sight I think I'd recall." He paused to take a last draw off his smoke before tossing it to the ground, glancing at David. "I had her promise me the best of the dances, for old time's sake, you know. Maybe we'll pick up where we left off."

David felt Liam's scrutiny. He and Seamus had always had an uneasy acquaintance. For whatever reason, lad was always spoiling for a fight, David was always willing to oblige. Liam needn't worry. He wasn't playing; not today. Seamus could look elsewhere.

"He's only messing with ye, Davey. He knows the lass is with you. Leave him be."

"Is she now? Hmm. She walked in unescorted. I'm sure of it."

David rearranged his face in an insouciant mask, and relaxed his hands down at his sides. Not going to spoil the day by wiping the smirk off the lad's face, not.

"She's free to dance with whomever she pleases, Seamus," he said, his voice pleasant.

"Come, let's get out of the heat, these clothes are roasting me alive," Liam said. "The kirk is bound to be cooler." He started up the path to the church door.

"Damned inscrutable Scot, the lass is wasted on him," Seamus muttered, walking to the bench to pick up his jacket.

"Bleeding heart *Eerish*," David muttered in return, his eyes following Seamus.

Liam turned back and grabbed David by the arm, jerking

at him to follow. "Out of the heat, aye?"

He followed Liam into the church, choosing a spot near the back where he could easily retrieve Elisabeth.

"When's the last time ye were in kirk, Davey?" Liam whispered.

"Sunday last," David said, turning toward him, raising his brows. "And you?"

"Don't remember. It's been a good while."

"Are ye serious, man? Why don't I know that about ye?" David asked, incredulous.

Liam shrugged. "Ne'er a topic of conversation I suppose. Quiet, here they be."

Spotting Elisabeth immediately, he went to meet her.

She smiled. "David, hello. I was hoping you'd be here now."

"I'm sorry I wasn't here when ye first arrived. You 'bout knocked me off my feet just now, Lisbeth. Ye take my breath away, how beautiful ye are. Come and sit."

Liam slid over to make room for her. "Sharing my mate for the day, are ye, Lisbeth? You look lovely, lass."

"Hello, Liam. You look very handsome yourself, as handsome as David. Well, almost. Oh, here she comes, stand up," she said, patting Liam's knee.

Annie come down the aisle escorted by one of her brothers, her father having died of smallpox shortly after they arrived in Philadelphia. Angus stepped forward to meet her. David settled on the bench, seeking Elisabeth's hand under cover of the fold of her skirts. They'd be here awhile. The lass was Catholic.

"ARE YE FEELING WELL enough, Elisabeth? You look—" He didn't finish, realizing too late it wasn't gallant of him to tell her she looked flushed or ill. Mayhap it was too warm for her outside the kirk.

She laughed. "What? Terrible? Grey?" Her gaze wandered from his eyes to linger on his mouth, her tongue moistening her lips. "It was just having you so close in there, touching you. I confess, I felt a bit faint."

He tensed immediately, tightening his hold on her, looking about for a place where they might have a moment of privacy. Then he saw her smile, the light of it reaching her eyes.

Relaxing, he grinned, squeezing her hand tight. "Ye did that on purpose. Have mercy, lass."

She laughed. "I'm going to have *such* a good time tonight, David, I'm so happy to be here with you."

"Truly? Seamus tells me ye promised your time to him."

"I did not! Why would you . . .? Oh, never mind. You know better I'm sure." She looked at the guests leaving. "Where are we to go now?"

"Annie's home. It's just a short walk from here."

They walked arm in arm in silence. The heat of the sun, the slight snap of coolness in the breeze that carried the salty tang of the Delaware, having her close. The day was perfect. She squeezed his arm and he looked down in question.

"It's nothing, I'm just assuring myself this isn't a dream."

His free hand covered hers as he stopped in front of a house no different than the others on the street, other than the pots of flowers adorning the entrance. Must be for the occasion; they hadn't been there last week.

It took a moment for his eyes to adjust to the dimness. The dining table had been stacked against the wall, piled high with sewing paraphernalia from Mrs. MacTavish's mending business. It blocked half the light from the only window. Seamus stood at the other end of the room with his fiddle, Ewan with his flute. There were others with them, one with an accordion, another with drums. Ewan called out something to Liam about needing him to take over the drums in an hour, Liam raised his cup to acknowledge him.

"There's Mrs. MacTavish, David." Elisabeth tugged at him, and they went together to thank her for her hospitality and to offer condolences on the loss of her husband, as well as compliments on the beautiful bride. It was agreeable, surprisingly so—the simple carrying out of small social niceties with her at his side, especially as she took care of the chattering. He led her to the group gathered around the small table holding the refreshments.

"Just a wee bit for ye, Elisabeth. We don't want tae send ye back lushey to your da," Liam said. He tossed back a whisky for himself, then moved from the table to allow others access.

"And speaking of the cove, are ye going to share how ye managed it, lass? Slumming with the lower sort for the afternoon? No' that we dinna appreciate the great honor, mind ye. Just curious," Liam said.

"Liam . . . " David said, both a warning and question in his voice.

"I apologize," he said, pocketing his flask. "It's no' my intent to . . . I . . ." His eyes darted around the room. Hands in his pockets, rocking back and forth on his heels, he brought to mind a caged animal. He shook his head quickly, as if shaking off a thought. "I am sorry, to be sure. Can I borrow her for a dance, David?"

David looked at Elisabeth. She nodded, a concerned look on her face. Handing David her cup, she allowed Liam to lead her to the dance floor. He hesitated, as if reconsidering, and she laughed, taking both his hands and pulling him into the group of dancers. David heard her say something about grabbing her chance to dance with him before he was snatched up by one of the six or seven ladies she'd noticed eyeing him. Liam didn't acknowledge her.

David looked around the room for the source of Liam's sudden change in mood. There were several young women he'd spent time with, as Lisbeth had pointed out, but none he knew to be of any more consequence than the other. He wandered toward the door where Rob was propped against the wall, watching the dance floor. Rob never danced, the only clue he ever gave that his lameness might embarrass him.

"'Fore ye got here a man from Dryman recognized us outside the White Horse, and he thought to renew the acquaintance. Close to our home, ken?" Rob said.

David nodded.

"He was one of the last of Liam's ma's 'special' friends, and thought it fitting to describe her charms to us. His two companions, now they were sober and wiser. He didna get more than a few words out 'fore they spirited him into a coach. I believe it's only out of respect for Annie that Liam didna follow. The look on his face . . . Mr. Oliver and I, well, we have stopped worrying over him, thought he was past it.

"And now that ye know he's not?" David said.

"There's no making it easier, he'll just shut ye out. On the other hand . . ." Rob canted his head toward the dancers. "Don't be stingy sharing your lass. She wears comfortable on him, no complications or expectations."

David looked, and indeed, Liam was laughing. "Thanks, Rob," he said. Preferring Liam didn't think he was being gossiped about, he walked away, having cause to regret it as soon as he saw Sarah Wallace making her way toward him. He'd encountered her several times since the passage, and each time it seemed she was heading down her da's path. He could tell from her gait she was already foxed, which only meant trouble. While he was certain he'd never done anything to encourage her, she didn't always see it that way, and this looked to be one of those times. Cockish wench. He'd not forgive if she ruined this one day he had with Elisabeth.

He looked back at Rob, hoping for help, but the lad just grinned and shrugged. Well, Rob wasn't at ease talking around the agreeable lassies, much less the difficult ones. He glanced toward the dance floor, hoping he could catch Liam's eye. But, of course, Liam had already seen and was whispering something to Elisabeth as he led her back to David.

"Sarah! It's lucky I am ye look to be free, two of the loveliest lassies in the room, one right after the other. Come, dance with me." Liam grabbed her by the hand and twirled her away before she had a chance to utter more than a word to David. He'd owe him double for this.

David turned to Elisabeth, watching her as her gaze followed Liam and Sarah. He took her hand. "Well?" he said.

Startled, she looked away from Sarah and up at him.

"I can see ye're working it out, lass. What's your decision?"

She laughed. "My decision, since you ask so politely, Mr. Graham, is to enjoy the one evening I know I have with you and to let lie any thoughts about what you may or may not do with the rest of your evenings. Don't you want to dance with me?"

"More than anything, Bess, and for the record, if I have any energy to spare in the evenings, I spend most of it working on letters to you or to my Ma."

"Oh my. Do step carefully, good sir. You mustn't expect the punch to dull my good sense."

He laughed and pulled her close, leaving no doubt to anyone watching where his affections lay. "Come," he said, taking her to the dance floor.

THE MacTAVISHES WERE an especially lively clan when one added whisky to the mix. He took Elisabeth outside for some space and some air. The temperature had dropped, and a strong breeze whistled up the street, sweeping the air of the stench lingering about the nearby tanneries. A good many of the street lamps hadn't been lit; those that were, illuminated the neighborhood only dimly.

"Are you going to kiss me, David? The night is fast going, and I'm tired of waiting."

"Och, ye're showing your bossy side tonight, are ye?" David said, laughing. She leaned with her back against the wall, the light of the streetlamp dancing across her face. He faced her, placing his hands atop the brick on each side of her face, trapping her, watching as her eyes flared, the sapphire darkening, absorbing the flecks of indigo.

The things she could do to him, without even trying. He blinked, backing up half a step.

"Ye're especially lovely tonight. I've been wondering why for hours. Could be your gown; it's especially becoming. I canna believe your Da let ye out of the house wearing such." He let his eyes linger on the soft, sweet expanse of skin left bare above her bodice. Creamy, flawless skin. He'd labored all afternoon to keep his eyes elsewhere, but, well, who knows when he'd have a chance such as this again. The lass always dressed so modestly. A taste couldn't hurt.

"I'm quite old enough to choose my own clothing . . . Polly modified the bodice for me a bit . . . and Papa was out . . ." she said, her voice catching as David's mouth trailed kisses across her skin.

He brought his attention back to her face. "Did she now? Hmmph, must no' have known it was me ye were to be meeting. It could be the color I was also thinking. The blue; it makes one notice your eyes, and your eyes are truly striking. Always have been," he said, kissing them shut in turn, the back of his fingers as light as a butterfly's touch as he caressed the swell of her breasts.

"Tell her I like the way she dressed your hair. It highlights the set of your bones, which are fine indeed. And your hair; over the years it's darkened just a bit. The color, it's like nothing I've ever seen before. I don't mind telling ye I dream of the day I can take out the pins and run my hands through the silk of it." He moved his hand from her bodice to her face, his fingers tracing a path from her cheek to the line of her jaw, down along the curve of her neck, then lightly across the neckline of her gown. She shivered.

"But I've come to the conclusion it's that ye're happy, ye fairly glow."

"I am happy today, and I'm quite refreshed now, so we may dance again."

He grinned. He was making her nervous. She ducked under his arm and started back into the house. She hadn't gone more than a step before he grabbed her wrist and whirled her back.

"No' just yet, lass. I wasna done."

"No?" she said, smiling at him.

"No." He lowered his head and kissed her, taking her mouth and molding it to his. His tongue gently traced her lips, and she opened hers, accepting it with small, hesitant touches of her own. He responded instantly, kissing her with an intensity he hadn't planned. Groaning, he wrapped his arms around her, moving his knee between her legs so that she fit even closer, running his hands down her back to pull her tight against him, cursing the petticoat that held her apart.

His pulse was beating a drum so fast he felt dizzy. He set her back against the wall and pressed up tight to stay steady, his body laying claim to the softness of hers. She arched up against him, and stars burst beneath his eyelids, the motion was so innocent and unexpected. Grinding his pelvis into hers, he reached for the shoulder of her gown, dragging it down, his hand molding her breast, his thumb caressing.

Dimly, slowly, it registered that someone had shouted, that she had stilled, that they were out in the street. With an effort he pulled away, searching her eyes before lowering his forehead to rest against hers, his breathing ragged. "I'm sorry,

Bess . . . I . . ."

"Shh, don't be. Please, don't be. I'm not."

"How do ye do that?" he whispered. "Jesus, kissing ye is no' like kissing. It's like drowning in a cloud. I canna think clearly."

She relaxed against the wall, pulling him to rest against her. "Why do you have to, think, I mean?" she answered softly. She ran her hands through his hair, pulling loose the tie, soothing him as his breathing slowed.

He raised his head, perplexed. "Well, I have ye in a compromising situation, out in the street in the dead of the night, and no' the safest street by far in the city. I think it mi' be a good idea to keep my wits about me. No' to mention . . ." He pulled up the shoulder of her gown and put her stay to rights. "I am sorry, lass."

She blushed and ducked her head. "Don't say that again. I told you, I'm not," she whispered. "Turn around, David." She smoothed his hair and quickly tied it securely. "Angus and Annie are leaving. We should say goodbye."

He took her hand. Others were leaving as well. The evening had gone by so fast, he'd been hoping for more time. Would she grant it, given what he'd just let happen?

"Bess, d'ye think—"

"There the two of ye are. We're headed to the Man for a spell. Will ye be joining us, then?" Liam asked. He appeared to have sobered, the dancing and the drums working off the lingering effects of the whisky.

David scowled. Why'd he have to bring that up? He'd been considering the City Tavern. "No, I thought—"

"I'd like to go, David. I'm not expected back home until later. I'd like to see where you spend your time."

"The print shop's where I spend my time."

"I want to go," she said, hands on her hips. "Might there be a reason you don't want to take me?"

"Nay, it's just—no, of course I'll take ye." He just wouldn't let her out of his sight, and he'd pray Liam's gaming didn't get him involved in a fight. As surly as he'd been earlier tonight, he'd have to pray hard.

He held back, not joining the others as they walked, not in the mood for the bantering it would require. He was down to counting the minutes now, the minutes before he'd have to give her up.

Stopping him at one of the frozen ponds still dotting the city, she pulled him aside to watch the skaters.

"It's beautiful, isn't it, David?"

"Hmmph." At night, maybe. The lanterns hanging about the pond cast a soft glow on the ice, leaving shadows to spill over the surrounding mud and refuse.

"Are you going to speak to me? Please, *please*, don't spoil the rest of the evening."

"I didna treat ye with respect, lass. How can ye let it go so lightly?"

She looked at him, her eyes narrowing. "Has it occurred to you I might measure respect by whether you heed what I say, in lieu of what you think I should be saying? I've a right to voice my own opinion, haven't I?"

"Of course ye do. It's just that—" He stopped as her mouth set in a thin line and she turned away. He reached for her, then dropped his hand. "I'm sor—" He sighed. "Do ye skate?"

"Some. Not as well as they do. Do you?"

"Nay, I don't think I'm light enough on my feet for that."

She relaxed her stance, placing her hand in the crook of his arm. "Of course you are. Maybe we can try together one day."

"Mayhap," he said, noncommittally. If they had the opportunity to spend such time together, he wasn't going to squander it making a fool of himself. He led her away from the pond.

"David, do you know Sarah's father?"

"No' well, why is it ye ask?"

"What is his trade?"

"Cobbler, when he's sober."

"Which isn't often, is it? How does he support her?"

"I havena a clue. Elisabeth, why are we talking about Mr. Wallace?"

"I saw him talking to my father at the market last month, when Polly and I were in the Dry Goods. Papa grumbled something about him expecting a handout. Does Sarah earn an income?"

"Truly, Bess, I don't know their circumstances. I'm no' surprised he asked your father though. From what I gather, he's the type that thinks he's due."

"Do you think he harms her? Some men take out their shortcomings on the weaker."

That gave him pause. He'd seen her with her face bruised from time to time, not uncommon for a lass who chose to frequent the places she did. But it could have been her father. He knew she feared him.

"Never mind, David. I just had the odd feeling she might be in trouble. I'm sure it's nothing."

"Do ye want me to look her up, check on the lass?"

"Only if I'm with you," she said, laughing.

A large group of seamen and dockhands were gathered around the door of the Tavern, laughing and jostling one another. He turned her about to face him and reached out, tugging on the shoulders of her gown. "Does this pull up some?"

"Stop!" She readjusted the bodice. "I thought you liked it."

"Oh, I like it just fine, to be sure. It's just it can be a rough crowd in there. Best not invite them to notice ye much. And they'll notice ye, mark my words."

She batted his hand away and unpinned a piece of fabric from around her waist. Draping it across her shoulders, she tied it in front. "How's this?"

He laughed. "So that's how ye got out of the house! That's perfect, lass, now come on."

Pushing his way through the crowd, he led her to an empty bench against a wall in the corner, near where Liam, Rob, and others had started playing cards.

"I'd hoped it would be more impressive inside, given all I've heard."

"Och, and what would ye be hearing of the place?" He motioned her to sit. "Stay here just a minute. Don't talk to anyone," he said. She frowned. "No one, Bess, I'll be right back."

He returned with two mugs of cider and sat, stretching his arm out around her shoulders, pulling her close. "Now then, why don't ye tell me the story of how ye made it here and why, when it's well past midnight, ye needn't be returning yet."

"It doesn't signify."

"Oh, aye, I'm thinking it does. Tell me."

"Very well, but I'm giving you fair warning you won't like it." She told the story, her voice so soft at parts he had to strain to hear her. Her eyes sought his when she finished. "Well, aren't you going to say something? Are you so disappointed in me?"

"I'm thinking. But disappointed, no. Why would I be disappointed?"

"That lying came so easily to me. I find that a bit worrisome myself."

"If it came easily, Bess, ye wouldna be worrying it now." He moved his fingers idly back and forth across her shoulder. "It does, however, give me pause that ye'd go to that extent to spend time with me."

"Truly? You should know how I feel about you by now. I may not choose to openly disregard my father's wishes, but I find I'm not above rationalizing when I choose to put my own first on occasion. And it *is* only on the rare occasion—I do honor my family, David!"

"I know you do, lass, I know."

"Papa has been through so much. I mustn't make it worse for him. When I come of age . . . well, then I won't feel so obligated, I suppose."

He wondered if that were true, if she realized how important her father's love and approval was to her. He roused himself, making an effort to lighten the mood.

"Then what, lass? Ye'll be joining the circus, become an actress?"

"No! I plan to become your wife." Her hand shot to her mouth, and her eyes widened. "Oh, drat." She turned away. "Forgive me. I know that was awfully forward of me. I fear I may have had more of the punch than was wise. You're probably quite weary of women throwing themselves at you."

David chuckled, shaking his head. He reached for her. "No one's throwing themselves, Bess, least of all you." He knew he should say more, but what? He certainly couldn't say what he knew to be true; she was papist, he was poor, what future was there in that? He pulled her close and stroked her back, choosing silence.

She looked up at him. "Will you just hold me for a while longer? Even if I fall asleep? I don't want to go home yet."

That he could do. He held her as she slept, content to have her in his arms.

"Looks like ye could use some help there, Davey," Liam said when he joined him later.

"I could. How did ye do?" David asked, nodding toward the others.

"Well enough. I'm thinking of following your lead. Perhaps I'll set it aside. A good friend has married today. Mayhap it's time to begin to plan for the future, no?" Liam said, grinning. "Now we best be going. She needs to wake. If ye carry her, we'll be stopped by the watch for sure."

"SLEEP OVER TONIGHT, Davey. Mr. O willna mind. It's late." They had just escorted Elisabeth home without incident. The night was quiet, the street empty.

David nodded. As they turned down Carter's Alley, he broached the subject that had been on his mind most of the day.

"Liam, how is it that ye know everything about me, yet I know nothing of your past?"

Liam exploded. "Christ Almighty, that's what spending the day with a woman will get ye. Leave it, David!"

Well, he couldn't say he wasn't warned. He held his hands up briefly, acknowledging the subject was dropped, and they walked the rest of the way in silence. Liam stopped him before he walked up the steps, his hands in his pockets, his eyes aimed toward the river.

"David, it's occurred to me ye're the best friend I've ever had precisely because I've no past with ye. Ye know me only as I stand here. I value that. Ye don't judge and ye don't pry. I trust ye with my life. I'd trust ye with my past if it mattered. It doesn't."

"Fair enough." He rolled back and forth on the balls of his feet. "May we sleep now, then?"

Liam hesitated, his eyes on David.

"It's cold out here. If ye plan to continue to bare your soul on the front stoop, could ye lend me your jacket?"

Laughing, Liam went up the steps, opening the door. "I think I'm quite done for the night." He motioned David in.

"And Davey? I stopped going to kirk the day my mother passed."

36

May 1786

"IAN, THIS ISNA RIGHT. THAT'S no' how 'tragedy' is spelled, and there should be a period here . . . 'Insurmountable' is spelled wrong as well; here, too . . . hell, ye need to redo the whole letter."

David had pulled the first copy off the press, and was looking it over before he handed it to Robert for proofing.

"Where?" Ian walked over, taking the page out of his hand. He looked where David pointed. "Are you sure, David? That's how he sent it in. I haven't time to change the whole damn page!"

Robert reached for the copy. "He's right, Ian. It's from Snodgrass. Man's notorious for his grammar and spelling, or rather lack of it. You know that. Mark it up, David, if you will, then give it back to Ian. Hurry, we're behind. I'll be back in a few minutes."

David spent the next five minutes marking up the copy, ignoring Ian as he grumbled about on and on about why it should be their problem if the 'gent couldn't write a fair sentence.'

When he finished, he handed it to Ian. "Here. It shouldna take ye long to fix. And you know well why, it'll look like Mr. Hall's the illiterate one if it goes out the way the gent wrote it. You're the one taught me that. We're to read it before we set it."

Ian mumbled an obscenity at David's advice, grabbing the sheet from his hand. Lad had been testy of late, having troubles with his lass.

"I'm not aiming to be a galley slave, David."

"I'm thinking we don't have a choice in the matter, Ian," David said quietly. Hall insisted the apprentices spend equal time at all the tasks in the shop.

Robert walked back in. "Go see Mr. Hall, David, before your supper. He's expecting you in his office. I'll handle the press."

Alarmed, David looked up from the machine. What had he done that required a summons from Hall?

"Best not to keep him waiting, David."

He sighed. "Aye." He walked to the basin and washed his hands, quickly drying them on the apron he wore. Taking it off, he hung it up, then hurried through the front to the small room under the stairs. Mayhap he shouldn't have corrected Ian. Mayhap Ian was right. He was senior to him after all. No, Ian had told him it was their job to edit submissions. Robert had never said otherwise. Maybe he knew David spent time in taverns with Liam. That was against the terms of the indenture, but . . . well . . . they all did. Even Robert had. Course he knew that. Could have been the cards. Not everyone gambled. Or the whores, but that wasn't so frequent, who would have—

"David, come in."

"Yes, sir. I came as soon as Robert told me."

"Sit. Now, Robert gave me an accounting of your output, and it seems you set forty-five hundred ems on Tuesday and five thousand on Friday, so that amounts to fifteen hundred ems over the daily four thousand, all of it accurate. I owe you thirty cents." He counted the coins out in front of David, then pushed them across the desk. David stared at him.

"What is it? Take it, David. It's yours."

"Nothing, sir, thank you." He reached for the coins, then drew back his hand. "Well, sir, that is . . . why are ye giving me this?"

Hall laughed. "Robert probably didn't explain. It's been quite a while since an apprentice has earned a supplement. I believe he was the last to do so, as a matter of fact, and that's been years. It's usually only the journeymen who are skilled and fast enough. Well, to get to the point, any day you set over four thousand ems, I pay you twenty cents per thousand ems. Any day you press over eight tokens, I pay you thirty cents per token. This is above your stipend."

"Honestly, Mr. Hall? I can get this each week?"

"Each week you earn it. Now, get back to work. You boys need to finish up before you burn my profits in tallow."

David pocketed the coins and backed out of the office. "Aye, Mr. Hall. Thank you!" He hurried back to the shop, calculating the difference the supplement could make to his annual savings plan, and what he'd have to do to increase it each week.

"I'VE PUT THE NUMBERS to paper, Liam," David said. They were walking along an abandoned wagon path just north of town, now little more than a game path. "And I'm bound to get faster at it over the next few years, so my budget is conservative. I think I can do it. It'll need to be a used press, for sure."

"Willna you need more than a press, though? What about

all those other things I see in the shop?"

"The type will be the most costly of it. I've worked that in as well. And listen to this. Thomas is leaving. Robert thinks Mr. Hall will let me assume his foreman duties on the two days a week Robert is over with Mr. Sellers. That will earn me fifty cents more a week."

"Foreman? Are ye serious? You've only been there two years. Well done, David!"

David shrugged. "I think I may be doing some of the duties now. I tend to be a bit driven."

"I've noticed. What about Ian? How would he handle that?"

"He wouldna begrudge me the chance. He's no interest in more responsibility. His mind's usually elsewhere."

"Are ye thinking of a paper? I'd like ye having your own paper."

"No' sure yet, but I think so."

"Where's Thomas going?"

"South. He's told me a journeyman can make up to twenty-five dollars a week in Georgia. Can you imagine that kind of money? Mayhap I could go there for a year or two when I reach journeyman. Save up the rest if I find I'm short."

"No, it willna help ye. A dollar in the South is worth about a quarter of what it's worth in Pennsylvania. Would probably just set ye back."

"Truly?" David said. He should have thought of that, given the confusing myriad of currencies in the market. "I don't think Thomas knows that."

"I'll tell Mr. O to toss in some economics in your tutoring." He jumped back a step, pulling David with him as a snake darted across their path.

"Poisonous?"

"Dinna ken. Listen, Lisbeth was asking after ye. Ye havena been by to see her, last couple of weeks."

He hadn't. He'd heard something in the market a few weeks ago that bothered him. He didn't want to think about it, and he didn't want to talk about it, both of which he'd have to do if he saw her.

She was having a debut ball. Well, if the rumors were true, and he had no reason to doubt them, a debut . . . and to what purpose? Of course, he knew the purpose and, of course, he could have no quarrel with it. Other than that, whenever he thought of it, his gut ached. He kicked a stone out of his way, watching it disappear amongst the wildflowers lining the trail. Not a cloud in the sky. Bonny day to be walking with one's girl, assuming one was permitted the privilege.

"David?"

"It's spring, isna it?"

"Aye, it is."

"Ye can tell her I'll be by this week."

ELISABETH LOOKED UP as David walked in, her smile fading as she took in his demeanor.

"Afternoon, Elisabeth."

"What's wrong, David?"

"No' sure. I saw Eliza at the market."

Oh no. Eliza was her dressmaker. She attended the same church David did. So he knew.

She'd been meaning to talk to him, she had. But she hadn't seen him for weeks, and really, whose fault was that?

"She could speak of nothing but the gown she's helped ye with for your debut. How 'stunning' ye looked."

Oh, drat that girl. How could she! She didn't have a brain in her head. She *had* to have known she wouldn't want her to discuss that gown with David, of all people. Or maybe she'd done it on purpose—she'd always suspected Eliza was attracted to him.

"I'm so sorry, David, I've been searching for a way to tell

you."

"How does 'David, I'm having a debut ball' sound? That's easy enough, isna it?"

"Don't! My grandmother insists upon it. It makes no difference to her that I want nothing to do with such an event."

"I understand it'd be important to her. And it's no' as if I'd be expected to be invited. I'm no' a fool. But ye kept it from me. I've always known ye deserve more. I did have hopes of hearing it from ye first-hand, however."

"What?" Confused, her hand flew up, pushing back at his words. "What are you saying? David, please . . . please don't make this into something it isn't. It's not easy for me to be pulled in two directions. David, don't walk out—"

Why . . . why . . . that *cad.* She was *not* going to run into the street after him, she wasn't. He hadn't even given her a chance to explain. She threw the slate she'd been holding at the door, barely missing Liam as he came around the corner. He ducked as he watched it fly past.

"Elisabeth, what did ye say to him? It's no' often he's rude. I know *I* did nothing to annoy him."

"Oh, hush."

He sat on the corner of her desk. "He's angry about your 'debut,' I take it."

She didn't care for his derogatory emphasis on the word. "You, too?" she asked, hands on her hips.

Liam shrugged. "Philadelphia? It's no' that big. I just heard this morning from one of the lassies hired to serve for the event. Odd. That ye hadn't mentioned it yourself, I mean."

"I'm only trying to make them happy, Liam. As long as I'm under their roof I feel I've an obligation to do so. They're my family. Is that so awful? *I* know it's merely a formality. I've already met all those invited. They've been invited to many of the functions at my grandmother's home over the years. Not one of those fops can hold a candle to David."

"Then why didna ye just tell me of it, lass? What made it so different ye felt ye couldna mention it?"

She swung around. He stood leaning against the door frame, his hands in his pockets, looking at her. "David, you came back."

He pushed off the frame. "I'm sorry, Lisbeth. I shouldna have left like that. Where're ye off to, Liam? I owe ye an apology as well."

"No matter, Davey. Spend it on the wee lass. Fetch me when you're done, and ye can do your groveling then. If ye have the time, we'll go for a pint," Liam said, walking to the small office he kept.

After the door closed, David continued, "Ye tell me so much; why not this?"

"Because, to others, it has so much significance. I was afraid it might to you as well. Don't laugh," she said when he smiled. "I know you've plenty of family in the cities back home. I don't know your customs, but I imagine your cousins will go through similar rites of passage. But don't you see? That's why I'm doing it. My grandmother can't imagine not going through with this ritual. She feels it would be a reflection on her if she didn't host a debut ball for her only granddaughter. And . . . and this is not the least of it. I'm embarrassed and ashamed I didn't stand up to them and insist you be invited."

He laughed at that. "Hell, Bess, I wouldna have accepted. That's no' for me. Not the ball, mind ye. I can clean up well enough, so as no' to embarrass ye. And my position at the paper allows me to converse intelligently on current events. I've even been raised to make meaningless polite small talk if the occasion calls for it. Nay—let me finish." He put his hand gently over her mouth when she started to reply. "And it might surprise ye to know that my ma insisted I learn some of those fancy dance steps you English tend to. But what I'm not up to is the task of feigning ye're a meaningless acquaintance and standing by calmly watching and waiting while others take the opportunity to court—"

"Elisabeth, would you see me before . . . oh I apologize, I didn't know you were here, David."

David stepped back. "No, it's I who apologize, Mr. Oliver. I shouldna be distracting her from her work. I'm just heading toward Liam's. It's good to see ye. I hear ye've signed on four more students for Rob's class."

"Yes! It's exciting. Liam's doing an excellent job recruiting. If I can talk Elisabeth into staying another year, we anticipate a whole new crop of young students. I couldn't be happier with how our little school is faring. And you, David, I just encountered Mr. Hall at the Coffee House. He tells me you're now a foreman. That's impressive indeed, for an apprentice of only two years."

Elisabeth sucked in a breath. Why, he hadn't mentioned that at all! And to think he was bad-tempered because she hadn't brought up a more difficult subject.

"Aye, well, it's just the morning shift two days a week, to relieve Robert. But I'm anxious for the opportunity. I willna keep ye. I see Polly's hankering for Elisabeth as well." He turned and winked at her as he headed in to see Liam. "It was good to see ye, Elisabeth."

"David?" Mr. Oliver said.

"Yes, sir?"

"Don't expect any leniency on your final exams next month, just because you have new responsibilities. I consider it my responsibility to see to it the up and coming youth are well educated."

"Of course, Mr. Oliver. I'd expect no less."

DAVID KNOCKED ONCE ON Liam's door before he entered, finding him with his feet on the desk, chair propped back against the wall and hands folded behind his head. "Sorry to interrupt ye, Liam, I can see ye're busy. Should I return at a more convenient time, then?"

"If that's to be the extent of your groveling, I shouldna have waited for ye. Let's go; I'm thirsty." He dropped his feet to the floor and stood.

"Wait just a bit, 'til Mr. O is finished in there and Elisabeth leaves. I'm thinking she's going to be a wee bit out of sorts she heard the news about foreman from Mr. O instead of me."

"Coward. Tell me, what made ye change your mood so quickly and return?"

"Aye, well, even as I was angry I knew I was behaving like an eijit. I'd been working myself inta it for the past few weeks, since I first got wind of the damned thing. Couldna seem to stop. But then, faced with her, it occurred to me it was no' to my benefit to have her attending this ball with that image in her mind."

"Ahh, fast thinking on your feet. Leave the 'behaving like an eijit' to the suitables her da will have attending. I couldna have steered ye better."

David peered through the crack in the door. Empty.

"Aye. Now, let's go; I'm thirsty myself, and I'm buying. I need to talk to ye about some tutoring. Mr. O's of a mind to be particularly challenging with my finals next month."

"Ye'll do just fine on your own. He's showed me some of your papers."

"Must have been those ye helped me with."

"Ballocks."

37

"POLLY!"

"Elisabeth."

Elisabeth skidded to a stop at the parlor doorway. "Good morning, Grandmother."

"Dear, you're apt to hurt yourself running down the stairs like that, and it's not necessary to raise your voice in the house. Now, Polly is busy with the preparations for the evening. Do you need help with your personal toilet? Perhaps I could assist you?"

"No, I don't need help just yet. But I do need to leave for an hour. My head is spinning. I'd like to get some air."

For weeks she'd managed to maintain an outward interest in this event, for her family's sake. But now the day was here, and it was real, with all its implications and repercussions. What if he washed his hands of her, decided their worlds were too different?

She must see him. She *needed* to see him.

"Oh, not today, Elisabeth! We have too many things we must attend to, all of us."

"Just for an hour, Grandmother. I fear I'll have a frightful headache if I don't take a breath of fresh air and some time to myself before this evening. Please understand. I must."

Her grandmother looked hard at her, and Elisabeth held her ground, refusing to squirm.

"Very well, Elisabeth. I trust I won't regret it." She picked up the bell and rang for a servant.

"Jane, please find Polly. My granddaughter would like to have her company on a stroll."

"MISS LISS? Where we be going?"

"I need to see him, Polly. I can't go through this without seeing him."

"Oh, no, Miss Liss, now how you gonna do that? Your grandma will have herself a fit if she knows that's where you be heading."

"She may suspect already. But provided I return within the hour and go through this evening with a smile on my face, she won't object."

"Where's he gonna be meeting you?"

"Well, I suppose as he's not expecting me, we'll go meet him. I believe he'll be at the paper today."

"He doesn't expect you?" Polly's mouth dropped open, her eyes wide. "You ain't never done that. Oh, my word, that's bold, Miss 'lisabeth."

"Too bold? Don't scare me. It won't take much to make me turn around. I just need five minutes of him, Polly, I'll go mad if I can't reassure myself. Five minutes and I'll be fine. I think we turn here. It should be on the corner."

Odd, that she'd never visited the print shop before. Would he welcome her interruption? Would it jeopardize his new position as foreman?

"There it is, Miss," Polly said, her finger pointing. "Well, ain't we going go in?"

Elisabeth stood rooted on the corner, staring at the shop.

"Hmmph, that boy sure is gonna be disappointed to find you lacked gumption at the last minute. I spose he don't have to find out. We should go back. Jane has a pile of chores for me to be doing."

Elisabeth grabbed her elbow, propelling her to the door. "Do we knock or just walk in?" she whispered.

Polly lowered her head, shaking it from side to side in mock wonder as she opened the door. A young boy looked up as they walked in, his hands full of boxes. "We're looking for Mr. Graham. Can you be telling him Miss Hale is here to see him?"

"Yes, miss." The boy set down the boxes and ran into the back room.

David hurried out, his hands wringing a cloth as he tried to wipe them clean. "Elisabeth? What's happened, lass?"

Tears filled her eyes. My word, but he looked so . . . so wonderful, so perfect, so strong, so handsome . . .

"What's wrong, Polly?" David asked, his face full of concern as he came from behind the counter.

"Nothing's wrong, David. She was aiming to see you today no matter what. Now cat's got her tongue."

Elisabeth laughed through her tears. "I just needed to see you, David. I apologize. I know you're working, but can I impose on you—just for a few minutes? Please?"

David walked to the door and turned the sign to 'Closed'. "Johnny, take Miss Polly and give her a tour of the shop. Show her the press, will ye?"

"Yes, sir! Come on, miss," said the young boy, excitedly gesturing Polly to follow.

"He's sweet. I haven't met him before."

"Aye, he's the newest apprentice on the floor. He's a good lad."

"I'm sorry I interrupted you. I was panicking. Tonight's my

debut, you know."

"Aye, I do," he said with a small smile. He pulled off his work apron.

"Would you mind holding me?"

He grunted and reached for her, pulling her into his arms. Resting her head on his chest, she breathed him in . . . ink, oil, leather, coffee . . . David; scents that swept through her with the promise she was treasured. This was where she belonged, and her heart clutched at the sheer rightness of it. She burrowed in closer, and he tightened his hold.

"David, don't be upset with me anymore, please?" she whispered.

He chuckled and reached down, bringing her chin up so her eyes met his. "I'm no', lass, truly, I'm not. It's glad I am ye value your family." He kissed her gently, so sweetly that her eyes filled, then he settled her face against his chest, stroking the back of her head and neck in a soothing rhythm, calming the temper that had plagued her for days. This was why she'd come. This was what she'd needed.

The church bells struck the hour. She didn't have much time. She lifted her head. "May I see the press as well, before I leave?"

"Of course, come back around this counter." They stood at the door, and he gave her a brief explanation of each piece of equipment. "Right now there's just me and Johnny at work." He called John over and introduced them.

Polly looked at her, and Elisabeth nodded and turned. "We won't be keeping you any longer, David. We need to get back." Polly stepped outside.

Elisabeth put her hand on David's cheek, standing on her toes to kiss him goodbye. He wrapped his arms around her, drawing her in, deepening the kiss until she melted, her arms tight about his neck.

"I love you, Bess. Don't be doubting it," he said finally,

pulling his mouth from hers.

Her eyes flew open as she tilted back her head to meet his.

"I must go now," she said. He grinned as she made no move to leave his arms.

Did he have any idea what that grin did to her insides? She ought to display some dignity before she found herself reaching for his mouth again.

"I don't think it's entirely proper for you to kiss me that way in the morning."

His grin only broadened, deepening his dimples, and she backed against the counter for support. "Stay an hour. It will be past noon. It will be proper then, aye?"

She pouted and he relented, releasing her and walking her to the door.

"I'll make a point of leaving the paper early enough Wednesday to meet you at the Academy, aye?"

"I'll count on it as a promise. Please don't change your mind."

"Aye, and Elisabeth? Thank you for coming today. I was needing to see ye just as badly," he said, placing a chaste kiss on her forehead.

She smiled and forced herself to go out the door while she still could.

"We got ta hurry, Miss. Hour's mostly done used up."

"He told me he loves me."

"He did? You sure 'bout that?" Polly looked at her, doubtful. "You sure that's what he said, now?

She nodded.

Polly smiled wide, her feet jumping into a skip as she clapped her hands together.

"Ha! 'Bout time that there boy got some sense."

HAD HE *truly* said that to the lass?

Liam stepped outside just as he reached the townhouse.

"David, I was just on my way to fetch ye. I thou' we should go to the Bull's Head for a bite to eat, then head to the quay. Rob will meet us later," Liam said, reaching back to shut the door.

David had gone to the townhouse to seek out Rob; he didn't wish to be alone. He hadn't expected to find Liam—Liam had taken to laboring at the docks until dark on Saturdays. David gripped his shoulder in acknowledgment of his change in plans, grateful for his company, even if it meant dinner at a tavern known for its greasy, sinewy, meat pies.

He broke the silence once they were seated at the bar. "She came to see me today."

"Who?" Liam asked, his eyes on the comely barmaid at the keg behind the bar, her full breasts threatening the promise of a spill from her gown each time she bent to fill one of the mugs stacked beside her.

So that's why he'd chosen this place. Though she didn't look worth the forfeit of a good meal. "Are ye sure ye want to eat here, Liam? We could have a pint, then go elsewhere."

Liam looked at him. "Nay, we'll try the fish. There might be some hope in that. Now, who came to see ye?"

"Who else would I be talking of? Lisbeth. Lisbeth came to see me."

"Elisabeth? At the paper? She came to ye at the shop?"

David nodded. He kept his eyes on his mug as he twirled it round and round in his hands.

"Well, go on, man, dinna make me drag it out of ye. That's out of character for the lass."

"I think she just needed reassurance I wasna holding this against her. I'm not sure, she didna actually say." And he had told her he loved her. God in Heaven, why had he said that? She'd likely believe it meant . . . why had he said that? The lass just . . . there was no accounting for the way she had him spinning.

"So she came to seek ye out, then didna say why? What else?"

"Nothing else."

"David?"

"It's nothing, she said nothing else."

Liam looked hard at him, then shrugged, conceding it was David's affair. "Then how d'ye know she wasna just looking to end it? I mean, that's been the speculation all along, aye?"

David's eyes shot from his mug to Liam. He chuckled. "Right then, I'll admit I was a bit of a fool. You were right. She's no' looking for a break. I could tell she was only looking for reassurance. I didna need the words to figure it out."

"'I was right . . . hmm, truer, sweeter words, and all that. Well now, now that we have that cleared up, can ye lighten your mood some? I've a full evening planned for ye, but ye must participate a bit, aye?"

David laughed. "It's glad I am that ye were available tonight, Liam."

"Pete's sake, Davey, I know well enough what tonight is. Where else would I be?" Liam called the barmaid over and ordered their meal. "Now, enough of the morose, aye? After we eat, we'll seek out James. Remember, I told ye about him. Black apprentice, works as foreman at a sail loft? Alex's friend?"

"Aye, the one who doesna acknowledge he's downtrodden, the lowest of the lower sort. I remember."

Liam laughed. "Aye, that's the man. The Negroes have a celebration planned for someone heading off to sea. China no less, can ye imagine? Now, that's music what will lift your spirits if nothing else will. It'll do ye good, something different. Ye and James can compare foreman experiences and so forth. Then Agnes has a cousin—dinna say it—ye dinna have to marry her, just dance with her now and again when we end up at the Man." He motioned to the barmaid to bring another round. Before David could protest he said, "I'm buying tonight, dinna fash."

"Hmmph. Well then, I'm verra thirsty."

Maybe there was no harm in telling her that on this night, it might serve to keep her mind on him instead of the swells paying court. And after a few days or weeks, well, by then she'd likely forget it was said. Especially if he remembered not to say it again.

LANTERNS LIT A PATH up the marble steps leading into the Hale's home. Tom, dressed in his butler best, stood at the door, receiving the guests one by one, ushering them into the home where candelabras and sconces were lit throughout. Flowers filled every available surface, and food and drink flowed freely.

The front parlor had been cleared of furnishings to create a dance floor and a spot for the musicians, while small groupings of chairs filled the hall. Polished mahogany woodwork and tables gleamed richly in the candlelight, setting off the flash of Mrs. Hale's silver to perfection. Little expense had been spared in the launching of Mrs. Hale's only grandchild.

"Papa, it's all so nice, thank you."

"I'm glad you're enjoying yourself, Elisabeth. Did you dance yet with Mr. York? His father is a good friend of the family. They've been anxious to meet you." His hands rose to his cravat, smoothing it, then down to his lace cuffs, pulling them into place. Elisabeth reached over to smooth his lapel.

"I think not yet." She consulted her card. "I'm to dance with him in the next set, however."

Her grandmother joined them. "It's a lovely gathering, Mother. I only wish Abigail could have been here to see it."

Elisabeth's eyes filled at the mention of her mother. Oh, how she wished she were here. She would have taken the

time to know David, looking past class and seeing him for
who he was. However, if she were alive, she herself would
never have met David, as they would never have left home.
God's plan was hard to discern.

"Yes, it has turned out well, hasn't it?" her grandmother
said. "Everyone has come." Her grandmother looked so
lovely tonight, her beautiful lilac dress complementing the
silver in her hair and the grey in her eyes. Amethysts glittered
beneath her ear lobes and around her throat.

"My word, Grandmother, I declare you have the eye of
every gentleman here, you look so beautiful. I was just thanking Papa for the party. I offer thanks to you as well." She
leaned over and kissed her cheek. "I'm so glad you decided
to forgo the expense of a chandelier. The candles we have
throw off such a nice welcoming light. They're precisely the
right number. And the musicians are quite talented, don't you
think? I shouldn't say it, but I know at Susan's party they
were not nearly so. The dancers had a time of keeping their
steps in order."

"Truly?" her grandmother asked, not above gossip. "Well,
Sheralyn was always one to pinch a penny. Never do so where
it shows, I say. But she does a wonderful job with the flowers
in her garden, don't you think? I believe she makes the most
beautiful arrangements I've ever come across. Those at the
front door are hers, she was kind enough to offer them."

Elisabeth continued on with her chitchat, well aware she
wasn't off the hook for this morning's escapade. Grandmother was nobody's fool, she knew that well, and she had
had the misfortune of encountering her before she left the
house. Perhaps she should have given up her plan at that
point, but she didn't regret it, not one bit, not after having
heard him tell her he loved her. That alone was worth the
risk. And the memory of being enfolded in his arms . . . she
smiled, remembering the sensations of his touch. Comfort-

ing, exciting, soothing, thrilling—oh no, she didn't regret it.

As the musicians tuned up, she looked for the next partner listed on her dance card. Making eye contact, she smiled at him, waiting for him to walk across the room and collect her, her mind filled with thoughts of next Wednesday.

DAVID STOOD ON THE fringes of the gathering with Liam's friend James, laughing as they compared the experiences of being an apprentice on the floor with those of being a foreman. James beat his stories without question. A Negro running a large crew of white men was much more challenging than a Scot running a tiny crew of English, Scotch, and Irish lads.

James nodded toward Liam, who was occupied learning dance steps with one of the girls. "That's a good man there. Not sure where he'll end up."

"Aye, he is at that. Probably shortsighted of me, but I like to think he'll always be nearby."

"I just can't see him in Philly forever. It'll be our loss. The town will only benefit from men like him. What are your plans, David?"

"I've several years left to serve out my term. After that, I'm thinking there's not much room for anymore printers in this town. I'm saving, though, I expect to have enough to open shop in another town." He was surprised as he said the words. He hadn't discussed it with any, save Liam. It made it more real to hear the words aloud again. "And you?"

"Oh, I don't think I'll be leaving Philadelphia. It's dangerous for one of my color to travel and start over in these States. And England's not for me. At least here, I'm known as a free man. I'll stay at the loft."

"I've never been anywhere in the States, other than Philadelphia. Your lass, is she free?" David said, nodding in the direction of the girl he'd seen with James earlier.

James chuckled. "She's not 'mine', just a good friend. But no, she's not free. Now her daughter, she'll be free when she turns twenty-eight. Assuming her master . . . " James turned his head and spat on the ground. "Doesn't sell her down South first."

"What are ye saying? Doesna the law say she'll be free once she's grown?"

"A slave is a piece of property. Would ye be giving it up for free next year if ye could make a profit this year on its disposal?"

David was silent, his jaw set as he puzzled this out. He'd thought a child born into slavery after 1780 would be freed once he or she reached their twenty-eighth year. If they could be sold first, to one living in a state not having such a law, well then, what was the point of the law? He would ask Mr. Hall first chance he got, because something seemed amiss.

"Ye got my mate all serious, James? The order of the day is revelry." Liam joined them, panting for breath, his dark blue eyes gleaming with excitement. He raked a hand back through his black hair, re-securing it in a cue with a quick motion. "Your drums, James, they bore their way into the soul, same as the pipes."

"When you invite me to a cèilidh, I shall be able to make the comparison myself, yes?"

"Aye, and I believe Friday next we can arrange that. Promise to come this time, no changing your plans again?"

"I look forward to it."

"Ahh, he trusts me now, David, now that he's spent some time with my solid, hard working mate."

"Well, I expect he has more cause to be careful than some of the rest of us, aye?"

"Aye, I expect so. Come, James, grab your lass. We're headed to the Man for a pint."

"No, thank you. I'll see you later next week, though."

"See there, Davey? There're some that take the terms of their indenture seriously."

James laughed. "Good evening to you gentlemen."

David and Liam thanked the host and headed to the Tavern. It was late when they arrived; patrons were already stumbling out the door. Liam had to shout to be heard when they entered.

"Over there, see Rob?"

David led the way, pushing through the crowd. He nodded to the man playing the fiddle, the lone entertainment for the evening; he often played on Saturday nights.

Liam grabbed Agnes, picking her up and holding her high as he kissed her. They settled in, ordering more pints of ale and gathering round for a game of hazard and high talk. None were better at it than Liam; he had an endless supply of yarns. David watched, amused, as Agnes hung on his every word. She wasn't much different than any of the other empty-headed lasses he chose to spend his time with; nice enough, fair enough, free enough with her favors. The lad went so easily, from one to the next, with nary a backward glance. He envied him that.

Why had he told her he loved her? He shouldn't have, shouldn't have said it.

He did his best to be pleasant to Agnes' cousin, Martha, including her in the conversation, dancing with her, even trying to remember her name when her brother came to collect the two of them shortly after midnight, escorting them home.

"Good effort, my friend," Liam said, slapping David on the back. "Agnes was happy. Ye can relax now. Let's see if we can spell any in this game."

"Her kin is agreeable enough. Ye could have done worse. That lass . . . last month was it? Now, ye owe me well for that one."

"Put it on my tab. I agree, ye can add three markers for the likes of that one."

38

"GOOD MORNING, MA'AM. MIGHT I be helping ye find a book of interest or perhaps with a
matter pertaining to the *Gazette?*" David asked, looking up
at the ringing of the bell. The woman looked a bit familiar,
though he couldn't place why.

He was uncrating the books that had just arrived from
London. He should have Johnny do it, but no matter how
patiently he explained that *Knox's Essays* might best be filed
adjacent to *Blair's Sermon's* as opposed to *Gay's Fables*, the lad
would invariably come up with his own incomprehensible
method of organization, a method none of the rest of them
could decipher when a customer came in wanting to see their
selection in philosophy or grammar.

The woman looked at him a moment before she handed
him her card. "I'd like to speak to Mr. Hall or Mr. Sellers
please."

"Yes, ma'am, Mr. Hall is available. I'll ask him to come
down." David barely glanced at the card until he reached the
steps. When he did, the name 'Mrs. Edward Hale' rose off

the vellum and announced itself to the accompaniment of trumpets.

Her mouth . . . she may be wearing some lines about it, but it carried a perfect bow nonetheless. Elisabeth's mouth. He slowly started up the stairs to fetch Mr. Hall, his heart sinking with each step, not sure if something had happened to Elisabeth or if her Grandmother was here to register a complaint against him with his master.

"MISS LISBETH, you shouldn't be out there in that sun."

Elisabeth tugged at the kitchen door with one hand, balancing the basket on her hip with the other. "Don't scold me, John. Will you look at what I picked? I did it; it grew this year!" She sorted through the basket, pulling out the asparagus. "See?" She held it up proudly, smiling as she displayed it. "There's more things growing as well, but I don't believe they're ready to be harvested yet. Has Grandmother come back from her errands yet? She could tell me, or maybe you could, John, if you've the time? Would you fry asparagus for supper?" She lifted her head, tilting it toward the hall.

"Whatever in the world . . . is that Papa? Who's he raising his voice to like that?" She looked at John, who turned away from her to tend to his fire. "John?" She walked to the door leading to the front hallway, opening it slightly.

"Miss Elisabeth," John said, "you come on back in here now. Leave your daddy to his business."

"Oh stuff, you can't tell me you're above eavesdropping. However else is one to find out anything? Now, shhh."

"How could you bring Abigail into this conversation, Mother? Her family may have fallen on hard times in recent years, but she was from good stock. The Powers name has a long and respected history."

"I know that, Edward. Abigail was a wonderful young woman. My only point, which you sidestepped quite neatly, was you would have married her regardless of her pedigree. You were driven to distraction by her. I'm certain neither your father nor I had much say in the matter; nor, I'd venture to say, would the treat of disinheritance. But it worked out well for many years. You were blessed with a happy life until God called for her."

"In large part because our backgrounds were so similar. I'm at an extremely delicate juncture in my career, Mother. I can't have gossip about my daughter jeopardize it. My alliances, and those include Elisabeth's, make no mistake—"

Elisabeth shut the door and went to sit at the table, her pride in her basket of produce forgotten. John went to her, patting her shoulder, and she reached up, clutching his dry, calloused hand.

"Do you think they'll forbid me to see him, John? Do you?" she asked, her eyes filling as she turned to him. "I did what they wanted, I had the debut. I was cordial to the boys; I was, John! I know I didn't receive any of them today. But I will. I just wasn't ready to pretend again quite so soon. I would have, though, if I had known how upset Papa would be."

"There's no telling, Miss Elisabeth, there's no telling. And don't be forgetting, you don't know for sure what they be talking 'bout. That's the thing 'bout eavesdropping. You don't be getting the whole truth of the matter."

"They were talking about David, John. You know they were."

John squeezed her shoulder, then went to empty her basket, setting the produce on his work table. "Mrs. Hale, I 'spect she'll know what's best."

39

"DID YOU REMEMBER, JOHN? DID you have the time?"

"Yes, Miss 'lisabeth, it's all packed right here. That boy will be so full he won't be able to move once he's finished with this here basket."

"Thank you!" She kissed his cheek before she ran out the door, calling for Polly. Her grandmother had had the most wonderful talk with her last night, and she was just bursting with news. It was going to be nearly impossible to wait until David came. She was hoping to find Rob or Liam free.

The front room was empty when she arrived. Rob was probably upstairs. Well then, Liam'd have to do.

My word, what a mess her room was. They must have let it out to seamen last night, for the floor was littered with mats. Mr. Oliver hired out the space to Alex and his crewmates whenever they were in the harbor, for a fraction of the going rate, she suspected. Usually they picked up before they left. She poked her head into Liam's office.

"Liam! I'm so glad you're here. Do you have a few moments?"

Liam looked up from the ledgers he was working on. "Lisbeth, is it that time already? I don't have time. I'm sorry; I must be at City Tavern to meet Dr. Schellsid at one. He's thinking of having his twins in your class. That's quite an accolade to ye."

"No, Liam, it's just past noon, I'm early. And you're the one who has courted the Schellsids. Enrolling their sons will be entirely your accomplishment. I have something to tell you; can you spare me the time?"

Liam wrote a last figure on the sheet and shut the ledger. Leaning back in his chair, he set his feet up on his desk and waved a hand for her to continue. "Talk away, lass, as long as ye don't have a complaint against Davey. I canna help ye there. Or if ye've decided on another ye met at your ball, I canna help ye there either, or if—"

"Oh, do stop, Liam, you know perfectly well I have no complaints about David, and I'll never decide on another. Now, listen, I'm so excited, I'm about to burst. You know I had my debut Saturday evening; yes, of course, you do. Well, on Monday I received all sorts of cards from gentlemen wishing to extend my acquaintance. I showed no interest in any of them and didn't return any responses. My grandmother was fit to be tied. On Tuesday afternoon she called me into her study. Liam, can you believe she went to visit Mr. Hall? Mr. Hall, David's employer?"

Liam dropped his feet and stood, coming around to sit on the corner of the desk.

"I know well who Hall is," he said. "Go on."

"Well, I was scared to death, so to speak. That must mean she knew I went to visit David Saturday morning. I suspected she knew, but suspecting and knowing are two different things."

"Aye. Get to the point, lass."

Elisabeth frowned. "She didn't say anything to jeopardize David's position, if that's what you're thinking."

"David's indenture requires no fraternization, no courtships; are ye aware of that, Elisabeth?"

"No, he never told me that. But I hardly think his attentions could be described as courting. We rarely see each other."

"I'm sure ye're right. Go on; what did your grandmother say to Mr. Hall?"

Elisabeth walked from his office to her classroom and he followed. No longer certain her news was good, she kept silent, busying herself with arranging the children's work for the day. He walked around the room and collected the mats, stacking them neatly in the corner, watching her every now and then until her nerves got the better of her and she started talking again.

"She asked Mr. Hall about David's character. She said she had a concern as he was showing an undue interest in her granddaughter."

Liam slouched against the classroom wall, dragging his hand down his face.

She stomped her foot, angry at him. He was spoiling it all. "Don't, Liam, please."

"Can ye get to the point quickly then, lass?"

"She didn't leave me with the impression she'd caused trouble for David. She said Mr. Hall spoke highly of his character, so much she was wondering if she should doubt his sincerity. But his testimony was verified by Mr. Sellers, who happened to walk in while she was there. They both told her that if she had any complaints about David, they were sure there must be a misunderstanding."

She looked at Liam, attempting to gauge his response. Surely he would understand now that Grandmother had not jeopardized David's position at the shop.

"Liam, she said she spoke to David when she first arrived. She didn't know who he was at the time, but they told her, Mr. Hall and Mr. Sellers, that is. She said, and I quote, that 'he was a man with presence, a man hard not to notice.' And she told me she could see the reason for my 'obsession.' My *grandmother* said this, Liam, I don't think you've any idea how remarkable that is."

Judging from his silence and the look in his eyes, he didn't think it remarkable at all. "Well, to get to the point, as you requested, the end result is I'm permitted to see him on a social basis, on the condition I also entertain the court-ship of others, others my father deems more suitable." She stopped and folded her hands, waiting for what he had to say.

"So . . . his master was questioned as to his character, and he's obliged to stand by while others court ye? This is what ye couldna wait to tell me?"

She sighed, dropping to her chair, head in her hands. His words had twisted everything.

"Is that how he'll see it, do you think, from your point of view?"

"Enlighten me, lass, what am I missing?"

"Well, we can spend time together, openly, for the first time in years. That means the world to me. I think he'll value that. I didn't know about that clause in his indenture." She picked up the stack of papers in front of her and flipped through them.

"And as for the others, my father's 'suitables'—they've always meant nothing to me. Spending time with them won't change that a bit. Except, of course, to make them more of a nuisance."

Drat it, this *was* good news, no matter what he thought. She rose, hands on her hips, and faced him, her eyes flashing.

"He has no cause to be concerned about them, none what-soever. Anymore than I have cause to worry about the girls

I know he sees while with you, true? And while I'm thinking about it, 'fraternization' doesn't seem so horrible a crime. Might his indenture also preclude frequenting taverns, drinking, and gambling?"

Liam burst out laughing. "Good God, lass, ye're too quick by half." He pushed himself from the wall and raised his hands in surrender as some of the children started to rush into the schoolroom. He said quietly, "Don't mind me, Lisbeth. Ye took me by surprise. Maybe ye should start with the last of it when ye tell him, though. I give ye fair warning he willna be obliging about the courtship of others. No man would." He put his hands on her shoulders and kissed her cheek.

"Mr. Brock kissed Miss Hale! I'm gonna tell David!"

"That's 'going to tell', no' 'gonna tell', Mr. Tell-Tale," Liam said, grabbling the boy and hanging him upside down by his feet, causing him and the others to dissolve into giggles. Turning the boy back on his feet, he announced, "I gotta work now."

"You mean 'have to work,' Mr. Brock," called out a little girl.

"Thank ye, Chrissy, yes I did. Women! Ye can never get a thing past them. Don't let anybody ever tell ye different, Thomas!" Liam said, tousling the boy's hair before he left the room.

DAVID RACED OUT of the printing office and ran toward the school, using the alleyways as a shortcut. He was late. The press had failed a couple hours ago, and he'd been delayed repairing it. The crew couldn't work without a press. Robert had been ill for two days, which left him. He probably should have stayed, in case it failed again, but he'd only be gone an hour. He'd return as soon as he visited with Elisabeth a while. He spotted her about a half block past the school.

"Elisabeth, wait!" he called out as he ran. Coming up beside her, he stopped, panting. "I'm sorry I'm late, Lisbeth, I had to take time to fix the press or half the crew wouldna be working this afternoon. I didna think it was that late, though. D'ye have to leave? Where's Polly?" He reached for the items she was carrying.

"I thought maybe you weren't coming. You did promise to be here early."

"I ken, lass, I'm sorry. It couldna be helped, truly. Can ye stay for a wee bit?"

"Yes," she said, and they walked back into the school, passing quietly through Rob's class.

"Are you hungry? John did go to some trouble to pack this," she said, taking the hamper from him, tossing the food haphazardly about her desk.

He eyed the food greedily. But best not dig in quite yet, something was wrong.

"Aye, but first, are you angry with me? Ye seem a bit. . . distant. Is there something ye need to tell me? Did something change due to Saturday night?" He sat on the corner of her desk and looked at her uncertainly.

"Oh, David." She came to him, reaching out a small, soft hand to touch his face, smooth the hair from his eyes. "No, no. Of course not. It's just . . . I was beginning to think maybe you didn't want to come today, due to my grandmother's visit."

Right then. Reassured, he reached for one of John's cold meat pies. "I've been waiting to talk to ye about that, Mr. Hall didna say a word after and I've been left to wonder why she came," he said, talking between bites.

Elisabeth turned away, walking to the door. "I hope her visit didn't cause you trouble with your employers. She left with a good impression of you. Mr. Hall was complimentary.

She's talked to my father, and they've agreed to allow us to see each other on a social basis."

"Bess! Why dinna ye say so at once? That's wonderful news." He put down the food and went to her, pulling her into his arms.

She put a hand on his chest. "Wait, there's a bit more." She walked away, her back to him as she said, "They've agreed—subject to the condition I no longer refuse the invitations of others."

He stiffened. The hell you say. "Nay."

"Nay? What the devil do you mean, nay?"

Rob's voice from the next classroom suddenly stilled. David circled her and shut the door.

"I mean 'no.' It's a simple enough word, lass."

She sucked in a breath and he watched, fascinated, as fury danced across her features. "How *dare* you! You're content to see me an hour a week in this classroom? And that's only if I merit the hour against all your other responsibilities, which more often than not, I don't? I'll have you know I'm not content! *I* find it trying to live this way. *I* find myself lonely a good deal of the time. *I* find that I miss you from one week to the next. *I* don't have the option of—"

"Ye might want to keep your voice down, lass," he interrupted, staring at her. Gone was the soft, feminine voice that marked her. He'd never seen her like this.

She pushed him into Liam's office and slammed shut the door. "*I* don't have the option of spending my free time carousing around this bloody town with my best friend, hoards of adoring men at my feet, secure in the knowledge that you're safe at home darning socks by the fire with your bloody *grandmother!*"

He couldn't help it; he knew he shouldn't, but he laughed.

"You think this is *funny?*"

"Nay, well, maybe. No, no of course not." Except for the

adoring men at her feet and darning socks part. He reached
out to touch her face; she was fuming. Her cheeks flushed
red and her eyes flashed fire. "God, you're beautiful."

Glaring at him, she slapped his hand hard before it reached
her, the sound echoing across the length of the nearly empty
room. "Don't you touch me," she said, spitting out the words
one by one. "You use that patronizing tone with me again
and I walk out that door."

That sobered him. He sat on the edge of Liam's desk.
"Aye," he said, nodding to show his attention. "What does
that mean then? Ye'll entertain the suit of those of your
father's choosing, those of a better sort than myself, I
assume?"

Her shoulders sagged as the fight went out of her, and she
turned from him. "Yes. I mean, I suppose that's the way my
father looks at it. I look at it as an annoyance, an inconve-
nience, but nonetheless a means to an end."

Just looking at her, he'd wager it'd be more than an annoyance. Not one of the knaves would be able to keep his hands
off her. "You're sixteen now, Bess. They'll be older still, no'
likely to settle for conversation at the end of the evening. I'm
to sit back, knowing that? That's what ye ask of me?"

"Precisely what are you implying?"

"That they don't care for you as I do. They willna be
content with your company alone. Ye'll be an irresistible conquest to them."

"Help me understand this, because I don't." She paced
back and forth, irritated once again, her voice rising with
each word. She raised a hand, her fingers counting out her
points. "First, do you think I would have no say in the matter? Second, last Saturday night, I happen to know where you
were and whom you were with. I'm assuming you don't care
for the unfortunate girl the way you care for me. Perhaps I'm
wrong, but you had just met her. Do I *also* assume, because

as you've just explained, this is just how things work, that you viewed her as a conquest, someone to prove to yourself you're a man? *That you ended the evening in her bed to show that you could, because you weren't content with her company alone?"*

David winced, staring at her, sure half the students had heard the last of that. Mr. O would have his arse for sure. How did she know where he was? Did she always know? She'd implied it from time to time, but he hadn't given it much credence. And she thought he'd bedded the girl? Could she really think that? When he'd been so wrought up with her and her debut? Hell, sometimes she ran circles around him. He couldn't keep up.

He always knew others would be courting her, that he'd have no say in the matter. Hell, he hadn't even offered for her, wasn't planning on it. But not now; he wasn't ready for it now. Maybe when his service was done, then he'd be ready. When he left Philadelphia.

Aye, and by then he'd have lost the opportunity of ever courting her. He wanted that, no matter what he might tell himself, he wanted it. It was past time. He studied his hands, picking at the ink that had dried around the cuticles.

There was the matter of his indenture, but he didn't foresee Mr. Hall holding him to the letter of the contract at this point in his service. Especially if it didn't interfere with his work, and of course he would see that it didn't . . . damn it all, how could she expect him to do this? Just the mere possibility of her kissing another made him want to throw the damn desk against the wall.

"Could you say something?"

She was still angry. Well, that made two of them.

"C'mere, lass, will ye please?" She did, and he pulled her close. Her face even with his, he placed his hands on either side, caressing her cheeks with his thumbs, kissing her forehead.

"I'm sure ye know well I was in no one's bed Saturday last. What I'm trying to say is, if I didna care for ye, I'd seek to bed ye. It would be all I could think of."

She closed her eyes, sighing, and pulled away. "Perhaps we should talk about this later. I don't find myself in a reasonable mood. You're only making me angrier by the minute, and I fear I'll say something I can't retract. And for God's sake, don't follow me! It will be embarrassing enough to walk through Rob's class."

And then she was gone. He flinched. The care she took in closing the door softly felt like a slap in the face.

Christ, he'd made a complete mess of that. That's not what he'd meant to say. Why on earth had he said any of that? He sank to the floor with his head in his hands, the press forgotten.

"DAVID."

Liam. David lifted his head and looked at him. Groaning, he dropped his head again. "You heard."

Liam slid down the wall to join him on the floor. "Aye, from Mr. Milne. Tell me."

Hell. Milne was the blacksmith two doors down on the opposite side of the street. He shut his eyes and exhaled a long, slow breath, then repeated the conversation as best he could.

"You didna really say that, did ye, Davey?"

"Which part?"

"The part where she didn't stir ye."

"I never said that!" He thought back. "Well, that's no' what I meant. I'm no' doing well at explaining it. It's just the thought of those knaves . . . hell, it makes me crazy, Liam. She makes me crazy. Why canna she just—" He stopped, not sure what he wanted from her.

Liam started laughing. David glared at him.

"My apologies, David. It's just that her mind . . . I love the way it works. She outdanced ye from the start; ye didna stand a chance. Think on it. I'll wager she didn't know anything about Agnes and Martha. She was just bluffing. But . . ."

"But?"

"Well, would you like it if she said she fancied ye, and therefore she had no interest in sharing your bed?"

"You know damn well what I meant. I don't mean to make her my whore. But good God, I awake to the thought of her most nights. It gets harder and harder to keep my hands off her. I canna imagine one of those shifting culls even making the effort to try."

Liam grinned. "Aye, but that's not what ye said, and if I know only one thing about women, it's that their vanity is fragile."

"Mayhap you're right." He ran his hands through his hair in frustration. "I swear, the lass still can addle my brain."

"Probably what keeps ye interested after all this time."

"Hmmph. Well, I've a press to attend to before I can explain she leaves me with a cockstand most of the time I'm with her." He grunted at Liam's expression. "Dinna fash, I've several hours to think on it. I'll manage a more poetic delivery by the time I see her. Truly."

He stood and walked to the door. "I'll drop off the ink I promised the lass then. Someone will be here, aye?" Liam nodded and followed him. She'd left without her hamper, the food still spread out on her desk. He picked up the pie he'd been eating and took another bite. "If Elisabeth will come on Sunday, can I count on you and Agnes accompanying us to the Schuylkill, for a boat ride and picnic?" He selected another of the meat pies and two of the sweet tarts, stuffing them into his pocket. "Take some of this food. Don't let it go to waste, aye?"

Liam bit into one. "Mmm, John does it up right, doesna

he?" He grabbed the last one before David could take it. "No' Agnes."

"No? Already?"

"I like her well enough. Just thinking of ye, mate. If Lisbeth wasna bluffing, aye?'

"Oh. Well, someone then?"

"Someone."

ELISABETH SAW HIM hesitate at the corner. She wasn't surprised he'd come. He wasn't a complete dolt after all.

She closed her eyes, reliving the shame of the afternoon. If word of the scene she'd made . . . if her father had even an inkling . . . furious was too tame a description of what his reaction would be.

She wouldn't be allowed to step foot in Mr. Oliver's Academy again, that was a given. What else he'd do to punish her, she wasn't sure. Countless times since coming home she'd gone over the names of those she knew were in Rob's classroom. She didn't think any of them were names she'd heard her father mention. But a scene like that would quickly make the gossip rounds, and if her father happened to be in the wrong place at the right time, he'd hear of it.

But then again, maybe no one had paid heed. Maybe Rob's lesson in physics had been so scintillating and spellbinding that he had had the full and undivided attention of his class.

"David?" He was so focused on the front door he hadn't looked her way.

Startled, he turned. "Bess, I've come to apologize." He came and sat next to her on the garden bench, glancing around.

"We're alone."

"I'm sorry, lass." He rearranged himself on the bench, his forearms on his thighs. Why, he was nervous.

"The thought of others touching ye; well it makes me

crazy. And I canna imagine they wouldna; touch ye, that is."
He looked up, his eyes meeting hers. "Honestly, I can't, given
how I ache for ye. Know that, Bess, you're the only one I
ever dream of, the only one I want to be with. It's been that
way since I first saw ye as a girl quayside in Bristol. I made a
mess of explaining it, and I apologize for that."

Well, why on earth hadn't he put it that way before? She
sighed, reaching for his hand. "I'm sorry as well. I was just
angry from the start I think. I know it won't be easy for
you. It's not easy for me." They sat in silence awhile, holding
hands.

"You noticed me in Bristol?"

He chuckled. "Ye know well I did. Ye turned when ye felt
my eyes on you."

"Oh, was that you?" She smiled at the look he gave her,
squeezing his hand. "I know. I did. I just wasn't sure you ever
remembered."

"Oh, aye, I remember well enough."

"I think I might have started falling in love with you right
then, when I looked back and you didn't look away."

"Bess?" He brought up his free hand to cover their hands,
his thumb stroking the back of hers. "'Fore, when we talked,
I encouraged ye to tell me everything. Don't now. It'll be
different. I can't . . . that is . . . well, I don't expect I would
care to hear any details of . . . I willna stray from this request.
Nor to see ye with—for God's sake, don't let it be Seamus."

"Who? Do you mean Amy's brother? Wherever would you
get an idea like that?" Before he could respond, she silenced
him with a kiss, tentatively touching his lips with the point
of her tongue. He brought her closer and kissed her back
eagerly, pulling his mouth away only when they heard the
clatter of kitchenware.

She moved out of his arms and stood. "There'll be nothing that bears repeating, David, I will promise you that now.

I should go in."

He stood as well. "Sunday next, if the weather promises to be fair, will ye accompany me on an outing to Gray's Ferry, for a wee picnic and boat ride? I can see we have others along, or ye can bring Polly."

"I'd be happy to accompany you. I shall look forward to it. Good night, David."

"Elisabeth?"

She turned, startled by the emotion in his voice.

"I didna think ye might be lonely, lass. I hope ye know I'd be there if ye'd be allowing it. Ye've only to ask."

Her eyes filled, and she managed a weak smile before she went inside.

40

June 1786

"YE HAVE WORK FOR SATURDAY?" David asked. He and Liam were sitting amongst a small stand of boulders, looking down over the harbor. He'd suggested the spot because he didn't want an audience. Mr. Oliver had asked him to intervene in a matter between Rob and Liam, a matter he wanted no part of, a matter he'd been delaying bringing up. Liam was bound to be explosive when he did, and if it had been any other than Mr. O doing the asking, he'd refused.

"Nay, it's scarce. Ye've only to look out there to see why, aye?" Liam threw his arm out, gesturing toward the harbor. "No' one ship from the West Indies, hasn't been in the last three weeks. No' one brig out there from anywhere at all, not one out of all of them."

Liam was right; the only ships in the harbor were the sloops and schooners that traveled up and down the Amer-

ican coast, trading state to state. International trade was at a
standstill. Congress didn't have the power to regulate it, and
the states weren't likely to grant it such. It was causing hardship to the artisans and laborers alike.

There was even talk amongst the print shops that the
wages of the journeymen would decrease from six dollars
a week to five and three quarters. David knew a group of
them, most of the journeymen in town as a matter of fact,
had met last night to issue some sort of demand to their
employers. He wondered if the journeymen had come to an
agreement, and what the masters would have to say about it.
Robert had declined to join them, telling David privately that
Hall and Sellers were fortunate to have obtained a lucrative
currency printing contract, and Sellers had already told him
his wages wouldn't decrease.

Six dollars a week; he could do a lot with that amount. But,
of course, he didn't have a family, and all the journeymen
he knew did. Nor did he have the worry of lodging, meals,
or clothing. He'd likely need more than six dollars a week to
marry someone like Lisbeth, whom he wasn't going to marry
anyway, so why did he keep speculating?

Best get on with it. Mr. Oliver had pulled him aside and
told him the lass Rob had been seeing from time to time was
with child. Rob was disowning it; Liam was furious.

"Liam, Mr. Oliver told me of the situation with Rob.
Don't—"

"I'm not having this conversation," Liam said, standing,
starting down the hill.

"What the . . .?" David stood. "Get your arse back up here
and sit down, 'fore I drag ye back! Ye be thinking I'm seeking
it, then?" He spat. "Think again."

Surprised, Liam backed up a step and sat, slowly, his eyes
never leaving David's face.

David walked the few steps that separated them, and

dropped down beside him. "Hell, Mr. Oliver is beside himself, what with the rift between the two of ye. You should at least talk to Rob about it."

"Oh, I have talked to him, David. He'll have no part in the child's future. He's made that clear enough."

"Aye, well, mayhap the bairn isna his to support. They're no' agreeable together."

"Be that as it may, he admits to bedding her. It's just as likely his as not."

"Ye'd have him wed her in spite of his aversion to her?"

"Mary's not a bad sort. Ye know her, David. And it's apparent he's able to overcome any 'aversion' to her when needs call."

"Nay, I've talked to him as well. He tupped her but once, when whisky clouded his judgment. It was a mistake; no' enough to base a lifetime on."

"There are women much more accommodating for a price, David; ye know that, as does he. He crossed the line, and this child may be his. His responsibility, not the Almshouse's. The bairn is deserving of a father, a family that can provide."

"I'm not arguing that point, only that it should be a father somewhat agreeable with being such." David shifted uncomfortably. "Liam, we have never talked of your father, and we don't need to be doing so now, if you're unwilling. But I'm trying to understand your thinking here." He held up a hand. "I concede from the start ye are far more knowledgeable than myself of the implications. But from where I sit, the lack of a father didna damage ye none. You're the most honorable, loyal, steadfast man I've the privilege of knowing. There's plenty with fathers who aren't fit to wipe your boots, and that's the truth of the matter.

Liam looked at him, his blue eyes wary. Standing, he turned away, watching the ferry below them make its way toward New Jersey.

"That's quite a speech, coming from ye, Davey."

"So mayhap ye should consider the possibility ye're wrong, especially as Mary doesna even want the lad."

"What?" Liam said, his hands forming fists. "Why no'? There's nothing wrong with Rob! She'd be damned lucky to have him!"

David fought a smile and shrugged. "Don't know if it's true or not, but I hear she chose Patrick Murphy and has named him the father. Patrick will be back from sea shortly; it's just as likely he'll choose her."

"How is it ye know of Patrick?"

"From Rob, as ye would, too, if you'd but talk to him. And Lisbeth said the lass confided in her that she never named Rob; her mother did."

"Hmmph."

Liam slid his hands in his pockets and paced back and forth in front of him. David stayed quiet. He'd said his piece.

"Do I need to warn ye against placing Elisabeth in such a state?" Liam asked, sitting back down.

He burst out laughing.

Liam smiled. "Aye, well, I've seen the way the lass looks at ye. A man can only be so strong, ken?"

"I'll manage, Liam. Ye needn't trouble yourself on that score, especially knowing if I didn't, her pa would likely marry her off tomorrow to another—with my child. I'll no' risk it. I make sure I'm never alone with her for more than a few moments."

"And what of the others who throw themselves at ye? There's been some fresh, agreeable lassies amongst them. Ye've had ample opportunity to take a flyer with any one of them."

"Speak for yourself. How did we go from condemning Rob to me? I missed the shift." David shook his head, smiling. "Ye know well I do nothing to encourage attentions from other than Elisabeth."

"Aye, and nothing to discourage them either."

"Only with the thought of helping ye out, Liam, that's all. Any 'other' is a friend of your lass of the moment. Don't be so ungrateful."

"Hmmph. The day hasna come that I need any help in that quarter. Should it ever, I give ye leave to bury me."

"Ease off. I've no intention of complicating my life by bedding any but one of the willing ladies that can be bought in Helltown."

"And best to keep that at a minimum, lest ye be bringing the pox to your marriage bed."

His brow furrowed as he looked over at Liam. "What the hell has gotten into ye? Are you my mother now?"

"Your ma talked to you of such things?" Liam asked, grinning.

A smile flickered over his face. "Nay, she didna. She would have passed that task along to Da." He paused, considering. "Have ye the clap, Liam?"

"No. Benjamin believes he does, though."

"Oh." David sat lost in thought. He had to admit that if he'd thought of the risk at all, it was only as some remote possibility. But Benjamin . . . Beni was a dockhand they'd met early on, and they'd spent many a night carousing with him as he'd guided them through the darker side of Philly. Maybe the time had come to give up that distraction, while he was ahead.

"Don't think too hard on this, I already have. The blowen that tipped him the burner works the ship yard. I've questioned him. We've ne'er been with her." He kicked at some pebbles, watching as they scattered down the hill. "I'm thinking armour might be a bargain at the price."

David scowled at him. Liam knew well his position on the use of condoms. "Or mayhap a widow."

"Is that so? Care to elaborate?"

David shrugged. "I suppose it makes no difference at this point." He drew up his knees, setting his forearms atop them. "The summer afore we sailed, my da sent me to set up wood for the winter for Mrs. Surley."

"She's your widow?"

"No' mine!"

"My apologies. Go on."

"Well, she had lost her husband the spring past and didna have any children to help her with chores."

"And a strapping, braw lad shows up on her doorstep, offering to lend a hand—"

"Do ye want tae hear this or no'?"

Liam made a quick motion of sewing up his lips, then held up his palms.

"I kept busy for the first few days with the chopping, her watching me all the while. Didna know if she thought I was taking off with her axe or what." He picked up a rock, began doodling in the dirt with its point. "When I finished, I asked did she need anything else, polite like, ken?"

Liam nodded, his bright eyes dancing with mirth, his mouth clamped shut.

"She, uh . . . well, uh . . . seems she felt she was lacking more than a bin full of wood and was fairly hungry for what she was lacking, I 'spose."

At this Liam couldn't contain himself and exploded in laughter. "And Davey . . . good sort that his is . . . felt obliged to oblige." He managed to choke out the words between snorts, slapping his knees in appreciation of his own wit.

David looked at him and grinned. "It wasna a hardship," he said, sending Liam off into fresh rounds of cackling.

"I wondered if my Da knew which way the wind blew, and that's why he sent me instead of going himself. She'd asked for him." Now that he thought of it again, he was sure of it. Da would have figured it would keep him occupied, away from the village lassies, and Ma need be none the wiser.

Liam struggled to still so he could talk. "Ha! Fortunate for ye, I say." He wiped his eyes with the back of his hand. "She was your first?"

"Aye, to both."

Liam chuckled. "Well, we canna all be so fortunate. Alex promised to bring a stash of condoms when next he arrives from London. Without taxes, the cost shouldna be too dear, and he willna mark them up for his trouble, since it's us. Think of it as an investment in your future. Why, a careful lad like you, you could make one or two last a year. Shall I say ye have a color preference for the ribbon?" he asked, grinning.

David grimaced. "The Kirk doesna condone the use of armour."

"And it condones rogering thy neighbor's wife? Why, ye are a veritable fountain of knowledge today."

"Widow."

"Ahh, a fine distinction, to be sure. Now see, I hadna known that. Leave it to the Kirk."

David laughed. "Right then. I'll speak to Alex next he comes." Maybe. Or maybe he'd just do as he should and stay away from the whores. He stood and stretched. "We should go."

Liam stood, and they climbed down from the rocks. "David? It seems I was wrong, far too quick to judge something that was none of my business to begin with. And Rob's a good friend. I would have suffered to have my poor judgment result in the loss. Sometimes I . . ." Liam stopped him at the bottom of the hill, hand on his shoulder, as he struggled with the words.

David looked at him, put his arm around his shoulders, and propelled him up the street. "Liam, tis no' necessary.

Come, let's gather Rob and settle in at the Man. I developed a fair thirst talking to ye."

"Ye did use more than your daily allotment of words."

"Hmmph." He changed the subject. "Have ye any word from Sean?"

"Not since the letter I told you of last. Mr. Oliver is talking of making a trip there next summer, if we still havena heard more."

"And ye'll go with him, I'll wager." David said. "I envy ye the freedom of that."

"You have your whole life ahead of you, young man, don't rush—" Liam said, his voice and stance parodying a stately matron.

"Shut up, will ye?" David interrupted. "You're fair full of homilies today. I scarcely recognize ye."

41

"WAIT, ELISABETH," DAVID SAID. "THE man is rarely here. I want ye to try this." He placed a hand on her elbow, drawing her back to the market stand they'd just passed.

"*Zwei*," he said, turning to the vendor.

"All, Mr. David?" the man asked. He scooped two pieces from his barrel and dipped them into a thick, brown liquid before sprinkling them with chopped nuts. Wrapping them, he then handed the meal to David, sticky and dripping with sauce.

"Aye, Mr. Henkel, *Danke. Ich werde zurückkehren.*" He moved away from the stall and handed Elisabeth a piece.

She wrinkled her nose. "No, thank you. John will scold me if I eat out again. You eat the both of them. What is it?"

"Fish."

"It certainly looks to be more than fish. David, what do you know of Liam's family?"

He held up a finger until he finished his mouthful. Breaking off a small piece of the second, he said, "Just that his mother died shortly before he crossed. Why?"

"Margaret was inquiring about his parents and I realized I didn't know, that he never talks about his family. I'm surprised you don't know more. Haven't you ever asked him about them? Uggh . . . no . . ." Her mouth open, he had stuffed it with food.

"Nay, from what Rob told me, years ago, I gathered it was a thing he preferred not to talk about. And ye shouldna either. Your mouth is full. Ye can nod, though, if ye like it."

"What did Rob tell you?" She passed her finger across her mouth, delicately cleaning off the sauce that lingered. "That's delicious. Can I have the rest of mine before you finish it?"

He gave her the remaining bite and wiped his hands down his breeches. "Lisbeth, I'm not comfortable discussing this, especially to satisfy the curiosity of a lass he hasn't shared the details with himself."

"He's your best friend, David. I find it hard to believe you're not curious yourself."

"One way or another, it's no' my business. Liam knows I'll listen should he choose to talk about it, I see no reason to press on the subject."

"Have you considered he might think you're not interested enough to even ask?"

That argument briefly gave him pause, then he dismissed it. "No, he doesna think that. And I don't have a need to know his private business, not until he shares it."

"Rubbish. You just don't want to talk to *me* about it. Do you know why Rob limps?"

Confused at the change in subject, he just looked at her, waiting. No doubt there was more meaning to the question.

"He was trapped in a stall with a frightened horse when he was four years old. He was kicked and stepped on for three minutes before they found him. Both of his arms were broken, a rib was cracked, and his foot was shattered beyond repair—ruined. He's been nervous around horses since, understandably reluctant to follow in the family farrier trade. His family had no use for him, apprenticed him to a chimney sweep when he was seven. Can you imagine, a mind like Rob's? Mr. Oliver snapped him up at nine, bought out his indenture, took him home."

David blinked. "He told ye all that?" He led her into the park, pausing at the water pump to rinse his hands.

"I asked him, he told me."

"Ye asked him why he was lame?" He squinted, looking at her, incredulous.

"Of course not, David. I asked how he injured his foot, how he came to know Mr. Oliver."

David exhaled slowly. There was a point here, and he imagined it had to do with Liam's parentage. He looked around to assure himself of their privacy, then reached for her, bringing her back against him, brushing the loose tendrils of hair off the back of her neck.

"Liam's no' so quick to share, lass," he whispered, holding her close. "He's told me nothing. And I did ask." He bent and kissed her neck behind her ear. "Once." He lifted his head and moved to face her. "Now I lost interest in this conversation moments ago, even knowing that you, like most women, are still burning to know. Ye're plotting when next tae catch me unawares and bring the conversation back round to your advantage. This, in spite of the fact that this park is fair deserted at this hour, and in spite of the prospect of spending our minutes in a more pleasing manner. Which is all I'm thinking of at this moment."

"Well, that just shows what you know. I'm only wondering how long you're going to talk about it before you kiss me properly."

He laughed out loud, then bent to kiss her properly. The

scent of the roses lining the pathway rose to mingle with hers, filling his senses, dizzying in their sweetness. He pulled back before he slipped under her spell and forgot the park was nary a block from her home.

"I have something to tell you," she said. She grabbed his hand and pulled him along the pathway.

"Oh? Did it require softening me with a kiss?" He was teasing, but when she didn't answer, he stopped, turning her to face him. "Lisbeth?"

"Let's keep walking." She pulled him forward. "First, though, I wanted to thank you for helping Polly last Saturday."

He tensed, wondering how much Polly had said about the incident, if she had mentioned the whorehouse, how lushey he'd been. "What did she tell ye?"

"That you ran off those men who were bothering her. Was Liam there as well? I'd hate to think you confronted them on your own, David. She said there were three of them. They might have been armed, you know."

Polly'd had words with her companion and had set off through Helltown alone, well after midnight. He'd seen her when she passed by, as had the other three lads who were standing about. It'd occurred to the men when they'd spotted her that they had no need of waiting, nor of paying. They weren't a bad sort, though; it hadn't taken much to convince them otherwise. A good thing, because Liam'd been occupied and might no' have come to his aid in a timely fashion.

"He was close by. Dinna fash, they saw reason fair quick. They'd just mistaken Polly for another sort of lassie. Now, what were ye to tell me of?"

"I'm going to teach again for Mr. Oliver."

"What do ye mean? Ye've no need to do that. Your studies have ended."

"I want to do it. He's agreed to keep me on."

"But . . . well . . . it's no' seemly, Elisabeth. Your family—ye don't—"

"Yes?"

He recognized the tone and backed down. He didn't need to point out to her that women of her class didn't work. She knew that as well as he did.

"Your father? He's agreed to allow ye to work?"

"I love it, David. It makes me feel useful. Can we leave it at that for now? Be happy for me?" She squeezed his arm and smiled at him.

His brought his free hand up to cover hers, returning her smile. Best not to comment further. Any of his thoughts would surely make her angry. Besides, she obviously had Mr. O on her side. He did notice, though, that she hadn't mentioned her father's acquiescence.

"I've also decided to teach Polly to read. She can't afford to go to school, and I've the time."

"She asked ye?"

"Well, no. But I volunteered. My summers drag by, you see, and she seemed to like the idea. She's certainly bright enough, though I think she may be just a little embarrassed. If I'm able to teach her, I was thinking of doing the same for other adults who haven't had a chance."

"It appears ye've been doing a lot of thinking."

"And what do you mean by that?"

"Don't get your dander up. Just making conversation." Reaching down, he plucked one of the wildflowers clustered in bunches about the park, choosing one to match the bits of indigo in her eyes, simply for the pleasure of watching her face light up at the gesture. He wasn't disappointed. He touched her cheek.

"Sometimes, lass, sometimes it's hard to place ye."

42

"WHERE IN THE HELL HAVE ye been, David? It doesn't take that long to get oil. Next door, now, go and wait for me," Robert said, jabbing his finger in the direction of his home, his black eyes snapping with fury.

"Robert? What . . .?"

"Now, damn ye! God in heaven, do what I tell ye *when* I tell ye, before I kick your arse all the way there!"

David turned and went down the steps, thinking irreverently that the man's slight frame would have a hard time kicking his arse anywhere. He hadn't a clue what he'd done to make him so angry.

"YE HAVE ANY IDEA who showed up at the shop today, David? Any idea?" Robert paced short, quick lengths in front of him, his hands flying about as he punctuated his sentences.

"No, sir."

"Don't be so damn polite. We gave you every leeway, every consideration, on account of your family. And this is how you repay it?" His hands went up alongside his head, holding it tightly in frustration. "God Almighty."

"It might help if ye tell me who showed, Robert."

"Shut up. I didn't ask you to talk, did I?" He grabbed a bottle of whisky from the shelf and poured himself a cupful. "You're goddamn lucky Hall wasn't there today. That's all I have to say. I'm goddamn lucky Hall wasn't there today." Slamming the bottle down, he started up his pacing again. "Damn it to hell and back, what am I going to tell John?"

His uncle? Why?

Robert looked at him, his eyes narrowing. "Well, don't you have anything to say for yourself?"

David grinned. He couldn't help it. It was better than pissing his boots.

"Impertinent rascal." Robert let loose a long breath and fell heavily into a chair, his anger spent for the moment, motioning David to take another. "Ye know of the Guardians of the Overseers of the Poor, David?"

David nodded, confused at the change in subject. "Of course, but first—can ye tell me why ye're so angry with me? 'Fore we talk politics? What do ye be needing to tell Uncle John?"

Robert grunted. He reached round to grab another cup, filled it with whisky, pushed it across the table to David. "They came for you, David."

"Huh? Why? I don't need any help. Why would they come for me?"

"You know a Sarah Wallace?"

"Aye," he answered, drawing the word out slowly, warily. "Is she the one requiring help?"

"You could say that." He took a piece of paper from his pocket and handed it to David.

David took it gingerly, looking at Robert.

"Go on now, read it," Robert said, waving the back of his

hand at him.

He opened it, read it quickly, looked up at Robert, then read it again, his face white as the blood drained from his head. "It's no' true, Robert, it's no' true," he managed to whisper, shaking his head.

"She says it is. That's all they need. Dammit, David, you *know* the terms of your indenture!" Robert stood, his anger hot again, kicking the few toys that littered the room out of his way. "I told ye to be discreet. Ye call this discreet?" He waved his arm abstractly at the window, then came to David, placing his hands on the table in front of him, leaning in to make his point. "Don't ye have sense enough to fuck a lass who's not going to turn ye in? What the hell were you thinking?"

He was thinking he'd need to fix Robbie's wooden horse before he got home. It had lost a rail when Robert kicked it. He was too numb to think anything else.

"Hall's not going to keep ye. Your uncle, he'll be blaming me. God knows this wouldn't have happened under his roof."

Hall's not going to keep him? He roused his mind, trying to throw off the shock of it. He looked at the whisky in front of him, picked up the cup, and breathed it in, then took a sip, letting the brew linger on his tongue, hoping the sting of it would wake him, help him focus.

An impending obligation of child support. The Guardians didn't have any legal authority, but they did have the ear of the legal system, and Sarah had sworn her child was his. His. My God . . . Lisbeth. He upended the dram and finished it.

"What happens now, Robert?"

"That's all ye have to say?" He sighed and sat, his anger gone. "They'll issue a warrant, to make the obligation legal and binding."

"Can they do that? I have nothing, Robert. You're saying

I'll no' even have a trade."

"Aye, they can."

This was the city's way of transferring the financial obligation of a bastard child from the state to the man responsible. He supposed it was fair. As long as the lass in question wasn't lying. And Sarah was lying. He hadn't seen her since Annie's wedding, that one fraction of an hour months ago. He hadn't touched her since the *Industry*, that one fraction of a minute years ago.

"I'll tell ye again, Robert, then I'll let it rest. It's no' true, it's no' possible. I have no carnal knowledge of Sarah, never have. She's a troubled lass. She's been dealt a hard hand, but all the same I'll no' go easy taking responsibility for this child. It's no' mine, I've no kind feelings for the lass. No' after this, anyway."

Robert looked at him, his hawk-like eyes taking his measure. Eventually he grunted, his eyes turning soft, and his shoulders slumped as he relaxed back into the chair.

"Well then, ye'll have to convince her she's better off without ye."

He'd been trying to do that for years, with much less at stake.

"When will Mr. Hall learn of it? Do I leave today?"

"No." Robert turned the cup in his hands round and round. "Maybe I was being hasty. I believe ye; chances are he will too. Aye, I was being hasty."

"Is this public knowledge then?" Lisbeth.

"Aye, to those who care to know. You'll be jailed until they have your bond."

Jailed. He tamped the panic down quick, before it overwhelmed him. "Have I no say with the law?"

"Talk to her. It has to come from her. Ye haven't a chance in hell in court. Ye'll likely just walk away with a fine for fornication, for your trouble." He held up his hand as David opened his mouth. "Don't bother, I'm sure it's a fine well earned, if not with this lass, then with another. Talk to her. Do it before they come back for ye."

The heels of his feet drummed the floor as he picked up the paper again, looking for her name, her address. "Do ye know where this is?" he asked, pushing the paper back toward Robert. "Looks like the Northern Liberties, but I thought she lived in Southwark."

Robert picked it up. "Aye, the Northern Liberties. Hell-town. Go tonight. It's Friday. They won't be back with the law until Monday."

IT WAS PAST DARK by the time he found the street, an hour more by the time he had found a boy who knew of the Wallaces and was willing to point out the shanty where they lived.

He stood in the open doorway; the door was hanging cockeyed on one hinge. "Mr. Wallace? Sarah?" he called into the shack. Nobody. He stepped back to the street.

"Are ye sure this is the house, lad? Looks empty. Ye'll no' be getting the penny less ye lead me to her."

"She's not there anymore. She done gone. I ain't to find her, that ain't what you said. The house, you said, and this is it," the boy said, his face scrunched up at the injustice of the bargain.

David curbed the impulse to shake the boy. He was so thin, he'd likely do damage.

"Very well then, do you know where she went?" he asked patiently.

The boy nodded, holding out his hand. David dug into his pocket, brought out a penny. "Where, lad?"

"Gimme the penny first."

"No, tell me first. Tell me the truth. Ye can join me for supper."

"I ain't joining you for nothing! Ma will skin me for sure, just for talking to you. They took her to the almshouse, on account of the baby."

"The baby? She has the baby now?"

"Don't know 'bout now. She's gonna soon, though. And they ain't got no food, Ma says."

"Where's her da?"

"Don't know. Now give me my money like you said."

David handed over the coin and went back into the house, using his feet to feel about the floor in the dark, searching for something that would tell him if Wallace slept here. Some rags in the corner, some empty whisky bottles, nothing else. There was no moonlight as yet, and he hadn't thought to grab his tinder box before coming. No way he was going to see a thing. He thought briefly of waiting, but at this hour, Wallace would show up lushed, if he showed at all, and there'd be no talking to him. He'd come back tomorrow, before dark. Or go to the almshouse. Or both.

He swore. Not more than five hours ago he'd had a future, a life he understood, Elisabeth—all of it in jeopardy now. He wanted nothing more than whisky and a whore to lose himself in.

But instead he went straight back to the print shop, not willing to jeopardize the gift of Robert's support.

Besides, he'd be needing the coins for a bond and child support. Christ.

"WHEN YE GOING TO be ready to talk?" Liam asked. "I'm getting weary of answering myself."

"That'll be the day." David sat on the riverbank, cleaning the fish they had caught. He wanted to talk, he did; he was fair screaming with the need to talk. But who knew what Liam would do? What if he went and married the lass, just to save him? He wouldn't put it past him. Tomorrow was

Monday, though, and he was no closer to solving this on his own than he'd been on Friday.

"Liam?"

Liam looked up from the fire, handing him the first fish that was ready. "It's still mighty hot. Grab this end of the stick. Now tell me."

"I want your word first. Your word, Liam, that ye'll do nothing to fix this without my say-so. Your word on our friendship."

Liam looked at him, warily. "Tell me first."

"Nay." He started eating the salmon. "It's undercooked."

"The hell it is. It's cooked just perfect. Why canna ye just tell me, Davey?"

David said nothing, grabbing the next fish as it came off the fire. He hadn't eaten anything yesterday; his appetite gone with the thought of his dilemma. Now it was back, in spite of the dilemma.

"All right, ye have my word."

"That you'll do nothing without my say-so. Say it."

"I'll do nothing without your say-so."

"Swear it. On our friendship."

"Jesus." He rocked back on his heels, then looked up at David. "Right then, I swear it on our friendship." He reached out and gripped the hand David had extended.

"Sarah's gone to the Guardians, says I fathered her unborn baby. They came to Robert Friday. The sheriff will likely show with a warrant tomorrow."

Liam just looked at him. "Get on with ye, Davey. Here I thought ye were serious."

"I am. I think they'll take me to jail tomorrow if I don't have a bond. Sometimes it takes days to get a bond, Liam."

"Sarah Wallace?" Liam asked, wrinkling his nose. He was having trouble grasping the situation.

"Aye."

"Ye didna . . . did ye? No, of course ye didn't." Liam looked at him for confirmation.

"No, of course I didn't. Doesna matter, though. It only matters what she says. And I can't find her, to make her take it back." He told Liam of the visits to Helltown, and of the visit to the Almshouse last night. "She wasna on the books. Else she just got there, and they couldn't find her name just yet. They told me to come back tomorrow. Watch that fish; you're burning it now."

Liam looked down, cursing. He took it off and set it aside, starting with a fresh one. "Ye're no' going to jail, ye'll be crawling the walls. I'll get ye a bond. Jesus, David, how'd ye get in a mess like this?"

"I'm done asking myself that, just wondering now how I'm gonna get out of it."

"And still have Elisabeth."

David grimaced. "Aye, and still have Elisabeth."

"Can ye make her take it back?"

"What do ye think?"

"How 'bout ye pray? That must work sometime, given its reputation, no?"

David didn't respond. He went to the river and washed his hands, splashing water over his face.

"Sorry. I can help, if ye let me. Let me talk to her, aye?"

"She'll be wanting someone, Liam. She needs someone. Her da's no help."

"I know."

David caught the look in Liam's eyes before he turned back to the fire. "It willna be you, Liam."

"Jealous?"

"It willna be you."

"Jesus, Davey. I have to do something!"

"Will ye get a bond? Act as my surety? I dinna fancy spending time in a cell."

"Aye, ye'll have it Monday morning."

43

"FOR THE LAST TIME, BOY, sit. They ain't springing ya tonight; they'd done already been here. Sheriff's done gone home, deputy ain't gonna do nothing even if yer friend does show. Best just be making yourself comfortable like the rest of us. Ol' Bertram of there, he's been three weeks awaiting."

How had 'ol' Bertram' stayed sane? He ignored the man, continued his pacing, two steps forward, two steps back. It was a cage, not a cell. How the hell could he be expected to pay the damn child support, locked up without work? He'd been better off running. Where in the hell was Liam?

The sheriff had shown up at the shop not long after dawn, surprising Robert and David both with his diligence. "What's got you up in a lather, Sheriff? The lad's not even had his breakfast," Robert had said.

"Guardians been after me since the warrant was signed."

"Doesn't seem like you'd be agreeable to having a bunch of busybodies pulling your chain."

"Boy's lucky I was feeling like relaxing a spell. Someone's

pulling their chain on this one, I suspect. Girl's father more likely than not. Do I need to restrain him?"

"Nay!" David had said, speaking up for the first time. "No, sir. I'm coming with you freely. Ye don't need restraints." He had reached into his breeches pocket for the small bag of coins he readied earlier, handing it to Robert, pulling his hand back quickly before the others noted its shaking.

"Robert, Liam comes, ye give him that, aye?"

"Aye. Don't fret, lad. You'll be back at the shop before noon," Robert had said, opening the door for them. "He'll have a bond this morning, Sheriff."

"Don't count on it, Robert. Like I said, someone's pulling their chain on this one. Everything's going to have to be in order before he's out."

And that was the last he'd seen of Robert. And he hadn't heard from Liam. The longer this took, the more chance Elisabeth would hear of it.

Ten hours and counting.

"WHERE WERE YOU ALL day, Liam?"

"Why are ye here, Elisabeth? I wasna expecting ye till next week."

She looked at him, arching a brow at his tone. "I'm preparing for next week. It's easier here than at home. I didn't think you'd mind. And several parents have stopped by with the semester payments. I didn't know what to do; Rob and Mr. Oliver were out as well. Are you quite all right?"

She watched him carefully. He was nervous, dancing on the balls of his feet, his eyes bright with worry, his mouth set in a grim line as he looked at her.

"Is it David?" David hadn't stopped by Saturday. He'd seen John in the market that morning and had asked him to tell her he had to break their plans for that night, and that he'd try to come by Sunday. He hadn't explained why, and he

hadn't come Sunday. She'd been disappointed, though not
worried. Not until now, that is; not until she saw the worry
in Liam.

"Why'd ye ask me that?" He ran his long fingers back
through his hair, creating an untidy mess as it came loose
from the cue. Hurrying past her and to his office, he turned
at the door to ask, "Did ye take the money or tell them to
come back?"

"You're certainly in ill humor today. I took the money as it
seemed they both thought they had an appointment with you
this afternoon. I thought they might consider it an inconve-
nience to have to come back. I wrote out receipts for them
and for you. The money and receipts are on your desk; I'm
sure you'll find it all accounted for." She picked up her bonnet, tying it on as she followed him into his office. "If it's
not an imposition, could you tell Mr. Oliver I could wait no
longer; I'll be back to see him tomorrow?"

"What d'ye need him for?"

"Liam!" She studied him. "He wanted to go over the curriculum, if it's all the same to you. He's purchased a new
primer." She stood quietly as he counted the money, placing
it in the small leather bag he used for banking. He compared
the receipts to his ledger and made a notation, ignoring her
all the while.

"Good day, Liam. Get some rest." He didn't respond,
didn't stop her as she turned to leave, his mind already elsewhere. She hesitated several times on her way out, standing
on the steps a few moments before she finally started down
the street toward home.

She went in the back door. "Hello, John. Do we have anything cool to drink?"

"Sure do, miss. I'll get it for you soon as I get this in the
pot."

"No, I'll get it." She took a glass from the table and

uncorked the bottle he'd motioned to.

"John, when you saw David in the Market Saturday, was he well?" She watched as his eyes shifted away, and he muttered something inaudible. "Tell me what you know, John, please."

"I don't know nothing I can tell you miss. Your Daddy, he done got home early. He's in his study. I expect he's looking for your company."

"He is? Well, that's a treat. I'll head in there to sit for a spell." She picked up her drink and started out the door. "Don't think I didn't notice your choice of words, John."

She found her father reading in his study. "Hello, Papa, it's good to see you home early." She kissed his cheek. "I've been at the Academy, preparing for next week. A new term starts, you know."

"Hmmm." He looked up from his paper. "I'm glad you're home, I wanted to talk to you." He folded the paper and set it on the desk. "Elisabeth, come Sunday, we're going to attend the Anglican service with Grandmother."

"What?" She was puzzled by the topic. "As well as Mass, Papa?"

"No, in lieu of Mass."

"But—"

"Being Catholic puts us in the minority, even more so than we were back home. Unfortunately it's sometimes a despised minority. It's become a constant battle for me to maintain my business relationships. This is one area I can easily rectify. I would have done so long ago, back when your Grandfather made the change, before you were even born, were it not for Abigail."

Her mother had been a devout Catholic. She had thought the same of her father. He noticed her hesitation.

"In deference to your mother, I won't object if you still wish to worship at St. Joseph's, Beth."

"No, I . . . " She searched for the words. "You just took

me by surprise, Papa. Of course I want to be with you and Grandmother for worship. I mean, that is, well—I'm willing to try it." Maybe.

"Good, then. That's settled."

Oh no, nothing was settled. No, no. She understood nothing.

44

"DAVEY?"

Rouse yourself, man, get up. Can't. Don't. Don't feel, don't think, don't feel, don't think . . .

"Davey, listen to me then, aye? I'm trying. I am, truly. Robert's trying, Mr. Hall's trying, Mr. O's trying. I don't know why; there's some obstacle to your bond. Hell, look at me, will ye? I need ye to release me from my promise, David. Ye need to. Pay attention, man."

Silence. Don't think, don't feel, don't think, don't feel, don't . . .

"Ne'er mind, I'm sorry. Drink this. Later then, aye? I'm setting it here then, for when ye want it, it'll help. Will ye take this? It's in your pocket then, Davey, a coin for a dram, aye?"

Don't think, don't feel, don't think, don't feel, don't . . .

Did he dream it, or was Liam here?

WEDNESDAY AFTERNOON HAD passed, his usual time off, and still she'd no word from David. Today was

Thursday, and she had tired of waiting.

"Go on home, Polly. I'm sure Liam's just been delayed talking with someone. You know well how he tends to go on. I'll have him walk me home."

"Are you sure, Miss? He may not have 'membered? I can wait with you." Polly looked around the empty rooms, her mouth puckering in concern.

"Don't be silly. I know you have things to do. Truly, Polly, I'll be fine."

Once Polly left, she ran up the stairs, all thoughts of respecting the men's privacy secondary to her own need to know. There had to be a reason as to why she hadn't seen David in over a week, and Liam knew that reason. Some hint was bound to have been left out and about.

Hmm. One main room, a small room in back, presumably where they slept. She walked to it. One bed. Did they all sleep in this tiny room? She searched; rifling through papers, opening books, picking up kitchenware and turning it over, rummaging through clothes, lifting the mattress, looking under the table and chairs . . . it didn't take long.

There was nothing—no slips of paper, nothing.

Well then, she'd wait. She'd wait days if necessary. She chose the rocker in the corner, sat down, and lay back her head.

"LIAM? WHY ARE you undressing? Don't!"

She must have fallen asleep. The room was dim now, lit only with a candle and a small fire. "Why did you start a fire, for heaven's sake?"

"Lisbeth?" Startled, he jumped, knocking himself off balance as he was taking off his breeches, landing heavily on the floor. "Christ, ye scared the bejesus out of me. What are ye doing up here? Turn your head, will ye? I need to change my clothes." He threw his breeches toward the fire and stood, drawing on another pair.

"Don't throw them in the fireplace! What's the matter with you? For heaven's sake, I wouldn't think you had money to burn." She stood, hurrying over to the pile. "Jane can launder them, if you haven't the wherewithal." She folded the discarded clothes neatly, turning her head as he'd asked, risking a brief look out of the corner of her eye, as of course anyone would.

"Nay," he said, taking them from her.

She looked at him, her glance lingering. Mary Jane had gone on and on about the man's chest. It appeared she wasn't so silly after all. Gone was the thin boy she remembered from the *Industry*. She hadn't realized. Though, of course, there was no reason why she should. She dragged her eyes away and looked down.

"Liam!" She turned to the fire and shook her hands vigorously over the flames. "You need to take more care with the taverns you frequent." She ran her hands briskly down her sleeves and shook her skirts. "I declare your clothes were carrying vermin!"

"I'll take that under advisement," he said drily, tossing the pile into the fireplace.

"Put your shirt on."

The impish grin that had been absent for days showed life once again. "Dinna trust yourself alone with me then, lass?" he asked, "Ye can put your hands on me, should ye be curious. I willna mind."

What would he do if she did? How deep did his loyalty run?

"Don't be ridiculous. I've been waiting for you. Now that you're here, you're going to tell me what you know of David's whereabouts."

The grin disappeared. "I've only seen him once this whole week, Lisbeth. He's been busy with some crisis or another.

He couldn't spare me even a word." He turned away, dismissing her as he reached for his shirt.

She picked up the nearest object, a pewter mug, and threw it hard against the wall. Startled, he looked back at her, watching her warily.

"Damn you. You certainly know more than that, and I want to know what you know. Bloody hell, I'm not stupid. I know something is wrong. Don't you understand how worried I am?"

"Of course I do, lass. Just let him handle it, though. It'll resolve itself. Ye know he doesna like ye fretting."

She gritted her teeth and reached up to tuck back her hair. "Don't treat me like this, Liam. I don't deserve it. I don't! I care just as much for him as you do, more I'd venture to say. Tell me." With an effort she relaxed her stance. "Please?"

Taking her hands, he stood before her, shirt in place. "If it were up to me, I'd tell ye everything. You're canny enough, no need to stoke the fire and leave ye wondering. But it's no' up to me lass. Trust me, aye?"

"Nay!" she said, throwing off his hands, throwing back his words. She ran down the stairs. She'd find out without his help. She'd go to the print shop, talk to his master, his indenture be damned.

Bloody hell again, it was dark outside. She called up the stairs. "You're to walk me home, Liam, it's late. And don't you dare say a word to me on the way. We're no longer friends."

SHE SET OUT FOR the market early Friday morning, avoiding everyone as she left the house. No one would worry; they'd think she was at the Academy, preparing for Monday. She chose a stall across the street from the print shop and busied herself with the produce, hoping she'd soon see the boy Johnny out and about running errands. She had only a few coins with her. There was only so long she could linger at the stand before the vendor shooed her along.

Drat, it was Robert who stepped out. He certainly would be of no help, though that did mean there should only be apprentices left in the shop. She'd just need to adjust her plans slightly. She hurried across the street and into the office, taking care the bell at the door didn't ring. Carefully, she lifted the countertop, stealing behind for a quick look into the shop. Someone tall and wide, brown hair tied back in a cue, stood at the press with his back to her. But it wasn't David; it was Ian. She had forgotten about Ian, but fortunately he hadn't even looked up over the noise of the press. She motioned one of the younger boys forward, the one standing behind Ian, looking toward the door.

The boy came out, and she put her arm around his shoulders, guiding him around the counter, pressing a penny in his hand. "What's your name, young man?"

"Tommy. What's the penny for, miss?"

"Tommy, can you tell me if Mr. Hall is available?"

"He's out."

"Do you know when he's likely to come in? I'd like to speak to him."

"I'm not sure. Can I help you, miss? Or I can get Ian," he said. "He'll help ye, seeing as how Robert's not here."

She stopped him with a hand on his shoulder. "No, that's all right. I'm sure you can help, come to think of it." She smiled at him, watching as he relaxed. "Do you know where I might find David Graham?"

"Aye, he's in the jailhouse."

She blinked. "Pardon me, did you say he was in jail?"

The boy nodded, eager to be the bearer of such shocking news. "Since they came and got him Monday. He was supposed to come right back, but he hasn't."

"But why? Did he owe money? Is he in debt?"

"Naw, Davey's tighter 'an a tick. It's on account of the bastard."

"Tommy! Where'd ye get to, boy? Oh. Elisabeth." Ian avoided her eyes. "Get on in back now, Tommy."

"Why's he in jail, Ian?"

"I don't know the particulars, 'cept there's a problem with the bond."

"Tommy seems to know the particulars. What bastard? What does he mean?"

"Don't know. The boy's one to listen to gossip. Never gets the story straight, who done what with who, you know the type. Listen, Elisabeth, I have to get back to the press."

"Of course," she said, her jaw clinched tight. "Thank you ever so kindly for your help." She made certain the door slammed on her way out.

THREE HOURS LATER she stood in front of the jail clerk for the second time that morning, hot, tired, and seething. Perspiration soaked through her gown, her bodice now a dark green in contrast with the light green of the skirt. She vowed she'd not be held accountable for her actions if one more man thought to leer at her, lie to her, evade her questions, or patronize her.

And she was no closer to knowing the details than she'd been this morning. She was, however, no longer certain she wanted him out.

The man behind the counter hadn't looked up at her, for he was preoccupied, his hand picking through his scalp, presumably searching for nits. She waited, her only sign of impatience hidden as her foot tapped a silent rhythm beneath her skirts on the dirty, straw-covered floor. As he pulled his fingers through the limp, greasy strands hanging loose to his shoulders, she discreetly backed up a step, safely out of range lest his search was successful. She managed a smile when he looked up at her.

"Here's the bond you requested, Mr. . . . Pryer, you said your name was Pryer, didn't you? Did you know it's much easier, Mr. Pryer, to go straight to the bondsman on Third? They couldn't do a thing for me at the almshouse. Well, no matter, it's done now. I trust this will suffice. Can you tell me when he'll be released?"

The clerk broke open the seal and opened the bond, comparing it closely to notations in his ledger book. "Ah, there's some particulars 'bout this here bond. Let me get my supervisor."

She closed her eyes and counted slowly to ten. Now was not the time to lose her temper; truly, it wasn't.

The supervisor came back and went through the same motions. He looked up at her.

"What did you say your name was miss?"

She smiled her sweetest smile, gratified to see the man soften a bit. "I didn't say, sir. I'm Miss Hale."

"Hale ? " He looked back down at the book, then took the bond and made notations in his journal. "He'll be released within the hour, Miss Hale. You should go and come back then. I hate to have you waiting in a place like this." He left, leaving her alone with the junior clerk.

"Sir . . . Mr. Pryer, might I trouble you for one more thing?" She smiled, reaching over to lay her hand softly on his. She had to—she had to know, never mind the filth the man carried. "What are the charges again? I know you've already explained, Mr. Pryer, but it's been quite a morning, and I just can't keep all these things in my head as well as you can."

"The Overseers of the Poor are charging the boy with child support."

"Thank you. I knew you had said something like that." She tilted her head, frowning. "Who did you say the woman was, the one who brought the charges against him?" She watched him as he looked back at the ledger, then as he opened the bond.

"Says here Wallace, Sarah Wallace."

She clutched the countertop, her knees giving way. She mustn't faint, not here. "Thank you, Mr. Pryer, you've been ever so helpful," she said softly.

She wouldn't fall apart, not just yet anyway. She had one more stop before she allowed herself that luxury.

SHE STORMED INTO the townhouse, heading toward the sound of the voices coming from Liam's office.

"—canna help him escape. Be reasonable, Liam. Mr. Oliver's gonna bring her here. He'll fix it. They'll drop the charges."

"Ye didn't see him, Rob. Huddled on the floor, crawling with vermin. He's mixed in with the lowest scum, no more 'an a square foot to call his own. The things the others were doing in there, Jesus; *I* had to turn my head! *Me!* God-fearing lad like Davey; he canna stay there. He can't. I have to do some—"

Rob held up his hand, stopping Liam midsentence as Elisabeth filled the doorway.

"I've posted the bond, they've accepted it. He'll be released within the hour. Liam, from this point forward, you and I have a professional relationship only. I trust you'll respect that and you'll remember it come Monday. You are no longer my friend. I ask that you inform David that his calls are no longer welcome, and I'm instructing Tom to turn him away should he show at my door. And if you mean to allow him in the Academy during the time I'm teaching, I will walk out of the classroom with no intention of returning. Do consider this warning my fair notice. Now, do I make myself perfectly clear?"

"Lisbeth, lass—"

"I certainly hope so. I'd hate for there to be a misunder-standing on your part. Good day, Rob."

As she left, she could hear Liam telling Rob, "She'll come 'round. Hurry, now—"

Men were such fools. It would be a cold day in hell before she'd forgive a betrayal such as this.

45

HE WORKED; IT WAS WHAT he had left.

He had tried three times that first fortnight to see her; the first two he was turned away by Tom, the man's face expressionless, his eyes expressing regret; the third time by Hale himself, the man's face expressionless, his eyes expressing glee. He scheduled his errands in the market hoping to see her, planning to linger at a time and place where he might. His forethought rewarded, he'd seen her earlier this week, tried to talk to her . . . tried. She had threatened to call out for the Sheriff, the look on her face giving truth that it wasn't a threat made idly. He let her be.

And so he worked. And there was plenty of work to be had. The northern states were in revolt again, and copy was coming in hourly, keeping him busy at the case full time. And when Hall refused to allow him to labor over the Sabbath, he found plenty of others without such scruples, plenty of masters willing to pay day wages for Sundays.

The mood of the country was tense, to match his own. The northern rebels, farmers the most of them, had had their fill of high taxes. Making their living by and large through bartering, they hadn't enough cash to pay the sums, and the amount levied continued to rise. Debtor's prison and foreclosures were the result, and they'd had enough of both. When Congress refused to fund any federal troops to resist the rebels, the states found themselves on their own. David set the copy as fast as it came in, though he scarcely digested the words. It just got him through the days.

Perhaps Liam had been right, perhaps he should have told her everything from the start. But he had expected to talk to Sarah, to convince her to drop the charges, to tell the truth, forestalling the need to rile Elisabeth about any of it. He hadn't expected the spin things had taken, to be left in jail for days. He hadn't expected his best friend to turn on an oath, to bring the wench into his own home. And he hadn't expected Lisbeth to be the one to finally release him, to find out the whole ugly truth of it the way she had. Truth be, he hadn't called any of it right.

So he worked. It was what he had left.

"LISBETH, YE'VE IGNORED the papers I set on your desk for four days running now. Take them, lass."

"They didn't look as if they pertained to Academy business. What are they?" As if she hadn't recognized David's handwriting immediately or noticed his distinctive seal, as if she hadn't reached for the letter a thousand times since Monday.

"Davey left them. The one is money for the bond, to repay ye; the other is a letter from him. He's asked me twice have ye read it."

"I've no interest in either. Are you ready to go, Polly? Good day, Liam."

"It's been over a month now, lass, don't keep on. Polly, here." He thrust the documents into Polly's hand.

"Leave the money, Polly. Burn the letter as soon as we reach home."

"Lisbeth, how can he explain if ye willna listen?"

"I quite expect you're right. It's a pity no one had reasoned that out earlier, isn't it?" She walked out; he followed.

"Is that what you're still angry over? That ye didna know? Mayhap ye should consider he was avoiding this reaction, aye?"

She turned on him quick, her eyes flashing fire. "Bloody hell, don't you dare presume to turn this back on me," she said through clenched teeth. "Don't you dare! You, you . . . wretch."

He reached for her. "Just read it, 'fore ye burn it. What's the harm in that?"

They both looked up the stairs at the same time, at the sound of a baby crying. Yanking her arm from his grasp, she reached for the letter Polly held in her hands, ripping it to shreds, wishing it had the weight of stones as she threw the pieces in his face. "Good day, Liam."

Halfway down the street, Polly spoke up hesitantly. "You wants I should find you some good bad words to use, miss?"

"That would be splendid, Polly. I'm certain I'll still have occasion to bring them forth."

She had gone to the almshouse a week after she'd given the bond, unable to sleep at the thought of Sarah living in a place like that, at the thought of David's baby living in a place like that. She hadn't any idea of the conditions previous to that first visit, had never given the place a second thought, period. She had brought food, blankets, and money, thinking to leave them anonymously for Sarah's use, only to find out that Sarah and the child were no longer there. She had been bound out to a man by the name of Mr. Oliver.

How cozy for them all.

46

SARAH HUMMED TUNELESSLY AS SHE cleaned up the last of the meal, wiping down the table so Mr. Oliver would have a spot to lay out his books. "I'm grateful for the help, Liam. The chores Mr. Oliver gives me, they're not much for me to offer in return." Pulling off her apron, she walked over to the cradle and retrieved the baby, taking him to the corner rocker, settling in to nurse.

"I'm no' complaining. It's my chores ye're doing." Liam glanced up from the book he was reading, watching her.

"Well then, maybe you could be friendlier. I could be friendlier, if you'd like." Her glance lingered on him as she loosened her bodice.

"Don't, Sarah. Jesus." He looked away. "What ye did was wrong."

"So? I had no choice!" Her pink mouth puckered in a pretty pout. "Besides, Charles will pay him back, just as soon as he returns."

He set aside the book, exasperated. Going to the window, he looked out over the street, watching the lamplighter go from lamp to lamp as the day slowly faded. "Where'd he sail to, China? He should have been back long before now. Regardless, it doesna excuse ye from naming David."

Her face closed, and she looked down at the baby, her red, chapped hand caressing his head as she pulled him closer, whispering cooing sounds as he whimpered against his mother's unrest.

"Who beat ye, lass? If it was this Charles, ye don't need his help, ever. Will ye never learn? And where's your da? He keeps changing lodgings. Seems I'm always a step behind."

Startled, she looked up. "What?" Her eyes widened. "Don't look for him! Why would you do that? How could you? Da mustn't know I'm here. You'll be sorry if he does, Liam, you will."

"Is that it? You're afraid of him then? Is he the one landed ye in the almshouse, bruised and broken? Ye shoulda gone to David before it came to all this."

"Ha."

"Aye, maybe no' David."

"If it weren't for her I could have. Her and that sotted ship. If I hadn't been tossing my oats day after day, I could have held his eye. I could have. She wouldn't have had a chance to take him, not if I'd been feeling myself."

"Ye're a lovely lass, I'll no' argue the point."

"I don't need David," she said stubbornly. "That was Da's choice to name him, not mine."

"Right then. Why not Annie? Ye must have some friends. I would have helped ye, lass, truly I would've, if I'd have known. Ye canna expect me to be happy the ways thing are now. Ye cost me the favor of my mate."

"I have no one. And Mr. Oliver bought my services, don't forget. I'm not here on my own free will."

"Oh? Didna ye just profess to be grateful no' more than five minutes past?" He moved from the window and went to the fireplace, rearranging the logs, stealing a look at her as he did, seeing the tears spill silently as she coddled the bairn.

Christ. "Don't cry, Sarah," he said, sighing. "I'm sorry. I'm sure Charles will be back soon enough and everything will be fine. And Mr. Oliver will release ye just as soon as ye're back on your feet and can take in mending again, ye know you're not bound here in truth."

And Davey would forgive. And Lisbeth wouldn't.

She sniffed. "I can't talk to her, Liam. I know well you want me to, but I can't. She looks down her nose whenever she catches a glimpse of me."

"Only as she's taller than ye. Wait 'til she's sitting, then talk to her."

Sarah giggled, wiping her eyes on her sleeve. The baby protested, waving a small arm in the air until she petted him, cooing until he was quiet again. Liam went to her and looked at him, running his fingers down the back of the baby's head.

How had she thought to get away with naming Davey the father?

47

"DAVID?"

"Aye, Mr. Hall?" He looked up from under the platen.

"Can you fix it?"

"Think so. Just a bit loose here again. Shouldna need any parts."

"Good, they're getting harder to come by. Listen, Mr. Oliver came by earlier."

David grunted, turning back to the bolt.

"David, Mr. Hall's talking to ye, give him your attention, aye?" Robert said.

"Aye," David answered sullenly. He came out from under the press and stood in front of Hall, brushing the loose dirt from his shirt. "He told ye I havena shown up for tutoring, I'm guessing."

"He did. I'll admit it surprised me."

"Mr. Hall, how can I?" David said. "He's bought the wench out, has her and the bairn living there, for Christ's sake."

"David," Robert warned.

"Sorry, Mr. Hall, but truly, d'ye blame me?"

"I want you there starting Monday. You need to put this behind you."

David stood openmouthed, watching him as he left. He turned to Robert. "He canna be serious, Robert! I'll swing for murder, should I have to sit in the same room with the baggage."

"Bring your own candle. Offer to light up the downstairs."

"Ye think this is funny, then? Can ye be giving me an advance on my pay, so as I can afford to buy tallow? I've four years and ten months before the bairn can be indentured, and I'm free of support, I'll wager ye can't.

"I've written your uncle."

"You didn't! God Almighty!" He threw the wrench across the room, barely missing Robert's galley. He started pacing. "Why'd ye have to go and do that, Robert?"

"You topple that case, boy, you'll be more than sorry." Robert walked over to confirm his metal hadn't been disturbed, then turned back to David. "I haven't posted it; I've only written it. I don't like the changes in you, David. I never expected you'd be one to turn bitter the first hard knock life throws your way. Granted, it's an uncommonly unpleasant knock. But you're not even fighting back. You haven't reasoned with her, and you've stopped seeing your friends. You're simply content to sit back and blame the world. To bask in your self-righteous self-pity. It's a waste. Maybe John can talk some sense into you."

"Don't mail it. I'm entitled to a month or two of anger, aye?" He reached down to pick up the wrench, looking at Robert. "Not yet, aye?"

"I'll wait a fortnight. Believe me, I don't want to worry him if there's no cause."

HE KEPT AN eye out the front window as he manned

the counter the next day, watching and waiting for John Black. He'd show within the hour at Mr. Hank's produce stand. There wasn't a reason he wouldn't; he had for years.

There, he'd come. He called back to Ian, let him know he needed to step out for a second.

"David! Where you been, boy? I—"

"Take it, John, please," David interrupted, holding out a letter. "You're my last hope in reaching the lass. Just lay it in her room while she's out and about, so as she doesna need to acknowledge to any she's read it. She willna know ye were the one left it. Please?"

John looked at the letter as if it were a live animal and at David's fingers as if they were teeth to snap off the tips of his own, should he reach for it. David leaned over and tucked the letter in his shirt.

"There," he said, patting John's shirt. "Ye didna even take a letter from me. All ye know is ye came across something with the lass's name on it, needs to be delivered."

"There's talk, David. Talk that—" John began, his hand going to his shirt.

"I'm sure there's talk aplenty, John," David interrupted. "I'm on a tight string right now, though, aye? I just have been watching for ye. I have to get back to the shop." He crossed the street and opened the door to the printing office before John could return the letter.

"You be at the wharves come Sunday, boy, I wants to talk to you," John called after him.

"Get the letter to her for me, will ye, John?" He raised his hand in parting before he closed the door.

DAVID QUICKENED HIS step, more to keep warm than out of any wish to reach his destination. Well past dark, a damp fog lay heavy and a cold wind whistled up the empty street, carrying the salty scent of the river as it bent the flames in the lamps and rattled the signs on their chains. He lowered his head against the sting of it.

He couldn't believe Hall was requiring him to go to Mr. O's. The man was daft if he thought he'd get any learning done, completely daft. As he opened the door to the tavern, the familiar smells and sounds assaulted him, and he rolled his shoulders defensively, shrugging off memories of life before his self-imposed isolation. He stood by the door a moment as his eyes adjusted, then headed to the bar. Nodding to the bartender, he took a seat.

"Haven't seen you in awhile, David. How you been getting along?" the bartender asked, setting a large pewter mug in front of him, filled to the brim with ale.

"Just fine, Will." Sweet, someone in town who hadn't heard. He glanced about, spotting him in the far corner at the same time he glanced up, then watching him as he laid down his hand and said something to the fellow next to him. Turning his own eyes back to his drink, he waited until Liam filled the empty stool beside him.

"You send Oliver after me?"

"I didna," Liam answered, his eyes studying David. "He's been known to do a thing or two on his own, he thinks it needs doing."

David didn't respond. He was inclined to gulp down the ale, but he only had the coins for the one, and he thought he might stay awhile; the fiddle in the corner, the shouts from the men gaming, the laughter from the group of couples watching the fellow dancing a haphazard jig, the clink of the bottles as the bartender plied his trade, all of it pulled at him, and he found he didn't want to shove back anymore. He looked at Liam.

"Such as?"

"Ye know Mr. O. He's apt to pick up any stray what needs a helping hand."

He grimaced. "Such as you." And Rob. Even him.

"Aye, such as me," Liam agreed.

"I don't care to go to the townhouse, Liam."

"Ye need to. Ye need to talk to her. Ye were all fired up to 'fore; what set ye off from it?" When David didn't answer, he went on. "Ne'er mind, ye still need to. Just know she's one with a stubborn streak, thinks ye think her lower than dirt."

David shrugged. He did.

"David, she just wants to be treated as someone who matters, no different than the rest of us. She was wrong, and I'm guessing she'll own up to it, should ye talk to her like she was a person, no' a roach. It's your Christian duty, aye?" He crossed his forearms and raised them to the ceiling, as if warding off punishment from the heavens for speaking out of turn.

David smiled slightly and studied his drink, turning the mug round and round in his hands, busying himself tracing the valleys of the many dents marring the surface of the well-used pewter. He'd pushed back at Liam, largely ignoring him the times he'd come to the print shop for him. It occurred to him, and not for the first time, that Liam, for all his irreverence, was a better Christian than he'd ever be. What would the Kirk have to say about that?

MONDAY NIGHT CAME, and he went. Not the first Monday, though, but the Monday before Robert's deadline. He had a stubborn streak himself.

"David, good, you're here," Mr. Oliver said, opening the door wide. "You've got some catching up to do. Come upstairs; I'm loaning you a book I want you to read. For the first few weeks our discussions, and your essays will be based on the principles of . . . ."

David didn't hear the rest as he followed Mr. Oliver up the stairs. All his concentration was focused on controlling the anger that threatened to overtake his reason with each step that put him closer to her and that baby.

"Sit, sit. Liam? He's here, come in now. Liam's joining us for this. He hasn't studied these readings yet."

David watched as Liam came in from the other room, followed by Sarah. Snug. He swallowed and sat on the bench, placing the book Mr. Oliver had handed him on the tabletop in front of him.

"Davey!" Liam gripped his shoulder and dropped down next to him. Mr. Oliver settled in across. Sarah busied herself by the fire, he busied himself with opening the book, curling his hands around the cover in tight fists. Not his book, take care. He relaxed his fingers.

Did Mr. O truly not notice the tension vibrating round the room, bouncing from one wall to the next, from the ceiling to the floor, now circling round the table faster and faster until its vortex threatened to engulf him if he just sat there?

"Would you like some tea, David?"

He bit his lower lip as she set a cup in front of him without waiting for an answer and another in front of Mr. O.

"Liam?"

"Nay, thank ye, lass."

"Mr. Oliver? Mayhap I should just read this chapter first, then come back better prepared, aye?" David asked, rising from the table.

"Of course not, David. Sit down. We're only skimming at this point."

He sat. His knees moved in a silent rhythm under the table, as his legs bounced up off the balls of his feet. He tugged at his collar, turning to Liam. "Can ye open the window?"

Liam got up to comply.

"But the . . ." Sarah started, then stopped.

David's eyes followed as she went to the corner, hovering over a cradle as she adjusted the blankets. "Ne'er mind,

Liam, just sit. Let's get on with it." He focused on the page in front of him, doing his best to come up with an appropriate question for Mr. Oliver, so that they could begin, and then end.

And it got easier. By the following week, having been there twice already, he could look her in the face, albeit quickly, and not even flinch when she walked to that cradle.

48

ELISABETH HURRIED INTO HER NIGHT-CLOTHES, kissing Polly's cheek and bidding her good night quickly, anxious to burrow under her bedcoverings. It had been a tiring day; she had known it would be from the moment her students filed into the room, one after the other asking if she knew it was snowing, had she seen the first snowflakes, did she think they would stick.

She had lost their attention before she'd even had a chance to gain it, their thoughts only on getting their fathers to pull out the sleds, to ready the skates, to find their mittens. Handwriting drills and vowels had no chance competing with the first snowfall of the season. She'd been grateful when Mr. Oliver decided on an early dismissal.

She saw it as soon as she turned down the bed, glancing back quickly to assure herself Polly hadn't seen it as well. She wasn't sure she had the willpower to leave it sealed, untouched and unread . . . she missed him so.

She could read it, then burn it, with no one the wiser that her resolve was faltering, that she was ready to forgive, that she was ready to beg forgiveness for not understanding that men will be men, for not turning a blind eye as Polly had hinted she might, as so many women did.

No! She wouldn't read it. She was certainly stronger than that, and certainly worth more care and respect than he had given her.

She picked up the letter and took it to the fireplace. Kneeling, she placed it on the hearth just in front of the embers. Maybe it would catch, maybe it wouldn't; fate could decide. Going back to the bed, she climbed in, leaning over to blow out her candle. She lay back and clamped her eyes shut tightly, calling to mind the snowstorm, the rising price of ink, the increasing scarcity of paper . . .

The fire snapped as a spark flew up from the embers.

"No!" She raced from the bed to the hearth, berating herself for putting the letter in danger. Picking it up, she carefully wiped away all traces of soot and broke the seal. She knew the stationery; she remembered choosing it for him last spring. She sank to the floor and read by the fading light of the remaining embers.

Dearest Bess,

If you don't read this through before destroying it, I'll understand. It's likely no less than I would do, should the situation be reversed, should I think you betrayed me.

I have not had carnal knowledge of Sarah Wallace, Bess, never. Not on the Industry before you and I met, not after, not in Philadelphia—never. I freely admit to a brief caress, well before I first kissed you, but that is all.

I know not why she made the charges, I have not spoken to her, have not seen her since the time I ran across her and her father in the market last spring. I can only tell you the whole of it came as a complete shock, and I have felt myself spinning out of control since.

I love you, Bess, more than I can express, more than I had guessed.

The hole in my life without you is deep and frightening. My thoughtlessness in leaving you without knowledge was inexcusable. My only defense is that my mind was reeling. After the thought 'why?,' my only thought was of you, if you'd believe her, if you'd believe me.

I'm deeply sorry for what you must have endured whilst obtaining the bond for my release. How angry you must have been, how brave, as you went from place to place and accomplished what others couldn't. Robert avers you are remarkable, I agree; you are the most remarkable woman I know. My heart swells with admiration.

I'll not press, for I know I've hurt you. If I have to accept I've lost your love, I will, given time. Losing your society; that I'll struggle with. I'm writing to beg that you don't turn when you see me, that you don't avoid where you think I might be. You are my dearest friend. I don't think I can accept that loss.

All my love and more, now and forever.

Yours, David

Tears falling freely, she folded the page carefully, carrying it back to bed with her, clutching it tightly as she lay still on her back, her eyes fixed on the ceiling. Was it any wonder she was lost?

49

December 1786

"WHERE ARE YE going? Where's Mr. O?" David said, his gaze flying around the empty room as he reached the top of the stairs and Liam hurried past him, trotting down the steps.

"Back in a flash, Davey. Stay here and watch the fire, will ye?"

"No . . . Liam!" He turned back to the room when he heard the front door slam. Damn the man; he knew he was uncomfortable here.

Something smelled good. He walked over to the hearth and saw they were roasting a turkey.

"They were all so glad you accepted the invitation to supper, David. One might think you was royalty."

Sarah. He sighed, turning.

"Aye, I can see that," he said, his arm circling the empty room. "Good evening, Sarah." He studied her. She didn't

look well in the full light. She looked years older than when
he'd seen her last spring, her skin yellow about her eyes and
mouth, her hair brittle like straw.

"That's at my bidding. I didn't want an audience, see." She
went to the table and poured him a glass of wine, brought
it over to where he stood by the fire. She frowned at his
expression. "Take it. I wouldn't be poisoning a prime source
of support, would I now? You needn't be so bloody chary."

He scowled and circled her, taking the glass and setting it
on the table, stepping toward the staircase. "Tell the lads I'll
be back in a bit, will ye?"

"No!" She hurried after him, grabbing his arm before he
started down. "I'm sorry. You always get me back up. Stay;
I've some things need saying." She tugged.

"Stand off, Sarah."

She dropped her hands at the ice in his voice and stepped
back quickly, her eyes round.

"Stop that," he said, moving back into the room. "Jesus, ye
think I'd raise a hand to ye?"

She didn't respond, and he went to the table, picking up
the glass he had left, taking a slow sip. She watched him
warily. Her bodice was wet; wet with milk, her breasts full.
He looked away.

"Are ye having some yourself, then?"

"No," she said, giving him a wide berth as she circled back
to the fire to check the meat. "It was one of Mr. Oliver's
conditions, were I to stay."

He nodded and sat, waiting.

"Would you like to see him?"

"Nay," he said, shifting uncomfortably on the bench, his
eyes fixed on the glass in front of him. He had avoided all
contact with the bairn so far. But he should ask her *why* now;
he should look up at her and ask her why.

She sat opposite him and pulled a small bag from the folds

of her skirt, placing it on the table. "This is yours. Take it."

He looked at it, then up at her, careful to keep all expression from his face.

"Charlie's back. I don't need your support, you see. He was at sea when my father saw the baby was coming. Someone had to pay; Da chose you. I couldn't do a thing about that. No matter what you're thinking, I couldn't. And after the baby came, well then I was too frightened to stop it. I had to protect my baby, don't you see? The Guardians, they would have nabbed him, Da would have let 'em."

His mouth watered at the smell of the turkey roasting; he wondered what else was coming with the meal, if that's where Liam had gone, to get extra for the table.

"David? Did you hear me?" She reached out a hand, then pulled it back. "They would have taken my baby David, bound him out, if I couldn't show a means of support for him. I couldn't let them take my baby, he's all I have."

"What about . . ." What had she called the man, the sailor? "What about the sailor?"

She shrugged. "He'll stay, for awhile anyway. Charlie's the baby's father, I think. What matters is that he thinks he is."

"Why couldna your da name him, then? Why me, Sarah?" He got up and walked to the window, looked out into the street, wished he were anywhere but where he was. "I've never been—" He stopped, on unsteady ground, unsure of her commitment in taking it all back, sure she'd be quick to take offense at anything he might say in anger or recrimination. "Will ye be all right, Sarah? With Charlie?"

She snorted, getting up to turn the meat a quarter turn. "I'm back on my feet, don't you see? I don't need him, if I decide I don't want him. I'm about healed up. I can take in mending; I may even decide to take a position of wet nurse. Plenty of rich nancies without enough of what I've got in abundance." She caressed her bosom, glancing at him to see if he appreciated her ampleness. He looked away and her voice hardened. "I've been taking care of myself long enough. I just lost track of things for a while at the end, Da took advantage."

She refilled his glass and went to the work table to cut the greens she'd laid out. "Liam went to fetch Charlie to come for supper. You're to be civil now, aye?" She turned to him, the knife she held flashing as it caught the light of the fire. "The money's from him. He plans to change over your bond first thing come Monday next. Doesn't want you named the father of what's his, so he says." She turned back to the greens. "Are you ever going to say anything?"

He had, hadn't he, asked after the sailor, asked her why? He never knew what Sarah wanted of him, hadn't from the start. He was afraid to trust the stillness that had settled over him, the calmness that was slowly pooling its way down to the soles of his feet, the tips of his fingers; he'd grown so accustomed to living with the spinning sensation that had accompanied the news of the Guardians' visit months ago. He heard the baby mewing in the corner and went to it, feeling her eyes on him as he did, recalling the knife she held.

He reached into the crib with his hand, letting the bairn grab his finger and pull. Strong, healthy little fellow, he thought, looking at the baby, a laugh starting from somewhere deep inside him. It startled the child, the laugh, and he clutched David's finger tighter, his little hand bobbing up and down. David dropped to the floor beside the cradle, back against the wall, doubling over as he laughed until he cried, the baby still clutching his finger, pulling it to his tiny mouth, sucking on it with a strength that surprised him. God Almighty, what a fool he'd been.

50

February 1787

"PULL!"

David stood at the press, content, pulling the lever over and over with a single-mindedness and rhythm that had the copies flying.

The new year was here, and the presses were humming. Once again, it looked as if neighbors would be slaughtering neighbors. The rebels in the north hadn't backed down. Two thousand men, farmers most of them, had organized and marched to Springfield, Massachusetts, with the aim to take over the arsenal there. Having few weapons of their own, they reasoned they'd need arms if they were to be a force to be reckoned with. The newspapers were calling it Shays' Rebellion.

"Pull!"

Lisbeth had softened her stance, still not ready to have him back, but at least she talked to him, though it was with caution. It was more than he'd expected, more than she did with Liam. Although Liam had reported that she had greeted him 'good morning' Friday last, before she remembered she wasn't speaking to him. He smiled, Liam had taken the brunt of her anger.

Sarah had left, gone off with her Negro man, her mulatto bairn. Left without thanking Mr. O, left without talking to Elisabeth. Mr. O had just shrugged, saying something about the Lord giving each of us choices, and one couldn't make the choices of others. He wasn't one to argue with that. Sarah and her man had taken care of releasing his bond before they took off; thankfully that was done before she'd started in with the bottle again.

"Pull!"

The masters were all up in a lather about the coming summer, certain the presses would be printing from before dawn to well past dusk. Congress had called for a Convention to be held in Philadelphia, to look into the 'embarrassment of our national affairs.' The Articles of Confederation had to be adjusted. If they weren't, not many held out hope for the nation to survive. Most thought it too dear to lose, but it wasn't a given the delegates would show.

"Ease up, lad, we're out of paper."

He looked up as Ian drew off the last sheet. "We done then?"

"Aye, think so. You ready for supper?" Ian asked.

"Past ready."

"David? Get on up here, will ye?" Robert called from the front.

"Coming, Robert," he said, hanging up his apron.

Ian grinned. "What'd you do now?"

"I'm past ever speculating on that again," he said, sighing. He picked up a rag for his hands and walked up front.

He stopped still. "Elisabeth." Why was she here?

She arched a brow and reached down, lifting a sled. "You won't skate with me. I've come to see if you would ride a sled?"

He came out from behind the counter, taking the sled from her hands and setting it down. He looked closely at her, taking in the set of her mouth, the look in her eyes. He glanced down at her hands, relieved to find they were at her side, relieved she wasn't mangling a defenseless bit of cloth. He looked back up, letting the question show in his eyes.

She smiled then. She smiled the smile that turned his world sideways, set his heart soaring, sent his blood racing. Picking her up, he covered her mouth with his and kissed her; kissed her until she stopped her half-hearted struggles against him at the sound of Ian's hoots of encouragement and Robert's discreet coughs of warning, kissed her until the room spun and he could no longer recall the months without her, kissed her until he wanted too much more and he had to stop before he took. She pulled away then, laughing, protesting that he must put her down, for he left her quite breathless and don't think she hadn't noticed he hadn't answered her question.

Would he ride a sled, indeed. He'd marry the lass with the Pope presiding if it meant he'd never lose her again.

51

April 1787

"WITHOUT MONEY, WE'VE NO TEETH, Davey. The Brits and the Spaniards have locked off our trade to the west, we've no' the might to stop them. Sean writes that, without the river, western Pennsylvania will ne'er prosper. They're doomed."

"Aye," David said. Liam was in a mood. There was nothing for it but to listen.

Shays' rebels had been defeated, but the political impact of the rebellion was immense. The Declaration of Independence was little more than ten years past, and the nation was dissolving into bitter political factions. To some, it had never had a chance, without a national currency or a united military force. Taxes, trade, the distribution of political power—none of it had been handled fairly.

Liam continued his rant. "We need roads, and where's the money for that, I ask ye?" He stood and paced, gesturing angrily toward the east. "And then there's the damn black-

mailing, blood-sucking pirates." He threw up his hands in a
display of exasperation. "So the Barbary States have seized
our ships and our men. What can we do but ask them,
politely mind ye," he said, pointing a finger at David, "to
give 'em back? I'm no' saying we should give in to the Muslim whoresons' blackmail, no' at all. But we could fight them,
should we have money for a navy, that is. We're weak, and the
whole world knows it. Thumbing their collective noses at the
grand experiment."

David raised his brows, fighting back a grin. "Muslim
whoresons? Just remember ye said it, no' I."

"Are ye questioning a bye-blow's use of the term, then?
And who better to use it, I ask?"

"No!" David said quickly. "No, no' at all. I didna even
think of that. Just the slur against the Muslims. Ye generally
don't slander a man's religion."

"It's nothing to do with religion. I couldna care less who
they call God or how they go about it, but you know what
the envoy from Tripoli told, nay threatened, Mr. Adams.
We need a treaty with them cause we're at war. No one
declared war, mind ye. We're at war just by virtue of trading
in the Mediterranean without paying the price of a treaty."
He stopped for a moment, shaking his head in disgust, the
illogic of the position giving him pause. "'In a war between
Christians, the prisoners are treated with humanity, but a war
between Muslim and Christian, well, it could be horrible.'
Tell me now, Davey, what kind of a man would *say* something like that? He's the one framed it in terms of religion."
He started his pacing again.

"But I can call them . . . what d'ye think of Barbarian
whoresons? That suit ye?"

"It's apt." They were both worried about Alex. They'd
had news it was likely he was in the Mediterranean when an
American merchant ship and its crew had been seized, so it

was possible he was now enslaved by the pirates. Most of Europe had paid tribute to the Barbary States of Morocco, Algiers, Tunis, and Tripoli, just so they could sail unmolested through the Barbary waters and trade with Africa. But the Americans had not paid. And, to make it worse, they were no longer under British protection.

"Liam, I think there are better than even odds Alex hasna been captured. The British are playing up the affair, to make us rue throwing off the crown. That's what Sellers says anyway, and he's lots of connections with the press in London. We may have had ten ships in the Mediterranean, ken, and if it's true only one has been captured of late, well then, Alex is likely on his way home, aye? And no one wants the Union to go down. I don't think so anyway. I've got a lot of hope in the Convention they've called. Shays' trouble, it's turning the tide, I think. The states are realizing they need a strong national front. They'll meet next month, and this time with a quorum, I'm sure of it."

"I hope ye're right. No' only that they meet, but that they manage to do something worthwhile while they're at it. It'll likely be too late for Alex, though, if he's captured. Pray for him, aye, Davey?"

"I do, each night."

Liam grunted. There was nothing for it, so David switched the subject. "I'm to go out of town Friday, pick up paper from the mill. They shorted our last delivery. Want to come?"

"Can't. I hired on for three days. I was lucky to get the work. Take Lisbeth."

"She's coming, just thought you'd like to get out of town, as well. It's hellish hot, and it's only April."

"Ye'll get no argument from me there. Let's walk a ways up the river, aye? Go swimming before dark."

DAVID SLID OUT FROM under the wagon and dusted

himself off. Wheels looked good. He harnessed the horse, running his hands along the leather and whispering to the beast as he did. All in order, now where was Lisbeth? He paced a bit, debating how long he should wait. Maybe her father had changed her plans for her.

"David! Are you ready?"

He turned and grinned. "Yes, Bess, just deciding whether to leave ye or not. Ye're late."

"No, we're not," she said, shaking her head. "We've been admiring the horses in the stable, haven't we, Polly? You looked so engrossed under that wagon I didn't want to disturb you. Now, where should we sit?"

He helped them into the wagon and jumped up himself, setting the horse off in the direction of the mill. He was glad it hadn't rained all week, that he didn't have to navigate a muddy bog of a road. It was riddled enough with holes and ruts. He started to question the wisdom of inviting Elisabeth, as most of his attention was devoted to keeping the wagon from overturning. But he enjoyed having her near. It was a gift, and he was thankful for it, just as he was thankful to leave the closeness of the city behind and travel through the open country of Pennsylvania. He glanced down to make sure Mr. Hall's rifle was still at hand.

Polly and Elisabeth chattered nonstop, about what he couldn't repeat with any degree of accuracy, but he liked the sound of their voices. He wondered if the foreman would give him any argument about the shipment shortage. Ian hadn't counted it when he accepted it last Friday, but had gone ahead and signed his name anyway.

Maybe he should buy a paper mill. The work was steady, paper always in demand. One could work and live in the country, next to water likely rife with fish. Aye, that was an idea. Maybe Liam'd like to partner up with him.

"Look, David. Isn't that where you took me last February?" She pointed to a game path off to their right, one that snaked around one of the tributaries of the Delaware. "With Ian and Liam? I don't remember the girls' names, but you remember, don't you? Polly, I told you all about it. We . . ."

David nodded and she turned her attention back to Polly. He did remember. It was the Sunday after a three day snowstorm. He had handed her a borrowed woolen petticoat, a pair of wool stockings, and a set of homemade snowshoes. She had looked at them skeptically.

"The wool will keep ye warmer, Bess. Ye'll need to take off your own petticoat. The shoes will ease your stride through the snow."

"Very well. I've always thought of trying it if the opportunity were to arise. I suppose it has. Although I wonder why you're still against skating with me if you plan to spend the afternoon tromping through the snow."

"I know how to fashion a pair of snowshoes well enough, I havena a clue how to go about a pair of skates."

That afternoon had been one of his favorites, full of laughter and friends.

The trees had been cleared ahead, and he could see the buildings of the mill from the road. He turned down the drive, bringing the horse to a halt at the end of it. Jumping off, he turned to help Elisabeth and Polly down from the wagon.

"I'll be back shortly, ladies. I need to talk to Rory Smith, the fellow ye see standing by the doorway there, aye? Wait here?"

"Miss Liss, look! Puppies!"

"Where, Polly? Oh!" Grabbing Polly's hand, she hurried toward the dogs, turning back to call out to him as she belatedly realized he was waiting for acknowledgment. "Certainly, David."

"Didna hear a word I said." He snorted and shook his head,

then walked over to talk to the foreman. They exchanged pleasantries, then David got to the point.

"I've got payment here for the mill, Rory. But I have to tell ye, I couldna bring it all. Mr. Hall wouldna release it. I'm to tell ye this pays for what ye sent, less the hire of the wagon ye see there. I'm to bring back the rest. He'll release the balance then."

"Are you saying we cheated you, David? I'm sure my man had someone sign when it was delivered."

"Of course not, Rory. We've done far too much business in the past. I'm just thinking your dock hand read this eight as a three. See here? In a certain light anyone could have made that mistake. Have ye done an inventory on your end?"

Rory finished his cigar and tossed it on the ground, grinding it under his boot. "No, not until month's end. The tow-head; who is she?"

Belatedly, David realized the man had his eyes on Elisabeth. "She's mine," he said, his tone even, discouraging further discussion. "Now, do ye propose to make up the difference?"

A small smile turning up the corners of his mouth, Rory grabbed the slip of paper, eyes scanning the numbers. He excused himself and stepped into the warehouse to compare it with his records. When he returned he handed it back to David. "It's possible. I asked the crew; they read it as a three, the clerk read it as an eight. Take the wagon around back, will you? They've instructions to make up the difference." He walked toward the women.

David looked after him, undecided for a moment. She had to be accustomed to dealing with attention with a face like hers, wanted or not. It was just that Rory caught the eyes of a lot of women in town; he saw no need to set Lisbeth's eyes on the man as well. Well, he should have thought of that before he'd brought her; there was nothing to do for it now.

He'd come to collect; he should collect. He'd just make sure the man in back was quick about it.

"DAVID, LOOK!" she said, laughing, lifting her face as the puppy lathered his tongue over her. "Mr. Smith says they're spaniels, and very easy to keep. Aren't they beautiful?"

He looked at Rory, not liking the glint in the man's eye, then down at her. Radiant over a wee puppy. "Very much so, Lisbeth. Are ye thinking of owning a dog, then?"

"No, I can't," she said, hugging the wiggling puppy close, her face pressed into his coat.

"Mr. Hale, he don't like dogs, 'specially puppies," Polly said. "Says they—"

"Shhh, Polly, it's all right." She set the dog down and patted Polly's arm. "Do we need to head back now?"

"Soon. Rory, I thank ye," David said, turning and shaking the man's hand. "I left payment with your bookkeeper. Would it be all right with ye if I left the wagon here for just a bit, so as the ladies can walk along the creek before we head back?"

"Of course," he said, looking at Elisabeth. "Come back anytime, Miss Hale, if you change your mind about the dog."

David offered each of the girls an arm and started down the short path to the river. Polly excused herself when they reached the bank, stating she wanted to sit on soft ground for a spell before getting back into the wagon.

"I'm glad you asked me to come today. It's wonderful to get out of the city. I love the countryside!" She turned to look at him, her blue eyes dancing. "And the puppies; my, I haven't held a puppy since I left home. I'd forgotten how they all smell alike. Don't you think so? It brings back memories, such good memories."

"They do, aye. I don't think one would think it a pleasant smell, though, if it didna come with such a pleasing package.

Is your da afraid of the damage they do?"

"So he says now, but he didn't used to think that way." She reached for a flower in their path, brought it up to her nose. "We had three dogs, and they were one of his passions. They died of old age within weeks of each other, shortly after Mother passed."

"So he associates them with loss, ye think?" That would make the man more human, in his eyes at least.

"I do. He's becoming so bitter, it . . . well, never mind. Time may still change things."

David stopped her, turning her to face him. He took the flower from her fingers and fastened it in her hair, behind her ear. "I'll get ye a wee puppy someday. Do ye like them big," he asked, placing a palm mid-thigh height, "so as they offer protection as they grow? Or small, to warm your lap in the evenings?"

She brushed the hair back off his forehead and brought her fingers to trace his mouth. "I'll have you for protection, won't I?"

"Hmmph, I 'spect it's more than likely I'll be your lap dog."

52

May 1787

"I'M THINKING LISBETH DOESNA CARE for that type," David said, coming up from behind, laughing when John jumped and almost dropped his selection. He'd spotted him half a block back, picking through a mound of early berries at the fruit stand, carefully choosing only those that passed his close inspection.

"You don't know nothing 'bout what my girl likes to eat, boy," John said, taking David by the elbow and moving him away from the stand. "But you do got first-hand knowledge of the happenings at the Sun last night. Fill me in."

Not surprised that John had already heard he was at the meeting of the Pennsylvania Abolition Society, David obliged. "Didna get there until late. Dr. Franklin'd already had his say. We caught Rush, though." With the delegates arriving daily for the Constitutional Convention, the print shop was full of constant interruptions, from newcomers and locals alike, and he and Ian hadn't arrived at the Rising Sun Tavern until well after dark the night before, just in time to catch the last of the meeting. The PAS had reorganized earlier in the year, and the membership now included a large number of artisans at its core. David attended when he could.

"They plan to petition the group of delegates to ban the international slavers. I think they might have more of a chance in mending the law as it stands, John, but something's better than nothing, aye? Mr. Baker spoke up and argued that—" He stopped, his eyes following the sheriff as he hurried by, armed and accompanied by three deputies. He shifted his shoulders, shaking the sensation seeing the sheriff brought on nowadays.

"D'ye know what's going on?"

"Another highway robbery. This time they say they killed them a traveler. Lots of talk 'bout vigilantes, hanging 'em all. You know the talk. Mrs. Hale, she's bound to be up in arms."

"Why's that?"

"She done up and joined the—wait, I got to remember so as I get it right. The Society for Alleviating Miseries of Public Prisoners. I think that's it."

"Did she now? So she'll be knitting them slippers once the sheriff rounds them up?"

"Something like that. Though I'm sure she'll tell it different."

"Nothing wrong with a good heart, I'd be thinking." Prisoners had misery in abundance, he could attest to that.

"Got that right, boy. Git now, 'fore your loitering ends you up in the Debtor's Prison, and she's knitting you a cap."

"Aye, aye, Mr. Black," David said, saluting John and hurrying on; he still had to get the mail. He passed a boy struggling against the weight of his cart, bent double with the effort of pulling it up the hill from the river.

"What're ye bringing in, lad?"

"More wine it is, for them delegates that's coming."

David looked at the lettering on one of the boxes. "The vessel; where's she hail from?"

"Tenerife."

David laughed and turned, following the boy to his destination. Mr. Oliver had mentioned this particular wine over and over. It was the same David had delivered from Hall to celebrate the opening of the Academy. Uncle John had arrived this morning, in town for a gathering of the Presbyterian ministers. They could have it when they all joined for supper tonight.

"How much for the wine, Mr. Easly?" David asked the shopkeeper as the boy unloaded the cart.

"Seven shillings, David."

"Och, ye must be joking. I know well this is from Spain. Now, a French wine ye might get half of that, but no' for this. It's inferior, man. I'll give ye five shillings for two bottles, get 'em off your hands."

"Not likely, lad. I'll give you one for five, only because of past patronage, mind ye."

"Well, I can see then it's no' been much appreciated, I should be looking elsewhere it appears!"

David left twenty minutes later, grinning, toting his three bottles for ten shillings. Maybe he should space out the gift, for the times he might need a peace offering. Only thing was, Mr. Oliver never got angry . . . well, rarely.

He stepped aside to make way for the large group walking up the street. Out of towners, from the looks of it. This Convention might just get Philly back on its feet. The hard times weren't easing, just getting harder, what with the staggering debt left over from the war and the strong opposition to any new taxes to repay it. He heard the complaints day in and day out. Everyone was worried about the future.

There was talk the end result of the Convention would be

to divide the Union permanently, that the states would never find a common ground in the never-ending arguments over free trade. They all had their own to protect; New England with her fishing and shipping, the middle states with their grain and manufacturers, the South with her rice and tobacco. It'd seemed damned near impossible the delegates would hand power over to a national government. From what he'd observed at the printing office, most of the culls couldn't even manage to discuss the issues without the conversation deteriorating into a shouting match, much less come to a mutual conclusion.

Mayhap the country should split into regions based on economic interest. Mayhap that would get them all back on their feet. He sure didn't have any answers; he was still in the stages of reading and listening, he'd leave the debating to others for now while he thought it out. Liam was done with thinking it out. He was one for keeping the Union.

Once the group passed, he ran the rest of the way to the post office. Haggling with Mr. Easly had taken more time than he'd planned for, and he needed to get back to the *Gazette* and get the day's work done. He was hoping to have time to join Uncle John and the rest of them at the river before supper. Fitch was planning on showing off his new steamboat, a trial run up the Delaware before he presented it to the delegates later that summer. He wanted to see it. Lisbeth might even come.

Though that could be awkward, seeing as how he hadn't mentioned her in his letters to Uncle John.

53

"DO YE NEED TO SPEAK to Reverend Green again, Uncle John?"

"No, we're meeting later for dinner, before I head back." Wilson readjusted his coat collar as they walked out of the church, probably hoping to air the perspiration that had gathered and soaked them during the long service. "He gives a fine sermon."

"Aye, he does. Kirk is full every Sunday."

This was the last he'd have time with his uncle, before he returned to New York. David knew what was coming. He couldn't stall any longer, and he thought he was ready. He only hoped it would be limited to the 'Elisabeth matter,' that his uncle hadn't somehow got wind of the 'Sarah matter.'

"Let's walk, shall we?"

"Aye," David said, retrieving a sweetbread from his pocket. "Ye want anything, Uncle?"

"No, thank you." He waited until David finished eating before he spoke again. "David, I was surprised to see you and Elisabeth together. It was apparent the two of you are quite close, that you've kept the acquaintance all these years."

"Aye."

"You've never mentioned it in your letters."

"Aye."

"Enough, lad," he said, an edge to his normally placid voice.

"Sorry, Uncle John. I know well what ye want. And I just can't. She's . . . well . . . I struggled with it for years, keeping her at a distance. But I find she's necessary, like the air I breathe." Christ, that hadn't come out right. Now he sounded like a lovesick ninny. He tried for a different tack, the one he'd prepared for.

"There's so many here in Philadelphia; it's no' like back home. Any block I walk, I might find a different house of worship. Right there, see?" he said, pointing. "The Quakers meet, and off to the south ye'll find the Catholics." He canted his head to the north. "Just over there are the Lutherans and the Baptists. Round yon corner, ye'll find the Hebrew church. And good men can be found in all of them. Good men and good women. All law-abiding and charitable. It's part of what makes this county different, Uncle John, what makes it special."

Wilson sighed, pulling off his hat and mopping his forehead with his handkerchief. "I'm more concerned with what makes you special, David, with your salvation, not the country's."

"My faith hasna changed. It ne'er will. You can count on that. I'm not suddenly going to pick up the trappings of popery, nor to forget my path to salvation." They had reached the banks of the Schuylkill and could hear the roar of the falls in the distance. "Ye want to walk to the Falls, stop at a tavern? The catfish are running . . . we could have some catfish and coffee."

"Nay, I've too many matters to attend to."

David turned back. "I'm sorry I canna comply, Uncle John. With your wishes, that is; I've nothing but respect for them, though I don't agree with them. Just as I've come to find I have nothing but respect for the beliefs of other good men. And women. Though I may not agree with them." He glanced at his uncle. The man hadn't said much. He didn't know if he was making any headway.

"I pray for ye nightly, David. Ye're a man now. There's not much more I can do."

David rolled back his shoulders in discomfort. He hated the idea of Uncle John leaving town like this. His approval was important. On the other hand, he couldn't give falsehood to obtain it.

He pointed to the State House as they passed, where the delegates were gathering for the summer's Federal Convention. "Can ye believe the future of the country will be decided right there this summer? The paper's full of nothing but speculation."

"Hmmph."

"She's a good person, Uncle John. You know that, you know that first-hand."

"I do, David. That's what makes it hard."

54

August 1787

"LISBETH, THERE'S A MR. SMITH up front to see ye. Will ye be all right? I have to run an errand for Mr. O," Rob said, sticking his head through the doorway of her classroom.

"Certainly, Rob." Smith . . . was that the name of one of the parents? Mr. Oliver hadn't given her a class list yet for the new term. She couldn't recall if Liam had mentioned a 'Smith.' "Should I lock up, Rob? I'm almost finished."

"Nay, I'll be right back."

She followed him into the front classroom. A tall, slim man stood with his back to her, hat in hand. He turned as she walked toward him. Ah, yes, from the mill.

"Why, Mr. Smith! What a surprise to see you again."

"Miss Hale," he said, taking her hand and inclining his head. "And please, call me Rory."

"Very well then, Rory. You must call me Elisabeth. Are you in town on business? Did you perhaps remember my plea?"

"Not shy, are you?" He laughed. "Yes, I've brought some paper scraps for you. Not sure that they're suitable for use, though. I'll leave that up to you."

"Anything will help. The boys and girls just need bits to practice on with ink. Thank you, that was so kind of you to remember."

He smiled, his eyes sliding over her. "Oh, I'm thinking you have all manner of men remembering what might make you happy."

She stepped back half a step. She hadn't planned on this when she'd asked the favor. He held up his hand.

"There, now, I didn't mean to make you uncomfortable. It was only a jest. I do have a proposition for you, though. I'm in town to pick up a load of rags from the workhouse. Should the Academy have its own load ready and waiting next time I come, I'll set aside more suitable paper as a contribution for your class. Perhaps you could ask the parents to bring some in?"

"That's a wonderful idea. I will." All the mills were perpetually in short supply of linen. There was no reason she couldn't channel some of the cast offs toward Mr. Smith's mill.

"Perfect. Now, might I interest you in sharing a pot of tea? We can discuss the particulars."

"Well, I suppose that would be fine. We do have a business arrangement after all, and I was headed home for dinner."

He laughed. "Your enthusiasm overwhelms me."

Obviously the man shared Liam's affliction of assuming women would fall at his feet should he glance at them twice. Well, no matter. Perhaps the availability of paper wouldn't be such a struggle this year.

She smiled sweetly, taking his elbow. "Would you mind the tavern at the corner? It's always looked inviting; I imagine the window offers a nice view of the harbor. I believe other establishments will be quite busy at this hour." And it wouldn't be unheard of for David, or someone he was close to, to be at the busier taverns this time of day, replenishing the supply of the *Gazette*.

"You're quite right, of course. The delegates should be adjourning for the day any minute now. I hadn't considered that. Philadelphia must be an exciting place this summer."

"It's certainly busier. But we know no more than the rest of the country. They've all vowed to speak nothing of the proceedings."

"Hmmm, I've doubts they're managing that well. From what I know of some of those gentlemen, they love nothing more than the sound of their own voices." He swept his hand toward the doorway. "At your service, Miss Hale."

She felt his hand at the center of her back as they left the Academy. No, she certainly hadn't planned on this when she'd asked the favor.

"IT'S HARD TO BELIEVE ye don't know *anything*, David. Surely someone's come in and said something. It's no' natural, those coves staying closemouthed for months," Liam said, studying the windows of the State House.

Only about half the delegates had arrived in Philadelphia by May 25th, but it had been enough to start the Convention, and all save those from Rhode Island had come at some point. They had immediately voted for a code of silence. Nothing of the proceedings was to be printed or spoken of. All wanted to get in their say, without the worry of any spin the public or the press might put on a remark taken out of context. The wonder of it was, they had held to it.

"I agree, Liam, but no one's said anything. Ye've seen the sentries they've stationed whilst they're holed up in there. They've even kept the windows closed, hot as it is, lest the sound carry. All I hear is speculation, and we've all heard that for months. Soon though, don't ye think? They look a bit more at ease at the end of the day."

"As soon as ye know, David, promise me, just as soon as ye

have copy, ye'll bring it."

"Aye, if I can." He laughed as Liam turned fast on him, his blue eyes flashing. He held up his hands in surrender. "I will, I promise. But Hall and Sellers aren't printing the draft. It's likely I'll know no sooner than you."

"Ye'll know, ye'll bring it."

55

September 1787

"FINALLY, MAN, WHAT KEPT YE? It's nearly past midnight!"

David feinted a turn. "I'll come back tomorrow, then, so as I don't interrupt your sleep."

The delegates had finally finished their summer's worth of work at four o'clock that afternoon. Printers Dunlap and Claypoole were in the midst of printing the final copy, readying it for the ten o'clock morning stage to New York, everything timed to reach the New York readers by Wednesday—the same day the Philadelphia newspapers would be including it in their own editions. David was able to get a draft copy from Angus, a friend at Dunlap's *Packet*.

"Get back in here, ye . . . ye . . . ye son of a farmer!" Liam said, grabbing his arm, hauling him through the door, pushing him up the steps while he followed, holding his candle high to light their way.

"Son of a farmer?" David said, laughing. "That's the best ye can come up with?"

"Aye, I fear I'm becoming too civilized. It's a point of contention, don't embarrass me, aye?" Liam led him to the table where Rob and Mr. Oliver sat, student essays piled high in front of them. "Here he is at last, Mr. O." Liam motioned impatiently for him to sit. "So is it true then, Davey? It's no' a modification of the Articles of Confederation. It's something fresh?"

David grinned. "It is, which explains the secrecy. But ye have to read it. It's remarkable."

"Ye read it, David. Ye've probably got it memorized by now," Rob said.

"Thank you for coming, David. We're fortunate to be among the first in Philadelphia to hear the details." Mr. Oliver lit an additional candle, placing it on the table in front of David, alongside the mug of small beer Liam had set before him.

David read it slowly over the next hour, stopping again and again to repeat a phrase when Mr. Oliver raised a hand, the room quiet except for his voice as the three others considered the implications. He finished as the light from the candle dimmed, the flame flickering in the pool of tallow at of bottom of the save-all.

"Read the first of it again, will ye, Davey?" Liam asked.

Obliging him, David read, "We the people of the United States, in order to form a more perfect union . . ."

"It's brilliant, don't ye think, Mr. O?"

"It is, it is," Mr. Oliver said thoughtfully, "'We the people', not 'We the states'."

Rob rubbed his chin. "The issue of fair representation; it's quite the compromise. I never would have guessed they'd all agree." It was no secret the smaller states had vehemently opposed any move to reduce representation in the legislature, while the larger states had bitterly resented the one state, one vote system. Now they'd have the best of both. Rob rose from the table, stretching his hands over his head and yawning. "D'ye think Washington will be the first President?"

"Course," Liam said.

"Nothing about slavery, though, except reducing the slave to three-fifths of a man."

"No. It's not perfect, David, but maybe as close as it could be, given the circumstances," Mr. Oliver said. "I would think the whole thing might have fallen apart, had the abolitionists insisted. The southern economy is too dependent upon slave labor at this point, shameful as it may be. But we've come many steps further. It's a good start, and the move toward the abolishment of slavery can evolve from this."

"I've just three hours to sleep before daybreak. I expect tomorrow will be a busy day. The office will be full of those stopping by with rumors and opinions," David said, rising from the table.

"Sleep here. No sense waking the floor coming in at this hour. I want to know everything ye hear, Davey."

"Course ye do." He settled down on the blanket Liam had tossed his way.

"Ye're likely to hear who proposed what, who argued what; it's important, aye?"

"It is. However, I'm apt to be too weary to pay heed," David said, "if ye don't shut up so I can sleep." Liam had always been interested in what and who made things happen, but this summer, his interest had been intense. Not for the first time, David wondered about his parentage.

"All right, we'll talk more tomorrow then, and Wednesday, you'll be free early on. I'm going to tell Lisbeth you're busy with me. She had ye all day Sunday, she can spare ye."

David snorted and rolled over, asleep in an instant.

THE *Evening Chronicle* SCOOPED the other newspapers Tuesday afternoon with a hasty printing of the 'Plan of the

New Federal Government.' The printer, Smith, had previously worked for Dunlap; David speculated he had received advance copy from someone there just as he had.

"You weren't suspected, were you, Davey, you and Angus?" Liam had brought him in some supper and drink, along with a copy of the *Chronicle*. "Go easy on that ale, mate. This copy I'm holding, it's riddled with spelling errors. Ye need to do it justice there."

David scowled at Liam before taking a long swallow. It was well past suppertime, and he was still standing at the case, fingers busy selecting type for the last paragraph. Mr. Hall had decided to leave the type standing for this printing, uncertain of how many copies might sell, deciding it was worth the investment in time to get the spare type cleaned up and in place this morning, pushing them all as they ran behind. The rest of the crew had taken a supper break as soon as Hall was called away. He and Liam were alone in the office.

"Nay, their newest lad, Johnny, they think. He didna show today. The *Seagrass* sailed early this morning. He was likely on it, with a good bit of cash. Smith willna turn a profit, I shouldna think. He didna have the time to press enough copies to make it worth it."

"He didna charge ye much, did he, Davey, young Angus? I need to make ye square."

"No' much; just a meal. He knew I wasna interested in scooping Dunlap. Now you, he wants an introduction to each of your five next lassies, so as he'll be standing ready with a shoulder to cry on when ye tire of them."

"Ha, verra funny."

"I believe he's serious. He's got a theory 'bout women on the rebound. I'm sure he'll share it with ye, should ye ask."

"I turn 'em up sweet. They don't need a shoulder to cry on. 'Specially his."

David looked at him, eyes narrowing. "You welshing, Brock?"

Liam sighed. "Nay."

"Right, then. Thanks for bringing me something to eat."

"Hmmph. I'll leave ye to your work; tomorrow, then, remember?"

"Aye, but I aim to visit with Lisbeth for a bit, when I come to fetch ye."

56

"GODDAMN RABBLE. THEY'RE MAKING US a laughing stock," her father said, tossing down the offending paper.

"Edward, your language, please," Grandmother said, looking up from her mending. "Elisabeth, watch your stitches, child. That row is straying a bit on the large side."

The Constitution needed nine states to ratify before becoming the law of the land. When Pennsylvania lacked a quorum to call their own state ratifying convention, a Philadelphia mob solved the issue by dragging two anti-Federalists members from their lodgings, through the streets of the city to the State House, completing the quorum necessary.

"Yes, Grandmother. Papa, Mr. Wilson is giving a speech next Saturday. I'm going to attend with Mr. Oliver and Liam. Dr. Rush will be there also. Would you like to go with us?"

"Elisabeth, you know I can't abide crowds."

"That's what Grandmother said as well. Well then, I'll give you a full report on Sunday, so as you won't feel as if you've missed a thing. Everyone is saying Mr. Wilson was instrumental in leading the direction of the Convention toward the interests of the Federalists."

"Indeed, he's a man to watch. You needn't get too involved,

young lady. I don't want you to end up like that Devonshire
woman. It'll be damned hard to find you a suitable husband
at that point."

"Oh, Papa, men have evolved past that; that was years
ago." The Duchess of Devonshire had been ridiculed and
vilified in the London press for her unseemly interest in the
politics of Britain.

Her father laughed, reaching out to cup her chin. "Four
years ago pudding, and men haven't forgotten."

Her heart went to her throat; he hadn't called her that
in years. "Well, I shall certainly try to appear as if I don't
understand a word of what the man is saying." Feeling her
Grandmother's eyes on her, she lowered her own back to her
mending.

"We'll look forward to your account, Elisabeth," her
grandmother said. "I trust it will be given with your usual
candor and understanding."

"Indeed we will. There's no need to wait until Sunday. You
can fill us in Saturday night."

"Edward, Elisabeth is going to the theatre on Saturday
evening, remember? Now, if you wouldn't mind, would you
pick the paper back up and read us the last bit? I believe there
was a piece about Catherine in Russia."

"Another woman out of her place," her father muttered,
distracted, picking up the paper.

Elisabeth looked at her grandmother, thanking her silently.
She was spending the evening at the theater with David,
something bound to reverse her father's good humor toward
her.

"JESUS, POLLY, COULDN'T ye have rushed her some?
We're going to be late." Liam had run up to meet them as
soon as he spotted them at the corner.

"We most certainly won't, Liam. You just won't have the

time to talk to half the people in the crowd before Mr. Wilson begins. Is Mr. Oliver ready?"

"Mr. O's there already, saving us a spot."

"Thank you for walking with me, Polly. I'll see you later this afternoon. Remember the blue gown? I've changed my mind. I think you're right after all, I'd like to wear that one. Could you get it ready? Do you think you'll have the time?" Polly nodded and left.

"Right about what? Lass never says a word," Liam muttered, taking Elisabeth by the elbow and walking swiftly in the direction of the State House.

"About the color matching my eyes, as opposed to the green, which I thought complimented my skin, but she thought—" She broke off as he glared at her. She'd been teasing him, though why it irritated him when she played the empty-headed girl she wasn't quite sure. Lord knows he pursued quite a few of them.

"Stop prattling, Lisbeth," he said. "Did ye see the box of rags on the doorstep? Mrs. Hambershin dropped them off for ye. Ye probably have enough now for the mill to pick up."

"I didn't notice them. You were in such a rush. I'll be sure to thank her. Shouldn't you have set them inside? What if they disappear?" She had started a campaign for rag donations, asking parents, friends, and friends of friends, to donate their old linen to the school. Perhaps she had enough now to justify a year's worth of paper. She actually had no idea how much each box could produce. She'd have to ask Rory.

"Who wants a box of rags? Dinna fash."

"Mr. Smith said he'd stop by at the end of October to collect them. I hope Mr. Oliver doesn't mind storing them."

"Nay, he's just surprised at how many ye received. Guess he hasna caught on to the powers of persuasion ye hold. We're here. I see Mr. O over there, by that woman with the red hat."

Liam pushed through the crowd to where Mr. Oliver was standing, arriving just as Philadelphia attorney James Wilson stepped up to the podium. The man wasted no time in delivering a stirring speech in favor of the Constitution, and the crowd was wild in their support, applauding enthusiastically at each point made. Dr. Rush, a prominent Philadelphia physician, followed Wilson with a speech no less stirring, though Mr. Oliver left midway through it, telling Liam and Elisabeth he'd had enough excitement for the day.

"It was something, wasna it, Lisbeth?" Liam said, guiding her through the crowd as they left. "The man's intense. Now, Rush, I agree with most everything he was saying as well. But I think he might be overstating it some to say this will make bedfellows of the Feds and Anti-Feds."

"I don't think that's quite what he said."

"Close enough. Listen, d'ye think Davey can claim kin with Wilson? I'd like to meet him."

"He's never mentioned it nor called on him, not to my knowledge anyway." That reminded her of Reverend Wilson. "Liam, why do you think David changed his mind about the theatre? He told me his uncle spoke out so strongly against it during his last visit."

Liam shrugged, usually a signal he knew and wasn't sharing. A thought occurred to her, and she tightened her grip on his elbow. "Liam, you haven't mentioned my rag campaign to David, have you?"

"Why?"

"I think perhaps he doesn't care for Mr. Smith."

"I may have; don't remember. 'Sides, Davey has no quarrel with Rory."

"All the same, I'd appreciate it if you didn't bring it up." She regretted saying it before the words were out.

"Och, ye're not stepping out with the man, are ye, lass?"

Liam said, stopping abruptly and turning to face her.

"So what if I am? It doesn't mean anything," she said, somewhat defensively. "And David doesn't want to know, so don't tell him." Rory was persistent, and she had finally accompanied him to the theatre a few weeks past.

"He's too old for ye, Lisbeth. Ye're safer with the nitwits your da picks for ye. That's the truth of the matter."

He did have a point there. She had much preferred the evening with Rory over any of the evenings she'd spent with those boys, and she wasn't comfortable with that. "As I said, it doesn't mean anything. Now you're creating a disturbance, it's far too crowded to loiter in the midst of the footpath. Let's continue walking please; I need to get home. I might still change my mind about my gown."

Liam shook his head, muttering, but did as she asked.

IF THEY didn't want to talk about it, they wanted to write about it. The Constitution was the only thing on anyone's mind nowadays, and *everyone* had an opinion they were passionate about. He picked up the next letter, reading it slowly, underlining the misspelled words and making a note of his best guess for the illegible ones. He looked up from the desk when he heard the shop bell ring. Hell, not another; he'd never get out of here.

"Ye were right, Davey, the man's something to hear. Ye shoulda been there," Liam said as he came around the corner. "What are ye doing? Why aren't ye working?"

"I'm reading. I can set these faster if I know where the errors are ahead of time."

"Canny lad. Listen, does Hall know him? I'd like to meet him."

"Who? Wilson? Dinna ken. He's been in the print office a couple times, but I wasn't the one helping him."

"Mayhap he's kin. Does the Rev'rend know him?"

David laughed. "I think he would have said something to us last May if that were the case, Liam."

Liam looked thoughtful. "Well then . . ."

David turned up a corner of his mouth and grunted. He knew that tone well enough. "Well then, what?"

"Just thinking, Davey. I may find ye a long lost cousin soon, aye?"

David snorted. "I've work to finish up. Scat, I'll see ye later. We can talk at supper." He stood and stretched, the tips of fingers reaching to the ceiling.

He was taking Elisabeth to the theater tonight, and Liam and his lass were to join them. He hadn't been keen on the idea at first, knowing full well how his uncle felt. And Uncle John wasn't the only one. There was a ban against such within city limits, for the 'prevention of vice and immorality.'

Aye, well, maybe it wasn't so immoral as all that; it was being billed a musical entertainment after all, not a play. Liam had shamed him into asking her. She loved going and, if swells were the only ones taking her, well then . . . Liam had left the 'well then' up to his imagination. And now that he was committed, he found himself looking forward to it. Couldn't be any harm in enjoying some music with your lass on your arm. Could there?

Liam didn't move. "'Member Lisa, David?"

"Sure, I remember Lisa. She's one ye shoulda kept near. Is that who ye're bringing?"

"Course not. I don't need any near." He sat in David's chair. "But she's a good sort, deserves what she's looking for. I'm thinking I should introduce her to Rory Smith."

"Rory? From the mill? Why'd ye think of him? Never mind, I don't have time for this right now." He shoved Liam out of his chair, sat down and turned to the pile of letters. "I'm working, mate. Save your matchmaking for conversation with the lassies tonight; they welcome that talk."

"Nay, don't bring it up. No' polite to discuss one lass in front of another. Do I have to teach ye everything? See ye in a wee bit, aye?"

"Aye. I'll stop by to fetch ye."

57

June 1788

"DAVID, I'VE JUST RECEIVED WORD New Hampshire will ratify the Constitution today. Can you believe it? Granted, we won't know for sure for several days, but we'll proceed as if it's to be. We haven't much time."

Mr. Hall was as excited as David had ever seen him. The Federalists, and Mr. Hall counted himself among them, had met at Eppley's Tavern earlier that month to celebrate the progression of the Federal Constitution through the various state legislatures. The lot of them had decided that Philadelphia would celebrate the formation of the new Union on July 4th with a grand parade and picnic—if the ninth State signified its acquiescence. Ever since, the entire town had been speculating on whether that would happen in time for the Fourth. And now, New Hampshire was the ninth.

It had been a long struggle, close to a year. Pennsylvania had voted to ratify last December, right after Delaware's ratification. But the vote hadn't ended the bitterness. Benjamin Franklin declared the letters circling the newspapers were giving the impression that Pennsylvania was "peopled by a set of the most unprincipled, wicked, rascally and quarrelsome scoundrels upon the face of the globe." And on some days, he'd have to concur.

The Federalists had the support of the likes of Washington, Hamilton, Jay, and Madison. The Anti-Federalists had no leaders of any stature, or indeed anything resembling a united, organized front. But they did have the people on their side in several of the key states. So the Federalists had agreed to recommend a list of amendments comprising a Bill of Rights. Only then did they have hope of a victory over the Anti-Federalists, and now, finally, it looked as if they would come out on top.

All the trades were planning on participating in the procession, and the apprentices in the shop talked of nothing else. David was excited as well, but he did not, under any circumstances, want to ride through town on a stage as the others apparently did.

"Mr. Hall, I'll be more than happy to organize the building of the thing, or whatever ye ask, but don't oblige me to ride on it!"

"Don't listen to him, Mr. Hall. He should be on the stage. He's been a part of your paper for years now, aye? It's not fitting he should be excluded," Liam said, adding to the debate as he walked in.

"Liam, what are ye doing here? Wait outside, will ye?"

Mr. Hall laughed. "It's Saturday, David. Liam has shown up here each Saturday at about this time for the last four years, hasn't he? There's no call to be rude to him. Now, if called for, you'll be on the stage with the rest of us. You'll regret it years later, having been here and not participated. Consider it part of your job duties. And I appreciate your offer to build the damn thing. I'm going to take you up on that. Use whatever resources we have, I want Hall & Sellers to contribute more to this effort than all the other printers in town. Sellers is sure to have some ideas. Consult him, will you? Consult whomever. Enjoy yourselves this evening, gentlemen." He left the room, winking at Liam on the way out.

David sank to the floor, groaning, head in his hands. He had enough to do already, didn't he?

Liam plopped down next to him. "Sorry about that, mate."

"Don't even pretend; ye're enjoying it as much as he is."

"Well, truth be, mayhap." Liam laughed. "He's right, though, ken. This will be one of the biggest parades in the country, one year after our Constitution. It's history in the making, my friend, and ye must participate. So come out of your shell. Mr. O's Academy will be there, James and the sailmakers will . . . *everyone* is to be there. It'll take the whole morning for the lot of us to get a few blocks up the street. And think of the fun to be had after! Everyone's talking and planning. Now, I came to fetch ye cause I have been invited to the Hale's parlor for the planning of the Academy's exhibit, and your attendance has been requested. So go clean up."

David looked at Liam. "Get on with ye."

"Seriously. Mr. Hale willna be there, but Mrs. Hale will. Lisbeth says she's excited about getting involved, a creative soul untapped or some such nonsense. Two trades to help plan, that will tap her no doubt. And give ye an opportunity to make a good impression on your intended's kin. She's expecting ye."

David groaned again, placing his forearms over his head. "Can this day get worse?"

Liam stood, giving David a kick. "Stop your whining. We only have two hours 'fore we're expected. Time enough to fortify yourself with some liquid courage if need be. No' enough to make ye lushey, though. Lisbeth willna forgive that. So again, clean up and let's go. Ye can thank me later."

"Liam, when will I ever be able to return all the favors ye've dealt me?" He stood and walked to the wash basin. Washing his hands and face, he then ran his fingers through his hair and tied it back neatly. "Wait a minute while I see if I have a clean shirt, aye? Let's go to the river, sit outside." He rolled back his shoulders. He needed space.

"STILL CLEAN?" David asked, fingering his neckcloth. Though they were standing outside the Hales' front door, he didn't know what he planned to do if it wasn't.

Liam examined him. "Aye. Ye'll do fine mate, just don't lose your tongue. Ye tend to do that. Did Lisbeth ever tell ye Granny thought ye fine, a 'man who had presence?' I believe she said she could see why her granddaughter was 'obsessed.' Aye, I'm sure that was the word used, 'obsessed.'"

"Hell, Liam. Ye're no' helping."

"My apologies." He raised a hand and banged the knocker.

Tom opened the door. "Good evening, Tom, do ye know Liam?"

"Mr. Graham," he said, inclining his head. "I'm told you are expected. Mr. Brock, I presume?" He took their hats.

"Aye."

"Tom, don't keep them at the door. Come in, David, Liam. Grandmother's waiting in the parlor." Elisabeth ushered them in, taking David's hand, squeezing it. He had never been farther than the hall. Likely by design, though he didn't dwell on it.

The parlor was a comfortable room, not formal as he'd expected. Vases of fresh flowers were scattered about and books littered the tabletop. The walls were cluttered with paintings that reminded him of home; landscapes of lush green hills dotted with sheep, cottages and the like. He liked them, much more than the dour portraits that had decorated the walls of homes he'd grown up knowing. Mrs. Hale sat next to the fireplace, a small fire providing her light as she worked with her needle. She set it aside as soon as they entered the room, standing to welcome them both.

She was trim and held herself tall, not stooped like some of the old woman he could think of. From a distance he wouldn't have even thought her old, if it weren't for the gray hair. Only close up could one see the lines that marked her face. Nice lines, though; lines that deepened around her eyes and mouth when she smiled, as she was doing now.

Brief pleasantries about the weather and their health were exchanged, then there was silence as Tom brought in a tray of refreshments and set it in front of Mrs. Hale.

"Would you gentlemen care for a cup of tea?"

"Thank you, ma'am, I would," Liam said.

"Yes, ma'am," David answered. He squirmed a bit on the low sofa.

Silence again. He noticed Elisabeth wringing her handkerchief round and round in her fingers. Wait. He looked again. That was *his* handkerchief; he recognized Ma's embroidery of his initials along the corner. He drew in a deep breath. Best get started, before he lost another one to her worry.

"Mrs. Hale," he said, "Liam's told me you've expressed an interest in offering counsel for the procession exhibits. If this is truly the case, I for one would be most grateful for any assistance you could provide. Other than my hands and my back, I don't have much to offer in the way of creative support to this endeavor, and Mr. Hall has entrusted me with the firm's contribution to the production of the printer's exhibit. It would grieve me to let him down, he's done so much for me, but quite honestly, I feel unequal to the task."

He took a sip of his tea, then set the cup down. He noticed Elisabeth's mouth had dropped open, and Liam was grinning ear to ear. Eijit. Just because he didn't choose to chatter didn't mean he couldn't.

Mrs. Hale's eyes hadn't wavered from him during his request, but he'd warrant he saw something resembling a twinkle in them by the time he'd finished. She glanced briefly at her granddaughter, then back at David. "Indeed, young man, I think between us we could accomplish quite a bit. Elisabeth and Mr. Brock have shared a few of the parameters of the exhibits, and Elisabeth mentioned you possibly would appreciate some comments as well. So I've been thinking." She set down her cup, and the conversation flowed fast and freely from that point on.

THE STREET WAS QUIET when they left, lit softly by moonlight. Liam was full of prattle and plans, having come up with several scenarios using Mrs. Hale's input.

"She's quite resourceful, isn't she, David? I can see where Elisabeth gets a bit of her spirit. Ye havena said a word since we left, by the way."

"Hmmph."

"Let's stop in here for a pint, 'fore ye tuck yourself in for the night."

David upended his mug as soon as he settled. Liam looked at him, questioning, then slid his mug to David as he signaled the barkeep for two more.

"That was exhausting, Liam."

"Ye gave no indication of such, I thought things went well."

"Good, then mayhap Lisbeth did, as well."

"Course she did. Ye didna care for her Grandmother?"

"Nay, I did. She's a remarkable woman, to all appearances. I've only met her briefly on other occasions. I just felt as if my every move was subject to scrutiny, no' only by her, but by Elisabeth as well."

"Och, I didna see that. Course I didna see ye shaking in your boots either, and I thought I knew ye well."

He laughed. "Oh, ye do, no doubt there. I wasna shaking in my boots. No' nervous, just careful. And three hours of careful wears on one a bit, makes one thirsty, ken? I've known the lass for close to four years now, and have ne'er talked more than small brief pleasantries to the woman who stands in for her mother. I knew it an important meeting for Lisbeth. I didna want to disappoint her."

"To my knowledge, ye're always exceedingly careful. Ye might be careful no' to let it lead ye to drink to excess," he said as David started on his third and signaled for another round. "Mr. O warns me often of subjecting ye to additional temptation."

"What the hell are ye rambling on about now? He thinks I drink too much?"

"I never told ye, Davey? The temptations of the print shop?"

David just looked at him, raising his mug to take a long, deliberate, swallow.

"Well, surely ye've heard the print shops are full of journeymen and 'prentices who imbibe to excess, and in spite of their high wages are doomed to die an impoverished lot because of it?"

"Oh, that. Well, surely ye don't believe it. Even if one could follow the copy, I don't see it possible for one to pick up the type without dropping it all over the floor or to justify the lines if lushey. That type is verra tiny if your coordination is off. And that's assuming the copy is perfect. Which it rarely is. I also doubt it possible to read and copy a manuscript full of bad grammar, poor spelling, and no punctuation if lushed. No' that we're ever allowed to print it as it's written. We'd be deemed the ones illiterate, no' the writer." He paused, warming to his subject.

"So we're charged with reading barely legible copy, correcting it, and setting the type, and doing it all without error on the first round because the paper and ink are damned expensive, ken? Intoxicated? No' possible, the master wouldna let ye near the type, nor the press. And as for high wages, have ye ever had a conversation with Robert regarding the adequacy of a journeyman's wages?"

Liam grinned and held up his hands in surrender. "Leave off, I know all that mate. Ye've educated me over the years. Probably why I ne'er thought it worthwhile to repeat Mr. O's concerns."

"Well, set him straight for me, will ye? I hate to have him foster a poor opinion of me."

"Ye missed the point. It was me he was cautioning. Ye will never do anything wrong in his eyes, unless I lead ye to it, that is. In which case I will still be the one responsible, and ye will still no' be to blame." He sighed dramatically. "Ne'er mind, there's no use reasoning with ye when ye're in this condition. Here, our man has arrived. Have another."

David laughed. "Is Rob to participate in this procession?"

"Aye, and why wouldna he? I tell ye again, Davey, this is an opportunity that willna come twice."

"I doubt that. The country will likely have Independence Day parades for the next twenty years."

"No' a special one, not the first year after our new Constitution. Where's your patriotism, mate?"

"I've no recourse but to enjoy it, so I shall. I liked Mrs. Hale's ideas. The *Gazette* will make a contribution to be proud of. I plan to go over it with Mr. Sellers tomorrow and get started as soon as possible. It'll be a big undertaking on top of the rest of the duties, and we have no' much more than a sen'night."

"That's the spirit; I knew ye had it in ye."

58

ELISABETH STIRRED SLOWLY, PLACING THE day in her thoughts. Sunday. Her eyes flew open. *Sunday*. She jumped out of bed and ran to the window. Oh, it's perfect, just perfect. There wasn't a cloud in the sky, and the storms of the past week had washed away the heaviness in the air. The day was dawning with more promise than she could have even prayed for, if she had prayed, which she hadn't. She was fairly certain God wouldn't approve of her plans for the day, especially as her plans included skipping the morning service.

She had one priority this morning, and that was her morning toilet. She couldn't keep David waiting when he arrived, couldn't give him time to think or to question. She called for Polly.

"THANK YOU FOR helping me so early in the day, Polly. I want you to take the afternoon for yourself as soon as we finish here." She ran a bar of perfumed soap down one arm and up the other.

"I can't be doing that, missy. I needs to go with you and Mr. David."

"Of course you can, you deserve it. Don't you want to

visit your friends?" Elisabeth asked. "No one need know,
and you could certainly use some time away. I swear we work
you to the bone. You could spend it with your beau. Will Leo
already have plans for the day?"

Polly picked up one of the pitchers by the bath and poured
it carefully over Elisabeth's hair, pulling the soap suds down
with her free hand as the water flowed over it.

"Polly?"

"I know what you be doing, Miss Liss, and it ain't right.
Tempting me thataway."

"I think you ought to fill a basket alongside mine, John
always prepares so much, David won't miss a bit of it. And
take a bottle of wine from Grandpa's cellar. Why you'd make
that boy's mama talk of you from sunup to sundown. What a
thoughtful girl that Polly is, how he ought to treat her right."

Polly giggled. "I declare, missy, you're letting that Liam
color your world somethun fierce of late."

"You'll go?"

Polly nodded. "I'll go, even though I'll spend most my time
hoping nothun comes of it. You don't be getting yourself
into trouble now. You remember all I taught you bout the
ways of boys."

"Don't worry about me. Just enjoy yourself and the day.
Can I get out now? Is all the soap out? You get in next. I'll
wash your hair while the water's still warm."

"DAVID! GOOD MORNING. Will you carry this?"

He grabbed her basket and blanket, peering behind her as
she closed the door. "Why're ye on time? Where's your staff?
Ye're manning the door yourself today? Isna Polly coming?"

"No. You're my sole escort today," she said. "But I feel
quite safe with you. One of Grandmother's friends in Darby
scheduled a house party. Everyone's gone. I begged off with
a headache."

"Ye feel ill? And Polly left ye?"

"No, I'm fine. I just didn't want to miss our outing. The weather is too perfect, so I fibbed a bit. And I told Polly to take the day off to visit her beau. What's the matter, David?" She smiled, her hands on her hips. "If I didn't know better, I'd think you were afraid to be alone with me."

"Hmmph."

"Well, that certainly clears that up. Let's go then, shall we? Before the neighbors start gossiping?"

They headed to the Schuylkill, then started along the path beside it, passing the Falls, passing the jumble of taverns that catered to the tourists. He told her that the printers in town had decided to share a stage for the parade. "Mr. Hall wasna keen on it, he said the others were just envious we'd planned for an impressive showing where they had not. But he's reconciled to it now. Tell your grandmother we're using some of her ideas."

"Grandmother likes you. I'm glad she spent time with you."

"I like her as well. I wish we had earlier. No, don't apologize," he said, placing his finger over her lips. "It's too fine a day." He stepped off the path, guiding her along a game trail flanked by grasses waist high, stopping when they reached the creek.

"This is a beautiful spot, David. You haven't brought me here before."

"Nay, we just encountered it last week. Caught seventeen fish in yon pool," he said, pointing to a deep spot along the opposite bank. He and Liam always had to take care where they fished on Sundays. It wasn't allowed within town limits on the Sabbath. But he had said it gave them cause to explore, and the days were the better for it.

"Oh, I wish we had poles!"

"Stashed them 'round yon brush. I'll rig them while ye get

the picnic set."

"Have you ever seen so many flowers?" She danced around the clearing. "I'd love to come here in August, David. Can you imagine? I'll aver I could harvest twenty or thirty varieties of seed. Will you bring me back?" She came up behind him and looked over his shoulder.

"Aye," he mumbled, intent on rigging the poles. He and Liam must have fashioned them from branches last week, and it looked as if something had been gnawing on the ends.

She left him to unpack the hampers. "I'm going to have a sip of wine. I hope you don't mind. She tugged off the bottom of his flask, using it as a cup. "Mmm, this is good. What's the occasion?"

He looked up as he finished with the poles. "Spending a beautiful afternoon beside a lucky fishing hole with the girl of my dreams."

She smiled, spreading out the blanket, arranging the picnic along one side. "Faith, it *is* a beautiful afternoon. Sometimes I'm just so happy, I want to throw up my arms and embrace the sun."

He came to her. "Will I do then? I don't want to see ye burn."

"Oh, yes." She reached for him and pulled him down. "Have some of this," she said, handing him the flask.

He took it from her, reaching for a piece of cheese from the spread beside her. "Ye look different, your dress is . . . softer?"

She laughed. "You've seen this gown a hundred times. If it's softer, it's from washing. Do you like that cheese? I purchased it at the market yesterday from a woman I haven't seen there before. But her milk was delicious, so I thought I'd try it." She reached across and brought his hand to her mouth, biting off a bit of the cheese and licking the crumbs from his fingers. She almost laughed aloud at the variety of expressions crossing his face, not the least of which was wariness.

"Mmm, it is good." She ran her tongue around her lips, then took a long sip of wine. Setting down the cup, she untied her cap, loosening her hair until it fell around her shoulders in soft waves. "There, much better. The pins were a bother. So, did you eat all those fish? That's a lot, even for a man with your appetite." She moved the cheese to the hamper, out of the path of the ants that had sniffed it out.

"David? Are you feeling all right?"

"What? Ah, fish, aye, we caught fish."

She smiled. "Yes, so you said. I was only wondering who ate them all." She brought her hands up behind her neck, under her hair. Polly had said that would enhance the shape of her bosom, draw a man's eyes, and my, it seems she was right about that. She lifted her hair off her neck as if to cool it, then combed her fingers back through it as she let it fall down about her shoulders again.

"I find it odd you noticed my gown. I was counting on you not being the type of man who places much stock in fashion. Well, I could hardly get myself in full dress without Polly. That's what you find different, not the gown, but what's under the gown. Or rather what's not." She reached out a finger, tracing a line from his chin to the hollow of his throat where she could feel his pulse racing. "It's so much cooler without all those petticoats."

Not sure how far she would have to go to tempt him, she watched his eyes carefully. It had taken years to get to this place; she wasn't about to jeopardize her opportunity by misjudging his response.

"Another thing I've noticed, I've found I don't like the distance they place between us when you choose to kiss me." His eyes darkened another shade, and he swallowed, his whole body tensing, still not saying a word. But she didn't need to hear the words; her eyes told her what she wanted to know. She took the flask from his hand, sipped from it before setting it aside, letting a bit of the wine settle across her lips. "Maybe you'd like to form your own opinion on the matter?"

"Bess, I . . . we . . ."

She almost smiled as she saw him glance toward the path they had come down. Was he actually hoping for someone to appear, to rescue him?

"No?" she said softly. "Well then, I'll have to reconcile myself to the possibility my curiosity is one sided. In which case I . . ."

Before she could finish she found herself on her back, cushioned by his arms under her, sheltered by his body above. She had a fraction of a second to smile before his mouth covered hers, then she lost all inclination to revel in her victory, lost all ability to think coherently as her senses took over. His mouth demanded, she gave, arching herself up as he pulled her against him. He kissed her again and again, his tongue probing, and she felt the world spinning fast above them. He shifted so he was directly over her, whispering her name as he kissed the sensitive spots along the side of her neck, his body moving against her. She knew now he wanted her. Polly had also explained that part.

But Polly hadn't explained how she would feel: breathless, dizzy, confused, unsettled, wanting, needing . . . She ran her hands down his back and pressed his lower body against hers, answering his rhythm without thought, turning her head to give him better access to her neck as his mouth traveled down her neck to her shift. Only when his hand untied her bodice, then traveled up her skirt, did she pay heed to the warning bells going off.

"David?" It took him a moment, but he stilled, his mouth motionless on her collarbone. She listened while his breathing slowed. He moved off her.

She curled to his side and put her hand under his shirt, running her palm up and down his chest before he covered it with his hand. "Lass, give me a minute."

She raised herself on her elbow so she could see his face. "I'm sorry, was that awful of me?"

"Nay."

She lay back down and gave him the minute he'd asked for, plus more. When it was apparent he wasn't going to talk on his own, she tried again.

"That's all you have to say? You've a right to be angry. You *should* be angry. I didn't . . . I'm confused, David. I thought I knew what I wanted, but I find I don't. I thought I wanted you to kiss me forever, then I thought I should stop you. Now I just feel flustered."

"I don't know what ye want me to say."

"Anything. Something."

"I can't. What're ye asking me, Bess? I'm wrought up as well."

She ran her hand up and down his chest again, ignoring it when he tried to still her. "David, please. You're the only one I can talk to. Just listen for a minute—before you refuse, please?" Sighing, she lay back.

"Many nights I go to sleep dreaming of being in your arms, of having you kiss me. Like you have before, like you did today. I only wanted the kiss to go on and on. Today it began that way, then quickly changed. I feel moody and unsettled, but somehow relieved you stopped when you did. But I still want you to kiss me, David, so I don't know why I had you stop. And I feel you may be angry with me. Maybe not angry, but . . . well, I don't know. That's why I'm asking."

Silence. She may as well just get comfortable and wait him out. He never talked if he didn't want to.

GOD HELP HIM. He'd known better, surely he had, but he had come anyway. Wasn't a reason in the world he couldn't have taken the picnic to one of the parks in town, not a one. And it wasn't her fault. She hadn't a clue what she did to him. But now she wanted him to explain it? Hell. He counted to one hundred, slowly. Then five hundred. Then backwards from five hundred, bringing to mind the slaughter of the chickens in market as he did so.

Right then. He was fine now.

He turned on his side to face her, his hand landing on her leg. She started a bit, and he realized it was her bare knee, her skirts still mussed up. He made to move it, then decided against it. He liked it. And he had himself in control now. She turned to her side to face him.

"I'm no' angry with ye, Bess, no' at all. It's just that, well, things moved along a little farther than they have before. Surely someone's explained these things to you?"

"No, who would? My father? My grandmother? Polly explained a little, but I find now, certainly not enough."

Without forethought, his hand fondled her leg. He found he loved the feel of her skin.

Eijit, course he did, should draw down her skirt and leave her be. He noticed with interest that her eyes had lost a little of their focus.

"Well then, I guess I'll try." Shifting his thumb to stroke the softness at the back of her knee, he watched her face for any sign of panic. She drew in a quick breath, but didn't stop him. "Give me leave. This is a difficult subject to talk of."

He moved to crowd her so that she lay back down on her back. "Surely you've seen animals mate."

Her eyes flared. "What are you saying?"

Perhaps that wasn't the way to begin. He grinned. "Just that a kiss is a mating call, that's all." He slowly inched his hand up past her knee. "When we kiss, ye feel it elsewhere, aye?" She nodded, her lips parting. "It can be verra satisfying, but will leave ye wanting other as well. Ye'll recall me telling ye that, when we've kissed in the past? No?"

He lowered his head, his mouth toying with her earlobe. She had opened her mouth to reply, but seemed to have lost her words as his hand moved higher up her thigh.

"I'm sure I have, lass. Were ye no' listening, then?" Slowly, he kissed her, his tongue tracing the outline of her mouth, trailing down the side of her neck to the curve of her shoulder. He pulled back . . . waiting, watching. Her eyes were soft, having lost all focus. He brought his hand up farther under her shift, lightly caressing, running it back and forth across the smoothness of her belly, under her stay. Very accommodating of her, leaving it loose like that.

"I have to agree, ken, I find I dinna miss the distance at all." He slowly brought his caresses lower until she arched up against him.

"D'ye seek my touch, Bess?"

Again, he searched her eyes for any trace of panic. Finding none, he moved his fingers over her, swallowing hard as he found her wet. She jumped a bit, but didn't move her eyes from his. He could see her breath quickening, her eyelids heavy.

"A kiss between two who are as bound as you and I, well, it appears it'll quickly lead to much more." His thumb found the spot he was searching, and his finger entered her. She cried out, panicked, and tried to move his hand. He stilled it for a moment, but didn't move it. "Ssh, it's all right, lass. It doesna hurt, does it?" She shook her head, blushing. He watched her, reveling in her responsiveness as he moved his fingers, dangerously close to soiling his breeches.

Deciding he was past caring, and well past talking, he bent to kiss her, his tongue finding hers before it slowly began to imitate the rhythm of his fingers. She closed her eyes, moaning softly as she arched to his hand. She cried out under his mouth, her hands pulling him closer, nails raking his back as her free leg came up over his thigh to pull him near. He ground hard against her and lost himself when she came, calling out his name, bucking up under him.

Groaning, he lay back, pulling her alongside him, running his hand through her hair until his heart slowed. Minutes past, maybe as much as an hour, he didn't know, before he could bring his thoughts to order. He rolled her back to the ground and raised himself on an elbow, bringing his free hand up to turn her face toward his.

"God in Heaven, ye're enticing. D'ye see? What ye do to me?" He gently took her hand and brought it against his wet breeches. "That's embarrassing for a man, lass, ken?" He moved her hand.

"It doesna hurt, aye? Quite the opposite. But it does cause complications. My seed, did ye feel it? It should spill inside ye." He reached down, pushing his finger in her for emphasis, and she gasped. He was growing hard again, and he brought her fingers back down to cover him. "I . . . my cock should be inside ye, Bess. But if I am, there are implications; ye could end up with child. Ye do know that, right?"

Gritting his teeth, he moved her hand. "I willna have ye and my child married off to one of your da's suitables, d'ye understand?" When she didn't answer he brought his hand up to cup her face, forcing her to look at him.

"Bess, do ye understand?"

She nodded, her eyes wide—with wonder, not fright. He let go and brought her head to rest on his chest, holding her close.

Sometime later she raised her head and looked up at him, placing her hand on his breeches again. Zounds, he was down to two hundred and fifty-nine. He'd have to start again. He quickly removed it, bringing it to his mouth to kiss her palm.

"Your 'seed' . . . umm . . . does that mean . . . did you like it as well, David?"

He snorted a small laugh. "Oh, aye."

"You're a wonderful teacher. I had no notion you could make me feel that way. I hope you feel inclined to instruct me further in the near future."

He laughed out loud and rolled to his back, releasing her. "By God, Bess, ye leave me speechless."

She supported herself on her elbow and looked down at him. "I hardly think that's such an accomplishment, do you?"

He stood. "Up with ye, lass, before ye tempt me further. And we're no' doing this again. If Polly canna join us, I'll bring someone, aye? Ye must tell me, so I can."

"Hmmph."

David laughed. "God help me," he said, pulling her up, helping her adjust her bodice, congratulating himself on his self-restraint when he allowed himself only a brief caress of her breast. He wanted so much more.

AS HE LAY AWAKE that night he began to make plans. The hell with her religion. He loved her, he wanted her. Surely her father would let her accept his suit. She had done his bidding for years. They couldn't marry for two years, but a long engagement was not unheard of. He needed to begin to make plans, and those plans must include her. He grinned. Knowing Lisbeth, she wouldn't be content to just trail after him; she was likely to have her own ideas on the paths they should take. And he'd welcome then all.

Independence Day . . . they could begin then.

59

July 4, 1788

DAVID TOOK HIS TIME WALKING the parade route to the printers' exhibit, backtracking and starting his trek down at the harbor. He thought he'd ask Elisabeth here, riverside, tonight. Many of the ships would be lit with lanterns; it promised to be spectacular.

Ten vessels ran the length of the harbor, from the Northern Liberties all the way to South Street, each honoring a state that had adopted the Constitution, each flying a white flag at the masthead calling out in gold letters the state honored, from the northernmost to the southernmost. All the other ships in the anchorage were dressed as well, and nature was accommodating with a brisk wind from the south to keep the flags and pendants flying large.

Aye, here would be good, a place they'd remember always.

The first cannon had discharged at sunrise, accompanied by the pleasing toll of the bells of Christ Church. The call could be heard for miles, and all of Philadelphia had answered, filling streets that had been tidied and trimmed the day before. He started back up Market Street, threading his way through the spectators who'd staked their spot and started their carousing late the night before.

He stopped to marvel at the federal ship *Union*, complete with a crew of twenty-five men. The exhibit had been started just this Monday. It was beautifully proportioned, with intricate carving throughout, and the bottom was the barge of the *Serapis*, taken from the British by none other than Captain John Paul Jones during the Revolution.

"Sir, I have no' yet begun to fight."

David turned, grinning at the quote. "Might of known ye wouldna be with your group."

"We're at the verra end," Liam said. "I didna want to miss anything. Why aren't ye?"

David held up the bottles of ink he was toting. "Look at all this, will ye," he said, waving his arm. "I'm glad I'm here after all. This is truly something to see. You were right."

"It is, isna it? The Grand Procession. Every one of these floats is nothing short of magnificent. *Eight days*, Davey. Eight *days*." He waved his hand back toward the Grand Federal Edifice, a roof supported by thirteen Corinthian columns thirty-six feet high, three of the columns left unfinished to represent the states that had yet to ratify the Constitution, all erected on a carriage now drawn by ten white horses. "Only eight days and look what Americans have accomplished. Every trade and profession in this city, every resource, every talent, every class . . . working day and night for this. Not for private gain, mind ye, but for this display, this tribute. It's astonishing, nothing less."

It was true, what Liam said. With a minimum of the usual fuss and preliminaries, Americans' energy and determination had accomplished the near impossible. And they were now a part of it.

"Look, the pilot following the *Union*, macaroni; recognize him?"

"Aye," David said, laughing. "His elegance has served him

well, I suppose. Here, I think this is James' group. D'ye see him?"

The sailmakers' group was a simple one—a flag detailing the men at work, followed by a number of masters, journeymen, and apprentices. They stopped to banter with James briefly before moving on.

"Slow down, Davey. I'm determining my future lot in life. No' often the trades are lined up for preview like this."

"Cordwainer, cabinet maker; hmmm, I think ye should have apprenticed yourself years ago."

"I'll give ye that. Painter? I could learn that easy enough, porter, that canna be too hard either. Any eijit will do."

"Keep your voice down. We havena time for a tussle."

"Clock and watchmaker? Sounds distinguished."

"Dime a dozen, no room for ye. Ye could lay bricks. But no, you're too pretty. Look, here be the tailors. There's far more than a few of them." David was lost in thought for a moment, wondering how his father was faring in the trade.

"Maybe a cooper, aye? Or a blacksmith. Now that, I could do that anywhere," Liam said thoughtfully.

"Sure, learn the wheelwright trade as well, ye'd be verra useful. Wait, look here. Dinna be forgetting the skinners and breeches-makers. Ye'd be indispensable on the frontier."

"Jack of all trades . . ."

"Master of none. Ye passed right over the professions, Liam."

Liam looked at him, puzzled.

David returned the look evenly. "Attorney? Right up your alley, I'd say. And also of use on the frontier."

"I canna . . ."

Liam shut his mouth, his habitual aplomb having deserted him. David raised a dark brow and grinned, not sure he'd ever seen Liam at a loss for words, not in all the years he'd known him.

"Look here, ye think these oxen know they're marching to their deaths?" David asked as they passed the victualers. Two axemen proceeded the oxen. A small band followed. "To the sound of music, no less. Ah, at last." He lowered his voice. "Look at poor Mr. Durant. Count your blessings, David."

They had reached the stage of the printers, bookbinders, and stationers. Nine foot square, it carried the tools of the trade, including a press. Ten printing offices were united, and 'poor Mr. Durant' was dressed as Mercury, in a white gown with red ribbons, real wings affixed to his head and feet and a garland of blue and red crowning his head.

One of the superintendents of the parade hurried by, the white plume in his hat dancing as he compared his notes against the order of the marchers, assuring himself all were in their proper positions.

Liam took his leave, and David jumped on the stage to replenish the ink stock. The pressmen were standing ready to strike off copies of the 4th of July ode that Francis Hopkinson, poet and civic leader, had composed for the occasion. David had helped set the type for the ode until late last night. Today he'd trail behind with the other apprentices. Mr. Sellers was leading the lot of them, his stock of white hair bright in the morning's sunlight. He'd been chosen to carry the standard of the united professions. He'd be followed by the masters, then the journeyman, and finally the apprentices, each carrying a scroll with blue silk binding and the words "Typographer." Spotting Ian in the horde, he jumped off the stage and joined him.

THE TOTAL DISTANCE they marched was about three miles, most of it in silence as the spectators viewed the procession in quiet awe. Watching those they passed, David could identify joy and pride on most every face. Federalist, anti-Federalist . . . nay. All Americans today. Would that it would last. A child darted out from the safety of the footway to offer him and others a cooling sip of water.

Those in front of the procession arrived at Union Green shortly after noon. A large circle of tables was filled with cold food prepared the day before by the committee of provisions. David helped secure the printers' stage, then watched as the balance of the trades arrived, waiting impatiently through a parade of biscuit makers, gunsmiths, brewers, barbers, plasterers, goldsmiths . . . it seemed it would never end. Then he spotted her, after the stay-makers. The schools in the city had united, carrying a flag inscribed 'The rising generation.' Mrs. Hale and Elisabeth had made robes for Mr. Oliver's Academy, decorating them with symbols representing the various scholastic disciplines, and Mr. Oliver, Rob, and Liam wore hats emblazoned with the school emblem. Elisabeth ran to meet him.

"I didn't see your stage, David. Is it still here?"

"Aye," he said, taking her elbow and leading her to it. He stooped to pick up one of the copies of the Ode littering the surface. "Here ye go, a sample of our trade."

"Very nice. It wasn't so bad now, was it?"

"No, no' at all." They rejoined the others to listen to the oration being given in the Grand Edifice.

"There's no whisky to be had, just American porter, beer, and cider," Liam said. "Someone thought this all out carefully, aye? They estimate a crowd of well over fifteen thousand this afternoon. Whisky willna mix with that. Did ye see the clergy, David?"

"I did. Why d'ye ask?"

"I was wondering if ye noticed the Presbyterians walking arm in arm with the Methodists, Catholics, Anglicans, Quakers, Jews, and the like," Liam said.

"Ye'll not get a rise out of me today, Liam," David said,

grinning. "Not all the Presbyterians lack tolerance, ken, and that's all I plan to say on the subject. Get us some brew, will ye, so we can join in the toasts?" Out of the corner of his eye he'd noticed Elisabeth watching him for his reply, and he took her hand. They'd never discussed religion directly, and he'd been surprised to find out she'd taken to attending the same church Mr. Oliver did. He was curious about that, but had been hesitant to bring it up, with her or with Liam.

"Did your grandmother come? I wanted to thank her for her help. The distribution of the Ode was a big success. The crowd loved it."

"She wasn't feeling well and didn't stay long; she doesn't take to crowds. She and Papa walked the streets early this morning to see the stages. You can see her tomorrow, if you intend to call on me."

He laughed.

"Well, you just might tire of me, seeing me two days on end."

His hand dropped to his pocket, and he felt for the ring, his grandmother's ring, sent out last year by Ma. "No' a chance of that, Bess."

"Here, David, grab this, will ye?" Rob said, appearing with two jugs of ale. He was with a young woman today, a woman he introduced as Jane. They all turned their attention to the stage as the first toast was announced by a trumpet's call and a round of artillery fire. The toast was to "the people of the United States," and was followed by a discharge from the guns of the *Rising Sun* at her moorings. The sequence was repeated for the next nine toasts, the trumpet and the artillery preceding, the guns of the *Rising Sun* following.

"My word, I think I'm grateful all thirteen states haven't ratified as of yet," Elisabeth said, putting her hands over her ears.

"Look, Davey, there's Rory, from the mill, over by that garden. With Lisa."

"They're to be married," Elisabeth said. "Sometime before Christmas."

David looked at Smith, then back at her, puzzled. How did she know that? She'd never met Lisa, far as he knew—Liam had disengaged himself fast from the lass, perhaps recognizing she was different. Had Smith—

"Whirlwind courtship, aye Davey?"

"What?"

"Rory and Lisa, whirlwind courtship."

David pushed back at the thought that threatened. Besides, the man was safely out of bounds now. "Aye," he mumbled.

BY SIX O'CLOCK the last of the dignitaries had spoken, and the crowd was dispersing. "I should stop and help Ian unload," David said as they walked past the print shop. "It shouldna take long. Come wait inside if ye like."

"Mr. Hall! Ye didna dress like a Gazette, I'm disappointed in ye," Liam said, greeting Hall.

"Come in, come in, boys. And women too, I see. Come in. I'm not sure what a Gazette might look like, Liam." Hall introduced them to the friends he'd gathered in the shop for a celebration and insisted they all stay for a toast. "The case can wait until Monday, David. Sit, sit." He poured them each a glass of wine.

Liam took a sip, raising a brow. "Quite good tae be sharing with the likes of us, Mr. Hall!"

"Rubbish, the 'likes of' you. You're the future of this new country, men like you, David, and Rob here. And unless I'm much mistaken, you know it well, and won't take the responsibility lightly. I've been saving this wine for an occasion such as this, and it's proud I am to share it with the 'likes of' you. A toast, ladies and gentlemen, to the bright and ambitious youth of this fine country!"

David went to Elisabeth as she sat quietly and sipped her wine. "Are ye weary, lass?"

"Oh no, David, I was just wishing . . . well, never mind, it's nothing. It's a compliment to have a man as important to this town as Mr. Hall singing the accolades of the three of you, that's all. In front of his own important friends, no less."

They stayed in the shop for over two hours, celebrating until after dark. David was the one to suggest they leave; he was beginning to get nervous about his plans to propose and wanted to get it past before he lost his nerve.

"Let's walk up the waterfront, look at the ships," Rob suggested.

"Aye," Liam said. "Then I'm off."

"Someone waiting for ye, then?" Rob asked.

"Hmmph."

They walked down the hill to the harbor. "Oh! Will you look at that! Isn't it beautiful!" Elisabeth said. The *Rising Sun* was illuminated from head to toe, and nature had added the display of an *aurora borealis* to the evening sky.

"It is at that," David said. They stopped, admiring the view of the harbor. "As ye are," he whispered, lowering his head to kiss her.

"Well, la de da. Look who's here, Charles," said a voice thick with drink. "That's the chit that threw you over at the Hastings last month. She's slumming. Appears you just weren't from the right part of town. She's giving it away easy enough on the quay."

Elisabeth tightened her hold on his arms as he slowly lifted his mouth from hers. He looked over at the two boys who stood at the water pump. The one speaking was pissing in the river.

"She didn't throw me over, I'll have you know," the other boy said, his voice slurring. "Did you, Elisabeth?" He hiccupped. "He'll find she's used goods soon enough."

Rage tore through him, washed over him, took a hold of him until he could no longer see clearly. Elisabeth was saying something, frantically clutching at his shirt, but he could barely make sense of the words as his vision clouded.

"David, no! He's drunk, he's lying. Just ignore him, David!"

He pushed her into Rob's grasp as he went for the lad. The boy stood stock still, looking at him, his eyes wide as David approached, his arms limp at his side, giving testimony to his incomprehension of the threat. David came in close, pounding his gut with his fists, finishing with a blow to his face when he felt him sagging. It took only seconds. Letting him drop, he drew back his foot to kick him for good measure, the kick not meeting its target as someone pulled him back.

"'Nough, Davey, he's down. Ye needn't do more. That's enough now. The lassies be here; it's done. Aye?"

David shook his head as if to clear it, the fury draining out of him as fast as it had filled him. He dragged his hand hard down the length of his face. The boy lay on the cobblestones, blood pouring from his nose. He looked to be unconscious, least he hoped that's all he was, that he hadn't hit the building behind going down. He probably shouldn't have hit the eijit so hard.

He looked behind him and saw Liam, his eyes intent, watching him carefully. Maybe it had been more than seconds that he had pounded on the lad; Rob's Jane was looking at him in horror. Elisabeth broke loose from Rob and ran to him, throwing her arms around him, sobbing. He put an arm across her shoulders as he looked for the other.

"Ye hit him, Liam?" he asked, nodding toward the second boy on the ground.

"Course I didna. He was yours to take. I might have, ken, if he'd looked sideways at ye. But he just crumbled, soon as ye let fly at the other. Smells like a distillery, likely passed out."

Rob stooped and checked the boys. "They'll be fine, 'pears they didna hit anything going down."

"David, I didn't . . . I wouldn't . . . what he said . . . it wasn't true, David," Elisabeth whispered between sobs.

Startled, David focused on her, lifting her chin. "My God, Bess, I know that." He wrapped both arms around her, holding her tight.

"Let's go, 'fore the Watch shows," Liam said.

The magic of the day was ruined, and he had only himself to blame. Tomorrow then; tomorrow they'd talk. Tomorrow they'd begin.

60

July 6, 1788

"LIAM, I'VE BEEN LOOKING FOR ye for over an hour. I thought ye were working down in Southwark ."

"No work there today. What can I do for ye, Rob?" Liam asked, picking up a bushel from the merchant's wagon, tossing it up on his shoulder.

"Mr. O sent me. Hall stopped by earlier, looking for David."

He dropped the grain on the waiting barge and turned to Rob. "What are ye saying, looking for David? He's no' at the paper?"

"No, he didn't sleep there last night. They havena seen him since kirk."

He grabbed another load as he thought. David had never missed a scheduled day of work, not once in the last four years. He was to spend Sunday with Elisabeth. Would they've taken off? He hadn't said a word to indicate such, though likely he wouldn't. He grunted as he threw the bushel on top of the growing pile. "Any from the Hales show up at the house this morning?"

"Nay. Look, Liam, Mr. O is beside himself, Hall wasna taking it lightly. I'll finish your load; will ye see what ye can find out?"

Liam grabbed another, covertly assessing the number remaining. Rob could finish well enough. It'd harm him more to turn him down. He dropped the bushel on the barge and went to the foreman, explaining Rob would fill in, forestalling any objection by quietly forfeiting half his morning's pay.

"I'll let ye know when I find out, Rob. Thank you for this," he said, waving a hand at the cargo.

AN HOUR LATER he stood on the Hale's front steps, hat in hand, knocking at the door.

"Good afternoon, Tom. Would you let Elisabeth know Liam, Liam Brock, is here to speak to her?"

Tom looked at him, his face drawn and weary, and something sparked deep in his eyes; surprise, and something else. Was it wariness?

"Miss Hale is not receiving today," he said, his words stilted and stiff. He shut the door.

What the hell? Liam stood still for a moment, staring at the closed door. He hurried down the steps and headed back to the kitchen entrance, finding John sitting outside with a bushel of peas, Polly on the ground beside him. Polly looked up at Liam, her eyes widening, and she cuffed John's arm before running into the kitchen. John looked at him and stood.

"John, don't go. I need to know what's happened. David didna show for work today, didna sleep there last night."

John was halfway through the door before Liam finished. He turned. "Young David's missing?"

"It's starting to look that way. I need to find him. Tell me what happened here yesterday."

John sank to the porch step. Liam sat beside him, turning his hat round and round in his hands while he waited.

"It was an awful row," John said, his sad eyes meeting Liam's. "Mr. Hale, I ain't never seen him that angry. Like to have himself a heart attack, the way he was screaming and carrying on. I thought he was going to take a switch to Miss Lisabeth. Don't know the whole story, but—"

"John, thank you for not sending him away. I'd like to talk to him."

Elisabeth. He turned to find her in the doorway, Polly cowering behind her, and he struggled to control his expression. Her face was swollen and red, her hair in tangles, more of it falling from the pins than held in place. Her gown was wrinkled and misshapen as if she'd slept in it. He stood slowly and followed her into the kitchen.

"Sit, please. John, would you get him a cup of coffee, please. Have you eaten, Liam?"

"Elisabeth, just tell me what happened."

"Very well." She reached for Polly's hand and pulled her close. "Do you remember Rudy, friend of Charles? The boorish character on Independence Day, after the parade? Of course you do. He took his complaints to his father, who relayed them to my father, a business associate of his. I shan't air the full details of my family's dirty laundry, but there was quite a scene. The end result is I'm never to see David again. Ever. Papa was livid when I told him I planned to marry David. He blamed my Grandmother, he blamed Polly, he blamed Mr. Oliver."

She looked at the door, averting her eyes. "He shouted at Grandmother, Liam, screamed at her . . . He'll sell Polly down south if I go against his wishes in the matter," she said softly, tears falling.

Liam looked at Polly. She moved a step closer to Elisabeth, fear flickering over the proud lines of her face. He turned back to Elisabeth. "David knows this, then?"

Startled, she looked at him, puzzlement showing in her

red-rimmed eyes. "Why are you here, Liam?"

"No one has seen the lad. He's missing."

He watched as the blood drained from her face, and her lips turned white. John came up behind her, guiding her down into a chair. "You has to eat something, missy. You hasn't eaten since breakfast yesterday."

"Find him, Liam, please. Find him," she whispered, clinging to Liam's arm. "And let me know he's safe."

61

"WICKED HOT, AYE?"
Liam stumbled out from the tangle of forest behind him and drew up short, his forearms to his knees as he struggled to catch his breath. The lad'd been worried; no other reason for the crashing about, given he moved like a cat.

"D'ye recall," Liam asked, pausing as he reached down to unbutton his breeches at the knee, pulling his stockings up tight, "the afternoon we caught a passel of fish in yon pool?"

David'd been recalling another afternoon, one where fish played but a small part. Was it only days ago? Lifting his slouch felt hat, he ran a large calloused hand through his hair to let loose the curls he could count on falling about his eyes.

"That was a good day. This is a good place." Finished with his tidying, Liam walked to the creek, kneeling as he drank, splashing his head and face with water. He turned back to David, one hand on his knee, one hand steadying himself against the ground as he studied him.

"I tried the taverns ye favor. Pete's sake, Davey, have ye any idea how many that runs to? Try visiting them all inside an hour." He untied the bit of leather holding back his hair and ran his hands through it, smoothing the inky black strands that had been plastered about his head at odd angles. Securing it again, he reached down, grabbed a few small flat stones, and brought them to David, placing them between them as he sat. He took one for himself and deftly skipped it across the water.

David ignored the challenge, his eyes fixed on the creek, watching the shimmer of sunlight on the water as it tumbled over the rubble in its path.

"That wench in Helltown?" Liam said. "She hadna seen ye. Looked mighty fine in the harsh light of day, too, ye'll be glad to know. She offered to soothe my worry for a bargain, but I didna have the time, tempting though it was. Told ye she favored me over you." He glanced at David before he went on, then selected another stone. "The harbor master, he hadn't seen ye either, but he assured me no ships had left since the Fourth. Thank God ye dinna like snug places, I was spared searching the holds of those anchored. And hell, speaking of God, I even set foot in your kirk." Giving up on the stones, he reclined back on his elbows, resting, waiting.

Too spent to hide the string of emotions playing across his face, David reached for his hat again, pushing it low on his forehead. The ache welled fresh, forming a hard knot in his chest, rising fast, threatening a sob if he didn't choose to release it in words. He tested his voice, hoping it didn't crack.

"I've lost her, Liam. She was a part of me; I'd sooner lose a limb. She's gone, and I don't know how to go on from that." He turned away as his eyes filled. "Honestly, I don't."

Liam was silent as he considered his response. When he spoke, his words came slowly, deliberately. "Aye, she's a part. And likely will always be; I canna see that she ever willna. But she's not the whole part, I think no' even the best part of ye, David. And go on ye will, as ye have no choice in the matter."

"There's always a choice."

Liam's body tensed, but his voice was even. "Nay, for you

there's no' a choice. God-fearing lad like you? Ye'll go on."

David stared at the mass of butterflies hovering over the wildflowers farther down the creek bed. There had been butterflies last week as well; she'd pointed them out. Laughing, she had parked herself in the midst of the flowers, delighted when the insects covered her, taking care to inform him the creatures had once been furry caterpillars, as if he were one of the young lads in her class. He'd never forget the picture she presented, Bess among the butterflies.

And naturally Liam was right, willingly or not, he'd go on. He stretched, extending his long legs, rolling his shoulders against the stiffness, welcoming the pain that traveled across the muscles of his back.

"Aye, I suppose ye're right," he said, sighing. "But in any event, I canna stay here."

"I'll agree with ye there. It'll be dark soon, and I'll wager ye havena eaten. Let's go." Liam stood, extending his hand.

"Here in Philadelphia," David said, not moving.

Liam froze. "What are ye saying? Ye have to stay. You must stay. Your indenture . . . ye're bound. Ye'd be branded a runaway, ye'd have no trade. What are ye saying?"

David looked up at him, curious. Surely he knew he was a runaway now? "I'd have no trouble finding work, Liam."

"A half-way journeyman? Nay! Not more than five, six days ago ye spoke of such with derision."

"Aye, well, sometimes I can be a bit full of myself." He looked down, reaching for one of the rocks, running its smooth surface between his thumb and forefinger. "Most times, truth be. Dinna ken how ye tolerate it."

"Ye stand a head taller than most, David. Ye think ye'd go unnoticed, should ye run? Hell, ye're no' even lopsided."

A slur against the pressmen. He was surprised to find himself almost grinning, though he lost the inclination before his muscles complied. He'd miss Liam.

Liam paced back and forth along the riverbank, savagely kicking the forest debris in his path. "Jesus, Mary, and Joseph, you can't throw it all away. Years it's been, years. Ye've only two left. Don't do this."

"I willna starve, Liam, I can round up work. It doesna have to be in a print shop," David said, puzzled by the note of panic in Liam's voice.

"I've no doubt of that. It's me I worry about, truth be, selfish bastard that I am." He sat, running his hands back through his hair, mussing it once again. "I need ye near. Ye're my family, my anchor, aye? Remember? Just until I grow up, become responsible?"

David smiled a faint smile, shaking his head at the thought of Liam ever needing him.

"David?" Liam said, his tone solemn. "I make light of it, but the thought of ye gone, it . . . well, just don't go yet. Please?"

He didn't respond, his attention fixed on the stones he was slowly tossing one by one into the river.

"Mr. Hall would be allowing ye back, I'm sure of it, if that's your worry. Ye may be soaking pelts in piss again for a while, but he'd be a fool not to. And Hall's no fool."

He held his tongue as darkness fell softly around them, and with it, the music of the night. Only when the harmony of the tree frogs gave way to the cacophony of the night predators did David stand.

He offered a hand to Liam.

62

August 1788

"WHY, MRS. HALE, WHAT A surprise. Please, do come in." Liam made a bow and swept his hand inwards. "I'm embarrassed. I canna offer ye anything in the way of tea or coffee, but I'm sure that's no less than ye expected, having deigned to visit those of the lower sort."

She walked into the room, her back straight, her head held high. "Don't take that tone with me, young man, I expect much better of you, you can be certain of that. I've come to speak to your guardian. If it's not too much trouble, could you tell him I'm here?"

Abashed, Liam took her elbow and led her to the chairs in the front of the classroom. "I apologize. Please sit. What can I do for ye, Mrs. Hale? Mr. Oliver is out for the morning." He took the chair across from her.

"Well then." She fingered her bag as if she were planning to get up and leave, then settled, her grey eyes soft as she looked at him. "While I have you, perhaps you could tell me how David has been?"

His expression closed. "How is David? Well, let me think how best to answer that, Mrs. Hale," he said, his voice hard as he rose to pace the room in front of her.

"Most of July was spent looking for the bottom of a bottle, then sporting for a fight from anyone willing. I'm glad to say that phase didna last longer 'an a month. I found it quite tiring. Och, we're still inta the whisky, mind ye, just not quite to that excess. And sporting women have replaced sporting for a fight." He stopped pacing and laid his forearm along the fireplace mantel, resting his forehead against it. He sighed, quiet for a moment, then turned to her, his face drawn, his eyes sad.

"Mr. Hall's patience is wearing thin and I barely recognize my mate. The most I can do to help is to follow behind and pick up the pieces."

"It grieves me to hear that. David was . . . David is . . . He's in my prayers nightly. He's a good man."

"Aye, just no' good enough apparently." He looked at Mrs. Hale and relented as he saw her face cloud with sorrow, her eyes glisten with unshed tears. "I'm sorry, Mrs. Hale, I just keep looking for someone to blame, and I tend to take it out on the nearest. I don't have it in me right now to ease your mind. Why are ye here, ma'am?"

"I hesitate to ask a favor, Mr. Brock, but I must. You may or may not know I've just arrived back from Charleston with Elisabeth. I took her there for several weeks to visit one of my dear friends, hoping a change of location would do her good. It didn't. I'm worried. The child is pining away right in front of me, and I can't help her. It breaks my heart every time I look at her. Her classroom, will the children be returning?"

"Aye, I'm to teach them until we find a replacement."

"Would Mr. Oliver consider asking her back, do you think? When I mentioned it, her eyes lit up, the first spark of life I've seen in her since this took place. But it was brief. She said you wouldn't have her, then she went back to bed. Mr.

Brock, she's been in bed for the last two months. She barely
eats or drinks. Frankly, even if Mr. Oliver agreed and she
consented, I'm not sure she could come back, given the state
of her health. But the possibility would give her something
to look forward to. And I've been given to believe it wouldn't
be a one-sided proposition, that she has contributed some to
the success of the Academy. Is she correct in assuming you
wouldn't have her back?"

"I can speak for Mr. Oliver with regards to this. He would
welcome her back on any terms. The children loved her. And
I would see her return as well, when I give off wanting to
wring her neck, that is." He held up his hands in surrender
as Mrs. Hale's lips tightened. "Nay, I've explained I tend to
look for someone to blame. But I can endeavor to behave
rationally for her sake."

"Would you come talk to her?"

He hesitated.

"She'd have to hear it from you."

He exhaled, running a hand back through his hair. "Aye."

"Soon, please. And Liam, I'm reluctant to ask this after
imposing on your goodwill—"

"Don't worry, I'll not come when Mr. Hale is likely to be
at home. Would ten tomorrow be fine, ye think? I'll use the
servants' entrance."

"I'm in your debt." She went to him, ignoring the hand he
extended. Taking his face between her hands, she kissed his
cheek. "Thank you."

"HELLO, JOHN. Long time and all that, eh?"

"Liam, come in. Young David, how's he been? Let me take
your hat there." John motioned him into the kitchen. "Sit,
have yourself some tea. It's a hot one today, for sure." He
placed a cup in front of him. "I hear stories, 'bout town.
Don't much sound like David. I don't pay them much cre-

dence, I don't, but I worry nonetheless."

"Believe them, John. Now, Mrs. Hale asked that I speak to Lisbeth. Perhaps I should just do that."

"Yes, suh," John answered, his face closing.

"Now, John, don't ye 'suh' me, hear? Discussing David's no' something I'll do in this house. I'd appreciate your help, though. He's always valued your friendship and acceptance. If I can get him to wet a line Sunday, would ye be willing to join us? "

"You white boys don't know nothing bout that subject. You join me and ole Barney, we'll show ye how it's done. Third pier, six in the morning come Sunday."

"Liam, you've come!"

He turned at the sound of her voice, reminding himself of his promise to Mrs. Hale, telling himself once again it wasn't her fault.

"Lisa—Jesus, Mary, and Joseph, what have ye done to yourself?"

She started crying at his words, covering her face with her hands, though not before he saw the deep hollows and dark shadows that surrounded her eyes. Her beautiful, graceful hands . . . chapped and red, nails bitten to the quick, cuticles angry and ragged. And where in the hell had she found the garment she was wearing? It wasn't more than a threadbare, shapeless cotton shift, and it hung without form from her thin, bony shoulders. Had the lass given over eating? Her hair was limp, dirty, and dull, and she had tied it back in the fashion of a man's queue, a tangled bushel of wet straw.

Beautiful, proper Elisabeth . . . looking the blowse. He turned back to John, his eyes wide and horrified. John gave him an indignant stare and waved the back of his hand, gesturing him toward her.

"Stap me, lass, I'm sorry. I havena seen ye in some time. Isna John here feeding ye?" John cuffed him hard on the shoulders, pushing him. He looked back at him, helpless. John just canted his head, motioning him forward.

He sucked in a long breath. "Lisbeth? Come sit." Putting his arm around her, he led her to one of the chairs. She pulled away.

"Now, Miss Lisabeth, Liam didn't mean no harm. You just—"

"Stop it! Do you hear me? All of you, stop it! I don't want to sit! And I don't want to eat! I don't want to!" She stamped her foot and made a weak effort to throw the chair against the wall, sobbing in earnest when it landed only a foot away, her thin shoulders shaking. Liam went to her, and she pushed him away.

"There's only *one* thing I want. Does anybody even *hear* me? Liam? Do you hear me? There's only one thing, I tell them, I tell them . . . I want *him*, Liam. I want him so, but nobody listens, I need . . . I need . . ." Her voice shook as she sobbed, and it was difficult to make sense of the words she choked out, but her meaning was clear.

"Aye, lass, aye, I hear ye, I ken," He held her tightly, pulling her head to his shoulder, refusing to relinquish his hold when she tried to push him away. He rocked her and murmured hollow words of consolation while she sobbed and pounded her fists against his shoulders. When her sobbing slowed, he realized she was speaking again, and he tried to make out the words.

"You . . . left me too Liam, I . . . I hate you . . . for that. I needed you . . . and you . . . left. I don't know . . . you never came back . . . if he's dead or alive. Did you think . . . did you think I didn't care to know? Are you . . . punishing me?"

He pulled away to look at her face, and she panicked, throwing herself at him, clinging to him. "No! I'm sorry. I don't hate you. Please don't hate me. Don't leave, Liam, don't, please."

He cradled her and spoke softly, stroking her back. "Lisbeth, shh, listen, stop crying, please. Shhh, I'm no' leaving. And I could never hate ye, lass. I love you. Ye're like a sister to me. I always tell Davey ye were my friend first. Irritates him a bit, I'll grant ye, seeing how it's only by minutes. And I'll grant ye I've been a bad friend to you. I'm sorry for that, I am. Now, John here offered me a bite to eat, I'd like to take him up on it, if ye'd join me. We'll talk over a meal, aye?"

She looked up at the mention of David's name.

"No. I'm not hungry. Weren't you listening? And don't use that tone of voice with me, I'm not a simpleton." She blew her nose on the handkerchief she carried and sat on the bench facing the table, exhausted from her crying spell.

Liam grinned and went to the water jug, pouring a bit of cool water on his handkerchief. Coming back to the table, he straddled the bench and faced her, thanking John with a nod for the food and drink he'd set on the table.

"C'mere, lass, look over at me now." Pressing the cool wet cloth around her eyes with one hand, he brushed the loose hair from her face with the other. Breaking off a bite of bread, he quickly placed it between her lips before she could object and placed his finger over her mouth. "Chew. I'm sorry I didn't think to see ye before now. It was thoughtless of me. I've no excuse. Truth be, I was angry, and I wasna sure of my reception." He followed the bread with a bit of cheese, and she chewed automatically, her eyes not leaving his face.

"I did leave word I'd found David, you know I did." She opened her mouth to respond, and he tucked another piece of bread in it, pushing her chin up with his hand. "Were ye aware classes were starting soon? It's kept me busy, ye know well how it is at the end of summer break." She didn't answer, still watching him, and he held the cup of ale to her mouth.

"Drink, there. Aye, well, this week the children have been stopping by to check in. Li'l John Talbot was fairly bursting with the news he memorized his threes over the summer. He was mighty disappointed to find ye gone." He put another piece of bread in her mouth. "Chew. Amy, remember Amy? Well she wrote a whopper of a book report on *Gulliver's Travels* over the summer. Ye have to read it. It'll make ye proud." He alternated bites of food with stories of the children until she'd finished most of what John had set out.

"Would ye consider coming back, lass?"

Tears glistened in her blue eyes. "I read *Gulliver's Travels* to David on the ship while he was ill."

"I ken, lass. I was there. It breaks my heart, all this." He waved his hand about.

"You would have me teach again? Mr. Oliver would?"

"Of course we would. You're a wonderful teacher, and the children miss you. I miss you."

"I'd love to. I think. I don't do much all day, anymore."

"Then get your strength back up. I'll tell Mr. Oliver within the month, aye?

"You're not going to speak to me of David?"

"Is there any hope?"

Slowly, she shook her head, her eyes filling again.

"Then, no, I'm not. But know that he's all right, and I'm watching over him."

63

DAVID SAT AT THE BAR, nursing a whisky, Liam beside him, as he'd been every night since . . . as he'd been every night. They'd just finished supper, and it was still early. Another long, empty night ahead.

He picked up his glass and stared into it, swirling the liquid around the bottom, remembering. "It's like a fine whiskey, aged years in a sherry cask."

"What're ye yattering about? We're lucky if this rotgut's been aged a fortnight in a topped chamber pot."

"My da brought some home once. It was quite the occasion; I just don't recall why. The color, though, that I remember well. It's the color of her hair. Havena ye noticed? Sometimes I'd look at her and think I was looking at a sunrise."

Liam choked, spewing the whisky in his mouth across the filthy bar. He looked askance at David. "Hell. I liked ye better when ye were threatening Big Jim over there with stuffing his ballocks down his throat for sitting too close to ye."

Reminded, David looked over at the man in question to make sure he remembered the threat. Satisfied Jim was indeed minding his space, he returned his attention to his whisky.

Liam pushed his own drink away and turned to face him.

"We're taking it easy tonight, mate. We've a date with the fish early on the morrow."

"So? I can handle it, and besides, tonight's Saturday. We've no call to be up early with the fish tomorrow."

"Aye, well, *I* canna handle it. I expect I'm not as resilient as ye. Ye're staying with me tonight. We're getting some sleep and we're meeting friends at six."

"What are ye rambling on about and why are ye so bossy the sudden? Ye remind me of . . . " He picked up his cup and took a long swallow. "I've no friends but ye, Liam; certainly none that rise by six."

He knew he looked like hell. He'd seen the puffiness about his face obscuring the lines of his cheekbones, filling the hollows beneath, rimming his bloodshot eyes. Saw it all last Sunday night when Robert had thrust the looking glass at him, disgusted with him for sleeping the day away, though he made no effort to stop him as he headed out the door to begin again. He'd had no call to stop him; he was the first in the shop each morning, the last to leave each evening.

He felt like hell as well, his gut aching, filling his breeches to the point of a new button—the first time he'd ever out-grown a pair around the waist before the ankles.

And the whores; he hadn't the stomach for that any longer, the image of Bess in his arms, her clear blue eyes so guileless and trusting, coming unbidden that last time up against the outside of the Man; rendering the distraction too filthy even in his self-loathing.

But work and whisky . . . now they dulled the pain, stopped the dreams, and he wasn't for giving either up just yet. Not while the barkeeps still honored his tab anyway. He'd just count himself lucky they weren't poxed, he and Liam.

He fingered his glass, taking a long swallow. Jesus, the places the man had tagged after him.

"I didna ask for company."

"Aye," Liam answered calmly. "But I did."

He motioned to the barkeep to refill their cups. Liam stopped the man and poured his remainder into David's.

"The Academy opens Monday."

David nodded, not concerned enough with the conversation to comment on the change in topic.

"I went to see Elisabeth yesterday, to talk to her about resuming her class."

David winced. "How is she?" he whispered.

"I've been so angry at her, David. Now I'm only angry at myself."

"Who are we fishing with?"

"John; remember John? Works at the Hales? And some mates of his."

"I let her down. I shouldna have hit the lad."

Liam made a sound of disgust. "Ye'd do it again, given the same. If no', I would have."

David nodded slowly. Unable not to, he asked, "Why'd ye need to talk to her about that? I told her it wasna seemly. I shouldna have said that, no' about something she loves." He shook his head. "I should never have said that. I should never have done a lot of things. The time I wasted fretting over her faith . . ." He tossed back the rest of the whisky, setting the cup down heavily on the bar. "She'll teach again, aye? She has each year."

"Dinna ken. She can't just yet."

"Why?"

"Well, it's just no' settled yet, but I think she will."

"Liam?"

"Hmmph?"

David sighed and got up. "Never mind, let's go." They walked out the door and stood in the darkness. "Ye think Mr. Oliver and Rob are up for a game of cards?"

"Nay, Rob's courting that Jane seriously now. Remember?

I told ye I thought they may marry soon?"

"Nay, I didn't. Good God, married?" He ran his hand down his face, giving his head a quick shake. "Damn, I've been full of myself. How can ye stand being with me?"

Liam just grunted. They walked slowly along Front Street, looking out over the harbor.

"D'ye still think about it, the passage over?"

"Aye, and still waiting for my copy of your journal."

"I havena forgotten. I was planning on filling it in a bit for ye. It's a little sparse on the details as it stands. Didna want to put anything in to worry or excite my Ma."

"Well it's been four years past. Ye'll have forgotten the details by now."

"No' likely. Did he strike her, Liam, her da?"

"What? Christ, no! No, nothing like that. I would have come to ye immediately."

"She's took to the bottle then? Been dragging her best friend through the dregs of society?"

"No' possible, ye occupy all my free time. She took to her bed, David, traded eating for crying."

They walked the rest of the way in silence until they stood outside the townhouse. David noted the new sign advertising the start of term on Monday.

"Liam, is she ill, then? Why is there a question about her teaching?"

"She's only feeling a bit peaked, dinna fash. She'll be all right, I'm sure of it. And ye will as well."

64

November 1788

"ALMOST HAD YE, MR. O."

"I'll agree, Liam, but only 'almost'. I'll warrant it's getting harder to hold my own against you boys."

David stood, stretching. "Mayhap against Liam and Rob, dinna ken if I'll ever master the game."

"They've been at my knee years longer than you, David."

"Ye'll stay for supper, Davey?"

David grinned. "Of course. Ye made soup, aye?"

He and Liam had found a marsh turtle earlier that day, a small terrapin that had had the misfortune to wander in their path as they made their way back into town from the creek. Liam had claimed he could make a soup to rival any of those made from the huge sea turtles brought in by the carrying trade, so David had snatched it up and handed it to him. Turtle soup was one of his favorites.

"HOW DO WE kill him? When he shimmies away like this?" Liam had asked, holding up the turtle shell for David's examination. "Makes it hard to wring his neck, aye?"

"I watched Miss Sue do it one morning, down at the market. The pot's what kills it, once ye throw it in."

Liam had blanched. "Och, that seems awfully harsh, now." He had set the turtle down, well off the path, hidden deep in the thick grasses. "No' hungry 'nough."

"Aye, and it's a good batch of potatoes, too," Liam said, grinning. He knelt by the fireplace, pushing the pot back over the coals to heat it up.

Rob snorted in disgust. "Ye should have brought the critter home. Ye willna find me turning my nose up at perfectly good game."

"Rob, stop tormenting the lad," Mr. Oliver said mildly. He lit the candle on the table and pulled forward his pen and inkstand. "David, as long as you're up, I have a list of books over there. I just thought of one I wanted to add to it. Would you mind bringing it over?"

Mr. O always had stacks of books going, some so tall they often teetered and fell should one walk too close. A loose paper near the top of the stack he'd pointed at caught David's eye, and he pulled it out, thinking it the list.

What the hell? He glanced toward the fireplace.

"Liam?"

"What d'ye have there, Davey?"

"Well, if I didna know better, I'd say it was notice of a reward upon my capture."

Liam jumped up and grabbed the paper from David's hand. "Ye weren't to see that. Rob and I . . ."

Rob spoke up. "We wanted to make sure ye were represented fairly by Mr. Hall, David. It was in fun—we never truly expected ye to take off for good."

"The notices ye print over there, well, we couldn't have ye characterized like that. It'd make us inta fools for keeping ye close!" Liam said.

David laughed and grabbed the paper back from Liam. It started out with lines he recognized setting himself. Some-

one bound would run, whether it be a servant, slave, or
apprentice, then their master would place an ad describing
the lad, or in some cases, the lass, and the reward they were
willing to pay to get them back. David agreed; the runaways
were characterized in such a way one wondered why anyone
would pay the dollar or two to get them back.

Rob had written out phrases from existing advertisements,
presumably as a guide in writing their own:

> *A down sour look, squint closed look, halt in his walk,*
> *one thigh smaller than another, sour visage, squinty eyes,*
> *lumpy face, much pock-marked and scarred, apt to tell lies,*
> *weaves stories, capable of fraud of any sort, wears women's*
> *clothes, seldom wears breeches on account of being round*
> *shinned, clumsily built, ungraceful carriage, hands stand out*
> *not in line with his arms, great gambler with smooth tongue,*
> *marked with smallpox, stole his indenture, wants for most*
> *of his teeth, apt to be impertinent, fond of strong liquor*

In Liam's hand was written the complete advertisement
they had apparently decided on:

> *FIFTY DOLLARS Reward.*
> *RAN AWAY from subscriber, apprentice lad named*
> *David Graham, a printer by trade, about eighteen years*
> *of age, six feet, three inches high, big, but carries himself*
> *well, dark eyes, dimples visible should he ever smile again,*
> *clear complexion. His dark hair is long. He ties it back,*
> *but may have cut it by now for concealment, in which case it*
> *will curl. He was inoculated for the smallpox, and the place*
> *can be seen on his upper left arm. Intelligent, but uses words*
> *sparingly. Should he choose to speak, speaks English, often*
> *with a Scotch cant, also speaks French and some German.*
> *Wearing a good white house-linen shirt, ticklenburg jacket,*

waistcoat, and breeches of copperas color, calf-shin boots
with copper-coloured buckles, and an old felt hat. Steady,
sober disposition, but has been fond of strong liquor as late.
Whoever takes up and secures said lad, so as his master
may have him again, shall have the above reward and
reasonable charges if brought home, paid by WILLIAM
HALL.

"Och, Mr. Hall'd ne'er be paying fifty dollars, even should his wife run."

"Nay, I expect I'd have trouble with that amount," Liam said.

David put the paper back in the pile and shifted uneasily. "Ahh, I ne'er told the lot of ye, that is, I appreciate . . . I'm verra lucky to have—"

"Cease. If ye mean tae be weeping, Liam will need tae be revising it again," Rob said.

"We're glad you stayed, David. Our lives would be much poorer, should you have left."

"Thank ye, Mr. Oliver, I'm glad to have stayed as well. Liam, have ye any 'strong liquor' on hand?"

Liam laughed. "Funny ye should ask; indeed we do. Seeing as how it's November, Mr. O thought we should celebrate a series of our own Thanksgivings this month, with good drink whenever good friends are on hand. "

"Nothing but the best Scotch whisky we could find for the occasion would do. We've all much to be thankful for since we've come to America, especially our recent news that Alex is safe and in London for the winter," Mr. Oliver said. "I've decreed a month long celebration in this household."

Rob cleared his throat. "Uh, I've an announcement, since you've declared a celebration, that is."

Liam sat back on the hearth, his mouth open. "Holy hell, ye're going through with it."

"Liam," Oliver admonished. He went to Rob and embraced him. "It's true then?" he thought to ask, pulling back.

"Aye, she said yes. We're planning on Saturday; that is, Mr. O . . ." Rob faltered, looking away.

"Don't be foolish, Rob. Of course you'll stay with us. You're handy enough; build a wall in yon room for the two of ye, if she's shy."

David shook his hand. "I'm happy for ye, Rob. Jane's a good lass. Though she hasn't thought to look me in the eye since last summer." There, he could jest about it; no need to worry about him, none at all.

"Well, ye do have a 'down, sour look' about ye after all, Davey." Liam had held back during the congratulations, keeping his eyes on the soup. David watched as Mr. Oliver laid a gentle hand on Liam's back. He rose then, and went to Rob.

Liam clasped Rob's shoulder. "It willna be the same ever again, will it?" he said, his voice subdued, his eyes on the floor. "But I'm happy for ye, mate, I am."

David watched them, feeling . . . something. He didn't know what, couldn't put a name to it. But again, he was glad he'd stayed, though sorry he'd dragged Liam through the hellholes of Philly after him.

"Well, if ye be pouring now, pour me one, will ye, Liam?" David asked, thinking to ease the emotions running through the room. "I'll be right back."

He hurried down the stairs and into the back classroom, careful to avoid treading on the floorboards he knew to squeak. The familiar scent of the room assaulted him as soon as he walked in, threatening to bring him to his knees, inviting him to give in to the grief that threatened to overwhelm him. Pulling out a small cloth bag from his shirt, he tucked it into the top drawer of Elisabeth's desk, then hurried out to visit the privy before he'd be missed.

65

January 1789

"ELISABETH? IS THAT YOU? WOULD you come in here for a minute please? And close that door, will you? No need to let the snow blow in."

"Sorry, Papa. I couldn't get my boot off." She closed the door and took off her coat and hat, hanging it on the rack. "I'll be right in."

Their relationship had been strained for months now. He hadn't forgiven her for the embarrassment he'd suffered at her hands last summer. And it seemed her "ridiculous" reaction to his "solution" after the incident had only further infuriated and distanced him. She was surprised he was making an effort to seek her out.

"Yes, Papa?"

"Sit, Beth, I need to talk to you about something. I'm leaving Philadelphia for a while."

"Why? For how long?" she asked, alarmed. "Am I to come with you?"

"No, I've spoken to your Grandmother and she's adamant that it's in the best interest of all of us if you stay here with her. She has no one now, and I'll be busy working." Seemingly as an afterthought, he added, "And I suppose you have that damn school you're so fond of."

"You'll be working? Where?"

"I'm going to New York first. A group of gentlemen and I will be making investments in land. It was decided that I'd be the scout, as I haven't a family."

Elisabeth winced.

"I didn't mean to say that. Of course I have a family. But the others have wives and young children. I'll be back often, to see you. And I've every faith you'll be in good hands with your grandmother."

She stood and walked to the window, her back to him. "When will you be leaving?"

"Within the hour. I have a series of meetings in New York in just five days, I haven't time to spare."

Within the hour, my. "I see. I'm glad you were able to spend Christmas here. Is it safe to travel in winter?"

"It won't be on a ship, so anything will be an improvement. I've bought you a gift." He laid a package on the table, but she didn't turn. "Well, then. You can open it later, once I leave. I expect to be back for a visit in May. That's only a couple of months away. In the meantime, I'll write, of course."

She nodded, not trusting her voice.

"New York is the place to be right now, Elisabeth. President Washington will be there, and all that follows."

She nodded again, wishing he'd go before the tears came.

"Well then." He cleared his throat and opened the study door. "You'll probably want to change into something dry, I don't want you catching a cold. Your Grandmother will need you while I'm gone."

She hurried from the room. It always made him angry to see her cry.

THE HOUSE WAS EMPTY when she returned from the

Academy. She went to his study and sat at his desk, closing her eyes, trying to summon up the happier times she'd spent in this room. Were there truly none? Had it been that long?

Sighing, she opened the package he had left.

A book; that was thoughtful of him. She did love books. It was brand new, quite a luxury. *The Power of Sympathy*, a novel. Smiling, she went to curl up in the chair by the fire. The title sounded familiar. It might be the one rumored to be the first American novel—and her papa had the thoughtfulness to purchase it for her, knowing she shared his love for books.

Hours later she stood, her mouth set in a hard line. She aimed the book toward the fireplace, then changed her mind at the last second and threw it across the room, out the doorway, and into the hall. It wasn't in her to destroy a book, no matter how distasteful. Running up the stairs to her room, she flung herself across the bed, crying as she hadn't since she'd lost David.

MRS. HALE RETURNED HOME from her meeting late, spotting the book on the floor as she reached to extinguish the lamp Tom had left burning. Recognizing it as the one Edward had purchased, she picked it up and opened it, turning to the introduction.

> *"Intended to represent the specious causes, and to expose the fatal CONSEQUENCES, of SEDUCTION; To inspire the Female Mind With a Principle of Self Complacency, and to Promote the Economy of Human Life."*

The author loftily maintained the book could teach young ladies to avoid scandalous errors.

"Oh, Edward, why?" she whispered. She laid the book down and started her slow climb up the stairs for the night.

66

March 1789

WHO THOUGHT TO ASSIGN THE wheelbarrow men to work the alley in front of the inn? He loped ahead to the two elderly women a few yards farther on, asking if he might escort them to the other side of the street.

"Just might be safer, I think."

"Prisoners, you say? Martha, did you hear that?" the taller of the two shouted, waving her cane at the men ahead. "Those men up ahead with the wheelbarrows? This young man says they're those vicious escaped prisoners, just like those we read about."

David grinned. "No ma'am, likely not the same as those who escaped." Given the wardens wouldn't be apt to send the same crew out in the streets again. He raised his voice some, so both could hear. "But it never hurts to be cautious, aye?"

"Oh, no. It most certainly never does, I agree with you, sir. More your age would do well to remember that."

"Milred, ask him about the dogs," the one called Martha shouted.

"Would you ask those men to pick up the dead animals,

sir? It's quite disgraceful. Martha counted six dead animals in that empty lot back there. One pig, two cats, and three dogs. That's one more than there was the day before."

If he asked the wheelbarrow men *that*, he'd likely wind up face-down in a rotting carcass. "I'll speak to someone about it, ma'am. I shouldna interrupt them about their duties." He left them outside the doorway of the inn. It wasn't an idle promise. He could talk to Mr. Hall; he was going to sit on City Council. And now that the city was incorporated, with rights to raise and levy taxes, well, just maybe they could get it right.

The men across the street hurled insults at him, one of them picking up the iron ball attached to his chain and dropping it back down on the ground in a menacing manner, hoping to provoke him. He responded with a half-hearted insulting hand gesture and hurried up the street.

He wanted to catch Liam before he left for the evening. He was anxious to hear how his day had been. He'd received a scholarship in December from the University, and today was his first day of classes.

Liam was exiting the townhouse just as he reached the steps. "David, I didna expect to see ye today. Have time for supper?"

"Aye, the City Tavern?"

Liam looked surprised, but shrugged. "Sure."

"Well, how was it?"

"Different, verra different," he said. "Here we are; I'll tell ye about it while we eat." Liam found them a table while David went to order the meal.

"The subject matter of the classes was no' a problem," Liam said, sipping from the mug David had placed in front of him. "Maybe it's due to my being a charity case, but it's a different world, and only two blocks down."

"Och, you're far from a charity case, Liam. You earned that

scholarship through merit, not need. And dinna disparage those who receive it through need."

"I know, I shouldna have said that. It was a bit of a shock, though, the day. Spending the whole of it with . . ." He stopped, searching for the word.

"Scholars, no' laborers? And ye're bound to think it a different world. It took ye months just to apply. Ye're used to thinking of yourself in a different light," David said. "Ye'll adjust, and quickly, no doubt."

"Ye're right, of course. Mr. Oliver is insisting I devote myself full-time to this, but I have to tell ye, his classes were much more demanding, and I managed working as well."

"It's only the first day; it'll become more difficult, I imagine." David raised his mug. "Well, here's to my learned university friend. May he still find time for the lower sort."

"Off with ye, David. I'll no' toast to that. None of this would be, but for ye." The meal came and Liam paused, black brows rising in surprise at the spread laid before him.

"We're celebrating, Liam. This is a big step," David said, grabbing one of the fried oysters.

"Well, now. I guess it is at that," he said, "and I see it's my favorites, no' yours. You don't even care for asparagus." He piled his plate with baguettes, smothering them in Welsh Rabbit. "Who will eat my leavings then?"

David grinned. "I'll have to force myself, no worries."

Liam snorted. "Now, come Saturday, we're meeting two ladies at the Bunch of Grapes for a late tea." He laughed, picking up his mug of ale daintily, for show. "Tea! Can ye imagine? I met them this afternoon and thought you might enjoy that."

"Course ye did," David said, scowling.

"Well, they were interesting to talk to. In town for a few weeks with their families from New York. Cousins, I believe. This is good. The quails are stuffed with oysters; did ye notice?"

David nodded. "Well, at least they're transitory."

Liam laughed. "Susan still pursuing ye? Tell Robert to threaten her with the loss of your position, should she show at the print shop again."

"I just canna rouse an interest, Liam. Women are a needless distraction. Annoying distraction, I'd go so far as to say."

"I'm sorry for ye there. Mayhap ye need to try harder," Liam said, serious.

"So ye keep saying."

"Mr. O's having Lisbeth take over my bookkeeping duties for the next few months. She volunteered, wants to learn how to be self-sufficient, she says. Her papa's all but abandoned her." Liam set his quail bones on David's plate. "Well, more to the truth, he's left for New York on business, doesna expect to return for several months. Warned her well against resuming her scandalous behavior whilst he's gone."

David picked the meat from the bones, careful to control his expression. If he revealed too much, Liam wouldn't talk of her, thinking to save him the angst. The man was fiercely protective—or like as not, he just didn't want to spend anymore time chasing him through the dregs of Philly. If he kept neutral, Liam's natural inclination to talk would win out.

"What's he doing in New York?" he asked, licking his fingers.

"Sounds like land speculation to me. She wasna clear."

"Well, I think she may be more suited to keeping the books than yourself, if she's the time for it. If she's no' too busy with other." Damn, too much. Fishing, and he's caught it.

"Aye. Have ye heard yet from the Rev'rend? He still planning a visit this month? Ahh, will ye look at this, pound cake." He grinned up at the server, reaching for the cake. "Ye do pay attention, don't ye, Davey?"

"Well, I wanted the strawberry rhubarb pie, but she said it's no' in season, the fruit. And you've said ye like it fresh. But she avers the raspberry shrub is good." He grabbed a portion of pound cake and put it on his own plate, dousing it with the shrub. "But no, he's no' coming. He must postpone it 'til May, when he comes for the Minister gathering. He plans to coach me on my options, so he says."

"Hmmph, sounds like him. He's always one with good advice, though. Just don't be joining the clergy."

David laughed. "No' likely, no' with the influence ye've had over me these past five years."

Liam grinned. "Glad to be of service! I can go to my grave a satisfied man, just hearing that." Finished, they left the table. "Are ye going to PAS tonight? I'll go with ye, if so. I heard they're going to address the issue of the Barbarian whoresons."

"Aye, let's stop and gather up Ian."

"Still working on enlightening the lad?"

"He tries. Did I tell ye when I went last I spent an hour with Mrs. Hale over coffee afterwards?"

Liam stopped abruptly. "Hell no, why?"

David shrugged and motioned him to keep walking. "She's an interesting woman, and she was alone. She's a large knowledge of the world. We talked a lot of the happenings in France and in Russia. Empress Catherine fascinates her. I walked her home."

"Pete's sake, David, I would've thought ye'd mention that sooner."

"Well, I'm mentioning it now, because it's likely we'll have coffee again tonight, and you're welcome to join us."

"Right then, I'd like to." He laughed, shaking his head. "I canna interest ye in a bonny young lass, but ye're more than willing to spend time with a woman old enough to be your own grandmother."

David shrugged again. "Like I said, she's good conversation. And she doesna want something I canna give."

67

April 1789

"LASS, HAVE YE SEEN . . ."

The deep voice drifted back, and Elisabeth cringed, sinking lower into the position she'd assumed to examine the china on the bottom shelf.

She knew that voice; she'd know it anywhere. It was a memory she summoned each night in a bid for sleep to come. Gravelly, harsh . . . melodic, soothing . . . it swept through her, enfolded her . . . What was he *doing* here at this hour?

"Och, ye say that to every Tom, Dick, and Harry comes in here, Mary. Ye think I don't notice the lads leaving this store all befuddled-like and knock-kneed?"

Mary laughed. "You do go on, David, that tongue of yours. Still waiting to taste it, mind ye. Is there something I can be doing for you today?"

"Well then, now that ye ask so sweet like that, darlin' . . ."

There was a brief silence, and Mary giggled.

Another pause, then David's voice aimed in her direction. "The shop empty, Mary? Seems—"

Elisabeth clamped her hands tight over her ears, closed her

eyes, and called upon God to do something . . . anything! An earthquake, a tidal wave . . . anything, God, *please*! She'd die if she had to listen to another second of their flirting, another second of their silence while she wondered what had stalled the flirting. And she'd die twice if he discovered her cowered here.

She recalled the conversation with Liam before she'd come, wondering if her sins against the country justified this degree of punishment.

"Lisbeth, the idea is to support American goods, no' to rush out and buy up a market's worth of British goods."

"So? I've had my eye on that china for months now. I should be start-ing my hope chest." She had declined to say what she might be hoping for. *"And with what you pay me, I can't afford an extra ten percent. It's ridiculous. It's highway robbery."*

"Och, so it's my fault then, ye support the enemy."

She stamped her foot. *"Don't make me feel guilty. I want that set! And I'm buying it before the duty sets in. Did you read all the items they're taxing? Did you? The list was endless. Who wouldn't go out and buy ahead? You yourself ought to stock up on playing cards. Ten cents the tax is on those!"*

MY WORD, she'd never look at this china again. Never! If she wouldn't have to pay for it, she'd break each and every last bloody piece of it. She'd vow she'd only buy American made goods from this point forward, no matter how shoddy, how tacky, how tasteless; if only he'd leave before she was discovered. Her face burned as she uncovered her ears and heard him make one last flirtatious remark before heading out the door.

She'd grow to love American made earthenware, truly, she would.

She waited a few moments until she could be sure David

would be back in the Print Shop. Why Mr. Hall permitted him to wander the streets, gallivanting about when he should be working, she was sure she didn't know. Now she was going to be late meeting her grandmother. The crowds were already gathering along the street, and Grandmother hated crowds.

General Washington was traveling through town today, on his way to New York to become the first President of the United States, and the whole city would be out in force to welcome him. From the sounds of the cannon, she suspected he'd already reached Gray's Ferry. Her friend Mary's home had a large, lovely window fronting Second Street, and she and her grandmother had been invited to watch the procession with Mary's family. It was said there were plans for a grand dinner at City Tavern before the General left Philadelphia. They'd have a splendid view of it all; if she could get there in time, that is.

68

September 1789

"WHAT ON EARTH?" ELISABETH SAID, losing her balance and falling from her knees to her back. The puppy covered her face with sloppy swipes of its tongue, its tail swishing in quick, happy beats as it balanced on her chest. She grabbed it around the middle, holding it up for view. "Where did you come from?"

"She's the runt of the litter. Can't get rid of her. I'm not looking to take her back, so she's either yours or the streets."

"Rory!" She released the puppy and struggled to a sitting position. He looked more prosperous than the last time she'd seen him, a year ago. His dark suit fit him flawlessly, the white linen of his shirt was spotless, and his boots had somehow made the trek still shining. The mill must be doing well. And, of course, he was as handsome as ever, with his swarthy dark looks and imposing stature.

"Hello, Elisabeth." He extended his hand and helped her to her feet. "Your garden's come a long way. I'm impressed."

They were standing on one of the flagged walkways that neatly separated the beds. Her grandmother had expanded her allotment of the garden to two squares now. John still had his three for his kitchen garden, and her grandmother had kept the remaining three for her flowers. She was trying a bit of everything, to test her skill, and she was indeed proud of how well it was faring.

Her wildflowers she kept in a less cultivated showing on the side of the house, below her bedroom window, their riotous display of color the first thing she sought to view each morning.

"It has, hasn't it? So much so that John threatens to feed me cauliflower for breakfast." She brushed off her skirts. "Rory, I was so sorry to hear about Lisa."

He grimaced, unable to look her in the eye. "It'll be a year this month, but I find myself still thinking of things two or three times a day that I need to tell her as soon as I see her again. I'll never forgive myself for not taking her out of this city as soon as she agreed to marry me."

"You can't blame yourself. Who's to say she still wouldn't have taken ill?"

"Well, if nothing else, we would have had months together." He shook his head and turned.

"No! Damn it, I'm sorry, Elisabeth." He hurried toward the puppy, who was busy uprooting one of the rose bushes growing alongside the house. Picking her up, he ran his hand over her head, cuddling her close. "Bad dog. How can I convince this nice lady to keep you when you go and show your true colors at the gate?"

"Hmm, I suppose she has no manners whatsoever, if that's how she's been disciplined."

He made a show of covering the dog's ears. "Shh, I haven't yet told her you're a witch of a schoolmarm."

Elisabeth laughed. "It's good to see you again, Rory. Come inside for some tea. Maybe I can keep her until you find a proper home for her. What do you call her?"

"Becca."

"OUR FIFTH YEAR, Lisbeth."

And her second without David. Elisabeth sat doodling idly on a piece of slate.

"Nice flowers. An admirer? Heard Smith was sniffing round again."

The years had taught her not to be surprised by what Liam knew. She looked at him, sighing. He was in the mood to talk, and he wasn't one to disappear on a hint.

"I brought them from home. They are lovely, aren't they?" Her wildflowers had been blooming for two months now; the seeds in the sack David had left had been prolific. Did he want her to be reminded of him constantly? Did he know the ache it brought? Did he ever still think of her?

"Our fifth year . . . my word. Did you know two of the students in my first class will be finishing up with Mr. Oliver this year? I'm becoming quite the spinster, aren't I?"

"Ye're the most intelligent, witty, practical, resourceful, beautiful woman I know. And charming; canna forget charming. Time doesna notice the likes of ye. Why, it seems only yesterday it was, ye were haranguing me about the conditions of a wee fireplace."

"Quite the prevaricator you've become. And you never have cleaned it; don't think I haven't noticed. You got David to do it for you that first year, and each of the last four you've managed to sweet-talk some poor girl into doing it."

"I've time on my hands, Lisbeth. My courses don't start for another few weeks. Ye think your grandmother would allow ye to take a short trip with Sally and me to visit her sister? Ye could chaperone us. Rob could cover your classes for a day or two if we time it proper, say Monday next, for instance?"

"Oh? You've progressed to the point of a trip together? To meet the family no less? The legendary, unattainable Mr. Brock, brought to heel?" She stood. "My, my."

"That's enough from ye, lass. I've my own reasons for making the trip. Meeting the family is no' one of them."

She began to gather her belongings for the walk home. "Hmm, I hope you've made that clear to Sally. She's a nice girl. Thank you, Liam, for the offer, but somehow I think watching the two of you won't lighten my mood, and I don't want to dampen her visit."

"Did I mention her sister lived in Baltimore? Ye'd enjoy it, I can take ye shopping; ye can keep Sally company."

Elisabeth laughed. "I'm sorry, but Baltimore doesn't entice me. Don't worry, I'm sure Sally knows you don't give a fig about her and has no expectations."

Liam grimaced. "It's no' that way. She's a friend. I'm sure she understands how I care for her." He paced—obviously a woman's point of view had worried him. "Lisbeth, ye'd have fun. Think about it," he pleaded.

She came out from behind her desk, tied on her hat, and called for Polly from the front room. "Did I mention I love you, Liam? You're the best friend a girl could ask for? Now, honestly, don't worry, I was only teasing you. Sally doesn't need me along," she said, hugging him

"Miss Liss!" Polly said, glaring at Liam.

Liam shrugged. "You're the only woman left can resist me, Polly. What can I say?"

"Don't pay him any mind, Polly. Let's go. In case I don't see you again, Liam, have a nice trip."

"WHERE'S LIAM going, Miss Liss?"

"Baltimore. You remember Sally?"

"The one we done saw at the dry goods?"

"Yes. She's a sister in Baltimore. Although I'm not sure that's why he's going."

"'Specially not as he done already started stepping out with that no account barmaid at the sign of the Swan."

"Truly?" She shook her head. "One of these days . . . "

"I don't think so, Miss Liss. Ain't none of 'em seem to mind overmuch."

"Would you? If Leo . . .?"

"Men done do what they do. Ain't got a whole lotta say in it."

"Hmmm."

"But my Leo wouldn't." She grinned wide, her eyes shining. "That man done knows what's good for him."

Elisabeth laughed. "Well, I'm certainly glad to hear that." She squeezed her arm tight. "You deserve to be happy, Polly."

"You do, too, Miss Liss. If it wasn't for me—"

"Don't you say that again, Polly, don't. You promised! If you think for one minute that I'd sacrifice you . . . that I'd risk Papa . . ." She couldn't even say the words.

"I know, Missy, dontcha start fussing now, I won't. Can we finish that book tonight? Do you have time?"

"Of course I do, especially if you help me grade the spelling tests."

"ELISABETH, HAVE you heard what happened?"

"With what, Mary? Don't forget, most of my time is spent with those under ten years of age." The heat from the summer had relented some, and she had convinced Mary to spend the afternoon in the park with her. Walks with David were one of the things she missed most; one of the several hundred things.

"More of those drasted wheelbarrows have escaped from prison. They robbed two men Thursday night coming home from Darby. One of the men may not even survive. Why, they were gentlemen who were accosted, Elisabeth!"

As if that fact made the crime more heinous. She kept the thought to herself; so many of her thoughts only distressed

Mary. The 'wheelbarrow men' continued to cause problems for the city, and several had managed escapes from the prison over this past year, committing highway robberies, household burglaries, and in a few cases, murder. The citizens were up in arms, maintaining the street work details allowed the prisoners too much freedom to survey the scene of their next crime, some even committing crimes while attached to ball and chains on the street.

"Have they recaptured them yet?"

"No, and not one of us is safe until they do."

In spite of herself, Elisabeth cast a nervous glance about the park. Seeing nothing untoward, she turned her attention back to Mary. "They will soon. They always do. Now, tell me about Charles. Has he called on you yet?"

Diverted, Mary proceeded to chat about her latest beau in waiting. While she rambled on, Elisabeth thought of Liam and his upcoming trip. What if those men attacked the stage? It was dreadful to travel; everyone knew that, what with highway robberies and Indian attacks, not to mention the appalling conditions of the roads. Why, just last week the stage to Baltimore had overturned at the river, killing the horses and injuring several of the passengers.

The thought of being without shelter, your mode of travel lost, subject to the conditions of the elements—it made her shiver. Liam was one of the only friends she had whom she could truly talk to. Well, him and Polly. She couldn't bear it if something happened to either of them. Maybe she should have agreed to go.

"You're not cold, are you, Elisabeth? Why, I declare, it's sweltering out here," Mary said, pulling out her fan and spreading it for effect.

"No, just a walk across my grave. Do go on, please. What did he do next?"

"Your grave . . . whatever are you talking about? Well, then he said . . ."

Elisabeth gave Mary her attention as she proceeded to chatter on. Because really, it was quite unlikely those men would make it outside town limits before the sheriff rounded them up.

69

THE HOUSE WAS QUIET WHEN she walked in. Polly had the night to herself, and her Grandmother was at one of her endless charity meetings. She supposed she'd soon be joining her in those meetings, something to keep her occupied in spinsterhood.

Goodness, she was in a mood.

She needn't be alone at all. She could be at the Spencers' fete for the evening. William had been quite insistent she accompany him. But she wasn't up to fending off his advances tonight. She would rather be alone.

And Rory; he'd been in town just a few days ago. She'd begged off an engagement, pleading the obligations of the new school year. She enjoyed spending time with Rory, and she wouldn't have to fend off unwanted advances. He could read her well enough.

And she could read him well enough to know her hands-off demeanor disturbed him. She might try, though, to be more agreeable next time. Perhaps it was just the thought that distressed her. There was no reason she shouldn't enjoy being kissed by Rory. Many women did, from all accounts. Yes, she might let her guard down next time. After all, it wasn't as if she were fated to enjoy the advances of one man only. If so, she faced a long life alone.

Tomorrow, truly, she must stop feeling sorry for herself. She headed to the kitchen to sit with John for an hour before she retired with a book.

BECCA RAISED HER head, growling from her position at the foot of the bed.

"Sshh, baby." Had that been someone at the door?

She listened for the sound of one of the servants as she fumbled for her flint and lit her bedside candle, but the house was quiet. Then she heard it again. It *was* someone at the door. Throwing on her wrapper and grabbing the candle, she met her grandmother at the top of the stairs.

"What should we do?" she whispered.

"Tom will answer it, child. You should stay out of sight."

"Not without you." She pulled her grandmother back into the shadows, extinguishing her candle.

"It's at the back door, Grandmother, hear it? And Tom's out, remember?" She started down the steps, the moonlight seeping through the transom lighting her way, Becca at her feet and her grandmother following behind. John was calling for whoever it was to hold their horses, he was getting there, fast as an old man could in the middle of the night. The next sound she heard was an awful keening, and she ran.

The back door was open, and two young black men were coming through, carrying a bundle. Her grandmother reached them first, taking John's candle from him and illuminating their burden. Polly; her Polly, bloody and bruised.

"No! No! Polly, no!" she screamed. John was on the floor, incoherent in his pain, moaning and crying, his arms wrapped about his head. She slid to the floor and held him.

"Lay her on the table, gently!" her grandmother said. "You men, one of you go fetch the doctor, the other the watch. Don't stand there, hurry, now! Jane, help me."

She had to stand. She must; she must help. Must not fall apart. She went to Polly and gently smoothed back the hair from her face. She was alive, barely, but alive. Sliding off her wrapper, she draped it over Polly. Her clothes were in tatters, her body bloody and beaten, the bruises already purple in the candlelight, but alive, thank you, Lord, alive. She took the damp cloth her grandmother handed her and gently blotted the blood from around her eyes.

"It'll be all right, Polly, it will. I know it hurts, honey, I can see how badly it must all hurt. I wish I could make it stop for you. I'd give anything to make it stop. The doctor is coming. He'll do something. He'll know what to do." She took her hand lightly, afraid of hurting her, and kissed her forehead.

John joined her, taking her other hand. Polly looked at him and closed her eyes, blood trickling out the side of her mouth.

"Don't you be going now, baby, dontcha be going," John said. His head shook from side to side, his eyes wide and terrified. She coughed, bringing up more blood. "No, no, baby, don't, please, baby, don't." Tears fell freely down the old man's face as he struggled to control his sobs.

Elisabeth continued to press the cool cloth about Polly's face, turning her own face to her shoulder to blot the tears that blurred her vision. Every breath Polly took was a struggle, but she still had the strength to cling to Elisabeth's hand.

Jane had filled the room with candles, and her grandmother began checking Polly's injuries, her face grim.

One of the men reappeared at the open kitchen door, unaccompanied. Her grandmother met him and pulled him inside. "The doctor?"

"He's a coming, ma'am. Arnold's bringing him. I done run. The watch, they ain't at their station. You want I should try the sheriff?"

"Did you see this happen?"

"No, ma'am, I ain't nothun to do with it." He shook his head, backing away, frightened. "Me and Arnold, we just brung her home, that's all, ma'am."

"Thank you for bringing her home, young man. Yes, the sheriff." She stopped him as he was leaving. "Wait. Do you know David Graham? Liam Brock?" At his nod, she said, "Bring one of them, or both, please."

Sometime later the doctor arrived and did his examination, asking John to step out as he prodded and poked his way around Polly's injuries, his expression grim. Elisabeth watched his face intently, searching for unspoken clues as to his diagnosis, wincing each time Polly cried out at his touch.

"Very well, you can bring him back in," the doctor said, repacking his bag. "Are you her father?"

John shook his head, numb.

"She's been badly beaten, as well as raped. Her ribs are broken. I believe one of them has punctured a lung." He covered her with the wrap. "Do you know who did this? Has the sheriff been sent for?"

'Over on Water Street, the man she was with, he's . . . he didna make it." Liam stood at the open doorway, his gaze on her as he responded to the doctor's question. David stood beside him. "The crowd's saying it was the 'wheelbarrow men,' but James, a friend, he's trying to find out more. Will the lass be . . . is she verra badly hurt?"

David. David was here. In her doorway. She watched him as his eyes swept the room, taking it all in, looking back at Liam, looking back toward her. He stepped into the kitchen and took Jane aside, whispering.

"How would the crowd know unless the perpetrators happened to commit the crime wearing their prison uniforms?" The doctor picked up his bag, and Elisabeth's attention snapped back to Polly.

"You can't go," Elisabeth cried. "You didn't make her well.

You didn't do anything but look at her. You can't go before you make her well!" She grabbed the doctor's arm, pulling him back. "Grandmother, don't let him go! Please!"

David went to her, wrapping his arms around her, pulling her close, away from the man. "Doctor, is there anything ye can give the lass to ease her?"

The doctor looked at him, his mouth tightening, and opened his pack again. He handed Mrs. Hale a small bottle. "This will help your granddaughter sleep the rest of the night." He walked to the door.

Jane came back into the room with another robe for Elisabeth, handing it to David. He wrapped it around her, then took two long steps to the door, blocking the doctor's exit.

"I'm sure ye just misunderstood me, Doctor. The lass on the table." He motioned with his hand. "Polly's her name. Polly's the lass that's broken, bruised, and bleeding. Can ye help her or no'?"

The doctor looked affronted. "No, I can't help her. Her lung is punctured. She's going to—"

"Keep your voice down, damn ye, man. Have ye no' a caring bone in your body?" David whispered, backing the doctor into a corner, his large frame towering over the man. "That man over there, Mr. Black," he said, stabbing his finger in John's direction. "He's raised her from a baby. Mrs. Hale, and Miss Hale are her family as well. Now, why canna ye help her? Will ye tell me?"

"She won't be able to breathe by morning. She's dying. There's nothing anyone can do. Step out of my way, sir."

"You're scaring the good doctor, David," Liam said, using his arm to back David away. "Doctor, don't ye have something that will ease her for the next few hours then, without making her insensible? She may want to name who did this. She may want to say goodbye. Can ye help her there?"

"If Mrs. Hale requests it. Now, I'll ask once again, step out of my way."

Elisabeth watched, her eyes frantic as her grandmother walked toward the doctor. Surely, *surely* she could make him help Polly. She wasn't going to die. God wouldn't permit it. She wasn't going to die.

Her grandmother touched Liam and David in thanks, then followed the doctor to the door, speaking to him quietly. She listened, then nodded, as he handed her something before hurrying out the door.

David walked to John, placing his hand on his shoulder. "John, the doctor; I think he gave Mrs. Hale something to ease the lass. Do ye want me to set her in her room? Is it nearby?"

"No, David, would you bring her bed out here instead?"

"Aye, Mrs. Hale. Jane, will ye show me the way?"

David carried out the bed and the linens, and Elisabeth watched numbly as he set the bed down, arranging the bed-coverings just so.

"Polly, lass, I'm going to lift ye, all right? I know well it will hurt, but your bed is bound to be more comfortable than this table. I'll hurry, and I'll be careful."

"Bess, let loose of her for just a minute," he whispered, coming up behind her.

She couldn't. She shook her head, whispering, "No." Nothing made sense; Polly so hurt, David so close. No, not one thing made sense. Liam came to her and held her, prying her hand away as David reached for Polly.

"Och, you're light as a feather. Ye Hale women must never eat," David said softly to Polly. She cried out as he picked her up, and he murmured meaningless words of comfort as he laid her gently on her bed, rearranging the wrapper to cover her.

"Leo?" Polly whispered.

"He didna make it, lass. I'm so sorry, I am. The world has

lost a good man." He wiped away one of his tears that had
fallen on her cheek.

Did David know him? Elisabeth pulled free from Liam.
Sinking to the floor by Polly's side, she enfolded her hand
softly between her own. She didn't know Polly's beau; how
could David?

"His ma?" Her eyes filled with tears and Elisabeth dabbed
at them softly with a handkerchief.

"I'll look out for her, baby. Don't you worry, I'll help her,"
John said, his eyes wide with fear.

Polly tightened her grip on Elisabeth's hand and whispered, "Good man, Miss 'Liss."

"Yes, he was, honey. I know I never met him, but Lord
knows, I heard enough about him to know he was."

"These two . . . good men . . . tell 'em."

"Oh, Polly, don't . . . very well, I'll tell them," Elisabeth said
as Polly's eyes flashed and she coughed again. She moaned,
fresh blood spilling from her mouth.

"Oh, honey, please don't try to talk anymore."

"Lisbeth, lass, allow me just a minute, aye?" Liam brought
her to her feet so that he could sit in her place. He reached
for Polly's face, gently turning it toward him.

"Polly, the doctor, well, he canna do anything. Your rib, it's
cracked, see? It's poking your lung, that's why ye're having a
hard time breathing. Mrs. Hale has something that'll ease ye
a bit. Before ye take it, lass, can ye name those who did this?"

She shut her eyes, opening her mouth. Liam bent to hear.
"White men . . . four of them, strangers. Dark hair, beards,
all of them . . . smelled."

"Scum usually does. They'll swing for it, Polly, they will.
Did anyone else see?"

She blinked. "Outsi' church. First—" She stopped in a fit
of coughing.

"I'll tell the sheriff. Rest, lass."

David took Liam's place and hovered over her, a look of helplessness written across his face, his big hand gingerly stroking back her hair. Polly opened her eyes at his touch.

"Watch over Liss. Wasn't her fault."

He darted a look at Elisabeth, and she avoided his eyes, not acknowledging she'd heard the request. "I know, Polly, I will if I can." Polly glared at him and he amended, "I will, I promise." He took his handkerchief and dabbed at the blood around her lips.

"No more talking. Polly, I want you to taste a bit of this. The doctor left it with me. I don't want you to worry about anything else, or anyone else, child."

Elisabeth moved away as her grandmother took over Polly's care.

"Make some coffee, lass," David said, coming up behind her.

She turned and looked at him, her jaw dropping.

He reached out and touched her arm, softening his request. "Ye'll feel better with something to do."

"I . . . it's just . . . " How could he possibly request sustenance now?

David raised his brows. "Ye don't know how?" he asked, his amazement apparent.

"Of course I know how," she said, pushing at him. Well, at least she thought she did, she had watched John often enough. She reached for the kettle just as he pulled her back.

"Hot, lass. Ye'll burn."

Will I do? I don't want to see you burn.

She sagged back against him as the pain of the memory shot through her, and her eyes filled.

John came to the fire, clucking his tongue as he reached for the kettle with his hook, assuming the task. She pulled away from David, forgoing the comfort of his arms, and went to the fire, kneeling to help John.

"Pete's sake, Davey," she heard Liam say behind her.

"Angry is better than falling apart, aye?"

She wasn't going to fall apart. This was all a dream, and she was going to wake up. Wake up and be grateful for life as it was. She wasn't going to fall apart. No, not this time, she wasn't. She set out mugs for the coffee.

"John. I . . ." David said. He stopped, his face filled with pain.

"I know, there's nothing no one can say," John said, tears falling fresh.

THE SIX OF THEM stayed with Polly, taking turns holding her hand, talking to her, soothing her. She died early the next morning.

70

ELISABETH INSISTED ON BEING THE one to prepare Polly's body for burial. She spent hours washing her carefully, lovingly, whispering hushed words of comfort as she removed all traces of the men who had harmed her, telling her softly that Liam had reported the sheriff had picked up one of the men so far.

Grandmother had sent Liam to procure the finest white linen he could find on the Sabbath, and so he did. Polly would have handled the cloth with awe, should she be alive to see it. Grandmother sewed the shroud until well into the night, refusing to sleep until it was complete to her satisfaction.

David and Liam stayed on, doing what, she wasn't quite sure, though they always appeared to be hurrying from one place to another. Her grandmother had wanted them there, especially when John left the house to comfort Leo's mother, and to offer her his help with the laying out should she have no kin nearby.

Grandmother sent David to find a carpenter for the coffins.

She climbed the stairs slowly to her room. My God, Polly was gone. They would put her in the ground soon.

SHE'D SENT A short note to her father, but she knew he wouldn't be able to make it from New York in time, even if he wanted to. So Liam and David accompanied her and her grandmother to the cemetery, following John and three other men as they bore the coffin to the gravesite on their shoulders. Grandmother was assuming the expense of burying Polly and Leo side by side, and she told herself to take comfort in that.

She listened vaguely to the service, her hands twisting the handkerchief she held, her mind replaying her memories of Polly. Polly laughing, scolding, gossiping.

She'd been teaching her to read, and Polly had caught on quickly, enough so that she could pass the knowledge on to her Leo. They had had such plans.

Why did God take good people early? Why didn't he discriminate? Was he even paying attention?

She glanced up when she could no longer hear the drone of the preacher's voice. She looked at a man kneeling, watching as he gathered a handful of soil. The memory rushed at her hard, and her fist went to her mouth to stifle a cry as her knees gave way. David was there, his arm encircling her waist, holding her tight as she slumped against him. He turned her away from the coffin, his big frame sheltering her as he pushed their way through the mourners, supporting her until they reached the shade of an elm bordering the graveyard.

"Dirt . . . they covered Mama with dirt . . . over and over," she said, sobbing. "Over and over, first with their hands . . . then with shovels, with *dirt*, do you hear me? Why does God permit it? Dirt . . . " Her voice trailed off as she gave in to the sobs, clutching handfuls of David's shirt.

He held her tight, one hand stroking her back. "Sshh, sshh. Dirt, it's no' so bad, now. It gives life to flowers and food and such, home and shelter to the wee creatures, a place to rest, aye? Tis only a place to rest God provides, that's all. Sshh, lass, dinna cry so."

His arms; what a comfort he was. Just for a moment, she wanted, she *needed* the comfort of his arms. It was only for a moment, Polly wouldn't begrudge her that moment.

Much later, as the sound of the others walking by roused her, she lifted her head and moved out of his arms, taking the clean handkerchief he offered. "Thank you," she murmured. Avoiding his eyes, she took his elbow, steering him to the street.

"How is it you've had so much free time, David?" she asked, wondering why it hadn't occurred to her before.

"I work odd hours and at night. Mr. Hall is verra understanding."

"So you haven't slept?"

"Have ye?"

Last night she had; she had resorted to the comfort of the small bottle of elixir the doctor had left. She smiled wanly.

"She had so many plans with her man, with Leo. She was free, did you know that? No, of course you wouldn't. I just found out myself. My grandmother did that, once the lawyers finally settled Grandfather's affairs. And she had plans to leave once I left home. But it was for naught, wasn't it? I didn't leave home, and now she's gone and can't live out her dreams, can she?" David squeezed the hand she had resting on his forearm. "Mother, you, now Polly. I know you're still here, of course, but, well, I've lost you. And Liam's going to Baltimore, who knows if he'll come back."

"Rest easy. He's no' going for a while now." He slowed his pace, his words rough. "I ache for ye, Bess. I know she was with ye day and night. Ye grew up beside her."

The tears started again, and she dabbed her eyes with his handkerchief.

"Thank you for taking care of us, David. Grandmother and I both appreciate your help."

"Ye havena lost me, Bess, I'll be here when ye need me."

"We're grateful. It's a comfort to know that."

He looked at her, then away. But she saw it, his hurt. They walked in silence the rest of the way. Once inside, he led her to a chair in the parlor.

"Do ye want me to make some tea, Elisabeth?"

She shook her head, looking down at the floor. David pulled out another chair and took a seat opposite her, his forearms on his knees as he leaned toward her. "Rest, will ye, Lisbeth? Don't make yourself ill. There's plenty of food in the kitchen, should ye be hungry. Liam and your grandmother will be here shortly, the carriage is always slower, ken. And remember, Liam is going to stay over a few days until John comes back. Should I stay? Until they get here? I'll be glad to do so, should you want."

Oh, she wanted. But again, she shook her head. He made a small attempt at a smile and touched her cheek briefly as he stood. She rose and followed him to the door, just as Becca ran in from the kitchen.

"This dog, she yours?"

"Yes, her name is Becca." She picked her up, watching as the emotions raced across his face before his mouth settled into a grim line and he walked out the door, shutting it softly behind him.

It's likely I'll be your lapdog.

She leaned back against the door, her eyes closed. She had made him angry. She hadn't meant to, truly she hadn't. But there was nothing left in her to mend it. She went to the staircase, her hand automatically going to the candlebox mounted under the sconce, mildly surprised to find it empty. She'd have to pay heed now, remember to bring down her bedside candle each morning, to see to her own needs now that Polly wasn't here. She climbed the stairs slowly to her room, each step an effort, her feet slogging through the waves of grief.

Walking across the pine floor of her bedroom, she sat at the window seat, leaning back against the wall as she looked out.

"He's stayed, Becca, see? Right out front by the corner there." Her eyes filled with hot tears as she watched him. "I thought he would. He's angry, but he's not one to leave me. He'll wait. He'll wait until Grandmother arrives and I'm not alone." She hugged the dog tightly as her tears fell. "He has your eyes, did you notice? Spaniel brown eyes, as sweet as the day is long." The dog wiggled to get free and she set her down. Sobbing now, she stood and kissed her palm, turning it to the window glass.

"I'm sorry, David, I love you so," she whispered, placing her palm on the pane.

But she couldn't let the need start afresh, not when she knew ahead the cost of letting him go.

She turned and crossed the room to her bed, to the nothingness sleep and the doctor's small brown bottle promised.

"I'm so very sorry."

TOWARD THE END OF September, all the escaped prisoners had been recaptured, but not before murdering another, a white man, during a household robbery. All five were convicted and sentenced to death.

They were hung at Centre Square before the month was out. David had seen the gallows waiting, but hadn't cared to witness the event, though he prayed the night before. He prayed they would remember the faces of a beautiful, young, sassy black woman and her beau as they fell to their deaths. He couldn't find it in himself to pray for their souls.

71

October 1789

"SET THE CORRECTIONS, WILL YOU, David? I
can't wait for Tom. Then have the lads press a hundred copies." Mr. Hall handed him the marked-up broadside.

"Aye, Mr. Hall." He went to stand at Tommy's case, composing stick in his left hand, the fingers in his right busy
selecting the tiny metal letters. That dog was one of Smith's
bitches; he'd lay odds on it. Had she gone to the mill, looking
for a dog then? Or had Smith run into her in town? He knew
his fiancé hadn't survived the fever last year, and he felt for
the man, he did, but that didn't give him call to sniff around
his.

But she's not his, never will be, and he wanted her to be
happy. Rory was a good sort, good future. His father had
passed; he owned the mill now. She could do a lot worse.
Had done a lot worse.

He should have kissed her. There at the house. He should
have. Backed her up against the wall and kissed her breathless, wiped that vacant look off her face, made her remember.
The shop bell rang and heard Mr. Hall greet the callers.

"David, come on up here. Have you met the Warners?"

Warner studied David, turning his hat round and round in his grimy, calloused fingers.

"I havena. It's good to meet ye, sir." He reached out and shook the man's hand. Ah, dried glue, then. Bookbinder?

"Mr. Warner owns the bindery at Third and Chestnut, just opposite the sign of the Moon."

"I've been in your shop, sir, a time or two. Ye have a good selection."

"Hall's told me a lot about you this last year, young man. It's time I finally met you. This is my daughter, Eunice."

"Miss Warner." He nodded to her. She murmured something; he couldn't make it out. Life hadn't treated the lass kindly, and her thin, sallow, pockmarked face reflected it. She had a pinched, unhappy look about her, and she didn't meet his eyes.

"I've lost my last lad, David. I'm not looking to replace him just yet. Don't have the business to warrant it. I'd asked Hall if he might have someone he can spare a day or two a week for the next few months. He thought you might be interested. Your wages won't suffer for it."

"I haven't had a chance to broach it to him yet, Silas," Mr. Hall said. "But we'll get back to you soon, all right?"

"Very well then, later this week," the man said reluctantly, turning to leave. He wore his brown hair short and it clung to his head in dirty strands beneath the hat he shoved on. "Eunice, let's get the market over with."

He turned back at the door, studying David again. "You feel free to come on over boy, sometime this week, see the place."

"I will, Mr. Warner, thank you." The bell rang as the door closed after them, leaving David and Hall alone.

"I'm sorry, David, I meant to ask you privately. Silas gets an idea, he's not one to let go of it easy."

"That's all right. What would ye have me do there?"

"Well, you could learn to bind books."

Sellers could teach him that as well. "Oh, right then," he answered, waiting for the rest.

"But I think he's mainly looking for a son-in-law, someone to share the shop with."

It took a moment for it to sink in. When it did, he looked at Hall, mouth open. "H . . . h . . her?" he stuttered, jabbing a finger at the door.

Hall laughed. "Everything has a price, David. He has a nice operation going, but the competition is more than he wants at his age. He's ready to turn it over. Think about it, will you? Get back to me tomorrow. You don't have to go, not by any means, I'm just presenting the opportunity."

"Thank you, sir," David said slowly. "I think." He knew it a lofty goal of most apprentices to marry the master's daughter. It was hard otherwise to set up shop. But hell . . .

"I THOUGHT YE SAID ye wanted to go 'fore noon, Davey."

"I do. We just need to wait for Robert to get back. Why're ye anxious?"

"I have a lecture in a couple hours. I wanted to eat beforehand, feeling peaked. Tell me again why ye need me with ye?"

"I didna tell ye the first time. Just come, please?" He reached for the flask of whisky Robert kept behind the counter, handed it to Liam. "Drink, then help me sort through these. The captain from the *Nancy* just dropped them off." Liam took a long swallow and came around the counter, grabbing a stack.

"From Dublin, are they? Can I read them?" He looked up as the bell over the door rang.

"Good day to ye, sir, miss. How might I be helping ye?"

"Hello, young man. Stuart Billings, my daughter Victoria,"

the man said, nodding in the young woman's direction.

"David Graham, pleasure to meet ye both." He noted the man was dressed well and appeared to be in his late thirties, early forties. His daughter looked to be in her late teens, black hair, dark eyes, full red mouth. Beautiful, he supposed, though her expression was a little haughty for his taste. She briefly inclined her head at his greeting.

Give the peasant his due. Well, then. "Will ye be wanting to place an advertisement, sir?"

"Yes, I do. We just arrived in Philadelphia a few days ago, on the *Commerce*. I've been advised the *Gazette* is my best source."

"Aye, that is, we've a large subscriber base. You may write your ad on this and I'll give you a price. It'll appear Wednesday next," David said, bringing a pen and paper up to the counter. "Ye'll be from London then? Winter's a hard time to cross." He glanced behind him to see if Liam was still in the room. He was being uncharacteristically quiet, if so.

"Yes. You're from Scotland, I take it? I've spent a fair amount of time there. My family owns property just north of Dryman. I've enjoyed many a holiday there in years past. The fishing is superb. Are you familiar with the area?"

"Aye," David said, "and it is at that." So that's it. Liam must have met the Billings at the quay sometime in the last day or two. The girl would surely have attracted his eye. Jesus, Mary, and Joseph, the lass might be his . . . sister? He spent the next five minutes securing the ad and moving Mr. Billings and his daughter out the door.

At the sound of the front door closing, Liam reappeared from the back room.

"Not now, David," he said, moving back to the stack of dispatches.

David was surprised. 'Not now' possibly meant later. "Here, we've finished with that stack. Start on these," he said, exchanging piles of paper with Liam. "Ne'er mind, here's Robert now. Let's go."

He gave Robert a quick update and headed out the door. "Lovely lass, the Billings girl."

"Hmmph."

"Ye know Warner's shop, right?"

"Right. But that's your business. Don't know what help I can be."

"Moral support."

72

"I WISH I HAD BEEN HERE to help you, you and your grandmother. I know it wasn't easy, coping with a murder on your own."

She hadn't quite thought of things in those terms. "You couldn't possibility have known in time, Rory. I knew that. Besides, David and Liam took care of all the arrangements."

"Graham. Right." His hand went to his face, long fingers stroking the sides of his mustache, black eyes considering, watching her.

She returned his look steadily, picked up her cup, and brought it to her mouth, waiting. He'd have something to say. Rory never dodged an issue.

"Would you mind if I had one of those teacakes after all?"

Surprised, she set down the cup. "Of course. Are you hungry?" She placed the plate in front of him.

"For something I haven't a chance in hell of having."

She blushed. Really, the man could be so forward at times. "Rory, I—"

"Don't. Save it." He smiled at her. "It's all right, Elisabeth. Honestly."

She was taken off balance as his hand reached across the table and covered hers.

"We enjoy each other's company, am I right? Good conversation, plenty of laughter?" He waited until she nodded. "Each of us, we've suffered a loss, neither of us, the first choice of the other, am I right?" Again, she nodded. "Well then, life's short, as we've both had the unfortunate occasion to experience first-hand. While I won't settle for being second best, I'm not such a fool I can't enjoy the company of a beautiful, intelligent woman if I've the chance." He waited while she placed another cake on his plate. "Would you like to join me for dinner tonight, Elisabeth?"

"But didn't you mention it was a business dinner? You were in town to meet your attorney?"

"Business combined with social. He has a wife you'd enjoy. I've no doubt you could hold up your end of the conversation."

"I think it's too soon, but in a few months, yes, I think I'd like that," she said, somewhat warily.

He squeezed her hand. "And who knows what may develop in time, between friends who like and respect one another."

She managed a smile. "Who knows." All she really knew was that she wished they'd finish tea quickly so that she could make her way to the druggist before he closed for the day. She hadn't been feeling quite herself; she needed to purchase another bottle of medicine.

"Are you feeling all right, Elisabeth?"

"Of course, Rory. I just feel the need for a little fresh air. Would you mind some company on your walk back to the tavern?" Becca's ears perked at the sound of the word 'walk,' and Rory laughed, reaching down to pet her head. "You don't need to walk us back home. I know you've business to attend to."

Rory shook his head slightly. She supposed the dismissal had been a bit blatant. But he rose and gallantly offered her his elbow, calling the dog to heel.

"The breeze feels good, doesn't it?"

"If you can get past the stench, I suppose it does," Rory said.

Elisabeth laughed. "I forgot, you've been spoiled out there at your mill. Here, Rory, let's walk through the church yard, instead of the street. Do you mind? It's a beautiful day."

She needed to make an effort. She'd never see the man again, otherwise.

"EVENING LISBETH."

She jumped, turning from the counter. "Liam! I didn't see you when I walked in."

"Wasna in here. I was leaving City Tavern when I encountered Smith. He said ye'd walked in here, so I took the opportunity, seeing as ye've been avoiding me. Tom says ye're resting every time I call for ye."

She frowned at him. Was it necessary to discuss her private business in front of the clerk? She put the bottle in her bag and walked out the door, Liam following.

"Yes, well, I haven't been feeling well. Good day, Liam." She started walking, clicking her tongue for Becca to follow. Liam followed as well.

"I was hoping ye'd come back soon. The wee ones, they miss ye, I miss ye."

"Oh, well, I don't know."

"Lisbeth, talk to me, lass." He took her arm and guided her into a small park. Leading her to a bench, he brushed the leaves from its surface, gently pushing her down. He sat next to her, taking her hand, lacing his fingers through hers. "I know it's hard. I know ye miss her. But it canna be easier, walled up in the house, can it?"

She didn't say anything, nervously fingering her bag with her free hand, staring at the panorama of leaves littering the ground. Red and gold. Autumn leaves? That was odd. Why would the trees have lost their leaves so soon?

"It's been over a month. Ye havena asked who's taking over the class. Are ye no' interested?"

She watched as his eyes dropped to the bag she was clutching, his jaw tightening. She forced her hand to still.

"No, of course I am." But he was right. She had no idea if her class was even being held. How had she let that happen? Puzzled, she looked at him. "Who is, Liam? Mr. Oliver? Somebody is, right? The children still come?"

"Aye, I am. And I'm happy to, though I'd like an idea of your plans, mind."

"Of course, I'm sorry. That was thoughtless of me." Her mind drifted as she stared at a nearby rose garden. She glanced down to make sure Becca was at her feet; the spaniel still had a fondness for uprooting rose bushes. "Were the roses blooming? In Center Square? Do you think they saw roses as they fell?"

"I didna attend. But no, I don't think they saw anything, given they're generally blindfolded."

"Oh." She colored at the foolish question, not sure why she had asked in the first place. "Of course."

"What were ye doing at the druggist?"

"I needed to purchase my medicine."

"I want ye back, Lisbeth. I need ye, the children need ye. And what of the night classes ye and Polly planned for the adults? She wouldna want ye to give up on that." He stood and paced in front of her. "She came to me, see, midsummer, told me of your plans, wanted to make sure Mr. O didna mind the use of his place."

She gasped. "Liam, I fully intended to ask, I did. It just wasn't certain yet, we . . ."

"Dinna fash, lass. Of course ye'd ask, I know that. She was asking on her own, and I admired her for it. When she wasna being your abigail, she was quite the saucy lass. Point is, Lisbeth, ye're letting her down, grieving like this." He waved a hand at her bag, and she clutched it tighter.

He knelt in front of her, taking her hands. "Don't do this again, Lisbeth. Come to school tomorrow, then let's work on a plan for the night class, aye?"

Her eyes widened and she looked at him, surprised. "But don't you see, Liam? I'm *not* doing it again! I haven't cried since it happened. I'm still eating. I get up every morning." She watched, fascinated, at the parade of emotions running across his face; he was usually so careful about that. Why was he so concerned?

"As soon as I'm feeling myself again, I'll come back, you'll see."

He sighed and reached for her bag, easily taking it before she could grab it back. He pocketed the bottle and stood, handing her back the bag.

"Liam! Explain yourself! What do you mean by taking my purchase?"

"I'm no' standing by again. Let's go." He grabbed her elbow and pulled her off the bench, leading her out of the park.

"But I've just told you. I'm not falling apart this time; you've no cause to worry. And it's because of the medicine I'm able to get through the day—the medicine you've just seen fit to appropriate. I appreciate your concern, but, in truth, it's *not* your concern." He wasn't listening. She could see that as she hurried to keep up.

"Come, we're going home, to your home. I'm staying. Mrs. Hale's there, aye? It'll be proper, then. We'll talk all night, if ye canna sleep without the laudanum. Ye'll come with me to the Academy in the morning, just to test the waters, aye? If ye find ye canna do it, I'll take ye home. Then we'll do it again, over and over, til ye find ye can sleep and find ye can teach."

"Liam, for heaven's sake, what's gotten in to you? Your behavior is completely ridiculous. Surely you've better things to do." She was beginning to get angry, the unexpectedness of the emotion surprising her. She yanked away her arm.

"Nothing at all better to do," he said, taking back her arm, continuing in the direction of her home. "Keep up, now. John will be setting supper soon. We don't want to miss it."

"Well," she said, sputtering, not certain what to say, then grasped at a possible solution. "David's certainly going to miss you, isn't he? If you're wasting all of your free time watching me."

"That could be a problem, no doubt of it."

So, he'd already thought of that, then. "What are you going to tell him, Liam? You won't say, I mean—"

"I'll worry over David, dinna fash."

He didn't loosen his grip, nor his resolve. She didn't protest further as it dawned on her, unwarranted or not, that he was sincerely worried about her. It didn't matter why. If she was responsible for that faraway look in his eyes, the pain in the grim set of mouth, why then, she'd do her best to erase it.

AND SO SHE FOUND herself surrounded constantly for the next six weeks; if not by him, then by her grandmother or John. She didn't mind so much, for after the first four weeks she was full of ideas and plans for the night classes she planned to hold in Polly's honor, and the three of them provided captive audiences with which to discuss them.

Polly would be proud of her.

73

"THAT'S A FAIR JOB. BUT see this here?" Warner shook his head, frowning. "That won't do."

David looked closely at the spot Warner was pointing to, finally discerning the cords across the spine of the book weren't entirely symmetrical by a mere fraction of an inch. This would be the second he'd ruined today. The man was a hard taskmaster. He'd get nothing for the day's labor.

"Aye, Mr. Warner. Ye have any tricks of the trade ye wanna share, so as I get it right the next time 'round?"

Warner glanced toward his daughter. "Leave us."

She hurried from the room, her thin fingers going nervously to her hair, scrambling to tuck in any strands that might have fallen from the severe bun she wore, so severe that, of course, none had. In the last five weeks he'd spent two days a week here, and the lass never once glanced his way, never uttered a word in his presence.

He'd watch her occasionally, when she was intent on her labors, folding the sheets so the margins met exactly, gathering the pages a book at a time, reviewing the gatherings with a practiced eye to detect any missing or out of place pages. She was competent and fast, only faltering if he left his eyes on her long enough so that she felt them.

Maybe he could ask her for instruction, over her father.

Truth be, from what he'd seen so far, she could run the shop on her own and likely resented the implication her father had had to bring in a stranger, an untrained one at that, to handle the business. He turned his attention back to the man.

"Boy, I've noticed you don't attend the afternoon service on Sunday. You got a good reason for that?"

"Ahh." Would relaxing on a riverbank be a good reason? He thought quickly. "I, uh, I use the time for independent reflection, sir. On whatever the minister was preaching in the morning hours. My uncle, sir, he's a reverend. He always told me there was value in meditation such as that."

"That so? Bible study, on Tuesdays and Thursdays. You know it all, do you?"

"No, sir. I can't say that. But with work—"

"This is Thursday; take Eunice. She'll be ready in ten minutes. I'll tell her to be up front." He walked out.

Hell, he was serious. David went to the basin and washed his hands. Was this worth it? Did he even like binding books? Not that he had anything against Bible study. He'd dropped out of the habit since coming across, had made the decision to occupy his time elsewhere.

And he was considering changing churches. Would Warner take issue with that as well? This week he planned to attend First Presbyterian. He had no quarrel with Second, but he didn't mind a change, and John Ewing was assigned to First. Liam had met Reverend Ewing at the University, said he was a brilliant mathematician and scientist, said he'd consider going to kirk just to hear more of him. David had called him on it, and they were going together this Sunday.

He took a chair and waited for Eunice, wondering if she'd get the courage to look at him, wondering what she was like out from under the thumb of her father, wondering how she'd feel about meeting Liam at the Man for a pint instead.

"WELL, WHAT HAPPENED?" David asked.

"Rob says he's leaving for Charlestown, so Mr. Oliver has accepted the position with the university. He's formally released me of any obligation to him."

Liam had made a stew, something he did every now and again during the winter months. He and David were sitting by the fire, waiting for Mr. Oliver to join them for supper. Mr. O had received an offer to teach from the University, and though his first inclination had been to decline it, he began to reconsider when Rob announced Jane was trying to convince him to relocate to Charlestown, where she had kin.

"And ye'll still continue with classes, then?"

"Aye, at least through December." Liam got up and walked over to the window, looking down the street. "There he is. He's talking tae Mrs. Gray, that widow two doors down." He grimaced, shaking his head.

David had escaped Eunice's company immediately after Bible Study that night, citing the need to look up an ill friend. Thankfully, Liam looked a bit peaked just now; he had no reason to belabor his conscience over the excuse, though in truth the lass had looked relieved. They'd gone to the class together for weeks now. He could tell being with him still didn't sit easy with her.

"Ye don't care for the widow?"

"Hmmph," Liam answered, mumbling something about fortune hunters.

"The woman keeps two taverns. She's likely to have her own fortune."

"She's no' for him." As if that settled it, he changed the subject. "Lisbeth has had several offers over the years. She should follow up on them. She's determined to support herself. Says she'll never marry; there're plenty of happy spinster schoolmarms. Ye ken, I think maybe—"

Surprised, David held a hand up quick, to stop him. "Nay, don't say it. I canna survive that again. I canna." Seeing Lisbeth through Polly's funeral had set the pain afresh for a few days, a reminder in the event he might have forgotten. She had made her choices clear; he wasn't going to forget.

So what if he only felt half alive?

Liam shrugged. "Her night school; it's flourishing, and only a month it's been. She's gone from four attending to fifteen."

"She's a remarkable woman." The pain ricocheted about his chest, settling in his gut. He shouldn't talk of her. He'd be paying for it in his dreams tonight. "Is it only Negroes attending?"

"Nay, she's four white women as well. None can pay, but no doubt she'll end up with all manner of lace trinkets."

"Can I help with paper, ink, anything? We've more than a few cracked slates unsuitable for sale."

"Aye, she'd appreciate it, to be sure."

David kicked a loose ember back into the fire. "I'm a free man at the end of August, Liam, can ye believe it? I'm still thinking of Baltimore. Would ye try your hand in Baltimore, ye think? Eunice's da wants me to set up shop there."

Liam wrinkled his nose. "It's a start, I 'spose, port city and all. I want to eventually make my way west. I want ye to come, too. But Baltimore is a start. It's west of Philly, aye?" He stooped in front of the fire, picking up a long handled iron spoon to stir the stew. "Are ye truly gonna marry her, Davey?"

"Seems I have to marry someone eventually; why not one with a father looking for a son-in-law to pass the business on to? I need a bit of help, and that tocher will help, mind ye. I'm still recovering from a few missteps. I can start as a printer of the odd item, maybe carry books in the shop. I think I might have a fair shot of it there, from others I've talked to. Mr. Hall thinks it worth a try. Less competition than there is here."

"She doesna like me."

"She likes ye well enough. She just doesna like the number of lasses ye sport."

"Nor the places I frequent, the time I take of yours, the things I talk of. Ye never laugh when you're with her, David. Do ye know that?"

David frowned. It was true, what he was saying. But having a wife would free him of a lot of distractions and entanglements, and this one came with the potential of a readymade shop. She was a good worker, their faiths were the same. Privately, though, he thought her a bit too pious, but that wasn't a bad thing. He'd do well to match her.

Uncle John would approve of her.

She didn't get his head all mixed up, so as he didn't know if he were coming or going. He had the upper hand, knew what's what when he was with her. All in all, he could do worse.

"Dinna fash, I find I don't welcome change," Liam said, watching him. "Ye've sense enough to choose your own wife. It was good of ye to wait this long, to stay in Philly. I may be able to do without ye for a few months. I've been preparing myself."

"Ye don't need me Liam. Ye never have. But I'm grateful ye had me stay. Ahh, I hear him downstairs. Just in time, I'm near famished."

"I'VE FOUND I DON'T like the distance they place between us when you choose to kiss me," she said softly, leaning over him, her hair spilling about him in silky soft waves as he pulled her down and over him.

David woke with a start. Hell, he hoped he hadn't said her

name out loud. The floor was full, several new apprentice lads having arrived in the last two weeks. He concentrated on slowing and quieting his breathing. Thankfully, though, Ian was making such a racket snoring, no one likely would've noticed any sound he might have made.

His dream had improvised some with her hair down around him; nice touch. That was one of his favorite memories of her, to be sure. But he had pages of others, somewhat less stirring, that he could pull out and flip through to lull himself back to sleep. He elbowed Ian in the ribs before he turned to his stomach.

Maybe he should try thinking of another lass. He ought to think of another; he needed to move on. Or how about he thought of Eunice? If he was thinking of taking her to wife, maybe he should try to work up some enthusiasm for it.

But thoughts of Elisabeth were the only thing that dulled the ache that plagued him each night, and he had a while until it was time to rise, and he could lose himself in work. He'd get through it by thinking of her.

74

March 1790

SUNDAY COMING. HE SIGHED, RESIGNED. It was bound to go slowly. He stooped to pick up the floor pi that Willy, the new hand, had left lying about before he ran out for the evening. Robert would go on a rant if saw it. He needed to write Da, tell him not to recommend any-more lads. Willy wasn't living up to Da's appraisal, and David felt responsible for having a part in bringing in such a sloppy workman. He set the tiny letters in an empty box in Willy's case; he wasn't going to distribute the type for the lad.

He didn't much care for winter. The days he wasn't working were hard to fill during those months. He searched through the shelves of books, hoping to find something he hadn't read yet that interested him. That was another thing about winter, though. Few ships came up the Delaware; therefore, few books arrived to restock their shelves.

Well, he supposed he could gain something by spending a full day in kirk with Eunice and her da. He shouldn't dread the thought. Not if he was considering a lifetime with her. The front bell rang, and he looked up as Liam walked in.

"What are ye grinning about? What's that ye have?"

Liam was holding up a fistful of strings, a large bundle dangling below. "Skates, Davey. I won the lot of them last night. Do ye know how to skate?"

"No," he said, gingerly taking the pair Liam had handed him.

"They won't bite ye; take them. We're going learn. Dock Creek is still frozen so' of Spruce. It'll be fun."

"Humph. People drown playing at that, ken. Who's the third pair for?"

"They were included in the lot. A bit small for us, though."

"I'll say."

"Sammy, come out from peeking 'round yon corner. Ye know how to skate?"

Sam nodded, his eyes wide. He was the newest of the apprentices taken on, still shy and unsure of his place.

"Good, come along now. You can teach us."

"WHY ARE WE WALKING way over here, Mary? We've passed several good ponds already."

"Yes, full of families and children. Society Hill is where the men are, Elisabeth. We're going to see and be seen."

Elisabeth smiled, shaking her head. So that's why Mary was in full dress, her blonde curls sitting just so under her prettiest hat, her new fur muff on display. Well, it couldn't hurt to try. As much as she told Liam she was looking forward to spinsterhood, in truth she didn't relish the thought. And though Rory still stopped by whenever he was in town, she knew his interest was waning. She couldn't blame him. She wouldn't be interested in her either, were she him.

And if she had a good time, she would have something to relay to Papa in her next letter. He never asked about her students or her garden. He always asked about her beaus. It was becoming difficult to continually evade the questions he pointedly posed in his letters.

"Here! Now see! Just look, Elisabeth. There must be a dozen young men our age!" They had reached the frozen pond off Third Street. They stood for a moment, watching the skaters.

Suddenly Elisabeth froze, grabbing Mary by the elbow. "Not here, Mary. I can't stay here."

"Whatever are you talking about? Of course you can." She shook off Elisabeth's hand and pointed. "Look, I think that's the tall, dark, handsome fellow you work with. See, over there? That's him isn't it? The one you've never introduced me to, though I've asked you a dozen times. This is the perfect opportunity." She turned to Elisabeth for verification, her blue eyes widening as she took in her friend's expression. "Drat. Whatever is the matter with you? All right, all right, we're going. Don't you faint on me, you hear?"

She looked back with regret. "And the fellow he's with? My word, will you look at how well he fills out his breeches. You'd better have a good reason for this, Elisabeth."

They walked several blocks back, stopping at a frozen patch full of families on skates. Elisabeth wondered who the young boy was with Liam and David. They seemed to be having a wonderful time, the boy directing the older two, all three dissolving into laughter as Liam and David ended up on their backsides.

She didn't resent him moving on, she didn't; she envied him. The sight of him today would have her crying herself to sleep for the next two weeks. She wouldn't wish the same on anyone. She only wished she knew when the longing would stop. It must eventually stop; surely it must. She turned to Mary, who was tugging at her sleeve. "Yes?"

"Elisabeth! You haven't heard a word I've said for the past five minutes. Is this spot acceptable to you? We'll meet no single men here, I tell you that."

"It doesn't signify. Yes, this spot is quite nice."

"Maybe to you it doesn't signify. Sometimes I just don't understand you." Mary sat on a bench, tying on her skates, grumbling all the while. She looked up at Elisabeth, throwing her hands in the air. "Well, tie on your skates, please? You won't make me go out alone, will you?"

LIAM STOPPED ELISABETH before she left the Academy the next Monday.

"Did Mr. Oliver tell you he's taking the position, Lisbeth?"

"No, I haven't seen him in over a week. I appreciate you letting me know." She continued walking to the door.

"Aye. Lisbeth, are ye all right? Ye havena been yourself today."

"I'm fine, thank you. I must be going now, though. We'll talk tomorrow."

He caught her elbow and brought her back, putting his fingers under her chin, pushing up her face to meet his eyes. "Your eyes; it looks as if ye've been crying."

She looked down at his hand, taking it in hers. "Your hand; did you hurt it skating?"

He grinned. "Aye, David ran it over. No more than I deserved, I suppose, talking a big lug like him out there." Sobering, he added, "I didna see ye there, lass. Truth be, I'm glad of that. It's no easier on him, ken."

She nodded blindly, tears filling her eyes. She kissed the cut across the back of his hand before dropping it. "I must go, Liam." She hurried outside, looking for the comfort of Polly before she remembered she wasn't there, would never be there again.

LIAM STEPPED OUT AND watched her go, still not sure if he should interfere and encourage David to approach her again. Sighing, he started toward the Market. He had told David he would bring his dinner to the print office. He knew they were behind, he'd seen him hunting up repair parts for the press earlier today.

"Liam! It was good of you to do this, man."

"Course it was." They sat on the floor. "Kentucky; what d'ye think of Kentucky, David?"

"Know nothing of it, nor do ye."

"I've been talking to that gent, that Billings. Sounds like I may want to know more of it."

"Billings, huh?" David raised a dark brow, pausing as he reached for another bread roll. "Did ye know the lass wasna his daughter?"

Liam looked up quickly and David laughed. "Thought that might interest ye."

"Why d'ye say that? I'm sure he named her as his daughter when we met."

"Mayhap. But I ran into them at the Coffee House with Mr. Hall last Wednesday. He introduced her to Mr. Hall as his stepdaughter."

"Hmmph. Well, that is interesting. Ian, come sit. I brought enough for ye, as well. Ye look like a sad hound dog over there."

Ian ambled over and sat. "Thanks, Liam."

"Now, what do ye know of Kentucky, Ian?"

75

"MISS LISBETH? WHAT YOU DOING with an apron on you?"

"Good morning, John," she said, kissing his cheek. She had risen early that morning and had run to the kitchen as soon as she was dressed. "John, it occurred to me last night that I have the rest of my life in front of me. Did you know that? I had forgotten; too busy being melancholy, I suppose. Well, I'm done with that."

"That's good to hear, Miss, but now, 'bout that apron?"

"Oh. Well, I need to learn how to cook, see? You'll teach me, won't you?"

"You don't needs to be in the kitchen, Miss Elisabeth. You to be the lady of the house, just like Mrs. Hale. You just plan the menus and such."

"Well, I do need to, if I don't want to starve. I doubt I'll have a staff. I'd like to be somewhat proficient by May. Now, I know I won't be near as good a cook as you are, but I think I should do passably well. So, will you help me, or should I ask Mary's cook to give me lessons?"

"Well, depends on who you're serving it to. Someone you care about or slop for the hogs?"

"Someone I care about, I'd venture to say. I'm not an

expert on household finances, by any means, but I don't think I should throw good money to the hogs, John. I doubt I'll be earning enough to afford the luxury of that."

John bit back a smile. "Well then," he said, still reluctant. He set the turnips and carrots he'd just brought up from the root cellar on the tabletop in front of her. "You can help me finish up this here stew. Start with these. We needs to get them just the right size 'fore they goes inta the pot. Too big, they won't cook enough; too small, they gets soggy." He went to the back door and brought over a basket, taking out two dead rabbits. He began to skin them as she watched, her knife in hand.

"You didn't have to kill them, did you, John? No, of course you didn't. What a ninny I am sometimes. You got them at the market. Didn't you? Yes, of course you did. And I can purchase them skinned and cleaned already, can't I?"

"Yes, miss, usually can get them that ways." He smiled. "Cost you a bit more, though."

Elisabeth started the slicing, looking to him for approval.

"John, I was talking to Grandmother last summer, right before . . . Well, you know she supports the Abolition Society? Of course you do. I'd asked her about you; I mean, why she kept slaves if she supported the PAS. She told me that none of you were slaves, including Polly. She granted each of you your freedom not long after Grandfather died, just as soon as she had the wherewithal to do so. I was upset she'd never mentioned it, but she said I'd never asked. And I suppose I didn't. I never thought to, and I'm sorry for that." She stopped slicing and looked up at him. "Well, I was wondering why you stayed; I mean . . . after my father . . ."

"Mrs. Hale be a good woman, one of the best. We weren't for leaving her, even at the trouble." John always referred to Mr. Hale's forcing the breakup between David and Elisabeth as "the trouble." Life had changed for all in the household at that point.

None could refer to Polly's murder in any manner at all as yet. She would try soon, though. It would be better if they could talk about her and how much they missed her.

"I'm glad to hear that. And I was very glad that Papa has no control over your welfare. I mean to say, I'm sure he would make good decisions. But I'm glad Grandmother took care of making all the decisions." She had finished with the vegetables, and he told her to fill a dish with wine.

"You can grind up these spices here," he said, setting out the mortar and pestle. When she was done he added the spice to the wine, sticking his finger in for a taste. He nodded his approval and handed her the plate of rabbit bits, tossing one to Becca where she waited in the hall.

"Now, this will soak overnight for tomorrow's dinner." He set it by the back door, well away from the fire, up out of Becca's reach. "I'll take it out in a bit, to keep it cool so it don't spoil. You done missed putting the turtle in the pot for today's dinner, so we's finished up for now, Miss."

She took off the apron and hung it. "John, would you know the receipt for some type of fish they sell in the market occasionally. It's covered with a brown sauce, stuffed with something soft, but it's crispy on the outside?"

"Ahh, Mr. Henkel's shad and oysters. I ain't ne'er tried replicating it. He guards the receipt, it being so popular. Young David, why, he lights up like a house on fire whenever—" John stopped, looking at her. "Whenever Mr. Henkel's in Market," he finished slowly. "Miss Elisabeth?"

"Not a word to him now, John, not a word, please? He might not be interested. I have to approach this carefully, with a plan," she said. She picked a knife up, turning it over and over in her hands.

"Hee! That's my girl! Ain't seen likes of my miss for a while." A big grin creased his face as he took the knife out of her hand. "All right, Miss Lisabeth. You take yourself a break now. This here has to simmer. I want you back here in three hours. We're going add some bread to it also, just 'fore ye eat. This here's a hearty turtle stew what makes any man happy, you does it right."

"I'll be back. I want to bring up some of my strawberries and make a pie, all right?"

"Yes, miss, if we have the time. If not, we can tomorrow morning. You can make the shrub if you wants."

"Thank you, John." She left him, smiling as she heard the sound of two pans crashing together, followed by a loud chuckle.

Liam didn't know it, but he'd changed her world in that one short sentence yesterday. He never talked of David with her, nothing of a personal nature anyway. She didn't know if he was married, engaged, or promised. Well, she assumed he wasn't married. She supposed she would have heard *that* from someone.

But she hadn't known if he hated the thought of her. By telling her 'it's hard for him, too,' well, she had all she needed to hope. She had broken this; she wanted to fix it, and it appeared it just might not be too late.

76

May 1790

"YOUR DA EVER RETURNING, LISBETH?"

"He writes that he's working day and night. Though he may have to make time to return for a brief while, to apply for naturalization. He says it'll make it easier to own property if he first shows intent to become a citizen. Are you applying, Liam?"

"Nay, no need. And dinna think I qualify. I've no' paid taxes as yet."

"Oh. Well, he says I'll be a citizen, once he is. And I've never paid taxes." She walked around the room, picking up the slates the children had left lying out, bringing them back to stack on her desk. "What are your plans for the summer, now that you don't have to recruit?"

"I've plans aplenty. Gonna line my pockets, Lisbeth. The harbor, she's full, have ye noticed? I'll warrant I can find work every day, should I care to. Now that there's talk on settling the government here, things are gonna change, ye wait and see." Liam paced back and forth in front of her, his eyes bright with excitement. "And I plan to fish every Sunday with my mate, get my fill 'fore he leaves for Baltimore. Mayhap I'll help him settle if I've time in August." He stopped, as if he were thinking ahead, then nodded decisively as he continued pacing. "Aye, I'll have time, long as I make it back 'fore term. That's what I'll do come August."

His mate? Was he referring to David? Puzzled, Elisabeth looked at him, her eyes wide. David was going to Baltimore? Granted, Liam didn't usually speak of him, but she'd have thought he'd have brought it up long before now that David was leaving Philadelphia. My word, he must have known for months, maybe years! And he'd never even mentioned it?

"Baltimore? Do you mean David?"

Liam looked at her, taking her measure. "Course I mean David. What other mate do I have content to fish the day away?"

"He's leaving? But he can't leave!"

A frown crossed his face, and he stilled. "Ye always knew he'd leave, Lisbeth. He's been thinking of it for years."

"No! I didn't; how could I? Well, maybe he talked of it in passing, but I never thought . . . it's just, well . . . I take some comfort in knowing he's nearby. He *can't* leave, Liam! My God, what will I do without him near?"

"Elisabeth, have ye gone daft?" He put his hands on the desk, leaning forward as he scrutinized her. "Ye havena spoken in years, other than at Polly's—" He stopped short at the look on her face. "Och, lass, I'm sorry. I know ye must have your reasons." He waited a few seconds for a response. "D'ye want to enlighten me as to what they are?"

She had to tell him. She stood, walking around the desk to stand beside him. "I love him, Liam. I've never stopped loving him. There's not a day goes by I don't think of him, not a night goes by I don't fall asleep dreaming of him, not a morning I wake wondering if I'll catch a glimpse of him, wondering if you or someone else will mention him, wondering if he ever thinks of me, if he ever forgave the way I treated him."

Liam stared at her. "Good God, lass." He reached for her. "Tell me now, I need to know," he asked. "Has something changed? With Mr. Hale, I'm meaning?"

She pulled away and looked up at him. "Do you know if he still cares for me? Will you tell me that?"

"Lisbeth, please, just tell me. Will it make a difference? I need to know if something's changed."

She pushed him away and slumped down on the desktop. "Go to your office and leave me be, will you?"

Liam shrugged and started to do as she bade. At the door he turned.

"Aye, well, maybe he should stay, just knowing ye're in the same city and thinking about him. Worship from afar, pining away at a distance and all that. He's always had an irrational bent where you're concerned, much against my counsel."

She straightened and looked at him, her eyes flashing dark and narrowing, her hand searching for something to throw. He grinned, ready for her attack.

She relaxed, shaking her head, helplessly returning his smile. "I shouldn't be telling you this. You'll only push me. And I don't want to be pushed. I'm still uncertain. But I began to think, Liam, maybe I'm ready to take a step. Maybe there's no reason to be miserable. Papa can't make good on any threats, and God knows I haven't changed the way I feel. Maybe David hasn't as well." She paused and tried again. "Has he?"

"I'll no' speak for the man."

"No, of course not. God forbid you put me ahead of him," she mumbled.

"We're having a celebration in two weeks. Bon voyage for the Academy. Have ye taken one of the positions elsewhere? No? What are ye waiting for?"

"I've a position in mind. You're always pushing—stop."

"Well, ye have to come to the event, bring Mrs. Hale as your escort. David will be here. I'll ask that he no' bring an escort. Will that suit ye?"

She paled at the thought that he might bring a woman when he knew she'd be there. If he'd do that . . . had she fallen so far from his thoughts?

"Would he?" she asked. "If you didn't tell him not to? Good heavens, would he do that? If he knew I was coming?"

"He's tried to move on; can ye blame him?" Liam's tone was serious. "Just don't take him for granted, Lisbeth. Don't even think of offering yourself if you're not sure, not completely sure. I won't ever forgive you. Ever. I tell you that now."

"I know," she whispered. She gathered her things and walked out of the room.

"SLOWER, MR. GRAHAM. Take more care."

"Aye, Eunice. Sometimes my fingers seem a bit too big for detail like this," he said. "And please, I asked ye to use David as my name."

"Well." Her hands went to her hair in her usual nervous search for nonexistent stray strands and she turned away, walking back to her work table. "Perhaps if you weren't in such a hurry to meet your friend, you might find a slower pace makes the detail work easier."

He made a show of slowing his hands to a snail's pace as he placed the next folded sheet on the sewing-press and opened it, passing his needle to and fro the back edge of the sheet as he attached it to the strings on the press. "Would ye like to come along, have some supper?" he asked.

"No, thank you. Perhaps next time." She tidied up the neat stacks of pages and stashed her ivory folder in the desk drawer. "Reverend Green is coming for supper tonight."

And here's where he'd do well to say something along the

lines of 'well, in that case, I'm sure Liam would understand if.' But he wasn't about to. The day had been long enough without the prospect of prolonging it into the evening. Besides, it wasn't even his Reverend. He could choose his own kirk well enough, couldn't he? He rolled back his shoulders, flexing the muscles in his back. No need to swallow him whole.

She waited briefly, then said primly, "Good evening then, Mr. Graham."

"Eunice," he said, with a grin and a small bow. Her mouth set in a hard line as she turned and walked away, her form erect.

Uncle John would approve of the lass; dimples held no sway. He grinned again, thinking an introduction was in order. The man was still unmarried, maybe a nephew-in-law would suit Mr. Warner. No longer under scrutiny, he hurried to finish.

BALTIMORE, MY WORD, why had she no one to talk to? Rhee was so far away, and none of the friends she had here came even close to the understanding she and Rhee shared. Liam, he was a dear friend, but he'd always be David's friend first. That's fine. David deserved him more that she did. And Mary? Well, Mary was just too scatterbrained.

Polly had always listened and had no compunction about telling her what she thought. Polly had listened endlessly; did she ever listen to her? Did she even know more than her man's name, if Polly dreamed about him, had made plans with him? Well, she did; of course she did. She knew how important he was to her. But she never went out of her way to meet her beau. Both Liam and David apparently had. It had been wrong—waiting until Polly would bring him to her, and now she never could.

All the plans she'd been making these past weeks, she'd

just assumed David would stay in Philadelphia. She hadn't even considered what he would want. She didn't deserve him anymore than she deserved Liam's friendship or Polly's loyalty.

Reaching home, she went to the back to sit on her garden bench, turning her face to the sun, closing her eyes and clearing her mind as she let the warmth flow through her. She took slow, even breaths, inhaling the sweet fragrance of her grandmother's roses as she relaxed and listened to the hum of the bees as they quivered over the flowers, flitting from one to the next. Summer was on its way.

Liam's news had only forced her hand, that's all. She had to make a decision quickly now, and it had better be the right one for David. He'd loved her, he'd loved her deeply, she knew that without question. Had she killed that, first with the breakup, then with remoteness when he stood by her at Polly's death?

She suddenly realized that Liam couldn't help her, not that he wouldn't. He couldn't be sure how David felt. The man held a lot inside, even from Liam. She must accept that she couldn't know ahead how he would react. Would she risk rejection? Yes, yes, she would. She had everything to gain, and nothing to lose but a bit of her pride.

Good Lord, she was doing it again. It didn't signify if she had anything to lose. The only thing that mattered was if she was the best choice for David. That's what she needed to focus on.

She sighed and stood, heading indoors. Grandmother was in the parlor, sitting at her desk by the window as she worked on her account books.

"Grandmother, I need to talk to you. It may take a bit of time. Do you have some time now?" Reaching into the mending basket, she picked up a stocking and turned to retrieve a needle from her sewing box.

"Of course, Elisabeth."

"You may be angry."

"Thank you for the forewarning. Now, what's on your mind?"

"I want to marry David," she said, somewhat defiantly. "It's been two years now, and I still feel the same. I love him, the sight of him still . . . Well, I probably shouldn't go into all that. But there's no need to tell me I can't marry him, because I will, if he'll have me. My problem is this, and I want you to be forthright. I'm prepared for your answer, truly I am." She set down the stocking and looked at her Grandmother. "Do you think I'm far too selfish to be a good wife to him?"

Mrs. Hale blinked, then laughed, one of her hands rising to cover her mouth. When she recovered, she said, "I'm sorry, Elisabeth. You've caught me quite unprepared. Perhaps the question should be if your father will permit it?"

"No, I've quite finished with worrying about that. Don't look surprised. I'm almost of age. I can certainly make my own decisions without my father. And if it comes down to it, I can support myself if he throws me out. Father was wrong to treat David as he did. David is a good man. He's kind, he's intelligent, he's caring, he's a hard worker—"

"And quite attractive, don't forget that."

"Grandmother!" Elisabeth laughed. "Yes, he is, isn't he? Perhaps you would understand the way—" She stopped, blushing.

"Of course I understand, I'm not dead yet, child! Well, it sounds as if you've decided. What did we need to discuss?"

Elisabeth stared at her grandmother, her mouth falling open.

"Close your mouth, child. If you weren't sure you loved him enough to fight back, there wasn't much I could do, was there? David doesn't deserve a namby-pamby for a wife. But, to get back to your first question, no, I don't think you're too selfish; a little self-centered perhaps, from time to time. Don't forget you told me to be truthful. Just be aware of it. You can overcome it. Now, what's your real hesitation?"

It was Elisabeth's turn to blink. This was a lot to take in. It appeared she'd been very self-centered; she hadn't expected this from her grandmother. "Well, Liam says he's leaving. He's going to Baltimore, as soon as his service is complete in August."

"And? You've an aversion to Baltimore? I wasn't aware you'd traveled there."

"Grandmother! You know very well I haven't. Don't you see? I'd have to leave you alone. And Papa already has, more or less."

"Don't you dare use me as an excuse, Elisabeth. I'm quite capable of taking care of myself. But see there? Just your concern shows you're not selfish. There's not one young woman in ten who would put her grandparents' welfare above her own desires. I'm not saying I wouldn't miss you. I'd miss you dreadfully. But the thought of you letting that man get away, out of some misguided concern for me, well, I'm telling you now, I don't want that burden."

"I can't believe you've never said any of this to me."

"Well, you've never asked me how I felt, have you? Or shared how you felt? Now don't cry, Elisabeth. Perhaps I'm being too harsh."

"No, no, you're not. It's just that, well, I've been feeling so sorry for myself, thinking I had no friends to talk to. You've been here all along, and I've wasted all this time not knowing. I'm so sorry."

"You've many years to make it up to me, God willing. Now tell me, how do you plan to approach the religion aspect of this dilemma?"

HOURS LATER SHE stood and kissed her Grandmother's cheek. "It's getting late. I'll have you know I feel better than I have in years, just talking to you, Grandmother. Do you want some tea before we go to bed? Oh, I forgot, Liam said to bring you as my escort to the Academy's get-to-gether, but I know that if you wanted to bring someone, he or she would be more than welcome."

"Why, yes, I believe I do."

"Really? Do tell, do I know him?" She followed her up the stairs, chattering all the way.

77

"STOP WATCHING ME, LIAM. I declare, sometimes you make me feel like a bug under glass,"
Elisabeth said, picking up the last paper and moving the pile
to a box. She helped him as he piled the desks inside his small
office to make room for the guests that evening, assuring
herself space was left for her and David to speak privately.

"Sorry, lass, just thinking."

"More like just wondering. I'm not telling you anything.
You'll have to be content with not knowing everything, for
once in your life." She dusted her hands off on a rag. "I'm
going now. I'll see you in a few hours, all right? Do you need
any help? Should I come early?"

"No, cleaned the fireplace Sunday last. Just go get beautiful
and hurry back. You're to be the hostess, ken."

"I am? But . . . well, I wish you'd mentioned that earlier,
Liam. I don't want to disappoint Mr. Oliver, but I need time
alone with David, I can't be—" She stopped as he grinned.
"Why, you cad! I daresay I've never known a man as under-
handed, as sneaky, and as conniving as you. You'll make a
perfect attorney."

"I havena decided to pursue law," he said, his eyes narrowing. "I'm just taking classes, that's all."

She slammed her umbrella down on the desk and gathered her belongings. "Oh, you decided that years ago, whether you're willing to admit it or not." She walked out of the small room, then stopped abruptly. Coming back in, she aimed a slim finger at him. "And I'll find twenty ways to make you pay if you breathe a word to David."

Liam grinned. "Go get beautiful, lass."

"I will, but I think I have a few minutes to go by Robertson's, I can use a new ribbon to match the dress I'm wearing. Do you know if Lenora is working today? I surely hope so. She's always so helpful." She reached up to tidy her hair, adjusting the pins as if she were picturing just the right ribbon. "Well, if I see her, I'll be sure to tell her how much you regret the loss of her friendship. Why, you haven't been the same since, pining over her night and day, though, of course, you're too embarrassed to approach her yourself, you feel so badly about the way things ended. You don't have another escort tonight, do you? I thought not. I just had a wonderful idea. I'll invite her to come with me. I'm entitled an escort, aren't I? Perhaps—"

"I willna say a word to him lass, I'm hurt ye'd even think I'd betray ye that way."

"Of course. Well, just look at all the time I've wasted chatting with you. I'd better hurry straight home at this point, hadn't I?"

SHE STOOD STOCK STILL outside the Academy, studying the front door as she waited for Mr. Coxcombe to retrieve Grandmother from the carriage. Mr. Oliver's Academy; the place where she'd do the unthinkable by asking a man to marry her, a man who had probably forgotten she existed, a man who would probably cringe at the sight of her, at the memory of the heartache she'd brought him. And that was assuming he even remembered his heart had once felt something for her at all.

"Breathe, child." Her grandmother patted her back gently. "Are you ready to go in?"

She nodded, numb, and walked up the steps, her hands wringing the handkerchief she held.

She was startled when she walked inside. She hadn't realized what an occasion this was to be. Someone, why on earth was it she didn't even know who, had transformed the place in a matter of mere hours. There must be fifty candles in these rooms, tables filled with food, punch bowls everywhere, beautiful arrangements of flowers—why, seating had even been provided to accommodate those who would want to sit. If she didn't know better, she would say she saw her grandmother's hand in this.

And, of course, it probably was. It hadn't even occurred to her to wonder where Grandmother was this afternoon as Jane helped her get ready, to even wonder if Grandmother needed Jane herself. She couldn't go through with this, truly she couldn't. David deserved so much more.

"She's quite a knack at this sort of thing, aye?" Liam said, coming up behind her.

"Why, good gracious, just look at you, Liam." She brought her hand to his cheek in greeting. "You'll have more women falling at your feet than even *you* know what to do with. I myself may even fall, you look so handsome. You bought new clothes?"

"Couldn't have Davey outdo me. The cove is togged in twig. Just wait til ye see him. Mr. Hall and Mr. Sellers dressed the lad like a swell on Chestnut."

Too nervous to chide him that now was not an appropriate time for a lapse from proper English, she asked, "Is he here?"

"No' yet. May I get ye something to drink?"

"Please. Oh look, here are the Harlows. I should tell them

what the twins did last week. They'll be tickled pink." She wandered over and talked to them, introducing them to the next set of parents who came in, entertaining them all with a story of how their children interacted. She continued to work the room, making the guests feel welcome, her eyes never far from the doorway.

He was here. She'd know him from any distance, even dressed as he was. He could be dressed in rags and he'd still walk across the room as if he owned the place, straight to the table that held the food. She smiled before she remembered how overwrought she was. Taking a deep breath, she excused herself from the couple she was chatting with and walked to him.

"Elisabeth, hello," he said, turning to greet her. "I imagine this evening is a bit sad for you."

"It is. I will miss being here. May I speak with you privately?"

He glanced down at her hands, and she stilled them, tucking the handkerchief in the fold of her skirts. But he'd seen. He'd know she was nervous.

"Would ye mind if I pay my respects to Mr. Oliver first?" he asked, a grim look settling over his features.

"Of course not. Perhaps we could meet in Liam's office in a quarter of an hour?"

He nodded and left, forgoing the refreshments.

She didn't. She walked to the punch bowl to refill her cup. A hand covered hers before she could bring the ladle from the bowl.

"You'll do better with your judgment unclouded, child."

Elisabeth nodded, setting down the ladle and her empty cup. "Did you see him, Grandmother? I find him intimidating, Liam was right. He's dressed quite the dapper gentleman."

"Oh. Well then, perhaps you should delay your interview

for a more convenient time, when you're more comfortable with his appearance."

"No! I've planned this for weeks!" She shook her head. "I declare, Grandmother, you are quite good at what you do. Maybe I should send you as my representative."

"If I were forty years younger, I'd be eager to do so; however, not on your behalf, I'm afraid."

She sniffed. "My word, I'd better get busy; you may take him right out from under me yet! Mr. Coxcombe appears to be looking for you. I hope to count on him as a distraction. He's very nice, by the way."

She'd been on such pins and needles she'd barely glanced at the man. But he'd been pleasant to her and she loved the way he looked at Grandmother.

"HAVE YOU BEEN WELL, David?" she asked, walking behind him to shut the door.

He shrugged, apparently deciding to forgo all small talk. That wasn't a good sign. She walked back and forth across the room, working out once again how to start.

She heard him sigh. "It's good to see ye well, Elisabeth, I think of ye often. But, if it's all the same to you, I'd as soon have ye speak your piece rather than torture myself with thoughts of what it may be for the next hour while we talk idle pleasantries."

He hadn't looked her in the eye when he spoke. She had no idea what he might be feeling. Well, best to get it over with and move on. He was right.

She swallowed and began, "I'm sorry, this is somewhat difficult for me." She stopped pacing and went to stand in front of him, her eyes on the floor between them.

"David, it was somewhat of a shock to find out you were leaving. I'm not quite sure why. I realize I should have known you probably would. However, I took some comfort in knowing you were nearby, in hoping I'd catch a glimpse of you from time to time and assure myself you were well, even if it left me in tears for days following. I can't change the last two years. I can't. But I find I do have control over my future. I'd like to ask you to marry me." She raised her eyes to meet his. "I *am* asking you to marry me," she amended. "If you'd like to, that is; if you'd consider it."

He looked stunned. "Pardon me?"

She hurried on. "I've learned to cook. I may not be exceptional at it, but I'm certainly adequate. You may ask John if you like. He has spent a great deal of time and effort teaching me. I've learned the basics of housekeeping, I confess I may need to send out the wash, but I've mastered most of the rest of it. In truth, it's not difficult, just a bit tedious." She stopped and raised a hand. "But not too tedious, I don't mean to imply that! I can do it. And bookkeeping. I've learned to do that as well. Mr. Oliver says I'm quite good. Even Liam admits so, and Grandmother is willing to teach me to keep the household account books. I won't mind if our children are raised Presbyterian, and I'll go to your church with you, but I hope you won't mind if I also attend my own church when I can—"

"Elisabeth, stop, please! Ye . . . ye have my head spinning, lass."

She hurried on, ignoring him. "I love you, David. I have from almost the moment we met. I've tried not to, I have, truly I have, as I suspect I may not be good enough for you. But I do, and I know, as surely as I know I'm standing here, that I'll always love you, until the day I die. I believe I can make you happy, that I can be a good wife to you and a good mother to our children." She folded her hands in front of her. "That's all. Now I'll stop."

There, it was done. She hadn't planned further than this moment. Though if she had, she most certainly wouldn't have anticipated this reaction. My word, was it indifference? He hadn't taken her in his arms. From all appearances he actually seemed to find her proposal amusing; the cad was fighting a smile. Her eyes narrowed, following him closely as he moved to sit on the corner of the desk.

"What of your father's wishes?"

"They don't signify."

He looked directly at her, raising a brow.

"They don't, David! He's all but abandoned Grandmother and me. He writes rarely. I've come to terms with the fact that he may never understand me or what makes me happy. I love him, so I can accept that. I know he loves me, but I realize now he began to leave soon after Mother died."

"Your grandmother? Her wishes certainly signify, to me anyway."

Elisabeth sniffed. "Grandmother is only concerned I may not be good enough for you. She . . . well, never mind, just know I have her consent."

She watched him as he thought, growing more impatient by the second. As usual, she couldn't tell the direction his thoughts were taking, and, as usual, it irritated her. She'd just bared her soul, and he couldn't be bothered to respond in an appropriate manner? She waited another thirty seconds while he looked at the floor and rubbed his chin before she decided she'd had enough.

Walking to the door, she announced, "Well then, when you frame your reply, please be sure to advise me of your decision." She opened the door and turned back to him. "And if it's not too much trouble, perhaps you could—"

"Aye," he interrupted.

"I beg your pardon?" she said, exasperated.

"Ye asked if I would marry you. Yes. Yes, I will. I accept your offer."

She shut the door, canting her head slightly as she tried to make sense of his words, so at odds with his actions. Somehow this wasn't what she had envisioned. He was still sitting on the desk, for heaven's sake. Shouldn't he . . . Stop, he'd said yes.

"Yes?" She took a deep breath. "Ahh. Very well, then. Might I inquire if you still lo—care for me, David?"

"Well, ye did present quite a case for a helpmate, I'd be a fool no' to say yes." He laughed as she muttered an obscenity and turned to leave again.

He sprang up and pulled her against him, just before she walked out the door. "Jesus, Mary, and Joseph, Lisbeth, give me leave, will ye? I came into this room certain ye were planning to tell me you were to be married to another."

"Would you just answer my question, please? It won't change my offer, but I . . . I would like to know," she asked quietly, her voice breaking. She wouldn't turn to look at him, afraid to see the answer in his eyes, afraid he'd see the tears pooling in hers.

He stood behind her, placing his hands lightly on her waist, bending his head, his breath hot on her ear. "Elisabeth, it staggers me that ye can even ask that. After all these years. How is it possible ye still have doubts how I feel? The verra air hums when you are in the room. I don't need my eyes to know ye're near. When you're as close as you are now, it fair sizzles. And this . . ." He reached around and cupped her face, turning her to face him, setting his mouth over hers, his tongue gently pushing past her lips to touch hers. She made a small sound in the back of her throat, leaning into him, and he pulled his mouth slowly away. "Darlin', that," he continued, "it's like a bolt of lightning chasing round my blood. It's a wonder to me ye don't know the effect ye have on me." He gathered her close and rested his head on top of hers.

"David?"

"Aye?"

"Don't call me darling. You never did before. It begs the question if you're certain to whom you're speaking."

He chuckled. "Did you hear any of the other hundred words I said?"

She pulled away. "I didn't hear what you didn't say."

"Come, I want to tell Liam, Mr. Oliver, Rob, Mr. Hall, your grandmother . . . I'll give ye no leave to change your mind. And tonight, in my prayers, I'll ask that Polly be told. And because I do love you, have never stopped loving you, and will *always* love you, I willna even say it was ye who proposed." He opened the door, then stopped, his forehead falling against the jamb. "Christ, I . . ."

"David?"

"You'll be angry, Elisabeth."

"I've no right to be angry, whatever it may be."

"We canna tell our friends just yet. There's something I . . . someone . . . someone I must tell first."

She swallowed, her mouth suddenly dry. "A woman?"

"Aye."

She staggered back a step, falling into the chair behind her, struggling for breath as the word slammed into her chest. He looked at her, a plea for understanding, her understanding, written across his face.

"Is she . . . do you . . .?"

"There's somewhat of an understanding between us. I meant to speak with her father on the Sabbath coming, to ask for her hand." He moved to kneel on the floor in front of her.

An anguished sound escaped her before she could stop it. She had no right, no right; the chant repeating over and over in her head as she rocked back and forth, her hand pressed to her stomach against the sudden nausea, bile rising with each passing second. She brought her fist to her mouth as she rocked, frantic, her eyes wide as she looked anywhere but at him.

"I have to tell ye the full of it, Bess, I have to. I feel nothing for her save respect. I don't know what she feels for me, naught more than mere tolerance, I suspect. It's more of a business arrangement between her da and me. He has no sons. But I owe her the courtesy of telling her first."

"Of course," she whispered.

"Ye are the only one I've ever loved, Elisabeth, the only one. Know that. I've never stopped. My heart never moved on."

Little by little, the nausea settled. She reached out, her fingers tentatively tracing the lines of his face while her breathing slowed.

"Thank you," she said, "for telling me."

"I'll do it tonight, lass."

"No, no, I don't expect that." She smiled slightly. "Maybe tomorrow?"

He chuckled and stood, offering her a hand.

"David? I think I should also tell you I've visited with your Reverend, and I believe he was quite scandalized you weren't with me. But I only wanted to know ahead of time, so as I could be prepared if you said yes, if he would have any objections to performing the ceremony, and if so, how I might overcome them. I hope you don't mind."

He looked at her, eyes wide, obviously taken aback. "Ye . . . ye spoke to the Reverend?" he asked, the color draining from his face.

"David, are you quite all right? I'm sorry, I shouldn't have. I've embarrassed you."

"Nay, it's just . . ."

"I truly am sorry. I've overstepped, I don't know what I was thinking." The butterflies in her stomach started up again, and she stepped back, wishing she could start the whole evening over. She was actually quite happy alone, looking back.

Her world hadn't tilted to and fro; she had her balance.

"Nay," he said, reaching for her. "C'mere." He pulled her into his arms. "What did he say?"

"Who?"

"Reverend Green. What did he say?"

What was he talking about? "But I thought, well, Liam had said . . . isn't the man's name Ewing, David? He said that he thought I should give serious and long consideration before making this decision, and that it would be best if my intended supported me in the choice." She backed out of his arms. "No wonder he was scandalized. Do you even know of a Reverend Ewing?"

He grinned, relief written across his face. "Aye."

"Oh, well then."

He pulled her to him and kissed her, his hands traveling everywhere, down her back, across her neckline, pulling fabric aside as his mouth claimed her neck, her shoulder, the tops of her breasts. As soon as a hand reached her hair, she pulled away.

"My word, David, who would have thought the mention of church could inspire you so?" Her hands went up to her hair, checking that the pins were still in place. "There's a room full of people out there! Do you know how long it takes to put myself together?"

And he was promised to another.

He reached for her. "Come back, darl—Bess. I willna muss ye further. Just let me hold ye a bit." She did, remembering he'd said the woman merely tolerated him.

No woman alive merely tolerated this man. She moved a step back.

"It wasna real to me, I think, no' until ye said that. That you're serious, that ye mean to go through with it. That ye'd consider my church." He reached out, running his fingers lightly up and down the side of her neck, and she shivered.

"We have the night, after the guests leave."

She smiled. "I wasn't completely sure you still wanted me, that perhaps you were saying yes out of some misplaced sense of duty."

He snorted. "Oh, aye, I still want you . . . if ye only knew." He brought her head to rest against his shoulder. "I still want you, Bess. Stay tonight, please. I've waited a long time to make ye mine."

As had she. She lifted her head and looked at him. "I know, David. But I will be married first."

"I dinna care to wait that long."

"Well then, speak to . . ." She didn't know the woman's name. She *never* wanted to know, ever. "Speak to your Reverend, because I *will* be married first."

Sighing, he smoothed her hair and helped her set her gown straight. "It's no' just him. There's the matter of my indenture. I've three months left. That's a long time. If ye want to be married first, perhaps next I see ye, ye wear something a lil' less enticing."

She laughed. "I'm not sure I remember how she phrased it. It was quite colorful, but Polly once told me I could wear sackcloth and still entice you."

"Smart lass, Polly was."

She took his hand and walked out the door. That was the first time she'd said Polly's name and laughed. Lord knows, she missed her still, but maybe she could begin remembering her without the overwhelming heartache.

78

July 1790

"COME HERE, BECCA." ELISABETH PATTED the empty spot beside her on the garden bench. The dog wagged her tail and jumped on her lap, standing on her hind legs while she covered Elisabeth's face with sloppy laps of her tongue. "No!" she said, laughing, moving her face out of the dog's reach. "You know quite well where I meant. You better not have mud on your feet." She kissed her, burying her face deep in her soft fur before she set her aside.

"We have a letter from Rhee here. You be a good girl now, and I'll tell you what she says." She opened it and started reading. "Oh! She's coming, Becca! Rhiannon is coming for a visit. Wait." She scanned the letter further. "I declare, I think maybe she's already sailed!" Elisabeth jumped up off the bench and swung herself around in circles, the letter clutched to her chest. "Oh, I can't wait, I can't!" Becca growled, and she stopped, the hair rising on the back of her neck at the sound. Becca so rarely growled. Lowering the letter, she turned slowly to look behind her, her heart going to her throat as she saw the man standing a few feet away.

"Mr. Wallace? Is that you? Of course it is. I scarcely recognized you. I'm sorry, you'll think me silly. I didn't see you coming up the path." Where had he come from? He *hadn't* come up the garden path.

"Where's your father, girl? Been waiting hours. Damn nigger says he's out."

"Tom, if that's who you're referring to, is correct. He is out. Is there something I can help you with?"

"He owes me," Wallace muttered. She couldn't make out the rest of what he said, but she could smell the whisky on his breath and see the red in his eyes.

"I'll just call for Tom, Mr. Wallace. He'll know when Papa's expected," she said, inching toward the back door.

Without warning he hit her across the face with the back of his hand. "Don't mess with me, girl."

Stunned, she stumbled back, hands flying to her face, as Becca launched at his leg, barking and growling. Tom stepped outside with her grandfather's rifle.

"Git, trash, 'fore I shoot your ass," Tom said evenly, the gun leveled at the back of Wallace's head.

Wallace kicked the dog, sending her whimpering across a garden plot, then turned on Tom. "Try it, boy. You don't think ye'll hang, shooting a white man?" he said, sneering, his face inches from Tom's as he leaned in over the barrel.

"What's it to you, mister? No satisfaction I hang; you already dead. Your choice, trash."

John materialized then, coming up from behind, throwing his arm around Wallace's neck and dragging him away with no more care than he would give a load of laundry.

Tom followed them down the path, the rifle still aimed and ready. "Sheriff's been sent for. Guess you decided to wait. Why don't you just settle now, 'til he gets here?"

"I just want my money. Hale still owes. We had a deal."

Elisabeth went to Becca, picking her up and stroking her, her fingers probing for injuries, all the while his words competing for her attention. "Owes . . . deal . . . "

"Stay Becca," she whispered, "Stay." She'd never been hit before. Her head was reeling, and she was struggling to set aside the pain. But she had to know, before the sheriff came; she had to know. John had the man secured, and she went to kneel in front of Wallace.

"Miss Lisabeth, git on in the house now."

"In a minute, John." She placed her fingers under Wallace's chin, pulling his face towards hers. "Mr. Wallace. What deal did you have with my father?"

Wallace spat at her, and Tom slammed the rifle butt against his head.

"Miss Lisabeth, you go on in now."

"I will," she said. "In just a minute." She changed position slightly, so that she could move faster if he were to spit again.

"Don't worry about my gown, Mr. Wallace, Becca's already put her muddy paws on it. A little phlegm won't hurt it a bit. Now, perhaps I could settle the debt, should you tell me the circumstance."

He kept his head down, the blow from the rifle having knocked the fight from him. She leaned closer, hoping to decipher what he was muttering. Something over and over again about his doing his part, Hale needed to pay.

"What was your part, Mr. Wallace?" she asked softly. "I'll plead your case with Papa."

He looked up, his small black eyes filled with hate as they peered at her through the fringe of dirty blond hair that hung in his face. "Overseers came, just like I said they would. I did my part."

She didn't hear anymore, falling back as if he'd struck her again. Tom lowered the rifle and helped her up, guiding her to the door where Jane stood waiting with Becca, her eyes round and white in her black face. Jane reached for her, pulling her inside.

She turned her head to look at Wallace again, sprawled out on the lawn, muttering to himself and growling obscenities at John and Tom. She waited by the window until the sheriff came, stood at the door while she answered his questions, watched from the porch as they carted him away. Then she walked back into the yard.

"Thank you, Tom, John. I don't know what I would have done without you gentlemen." She put her hands on their shoulders. "Thank you. What you heard, though," she said, shaking her head from side to side. "You can't repeat it, please. You can't repeat it."

"Didna hear nothing, miss," Tom muttered, turning to walk back inside the house.

"Please, John, he can't know. He'll kill him if he does. He will. He can't know."

"Now, Miss Lisbeth . . . young David, he's got more sense than that."

"He can't, John. He'll hang if he kills him. They'll hang him! He can't know, please, John," she pleaded.

She had watched him beat a man for slandering her; what would he do to one who had hit her, to one responsible for jailing him? And would he still marry her, should he know what the grandfather of any children they might have was capable of? Would he? No, of course not. He'd despise her.

"John, I'm begging you." She clutched the front of his shirt in her hands. "No good can come of him knowing."

"He won't know then, Miss Lisabeth. Dontcha be worried now, hear? He won't know," John said, patting her head, removing her hands. "You needs to tell Mrs. Hale. It's her property that man done hit you on. You needs to tell her."

"I will."

GRANDMOTHER HAD CRIED bitterly, and it nearly broke her heart to see it. They clung to each other, rocking back and forth as they sobbed, stopping only when Jane came to them with cold cloths for their eyes and whisky for the ache inside. Then Tom came in, helping her Grandmother up, insisting they both go upstairs to try to sleep.

The household helped with her excuses not to see David for a few days, until the bruises marking her face had faded.

The blow to her heart, though; she feared that would never fade.

79

"BE STILL, WILL YE? I canna think over the sound of your pacing."

"Och, you're testy. Ye need a night carousing, 'fore you're a married man. It'll make ye more agreeable and appreciative. What d'ye say to a few rounds at the Man, rouse up a game? Mayhap a visit to Helltown? A wench to take the edge off. Aye?"

David sat at the desk, pencil in hand, questioning again the wisdom in accepting Lisbeth's proposal. Eunice had seemed relieved, though that hadn't surprised him. He'd always had the impression he intimidated the lass. Her father, well . . . that couldn't be helped. The man's anger was fierce.

"Nay," he answered, continuing to tally the figures.

"Righteous cove." Liam went to the news stack and thumbed through next week's copy. "I've news. Are ye interested?" He looked at David. "Something I overheard. Nay? Very well, I'll just tell ye then, whether ye're interested or no'. Dr. Franklin left a codicil in his will. The culls at the Coffee House are thrashing it out." He waited a few seconds for a response. "Pete's sake, Davey, ye take all the fun out of being the first with news."

Damn, he couldn't afford a wife. He tossed his pencil aside

and gave Liam his attention. "He's left me a bequest, has he then, solve all my worries? Out with it, mate. Don't keep me hanging."

"Marginal effort there; however, I'll take it. Seems Franklin waxed nostalgic near the end. He remembered how he received help starting out and decided to pass it on. He's left two thousand pounds to Philly to loan out to those who've completed their indentures."

"Seriously? Ye know the terms?"

"Didna get that much. Mr. Hall will know soon, I imagine." Liam pulled David's paper toward him. "Piece work? Ye're calculating the rate of piece work? Why?"

"I'm budgeting, Liam. Remember I'm to be married?"

Liam studied the page further, his brow furrowed. "I don't understand. Ye were to set up shop, I thought. There's no' a sum here for a press, nor for your case." He turned the paper over. "What the hell! Ye know damn well Lisbeth willna expect a full staff of three! Give the lass credit."

"She has one now. More, if ye count the day help."

Liam studied him for a moment, his blue eyes hard. "Tread carefully, mate. Ye'll have her thinking ye're looking for reasons no' to marry." He pushed the paper back to David. "Why piecework?"

"It pays. I've no call to be choosy."

"Ye're stepping round the question, David. Come, let's at least get dinner, aye?"

Is that what he was doing, putting up obstacles? It had been a little over a month since she had come to him, and they still weren't married. He put the paper in a drawer and stood, walking out the front office and onto the street with Liam. "I don't think it's a good idea to set up shop, Liam. There are too many risks involved. I don't have enough money to buy a press and set up house both."

"What of her toch'r?"

"That's her da's money. I'll no' touch that."

Liam stopped him as they passed the new Library Hall. "It's almost complete. What do ye think of it?"

David shrugged. "It's different. I like it well enough."

"Some are calling it the new 'Federal' style."

"Hmm. That's all you heard of Franklin's money, that funds were available?"

"Ye have to use it to start a business and have someone to speak for ye."

"In Philly ye think, the business?"

"I didn't hear. I'm not sure the gents knew the details themselves."

He exhaled slowly. "Maybe there's some truth to what ye say, Liam. What do you think? D'ye think I'm looking for reasons not to marry?"

"Aye, I do, but only as ye're wary. Ye've learned to get by without her. A hard fought freedom, no doubt; one hard to relinquish."

"Hall and Sellers gave their consent. I havena told her."

Liam looked at him, surprised. He turned abruptly, motioning David to follow him into one of the taverns they had just passed. It wasn't crowded yet. They had their choice of seats. Liam led him to the bar, his gaze sweeping over the tables.

"Would ye mind if I asked to marry the lass then, if ye're throwing her off, I'm meaning?"

David turned on him fast. "Try it and you'll wish I'd let you drown."

"You're right, of course," Liam said easily. "My blunt's no less shy than yours." He nodded toward a table by the door. "But ye willna mind if William over there does, aye? The swell is well breeched. I have it on good authority he can provide at least six to staff the household. She'll be twice as happy as she is now. Ye can give him pointers so he has better luck with her this time around."

Jesus, Mary, and Joseph, how the hell does he do that? How does he manage to walk into a tavern where David could see two of the lads who'd tried their hand at courting Elisabeth, just from where he sat? He signaled for whisky, tossing it back as soon as it arrived.

Getting up from his stool, he left some coins on the bar. "You're on your own, Liam. I have some things to take care of. But stay here, aye, so as I can find ye in a wee bit?"

Liam had turned to watch the group of men playing cards, one of whom kept checking his pocket watch. "Later then, mate. I think I'll rouse a game. It's been a while."

David walked out and headed back down the hill toward the quay. The streets were full as the market was emptying for the day, but he needed the breeze from the river. He needed to clear his head.

Did he really think a woman like Elisabeth would remain unmarried while he took off to make his fortune? And even if she did, would she still want *him* when he came back? Hell, he wasn't even sure why she wanted him now.

Would he be content without her? Granted, he'd learned to get by day to day, sometimes without thinking of her for an hour at a time. Should he settle for that? It was safer. Safer is better, right?

"David, good afternoon."

"Why, Mrs. Hale, good day to ye. Hand me that." David took the package from her hands and looked around. "Where's Tom? Is Elisabeth with ye?"

"Tom's sister was getting married this afternoon. It wasn't heavy David, but thank you. I believe Elisabeth will be home by now. She was spending the afternoon shopping with Mary. Would you like to walk home with me?"

"Of course."

"I've been meaning to talk to you anyway. A little slower please, don't forget I have some years on you."

David laughed and slowed. "It's hard to forget, ma'am."

"Have you made any plans yet?"

"My intentions, is it now?" David grimaced. "Ye've every right to ask, of course. I wish I had it all worked out, Mrs. Hale." The words spilled out before he thought. "Sometimes I think her da was right. I can't give her the life she's accustomed to, no' yet anyway, no matter how many ways I put the figures to paper."

"Don't do her an injustice, David. The only thing that child wants is you. She's different than other girls her age, I had a hard time accepting that at first. Why, when Edward first wrote they were coming, I had visions of ten years filled with parties and beaus. But she's . . . well, I don't have to tell you what she's like."

"I ken, Liam's telling me the same, but I do know. He thinks I'm stalling, because of what happened two years past."

He watched as she opened her mouth, then shut it. They were passing a small park, and she guided him to a nearby bench.

"Sit with me for a minute or two." She lowered herself on the bench carefully, grabbing the back of it for support as she sat. "I wanted to ask you; perhaps you'll see it as pushing, but I'll ask anyway. Edward won't be back until November now. If you and Elisabeth do marry, I'd like you both to stay on at the house. Just until you leave for Baltimore, I know I couldn't count on having the two of you for long."

"That's verra generous, Mrs. Hale. But I do have enough money set aside to put a roof over my own wife's head."

"I don't doubt it for a minute, knowing you. I'm asking it as a favor to me. I'll miss her when she leaves. And you as well, David. I ask that you set aside your damn pride and consider the offer in the spirit it's given."

David grinned. "Why, Mrs. Hale, that's mighty strong language I just heard."

"Well, don't make me beg, young man. You know how much I enjoy your company." She took his hand, holding it in her lap, patting it. "Don't let the past rob your future, David," she said quietly, her small blue eyes sincere with concern as she watched him.

David was silent for a moment, considering all the things Liam had said. He looked at Mrs. Hale. Nice stock he thought, smiling slightly. His Ma would definitely approve. He recalled the rush he'd felt, leaping about his blood just moments ago, when first he spotted Mrs. Hale in the market, expecting Elisabeth to be just around the corner, and the disappointment he'd experienced when she wasn't.

Then there was the flare of anger he'd felt at Liam's jest on offering for her himself. He shifted in his seat, still guilt-ridden over his response. Never, not once in the last six years, had he *ever* implied Liam might owe him his life.

She made him crazy, that's all, and he was crazy to think he could do without her.

What an eijit he was, an eijit and a coward.

He jumped up and extended his hand to Mrs. Hale. "D'ye have some time? There's my church. I'd like to talk to Reverend Ewing about marrying me tonight. That's where I think I may have been headed when I ran into ye. Your presence can add some respectability to my request, aye?"

"Tonight? But . . . but . . ."

"Ye're no' going to have me go through a big wedding are ye, Mrs. Hale? Please say ye wouldna do that. Anything can go wrong by the time it's planned."

Emotions played out visibly across Mrs. Hale's normally composed face. He knew well she wanted to plan a big wedding. But he didn't think he could do that. He'd be expecting Mr. Hale at any moment to interrupt the process and whisk his daughter away. Perhaps he was wrong, but he felt the man had an irrational prejudice against him.

Graciously, her features settled into acceptance. "No, no, of course not. You just took me by surprise. It's your wedding, and Elisabeth will be only too happy to marry you tonight if that's what you want. Let's go speak to the gentleman, then you must at least allow me three hours to prepare. Will you do that, maybe four?"

"Aye, three. I've some preparations to take care of myself." Finding Liam not the least of them; hopefully he'd stayed put. "And Mrs. Hale, I'd be honored to accept your kind invitation for the next three months, no' tonight I'm thinking, but after." He watched her face closely and was relieved when all he saw was joy at the prospect.

"Well, then, let's hurry, David. Isn't that the Reverend leaving just now? I have many things to do. Maybe Mary will stay and help. It turns out to be quite an inopportune time to have Tom unavailable. Would you send Liam, if you can spare him? Can't you walk any faster, young man? My word, you must be twenty years younger than I am."

David grinned. He thought it might be a few more years than that.

80

CIT WAS ALMOST NINE. SHE should be here by now. He paced the footpath in front of the church, going over everything once again, making sure he'd left nothing out.

Liam was here, chatting idly with Mr. Oliver, over amongst the trees. He would have liked Rob here, but Rob was in Charlestown now. And Uncle John was in New York, which was likely for the best.

He'd paid for a room at the inn on Front, giving Liam some money to fill it with flowers and whatnot, asking him to see that Lisbeth's bag was there awaiting her. There was nothing else, was there?

"Good God, a ring. I forgot to get her ring. Liam! I'll be back. Tell her I'll be right back." He handed Liam his jacket and bolted up the path. His mother had sent him his grand-mother's ring a few years back. He'd forgotten about it, come to think of it, wasn't exactly sure where he had it stored.

"David, stop, I have it!"

David stopped, and Liam motioned him back. "Remember? I snatched it on its way into the Delaware? Nay, on second thought, ye wouldna." He brought it out of his pocket to show him. "Everything's in place, Davey, dinna fash. Here they are now, Mr. Coxcombe is escorting them."

David started toward the carriage, but Liam pulled him back. "Into the kirk with ye, mate. Ye're no' to see the bride. Mr. O will see to them."

"It's no' a formal wedding, Liam," David said, reluctantly following him.

"She'll appreciate some tradition nonetheless. Put this back on." He handed David his jacket. "Now take in some air. Don't want ye bolting halfway through the ceremony. Ye look peaked."

The Reverend met them inside, welcoming them, inquiring after the bride.

"Aye, she's here. Well, Liam wouldna let me make sure, but I think she is."

"Here she is now, Rev'rend," Liam said, canting his head toward the back.

She walked into the church, her eyes searching. The lass couldn't look more beautiful should she have had days to prepare. He should go meet her. He started back up the aisle, stopped when his knees threatened to give way.

She came to him, reaching out her hand. He clutched it tightly before she could notice his shaking. She looked at him, her clear blue eyes meeting his.

"Don't you dare faint on me, David Graham!" she whispered. "Why, given the amount of time it took me to get you to the altar, then you giving me three minutes to dress on my wedding day. Well, I declare if I had any pride left at all, it would be the very last straw." She brought her free hand up, caressing his cheek.

There, he closed his eyes briefly and relaxed. He could breathe again. He took in a deep breath and exhaled slowly.

"Now, lass, dinna exaggerate. Three *hours* it was I gave ye," he whispered back. He grinned, and she flashed that devastating smile back at him.

He could do this, he could, though he didn't dare take his

eyes from hers as the ceremony began, nor let loose of her hand.

LIAM JOSTLED HIM, clearing his throat. Somehow he didn't think it was for the first time. He tore his eyes from Lisbeth's and looked up. The ceremony was over. He must have said all the right things, as no one looked out of sorts.

Well then. He was married. He looked back at her.

Mine.

He had the urge to drop to his knees and shout his thanks. Might of, if he wasn't sure Liam would kick his arse all the way to the kirk door. Not that he could, but the man should certainly try, were he to see him start to do something so foolish.

Mine.

He grinned and gave his new wife a chaste kiss, his eyes promising much more later, before gentling his hold on her and turning to thank the Reverend.

Mrs. Hale told the small group that a reception was to be held at the inn near the Academy. "Mr. Brock was good enough to persuade them to allow us a room on short notice."

He followed the others up the walkway, looking down at her every few steps. *Mine.*

81

SO MANY HAD COME; HOW on earth had Liam and Grandmother managed it?

The friends they shared from the Irish community and the Academy, several Negroes, John and James among them, her girlfriends, Mr. Hall and others from the print shop, as well as friends she'd met through Liam's recent association with the University; they were all here. It took hours to greet them and thank them for coming. Hours . . . and he never once left her side.

Was this only a dream? They'd been ushered into a room off the inn's main room, a beautiful room full of flowers and bright with candles, complete with a large window displaying the view of lantern-lit ships on the river. Someone had even had time to see to food and drink. So fast . . . she could scarcely credit it.

She was married. To David. She might not have believed it, were it not that he hadn't once let go of her hand, were it not that he was right there every time she thought to question it.

People drifted into the public area toward the musicians the inn hosted on Saturday evenings. David led her there as well, twirling her into his arms. He always surprised her with how well he danced, graceful in spite of his size. She dropped back her head to look up at him, intending to comment on the musicians. Stopped short by the heat in his eyes, she was somewhat surprised to feel an answering need begin to pool low and languid, rousing her from her dream-like state.

She swallowed. "I'm growing rather tired, David. Are we to stay here tonight?"

"Aye. I should see ye get some rest, seeing as I hurried ye earlier." Cutting the dance short, he guided her toward the stairs.

"No' so fast, Davey, I'd like to dance with your bride 'fore ye leave, if ye'll let loose of her for just three minutes. I'll wager her hand lost all circulation an hour ago."

David looked at Liam, then to the stairs and back, before releasing her. "Return her straight to me then, will ye? She's tired."

"Hmmph, ye don't look weary, Lisbeth. Are ye sure ye want to be married to that possessive brute?"

"I'm sure it's not possible to be any happier, Liam," she said, watching David cross the room to her grandmother. She loved watching him move, she always had.

"I can see that, lass, I'm happy for the both of you. But I'm no' giving ye back after this, Mr. O deserves a dance as well. I'll keep the lad entertained, I expect."

"Did you like my friend Mary?"

"She's verra nice, Lisbeth, but rid yourself of any match-making notions, aye?"

"I have none. She's not for you, I know that. It's only that she's wanted to meet you for some time now."

"So. I'm coming to terms with losing my mate. This was sudden, aye? I'll have no one to play with."

"I'd never seek to alter your friendship with David, Liam; never. You're a part of who he is. I would ask, though, when you intend to include women in your outings, that I be invited as well."

He laughed. "Ye know well enough the lassies I tossed his way were no threat to ye. I wouldna have done it if I'd thought they might be. It was just my way of keeping him out and about, ken? So as he wouldna brood; he tends to fold into himself without ye. They were ne'er more than an annoyance to him, even after ye threw him over."

"I didn't 'throw him over,'" she said, bringing her cheek to his. "I do love you, Liam, I want you to know I thank God every night for the friend you've been to me." She turned her face to kiss his cheek, her mouth ending on his as he turned toward her at the same moment. He stiffened and drew back quickly, his face closed.

Blushing, she mumbled, confused at his response. "Forgive me, I didn't mean to . . ."

"Mr. O's waiting," he interrupted, taking her hand and leading her off the floor.

LIAM STOOD OFF TO the side and watched her as they danced, dazzling poor Mr. Oliver so he was as befuddled as a young lad. He sympathized.

Christ, their wedding day . . . his cock waits till her wedding day to make a stand for her? If the music hadn't stopped, would he have . . .? No, no, of course he wouldn't; he wouldn't. She was his sister, for God's sake. He snorted. If he were honest, he'd admit he'd stopped seeing her as his sister since that God-awful night last year, when he'd seen her in her shift, the candlelight from behind backlighting the luscious curves of . . . hell, that wasn't helping. He turned away.

David had pissed the turf years ago. There was no cause to debate this, wedding night or not. It was the whisky; he had just had one too many, that's all. She'd been so close; it'd been a while since he'd had a woman, a natural reaction. That and the emotions of this night, the room was fair buzzing with it.

"Are ye feeling all right, Liam? Liam?"

David. Answer the man. "Fine, fine. Just has been a long day. If I'd known ye were to become spontaneous and impulsive of a sudden, I would have rested up. Now, d'ye need any last minute words of encouragement? Instruction?"

David laughed. "I think I know what to do, ye can rest easy on that score. You did fast work with this," he said, gesturing to the room at large. "I shouldna be surprised at what ye're capable of anymore, but ye always manage to surprise me nonetheless."

If he only knew, which of course he never would. "I had help. Tell two people, they each tell two, ye know how that goes. Ye've lots of friends here."

"Aye, we're blessed. Now I'm relying on ye to run interference whilst I work on getting my wife upstairs, aye?" David's gaze followed Elisabeth as she left the dance floor, frowning as it settled on something else.

Liam turned in the direction David was looking. The Billings had just walked into the room. "Late night out," he said, turning back to David.

David shifted from foot to foot, his expression still set in a grimace of discomfort.

"Ye'll be wondering if I know she's been stepping out with Darcy?" Liam asked.

"Ye knew?"

"Aye, the lass thought to bring me to heel."

"Out of curiosity, if ye hadn't, should I have said anything?"

He thought for a moment. "I think so, yes. If she mattered I might've made ye pay for being the messenger, mind."

David snorted. "As if ye could, pretty boy." He looked again toward Victoria. "There's others, Liam. D'ye know that as well?"

He hadn't. He could feel David watching him.

"Maybe we should stay a bit longer. Lisbeth's no' met her yet."

"Nay, I'm a big lad now, all grown up, remember? Here comes your bride. Go, enjoy your wedding night."

David grinned, taking Elisabeth's hand. "Wait with Liam just a minute, Bess, while I speak to Mr. Hall, all right?" He kissed her, leaving her looking uncertainly at Liam.

"Liam, I didn't mean to make you uncomfortable earlier, if I said anything. I mean, I apologize . . . you are my dearest friend, that's all I . . ."

Oh, hell. "Of course ye didna, lass," he said, bringing his hand to her cheek, meeting her eyes. "I love ye as well," he said, embracing her. He drew back, his eyes sad, unable to hide the wave of emotion crashing over him.

"Keep him happy, Elisabeth. I'm releasing him to your care." He kissed her cheek as David walked back to collect her.

"HE DOESN'T KNOW YOU want her, does he? I wonder if she does. Though I'd imagine she does. Women usually do," Victoria said, coming up behind him.

Startled, Liam turned to her, his reaction controlled by the time he faced her. "It's probably difficult for a woman like you to understand, Tory. David and Elisabeth have been my closest friends since I was a boy. I love her, and I love him. I wish them all the best. It's been a difficult journey for them to get to this night. I'm nothing but happy for them."

Her black eyes danced as she looked at him. "Of course you are. None of which, however, stops you from wishing you were leading her up those stairs, instead of him."

"You have a filthy mind. I'll leave you to it. Good evening, Miss Billings."

She laid her hand lightly on his sleeve. "Actually, I was under the impression you had a fondness for my filthy mind."

Or perhaps that was my filthy mouth?" Placing a slender finger on her full red lips, she canted her head, as if considering, then shrugged as if the difference was of no consequence.

"I'm glad I encountered you. Do you like green Mr. Brock? I saw the most wonderful emerald green peignoir in a shop today. I had to have it, although Papa will have a fit when he receives the bill. There isn't much to it, not for the sum, but I thought the coloring suited. I'll leave my door unlocked for the next half hour, should you want to stop by and tell me what you think. If you're cordial, I'll even let you pretend I'm her." She dropped her hand and walked away, leaving him no opportunity to respond. The lass was fond of having the last word.

Nay, Tory didn't walk. Glided, she glided away. Jesus, what a night. He turned from the stairs and spotted Mrs. Hale alone.

82

"IT'LL BE SOME TIME BEFORE we have a place of our own I may carry ye into. This will do, aye?" He turned and picked her up easily, carrying her through the doorway.

She laughed. "It will indeed! Put me down now, so I may see. Oh David, look, it's such a beautiful room. Thank you for all the flowers!" She stood in the center of the room and swung around, arms outstretched. "I'm so happy!"

"Careful no' to drop that candle now. I confess, your grandmother and Liam did the leg work."

"When you say 'some time,' what do you mean exactly, David? We'll be together, won't we? Mr. Hall gave you leave? I don't care where you put me, as long as you keep me." She lit two of the candles in the room before setting down the one she was holding.

He laughed. "Oh, aye, I intend to keep ye, have no doubt of that. I'd been talking to Mr. Oliver about renting space in the townhouse, seeing as they have more room than needed."

"But I thought they had lodgers now? Liam told me a family had moved in downstairs."

"They've still room to let, but I wasna sure ye'd be comfortable there, given your association with the place and Mr.

O. But no matter, your Grandmother has convinced me we should stay with her for a time." He went to the table near the fireplace and picked up the decanter, pouring them each a glass of wine.

"She told me she wanted to ask you. I wasn't certain how you'd feel about it. I'm glad you said yes, for her sake."

"She has a way of asking, I'll give her that." He picked up the glasses and brought her one. "To my beautiful wife, and many long, happy years ahead," he said, raising his glass in a toast.

"And to my husband, who's suddenly full of surprises." She sipped her wine until he took it from her, reaching for her. She backed away.

"You'll have to tell me sometime what brought this on so quickly." She moved to the bed. Someone had brought her new night shift and laid it out. Hopefully that someone had been Grandmother. She pushed aside the thought that had been nagging at her and picked up the silk, fingering it nervously.

"Will you turn around, David?"

He looked taken aback. "Nay, I will not. Why would ye ask me that?"

"Please? Just this once, just this time?"

He sighed and walked to the window, glass in hand. Turning to the fireplace, she began working on the row of tiny buttons that traveled from the small of her back to the back of her neck. She heard his boots come off as he sat on the bed. Then his jacket. Now his shirt. Not his breeches, please, not just yet.

Why was she suddenly behaving like a ninny?

"Will ye give me leave to turn now?"

"Soon."

He sighed, louder this time, and she heard him rise from the bed.

She laughed, some of the nervousness leaving her. "I'm hurrying as fast as I can. This isn't easy, without my maid!"

"I'm willing to stand in for her, lass."

"No!" Why, she wasn't sure. It had taken a good deal of effort to procure the new stay she was wearing. It was a lovely blue silk, a shade that accentuated the color of her eyes, trimmed with a tiny edging of ivory lace that came close to matching the color of her skin. And it made the most of her figure, if she did say so herself.

"I don't recall ye being particularly shy, Bess."

"I know. It's odd, isn't it?"

Again, the sigh. She hurried, but it still took her some time to get out of her gown, washed up, and into the shift. She turned to him.

My. My word, but he's magnificent. All these years and she'd never seen him without his shirt. Her fingertips quivered as she anticipated running them across his wide shoulders, down the sleek muscles of his back.

"David?"

He turned from the window, grinning as he walked toward her. Removing the nightcap and pins from her hair, he swept the length of it down around her shoulders.

"Well, that will be a mess to untangle tomorrow."

"I'll help ye comb it. Ye are the most beautiful thing I've seen in my lifetime. I'm no' even sure ye're real."

"Well then," she said, reaching up to bring his head down, "you'd better stop talking about it and kiss me, if only to assure yourself I am."

"MRS. HALE, IT turned out well, don't ye think?"

"It did, Liam. Not a soul would have known we spent only two hours in preparation, were it not for the lack of formal invitations."

"But that matters naught, aye? I've never seen David happier. You and I; it's a fine team we make. May I see ye home?"

"Oh! Would you mind? Mr. Coxcomb was kind enough to delay his prior engagement, but he couldn't ignore it entirely. I'm sorry to impose. I saw that beautiful girl you were talking to. You have much better things to do than escort an old woman home. But I'm afraid I'm a bit worn out."

"Of course ye are. It's no' every day your only granddaughter gets married with an hour of notice. I'm happy to take ye. Come now, I'll see if I can get us a carriage."

They were in luck. The inn had a coach just outside. Any other part of Philadelphia this time of night and he might have struggled with finding one. He helped her into it and settled across from her.

"You haven't had much time to talk to David, I assume, Liam. I asked him to stay with me, him and Elisabeth, for the next few months until they go to Baltimore. It's going to be so quiet in the house when she leaves; I was very gratified when he eventually agreed."

"Aye, they'll leave a big hole in my life as well. I'll miss them, miss the Academy. A year of changes this has turned into. I find I may no' like change as much as I had in the past."

"I know, but things work out for the best, you'll see." She patted his knee in consolation as if he were a small boy and he grinned. "I decided I'm going to Charlestown tomorrow to give them time alone for a few weeks. I'll leave a note, of course, but perhaps you could explain to David as well, so he doesn't feel they've caused me to leave my home? I don't want him to regret his decision to stay with me."

"I've been thinking the same, actually, how to absent myself. Would you like an escort? I havena been outside of Philly since I came across. Ye needn't put me up. Rob is there."

"Why, I'd be honored. Alison will be pea green with envy

to see me escorted by such a handsome and entertaining young man." She looked at him, speculating. "But as soon as I get back to Philadelphia, I'm going to work on finding you a wife. You should have neither the time nor the inclination to escort an old lady around the country. Not that I'm anything but grateful you do, of course. Why on earth you haven't settled down with one of those countless young women my granddaughter talks about, I'm sure I don't know. But I'll find someone deserving, young man, mark my words. Why, I can probably even get started in Charlestown. As long as you're there as well, why not?"

He laughed, glad he'd had the opportunity to escort her home. She wore easy on him. He was a long way from wanting a wife, but he had to admit it'd be interesting to see who she came up with.

"Why not indeed, Mrs. Hale? Should I make a list of what I require, give ye something to be going by then?" They had arrived, and he helped her out, sending away the carriage.

"No, I don't think so," she said, considering. "I think perhaps you may not know what you require." She kissed his cheek and offered him her hand. "Good work tonight, Mr. Brock."

He took her hand, kissed it, and bowed. "Aye, we make a fine team, Mrs. Hale. Good evening to you." He turned and walked away, calling back to her before she shut the door. "I'll book the both of us first thing in the morning on the Charlestown Packet. She sails at one; I'll call for ye at eleven, if that suits."

"Oh, but I wish I were years younger. I do appreciate a man who takes charge. I'd snap you up in an instant. Eleven will suit. Goodnight, Liam."

Liam laughed. "Ye don't have to look far for my list of requirements, ma'am."

He started walking home. It was a warm night, cloudy and

damp. Not a breeze to stir it, the air upstairs would be stifling. He was glad Mrs. Hale didn't mind him accompanying
her to Charlestown. It would give David and Lisbeth time
they needed, if both he and her grandmother were gone;
give him time to adjust as well.

He sighed, realizing he'd passed right by home and was
standing outside the inn. She was using him for sport, nothing more. Slumming with the lower sort. Weak, that's what
he was. He'd overshot his half hour, for sure, but he was
willing to wager the door would still be unlocked. The lass
liked him well enough to cut him a wide margin.

This would likely lead to nothing but trouble, he cautioned
himself for the hundredth time as he opened the door and
entered the quiet lobby. The lad at the desk looked up at the
sound of the door, then down to his book when he saw it
was him. Liam set a coin on the counter as he passed, a token
of his appreciation of the lad's discretion.

Her last words rang in his ears as he trotted up the stairs.
I'll even let you pretend I'm her. That wouldn't happen. No way
any man could confuse the two of them. And she would
look past fine in green, he thought, grinning.

One last time couldn't hurt, and if he were lucky, she and
her da would have left town by the time he returned from
Charlestown.

83

ELISABETH LAY STILL, A SLOW, lazy smile spreading across her face. How quickly her life had changed in the space of a few hours yesterday. David was sprawled across her, head on her shoulder, one leg pinning her down, one hand cupping her breast, revealing a possessive side she hadn't known existed. Not that she minded; she didn't mind at all. It was a nice change. For now, anyway.

His hand began to caress her. Ah, he's awake, finally. She stretched, kissing the top of his head.

"Good morning. I'm glad you're awake. Shouldn't we be up, dressing for church?"

"We were there last night. Ye're thinking of kirk whilst ye're in your honeymoon bed? The Reverend will be delighted."

"Well, my husband has been asleep for hours. Know that I spent more than a few of those hours reflecting on his fine attributes, he having so many to reflect upon, before my mind moved on. Actually, it would probably frighten you if you knew the amount of time I spent thinking of you."

David chuckled, his mouth nuzzling her neck, moving up to her ear. "We're no' moving from this bed for some time yet, except to eat. I think I missed supper yesterday."

"There should be food arriving at some point this morn-

ing. Grandmother told me she arranged for our breakfast."
She shivered at the things he was doing with his mouth.
"Mmm, I like the way you wake up."

He brought his head from her neck to look at her. "Are ye
sore?"

She blushed, shaking her head, moving her hand to smooth
the soft dark curls on his chest. How big he was, how solid.
She loved touching him.

He ran his hand lightly down the curve of her waist, grabbing her hip as he rolled to his back. She barely had time to
blink before she was atop him and he was inside her. She
winced before she could stop herself. Maybe she was a little
sore.

He noticed and winced himself. "Sorry, lass, dinna move
if it pains ye then, though have mercy on me, aye?" he said,
breathless. The teasing look in his eyes had disappeared,
replaced by a hot, drowsy light, his eyelids heavy.

She laughed, delighted with her power. "Rest assured
David, I won't abuse you. But what do I do?"

"Ah, lass." His hands reached behind her head to bring her
down to kiss him. "Just be."

HE WAS NEAR FAMISHED. He looked greedily at the
table the staff had brought in, loaded with all manner of
victuals. Mrs. Hale was something, a fine addition to his family.

Elisabeth looked over the large selection and shook her
head. "I hope you're hungry," she said, taking a small slice of
toast and buttering it.

"I am. Ye're not?"

"Not this hungry," she said, laughing, waving her hand over
the table. "David, who was that woman Liam was talking to
as we left last night?"

"Victoria Billings. She and her da are staying here whilst he readies for a move out west, Kentucky I think." He stopped for a moment to chew a bite of ham he'd taken, then swallowed, following with a sip of small beer. "I believe she intrigues him because she doesna seem to care for him one way or another."

He'd stopped to look out the window as he made his way to the chamber pot just before dawn and had seen Liam leaving the hotel. He hoped he wasn't swiving the chit. It could've been a game of cards that kept him so late. He hoped it was cards.

"You don't like her with him."

"I didna say that, lass."

"The set of your mouth says it. She did seem rather cold and aloof, but, of course, I haven't even met her. I'll rely on your judgment, as it confirms my first impression. She's not for him."

David wasn't sure what to say. She was right, of course, but hell, he hadn't said any of that, and he'd hate Liam ever thinking he had. "Hmmph, well then, no matchmaking, lass. He willna like that."

"I just said she's not for him, didn't I?" She added more food to his plate and poured herself another cup of tea, which he hoped signaled an end to that vein of conversation. "What would you like to do today?"

He looked at her, making no effort to conceal his likes and wants. She laughed.

"I don't think I can, David. It was an effort to get up to this table."

"Hmmph. Right, then. I'll call for a tub full of hot water for ye after breakfast. It'll soothe ye. I'll wash ye." She blushed and he added, "You're not to be shy anymore, Bess, aye? Ye did say 'just this once.' Then I'll comb your hair and ye can show me how to help dress ye if I'm to act as your maid. We can stroll along the river; nay I'll hire a buggy. Ye need to rest up. We can ride, maybe to Darby, maybe to Egg's Harbor. Then we'll stop and have dinner at one of the taverns outside of town. If one's for hire, we can take a sail in the moonlight."

"A moonlight sail! That sounds lovely, but don't hire a buggy. It requires too much of your attention, and I want every bit of that today. Walking will suit me just fine. We'll walk until we wear ourselves out. You know where I'd like to go? Do you remember the place along the creek, past the Falls?" She colored prettily, and he remembered. "Well, the flowers along the river are blooming in profusion now. You may pick me bouquets, and I'll dry some for keepsakes. That's where I'd like to walk."

"Aye, I remember. I was to be teaching ye some things, as I recall." He looked at her, his food forgotten as she blushed yet again. "There're things that willna pain ye."

She swallowed, looking away, and he brought a bite of ham to her mouth to ease her embarrassment. She recovered quickly, batting away his hand.

"And what shall I do for you, David?"

"I'll think of something, no doubt." He grinned. "Now eat, will ye?"

She ignored him, setting down her toast and coming around behind him, her hands on his shoulders. "When was the last time someone pampered you, took care of you?" she said softly. "The last time you had the opportunity to soak in a warm tub only because you wanted to, and it felt good?"

He made an effort to concentrate on the table before him, mentally cataloging the various foods, the style of the tableware, the sheen of the glassware—anything to keep his mind off the scent of her, the taste of her, the soft, silky texture of her skin under his hands. She was aching. He needed to remember that.

"The river's just fine for me, lass. I don't need a fancy tub."

She ran her hands down his chest, and he gave up; gave in to wanting her yet again as she bent to kiss the top of his head, her hair spilling over him in a tent of amber, silky waves.

"Needs and wants are two different things, David," she whispered.

Reaching around, he grabbed her, pulling her into his lap. His sunrise. "No' for me, Bess, no' when I look at you. When I look at you, I find they are one and the same."

CAST OF CHARACTERS

PASSENGERS ON THE INDUSTRY:

David Graham – Scotch-Irish, apprenticed to a Philadelphia printer

Elisabeth Hale –English, accompanying her father to America

Liam Brock – Scot, apprenticed to Mr. Oliver

Reverend John Wilson – David's maternal uncle, a Presbyterian minister

Edward Hale – Elisabeth's father, an English gentleman

Mr. Oliver – guardian to Liam and Rob, traveling to Philadelphia to open a school

Rob – Scot, apprenticed to Mr. Oliver

Sean – young boy under Mr. Oliver's care on the *Industry*, traveling to join his brother in Pittsburg

Mary Andrews – passenger on the *Industry* who offers to cook for David and his uncle

The MacTavishes: Annie, Seamus, and Ewan – Irish passengers with gift for music

Sarah Wallace – accompanied by her father, Sarah has her eye on David

Mr. Wallace – Sarah's alcoholic father

Mr. and Mrs. Kiefer and son Paul – German emigrants, Paul befriends Sean

CREW ON THE INDUSTRY:

Captain Honeywell – Captain
Sam Ritcher – First Mate
Alex Mannus – young sailor who befriends David and Liam

PRINT SHOP:

Mr. Hall – David's master
Mr. Sellers – Hall's partner in printing business
Robert Store – journeyman in print shop, David's superior
Ian – apprentice closest in tenure and age to David
Thomas – senior apprentice in shop when David first arrives in Philadelphia

HALE HOUSEHOLD:

Mrs. Hale – Elisabeth's grandmother
John Black – cook
Polly – maidservant and friend to Elisabeth
Tom Abernathy – butler
Jane – servant

OTHERS:

James – apprentice to sailmaker
Rory Smith – foreman (and later owner) of paper mill outside Philadelphia
Victoria Billings – in Philadelphia with her father, readying for a trip out west
Silas Warner – Philadelphia bookbinder

Eunice Warner – daughter to Silas Warner
Mr. Coxcombe – occasional escort of Mrs. Hale
Mary – Elisabeth's friend
Rhiannon (Rhee) – Elisabeth's close friend (in England)
Becca – Elisabeth's cocker spaniel

GLOSSARY OF

EIGHTEENTH-CENTURY

VOCABULARY

abigail – a female maidservant
baggage – an insulting term for a woman
bairn – a child
bawbee – a silver coin of minimal value (*cant*)
blowen – a woman of ill repute
blowse – a disheveled woman (*cant*)
boll – a measure of weight
blunt – money (*cant*)
bye-blow – a bastard
case – a shallow, divided receptacle in which metal type is stored
cèilidh – a social evening with music, singing, dancing, etc.
chit – a dismissive term for a girl
close – an alley
cove – man (*cant*)
cull – man (*cant*)
eijit – idiot
fash – fret, worry
galley – a shallow box in which type is placed after it has been set
galley slave – a term of derision applied by pressmen to compositors
macaroni – a fop or a dandy
pi – unsorted pieces of metal type

receipt – a recipe

sassenach – an English person

save-all – a type of candlestick used by our frugal forefathers to burn ends of candles

sen'night – a week

silkie – seal

swiving – to have sexual intercourse

tocher – dowry

whist – a trick-taking card game popular in the eighteenth and nineteenth centuries

whoreson – son of a whore

victuals – food

zounds – a mild oath, contracted from 'God's wounds'

ABOUT THE AUTHOR

LINDA LEE GRAHAM IS THE author's pen name.
VOICES indulges her passion for genealogy and
history.

If you have an interest in some of the stories behind the
story, be sure to visit www.LindaLeeGraham.com.

The series continues with:
VOICES WHISPER and VOICES ECHO.

Made in the USA
Middletown, DE
20 June 2019